ILLINOIS
WEDDINGS

ILLINOIS WEDDINGS

THREE-IN-ONE COLLECTION

BECKY MELBY
AND
CATHY WIENKE

BARBOUR
PUBLISHING

Published by Barbour Publishing, Inc., P.O. Box 719, Uhrichsville, Ohio 44683, www.barbourbooks.com

Our mission is to publish and distribute inspirational products offering exceptional value and biblical encouragement to the masses.

ecpa Member of the
Evangelical Christian
Publishers Association

Printed in the United States of America.

Dear Reader,

In *Illinois Weddings*, you'll meet three generations of head-strong, fallible, and passionate women. What a joy it's been for us to follow each of them on their faith and love journeys, and we're so glad you've decided to join us.

One message we have tried to convey in every story we've written together is that God is the author of second chances, and it is never too late to fall into His arms and experience the blessed freedom that comes with forgiveness. In *Pleasant Surprises*, *Parting Secrets*, and *Pure Serendipity*, you'll read Angel, Jeanie, and Ruby's struggles with believing they are worthy of another chance.

If you find yourself in that same place, feeling as though what you've done—or what's been done to you—makes you undeserving of a fresh start, our prayer is that you'll allow the truths in these fictional encounters to touch your heart.

None of us deserves a second chance, but God's grace doesn't hinge on our worthiness. It hinges on his free and abundant love. And only on that.

In *Parting Secrets*, Jeanie reveals the secret she's lived with for thirty years; a secret which profoundly affects the generation before and after her. Hers is the story of a woman who escaped a web of degradation that entraps millions of women every year. Most of them do not escape. Today, more than twenty-seven million people worldwide are enslaved by the sex trade industry. An unspeakable number of them are children.

As women, our hearts break over these statistics. In the face of such incomprehensible numbers, it's easy to feel powerless. We want to get involved, but don't know how. In an effort to "do something," we are donating a portion of the proceeds from the sale of this book to Women At Risk, International. WAR, Int'l is an organization with the goal of creating circles of protection and hope around women and children at risk of human trafficking, domestic violence, depression, loss, disease, and exploitation through culturally sensitive intervention projects. For more information, go to www.warinternational.org. We all need to pray for the women and children exploited daily by these hideous crimes, and to ask what part we might play in the solution. We love hearing from, and praying for, our readers. Please stop by our website and share your thoughts on these stories:
www.melby-wienke.com.

Blessings,
Becky and Cathy

PLEASANT SURPRISES

Dedication

To Mary Hughes—Thirty years ago you led us both to the foot of the cross. We are forever grateful.

"I thank my God every time I remember you. . . . I always pray with joy because of your partnership in the gospel from the first day until now, being confident of this, that he who began a good work in you will carry it on to completion until the day of Christ Jesus" (Philippians 1:3-7).

Love, Cathy and Becky

A special thank you to the Pearl Girls—Eileen, Patti, Lee, and Patty, and to Cynthia, Jan, and Paulette for awesome critiquing.

Thank you to Steven Hurley for his expertise, and to Becky's Bill, who just ran his thirtieth marathon.

Chapter 1

With each white dash that slipped east between Angel Cholewinski's pickup and the Chicago city limits, the knots of tension in her shoulders diminished. Glancing at the numbers that glowed red in the dark cab, she let out a long-held sigh. 12:03. The work week she'd thought would never end was finally history.

Angel ruffled the fur of the Irish setter enthroned on the passenger seat. "Starting to smell like home, isn't it, boy?" Sunny's slack mouth rippled in the wind as he sniffed the night air.

The late August breeze drifting through the window of Angel's sunburst orange Chevy Colorado had lost all hint of the city. She filled her lungs with the homecoming smells of cow manure and burning leaves and dipped into the bag of caramel corn balanced on her lap. "Catch!" She tossed a piece, and Sunny caught it.

As 12:03 changed to 12:04, "With a Little Help from My Friends" floated out of Angel's purse. Finally, a call from an old friend instead of a new enemy.

Sunny turned toward the source of the personalized ringtone, and Angel was sure he smiled. His loyalty wavered in the presence—and even the voice—of her roommate. "She's calling to talk to me, not you." Angel opened her phone. "Hey, Pugsley, what's up?"

A yawn answered. "I wanted to make sure you weren't suicidal before I go to bed."

"I'm fine."

"Liar."

"I'm doing denial like a pro—thinking of nothing but a weekend of carbs and sleep."

"Good. You just stay in la-la land."

"When all else fails run home to Mommy." Angel flashed a tremulous smile at the phone. All else was definitely failing.

"That's a beautiful philosophy, Ange. How'd your party go?"

"Smoke and innuendo-filled, as usual. But my part was clean. Feels good." A twinge of guilt reminded her, again, why she was heading back to her hometown for two days of escape.

"I'm proud of you, girlfriend. Drive safe and take care of you."

"Take care of you. 'Night."

Six minutes later, Angel was deep in denial and thoughts of Polish pastry

9

when her phone rang again. Not a smile-inducing sound this time. The "Mexican Hat Dance"—an annoying song for an annoying caller—jangled from her purse. She contemplated pulling over and tossing her phone into the Pecatonica River.

On the fourth ring, with what little civility she could muster late on a Friday night after the worst week of her life, she answered it. "Chuck?"

"Um. . .no. . ." The male voice stammering over music, laughter, and clanking dishes did not belong to her marketing manager. "Is this Angel Shle. . .Shlewhiskey?"

Angel's teeth gritted at the massacre of her name. "Cole-eh-win-ski. Speaking."

"Uh. . .yeah. . .I was hoping maybe you could clear up a little, uh. . .confusion I seem to be sharing with one of your employees."

"I'll try, Mr. . .?"

"Kilbourn. Jonathan Kilbourn. Maybe you remember me? You people did my bachelor party a year ago. I was thinking of hiring you to do my brother's party, but I'm sitting here at my in-laws' twenty-fifth anniversary, which I gotta say your people have done a bang-up job on, and one of your guys here, Chuck somebody, says you changed your policies and you don't do bachelor parties with. . .uh. . .girls. . .now. And he says you don't have the gin fountain anymore. Man, the guys loved that." The man snickered. "I gotta agree with Chuck here. There's no way this is gonna fly. But then, he goes and tells me your company's throwing a bash for Joe Hart and his buddies tomorrow night, so I'm just a little confused."

Angel took a deep, controlled breath and silently recited the Bible verse she'd taped to her office computer. . .and her dashboard. . .and her bathroom mirror. 1 Peter 3:15: *Always be prepared to give an answer to everyone who asks you to give the reason for the hope that you have. But do this with gentleness and respect.* She forced a smile. "Mr. Kilbourn. Of course, I remember you. How's married life?"

There was a momentary pause. "Fine. . ." Caution surrounded his brief answer.

"Wonderful. Well, Jonathan, it's because of our—because of *my* commitment to encourage strong marriages that Pleasant Surprises only coordinates bachelor parties that honor and value women and the sanctity of marriage. I'm sure that, as a married man, you support that, don't you, Mr. Kilbourn?"

"Um. . .yeah. . .well, sure, but a little harmless fun. . .and what about Joe Hart's gig? You can't tell me that's going to be some Sunday school picnic. Guess everybody's got their price." The man's voice was laced with sarcasm. "All that honoring women stuff goes out the window if your client happens to be a linebacker for the Chicago Bears, huh?"

Angel's stomach twisted. *What about Joe Hart's gig?* It was precisely because she didn't like the answer to that question that she was running home to Galena.

The words she came up with sounded weak even to her. "Pleasant Surprises is undergoing some policy changes that will affect all of our *new* bookings, Mr. Kilbourn. Now, if you'd like to talk about the kind of bachelor party you could video and show your wife, give Pleasant Surprises a call. I'll sit down with you personally to plan the details."

"Yeah. . .sure. . .whatever." The phone went dead.

Angel shoved a handful of caramel corn in her mouth. And the Hat Dance jittered her nerves once again. She chewed fast and swallowed hard. "Yes?" Could the man hear the enamel grating off her teeth?

"Angel"—this time the voice matched the caller ID— "about that guy that just called you. . ."

"On your company phone. After midnight."

"Chill, Ange. You're in debt up to your eyeballs, and he was a prospective client. I thought I'd give you a chance to make him happy, but you didn't even try, did you? You can't afford to lose anybody else, Miss *Shlewhiskey*." He laughed at his own wit. "I heard you fired Elly. Not a good move. If you keep shooting yourself in the foot like—"

"You told him about Joe Hart's party. What part of 'client confidentiality' don't you understand, Chuck? Joe Hart doesn't even know about his party. The guy could have been a repor—" Two deer suddenly entered her peripheral view from the right. They were fast approaching the highway and didn't appear to be slowing. Angel pressed on the brake and dropped the phone. Grabbing the steering wheel with her left hand, she stuck her right arm out to shield Sunny as the dog lurched forward.

Two yearling fawns pranced in front of her, one missing the front bumper by two yards, the other by a matter of inches. Angel darted a glance in the mirror then exhaled. Thank the Lord, there was no one behind her. She clamped onto the wheel and pushed the accelerator.

Sunny barked, and Angel jumped, then again let out a breath. "A little late for that, boy. They're safe in the woo—" The head and shoulders of a large deer flashed above the hood. A sickening thud shoved Angel into the door. Sunny fell across the console and slammed into Angel's shoulder. A tight inhale squeezed through Angel's throat as she mashed the pedal to the floor. Anti-skid brakes grabbed. The truck shuddered to a stop, blocking the westbound lane.

Sunny scrambled back to the passenger seat, and Angel tried to turn the steering wheel to the right, but it wouldn't budge. "We have to get out of here." Her teeth chattered, constricting her words. She had no choice but to crank the wheel to the left to get off the road. The truck bounced on the rim of the front tire, and rubber scraped against the frame as she inched toward the gravel and parked facing Chicago.

When she could wrench her hands off the wheel, she turned to Sunny. His tongue hung out. His breath came in quick pants. "Are you okay?" She ran her hand along the setter's sides. Sunny trembled but didn't appear to be hurt.

Angel touched her forehead. "Am *I* okay?" She felt her ribs, her arms. Her shoulder ached. She prodded it. She'd be sporting a colorful bruise tomorrow, but that was all. *Thank You, Lord.*

"Can you see it? Did I kill the poor thing?" With shaking hands, she opened the door. As she stepped onto the running board, her knee threatened to give out. With both feet on the ground, she leaned against the truck until she felt some strength come back to her legs. The air was balmy, in the seventies after a hot and humid day, but she was shivering. Movement drew her gaze to the ditch across the road. A doe rose up, swung her head slowly from side to side, and bounded across the highway.

The sight calmed Angel's nerves. Her shaking stopped. She walked around the front and stared down at the right fender. The headlights shut off just as she got there, making the night seem suddenly thick and black. As her eyes adjusted, moonlight revealed a concave hollow in the orange fender pressing into the flat tire. She skimmed her hand along the dent the same way she'd felt Sunny's flank.

She walked back to her door, opened it, then turned on the flashers and fished around on the floor until she found her phone. Calling information, she got the number for a towing company. A woman answered in a voice that said she'd been sound asleep.

"I just hit a deer. I need a tow truck."

"Where are you?"

"Highway 20 between Eleroy and Stockton."

"My husband's out on a call. There was a big accident on highway 73. I'll have him call you when he's free."

Angel gave the woman her number. As she closed her phone, the fear she'd held at bay for weeks crashed into her and buckled her knees. With the hum of crickets in the tall grass beside her and the rustle of wind in the papery cornstalks beyond the ditch, she gave in to pent-up tears.

Five months ago, she'd been named Small Business Entrepreneur of the Year. A week ago, she hadn't had enough in the bank to write herself a paycheck. *Lord, people warned me things might get harder, but this is too much.*

The phone rang again. She answered with a monosyllable that loosely resembled hello.

"What in the world happened?" Chuck's voice sounded more irritated than concerned.

"Almost hit a deer." Technically the deer had hit *her,* making it just a partial lie. She was too tired to explain, and too tired for the confrontation she couldn't put off any longer. "Chuck, I'm not having this conversation with you again. I'm really not in the mood to explain one more time that you're not a partner in this company. You work for me. Scratch that. You *worked* for me. Your disrespect just cost your job."

In the pause that followed, the night air smelled even fresher than it had just two miles back.

"You know, Angel. . .that might be the nicest thing you could do for your clients. They need an event planner who'll give them what they want. And ol' Chuck's new business aims to please." A skin-prickling laugh spit through the phone. "You can't make it without me, Miss *Shlewhiskey*."

The phone went dead.

ॐ

Waiting wasn't something Angel did well. She flipped the switch to keep the dome light on, found Sunny's leash, let him out of the truck, and started pacing, trying to settle her thoughts enough to pray again. Her thoughts and steps halted as a westbound SUV passed her, then slowed and did a U-turn, driving past her again and pulling to the shoulder three feet from her front bumper.

Sunny put himself between Angel and the vehicle. A deep, throaty growl hovered in the night air. Angel gripped the leash near the hook, ready to release him if she needed to. "Hang on, boy." He wasn't trained, but she had no doubt he'd protect her.

The driver's side door opened, and a tall man got out. In the dim light, Angel saw dark hair curling over the collar of a light-colored shirt with two buttons open at the neck, and sleeves rolled to the elbows. He was twenty-something, maybe nudging thirty, incredibly handsome, and tall—a good six inches over her five-foot-eight. In the shadowy light, he appeared to be looking at her with genuine concern. "Problems?"

It was at that moment Angel remembered what she'd changed into after the party—Disney princess pajama bottoms and a hot pink T-shirt. The ensemble accentuated every one of her twenty-three pounds over goal weight. She placed her free arm casually across her stomach. Two kernels of caramel corn stuck to her arm. Brushing them off, she stared down at her orange flip-flops and then up at the amused smile of the man who wanted to either help her or abduct her. "I hit a deer. The fender's bent and the tire's flat." She looked at the arms that filled out the shirt and wondered if he could straighten the fender by brute strength. *But what if he's not really a nice, concerned guy? What if. . .?* "I'm waiting for a tow."

"Where you headed?"

Don't talk to strangers. "Galena." The man had a safe smile.

"Where are they taking the truck?"

"Eleroy."

He rubbed his chin. "Want a lift home or to the garage?"

"Thanks, but I think I'll just wait for the tow."

"Want company while you wait? Not too smart to be out here alone."

Or to be alone with a stranger. It wasn't her conscience she was hearing; it was her mother. "Thanks, but I'll be fine. Got my trusty guard dog."

"You're sure?"

"Yes. Thanks for stopping."

The man nodded and got back in the Ford Explorer. Angel sighed. *There's such a thing as being too cautious.* Caution might just keep her single. Twenty-eight was pushing hopeless. . .at least in her grandmother's mind. She opened the tailgate and climbed up. Sunny jumped up beside her, and Angel rested her hand on his back. As the taillights of the Explorer shrank on the horizon, she sighed again. She'd spent her entire childhood dreaming of a tall, handsome rescuer. Until high school, her Prince Charming was the father she envisioned waiting for just the right moment to swoop in and claim her. Since then, she'd imagined a tall, strong, handsome hero. . .like the one that just got away. "Gotta quit chasing off the cute ones."

Suddenly, the brake lights that had all but disappeared blazed. The turn signal flashed, and the vehicle did another U-turn and pulled up facing her tailgate. Two car doors opened and closed. Angel's fingers cramped on the leash. She couldn't see a thing in the glare of the headlights.

"Hi, again." The deep voice had a smile in it. "I got to thinking that I should have mentioned I wasn't alone."

A tall, willowy girl in her midteens stepped in front of a headlight. The girl waved with her fingertips and said, "Hi," and Angel finally exhaled. The man stepped forward and held out his hand. "Wade Ramsey. This is my sister Taylor."

Angel took his large, strong hand. *Is this smart?* "Angel Cholewinski."

"Glad to meet you, Angel. It just didn't seem right to leave you sitting here. Who knows how long it could take that tow truck. If you feel safer knowing I'm just a guy driving his baby sister home, I'd like to extend the offer again. I live in Elizabeth, if you want to check my references." Wade Ramsey smiled, slow and slightly crooked.

Lord, give me wisdom.

"Please?" The girl spoke up for the first time. "He's been listening to old Beatles stuff since we left Wheaton and it's driving me crazy. He wouldn't do that if someone else was in the car."

Wade Ramsey's crooked smile broadened. "My sister didn't come with a volume control knob, so all I can do is drown her out."

Taylor put her hands around an imaginary guitar. Her head wobbled side-to-side. "Do you want to know a seeeeecret?" she crooned off-key. "*Please* come with us."

"Would you feel safer calling someone and giving them my plate numbers or something?" The guy was covering all the bases.

Angel shook her head. "I'd hate to have you go out of your way."

"We're headed to Elizabeth. Galena's not much farther. Why don't you give the garage a call and tell them you'll leave the keys under the visor. Nobody can steal it in this condition."

"The dog can sit in back with me," Taylor said. "I'd love some intelligent company." She wrinkled her nose at her brother.

Is this a setup? He could knock me off, throw me in the ditch, then come back here, straighten my fender, and drive off with my truck. Again, her mother's voice—*You can't get in the car with a complete stranger. You don't really believe she's his sister, do you? Maybe he kidnapped her, too. Maybe she has to play along or else. . . .*

The man's hand slid toward his back pocket. Angel wrapped both arms around Sunny.

"Here's my driver's license and my IEA card and. . ." He stepped toward her. "And my next barber appointment and my NRA membership. . ."

Angel looked from his easy smile to the Illinois Education Association card that topped the stack he held out to her.

What if they're fakes? Her mother whispered from Galena.

And what if it's time to start running my personal life the way I want to run my business? With crazy faith.

"Just let me grab my bag."

Chapter 2

Wade puffed a sigh of relief when he put the car in gear and locked the doors. Until that moment, he'd kept one eye on the ditch, half expecting the girl's boyfriend to ambush him from the cornfield.

His conscience—and his sister—wouldn't let him leave her there alone. But this had all the feel of a setup—helpless female on the side of the road with no one around for miles. He pulled onto the highway and shot a glance at her. Maybe there was no boyfriend. But maybe there was a weapon in the eighty-pound neon orange tote bag he'd lugged to the car for her. The silly pajamas could all be part of her MO. He turned off the CD player, stopping the Beatles on the first verse of "Baby You Can Drive My Car."

"So. . .what brings you to Galena?"

"It's home. I live in Oak Park, but Galena is *home* home. I work in Chicago."

For the mob, no doubt. Then again, she was kind of fair skinned to have an Italian godfather. And her tongue-twisting Polish last name sounded believable. Who'd come up with an alias like that? If she'd made up "Angel" and she was anything but, he'd have to hand it to her for that flash of genius. "What do you do?"

"I'm an event coordinator."

"Interesting." *Events. . .like the St. Valentine's Day Massacre?* "What kind of events?"

"Oh. . ." She paused. Probably scrambling to make it sound believable. "Birthday parties, bridal showers, anniversaries. We do weddings and corporate meetings, too, but we specialize in surprises."

Wade glanced at the tommy-gun-sized bag on her lap. "Surprises, huh?"

"Yes. How about you? You're a teacher, I gather."

Taylor reached over his shoulder from the backseat and hit the light above his head. "Just for a sec," she said with her I'm-almost-sixteen attitude. "Gotta change batteries."

"Put your seat belt on."

"Yeah, yeah."

Wade brought his focus back to the passenger seat. "I teach high school. American government, American history, and world history, and I coach basketball."

The girl whose hair matched her dog slid the bag to the floor between her feet and shifted in the seat to face him. "I'd love to go back and take history all over again," she said. "I blew it off in high school. So what are you teaching right now?"

He stole another quick look. She was staring at him. With eyes that were Old Glory blue. "I'm. . ." Taylor shut the light off, and Wade remembered the road he was supposed to be driving on. Muffled rap music from Taylor's headphones beat through his silence. What *was* he teaching anyway? Oh, yeah. . . "I'm starting a new honor's class on the twentieth century. Just finished World War One and prepping for the prohibition era—organized crime and all that."

"Have you ever brought your kids to Chicago for the Untouchables Tour?"

"More times than I can count. The kids call it the Gangsta Tour."

"I did a party at the old Biograph Theater—"

"Where Melvin Purvis ambushed John Dillinger."

"You know your stuff."

"It's what they sort of pay me for." He engaged the cruise control.

"What made you choose teaching?"

Wade kept his eyes on the cone of light his Explorer painted on the road ahead yet tracked every move the girl made. The way she'd turned in the seat, with one pajama-clad knee pointing toward him, surprised him. He tried to picture Angel Whatever-her-name-was in a business suit, but it was hard to do. From a distance, at least in her pajamas, she could easily pass for one of the twelfth graders in his U.S. history class. But up close her self-assurance was evident. An intriguing mix of fun and competence. . .in a not-hard-to-look-at package.

Angel cleared her throat and he glanced at her. An expectant look met his gaze. She'd asked him a question. "I'm sorry. . .what did you ask?"

"I was just wondering why you chose teaching."

"Oh. . ." *Focus, Ramsey. This is ridiculous.* "Teaching was supposed to be a temporary stop on my way to something bigger. I'm working on my PhD."

"It was supposed to be. . .but you've decided to stay where you are?"

"I don't know. Up until five years ago, I thought I wanted to spend my life traveling and researching and writing, but I'm finding out that God may have gifted me with sufficient immaturity and imagination to click with kids."

Her laugh was throaty, with just the faintest snort at the end. The kind of laugh people describe as contagious. She pulled something out of her ponytail, and Wade grabbed another quick look. Curly copper hair bounced to just below her shoulders. He wondered what it would look like in the sunlight. She slid her hair band onto her wrist. "The history teachers I had were as exciting as oatmeal. Give me an example of your 'immaturity and imagination.'"

Well, for starters, a few minutes ago I imagined a machine gun in your bag. . . . "I'm big on experiential learning. I do as much hands-on stuff as I can. Reenactments, living history museums, that kind of stuff. And at least once a week I show up in costume. Kids don't smart back at Abe Lincoln."

"Wow. I probably would have learned something if you were my teacher."

Wade's lips pressed together, holding back a smile. "So I'm taking you

17

home. . .to your parents? Husband? Boyfriend?" He'd managed a glimpse of her left ring finger. Bare. . .not even a ring groove.

"My mother and grandmother."

No love interest in Galena. That didn't rule out a guy in Chicago, but it was something. Something he really shouldn't be thinking about fifteen minutes after he met the woman. . .or at all, considering the responsibility that sat, none too still, in the backseat. "Are your parents divorced?" *Way too nosy, Ramsey.* The question had come to mind because of what his own parents were dealing with. "Sorry. That's none of my business."

"No. That's okay. I've been asked that question my whole life."

"Really?"

She nodded, curls swaying on the outer frame of his vision. "My mother never married, and I don't know who my father is. It's her little secret." A tinge of bitterness brushed her words. "My mother and I lived with my grandparents. My grandpa died when I was eight, so essentially I grew up in an all-female house."

"That had to have been. . .interesting."

She laughed. "Terrifying at times. Three generations of female hormones under one roof. We have fun together, but I missed out on a lot. I'm socially deficient in many ways."

He matched her easy laugh. "Like how?"

"Well, I've never seen a single *Star Wars* movie."

His jaw dropped in genuine shock. "You're kidding?"

"I'm not. Didn't see *ET* or *Jurassic Park* either. I stink at eighties trivia games."

"Wow. . .you need to do something about that. Have you ever tried to find your father?"

"No. Maybe someday, but it would upset my mother. For whatever reason, she doesn't want me to know anything about him."

"Doesn't that creep you out?" *Another great question.* And it came out the way one of his high schoolers would say it.

"Sometimes. But I try not to picture him as any kind of menace to society. When I was a kid I imagined he was someone incredibly famous, and my mom was just trying to protect him. . .or me. I decided they were secretly in contact, just waiting for the day we could all be together." She laughed. "I didn't give up on that dream until about ten years ago. When I turned eighteen and he didn't come to find me, I had to let it go."

"That must have been tough."

He sensed her sort of folding in on herself. Her arms crossed and she looked away from him. "It is." Her voice grew quiet. But after only seconds, she turned back to him. "I had more stability than a lot of kids. My mother and grandmother still live in the house I grew up in, still running the family bakery."

18

"Which one?"

"Angel Wings."

"I've been there. You have a bakery named after you?"

Her laugh had a cynical tinge. "I was named for the bakery."

"How sweet."

She groaned.

Wade let his arm slouch against the door and relaxed his grip on the steering wheel. Maybe she wasn't a *gangsta* after all.

§

The smell of frying onions woke Angel just after eleven on Saturday morning. Gratitude flooded her first few lucid moments. She ran her hand across four-hundred-thread-count sheets. Two years ago she'd sent her mother and grandmother on a cruise and had their house completely remodeled. Of all the changes, it was the sheets without holes and towels that weren't frayed that made her mother cry.

Angel, still in her pink T-shirt and princess pajamas, walked barefoot into the kitchen where her grandmother stood in front of the stove. Bending to Ruby Cholewinski's four-foot-ten height, Angel wrapped her arms around the little woman in a teal terry cloth robe. Fuzzy purple slippers covered her grandmother's feet. Her short hair, white at the crown and gradually changing to pewter at the nape of her neck, was still damp from her shower. Angel reached around and carefully grabbed a caramelized onion. "Smells wonderful, Bapcia."

Her grandmother twisted and planted a kiss on Angel's cheek. "It's easy to cook in the magic kitchen provided by my famous granddaughter." She swept her hand across the improvements—granite countertops, walnut cabinets, and new appliances. "Only the best food for you, Angelika."

"The best is making my jeans too tight."

"Ach. You're tall, you can carry it. When you were twelve and looked like a little round bear is when you should have worried about your weight."

Angel cringed. Her seventh grade school picture flashed before her eyes, and with the visual came the feelings. In the downward spiral her life was taking, she was revisiting the emotions that made food her best friend in junior high.

Her grandmother pinched her cheek. "Food is a blessing. You want to look like I did when I was young? Living on moldy bread and—" She laughed. "You've heard my stories too many times."

"I love your stories. You need to write them."

"Ach. How are you feeling? Sleep well?"

Angel nodded, picking up a knife and cutting board. "My arm's a little sore, but I sleep better here than anywhere else in the world."

Flipping a browned potato pancake, Bapcia smiled. "Probably helps to have a tall, handsome stranger to dream about."

"Ha! You ruined my chances with him. Where's Sunny?"

"Guarding the shop. He's always good for business; children run to the dog and their mothers smell the pastry. Back to your Prince Charming. . .blame your mother for ruining that man's first impressions; she asked more questions than I did. But she was right to invite him in last night after you were *maniaki* enough to ride with him. And he might as well see what he's up against before he gets too interested in you. Cholewinski women are not to be trifled with."

Angel rinsed a cucumber and set it on the cutting board. "Oh, you didn't scare him away; just the opposite. He's not scared of you, Bapcia; Mr. Ramsey is in love with you. Those were his final words as he drove off—'Tell your grandmother I'm in love with her.' That's why I haven't got a chance."

"He's in love with the angel wings; he ate six. You learn to make *chruscik* and he'll love you, too. Polish pastry reaches the heart."

"I make a pretty mean chruscik, Bapcia. You taught me well, but I still think the guy was more taken with you than your pastry."

As she lifted a potato pancake from the pan and set it on a plate covered with a paper towel, Bapcia batted her eyelashes. "What can I say?" she said coyly. "True beauty doesn't fade with time. Sixty-two and I haven't lost it yet."

"I hope I have your genes."

Her grandmother's smile froze for the space of a heartbeat. Her eyes darted to Angel's hair, then back to the frying pan. Angel knew her thoughts. She'd heard them whispered many times when she was little and supposed to be sleeping. Her grandmother would stroke her hair as she rocked her and mutter to herself—"Where did this hair come from? Whose long legs do you have, little one?"

Pointing to the tub of sour cream sitting on the counter, Bapcia said, "Finish the *mizeria* and come join me in back. We have to save some for your mother. I'll take it when I go to the shop."

Angel sliced the cucumbers, sprinkled them with dill and lemon juice, and stirred in a generous scoop of sour cream. Walking out through the sliding glass doors of the dining room, she set the bowl on the glass-topped table on the deck and took a chair. From the shade cast by the umbrella over the table, Bapcia smiled up at her, folded her hands, and bowed her head. "Lord Jesus, thank You for providing for our needs, and thank You for protecting Angelika last night. And since there is no such thing as coincidence with You, Father, thank You for bringing that nice man along just at the right time, and bring him back to our door soon. Amen."

"Bapcia! You're shameless. . .even with God!"

"Philippians 4:6 says, 'In every situation, by prayer and petition, with thanksgiving, present your requests to God.' It's no secret to Him that your mother and I want a good man for you. Somebody in this family has to have a real wedding! Meeting Wade was not a coincidence. It was serendipity, plain and simple. God can bring good things out of adversity. Did he ask for your phone number?"

"No."

Bapcia put a pancake on Angel's plate and gestured in the air with the spatula. "He knows where to find you. So what else do you know about him?"

Angel spooned cucumber salad on top of the pancake and took a bite before answering. Closing her eyes, she said, "No one makes this like you, Bapcia." When she opened her eyes again, her grandmother was still staring expectantly. "I didn't learn much more than you and Mom got out of him. He's twenty-seven, he likes classic rock music, he's been to Europe twice, and he has a passion for American history and glazed doughnuts, which is now probably replaced by Polish pastry. And. . .he wants to throw a surprise anniversary party for his parents."

"How convenient." Bapcia smiled smugly with what Angel called her "fortune-teller" look.

Angel rolled her eyes. "What?"

"I could see you married to a high school teacher."

"Not a high school teacher who lives in Elizabeth."

"The Lord may not have you in Chicago forever, you know."

Angel grimaced. "Don't go there, Bapcia. That's beginning to look only too possible."

" 'Don't go there.' I don't like that phrase. It's about as respectful as 'shut up.' " Bapcia's eyes gleamed as she took a long drink of iced tea, peering at Angel over the rim of her glass. When she set the glass down, her lined face rippled with a sympathetic smile. "God can bring good things out of adversity, my Angel."

"I know, but—"

"No 'but.' God is at work here." A finger pointed at Angel. "And that man is part of His work."

Chapter 3

We can't afford anything that fancy-shmancy." Taylor leaned over Wade's shoulder as he stared at the Pleasant Surprises brochure—and the dollar amount Angel had scrawled on the back.

"We'll manage." His little sister had no idea how much he had stashed away in savings. Though it was earmarked for work on his doctorate, he had a bit of a cushion he could use for other things. . .like a party for his parents planned by a feisty redhead.

"Says you."

Wade put his feet on the coffee table, knocking over a bowl and sending pretzels scattering across the carpeting. "Oops." Sticking the brochure between the cushions of his beige suede couch, he opened his laptop and read the latest e-mail from his academic advisor.

"Klutz." Pointing her toes, Taylor stretched out one leg, lowered it, and lifted the other, walking catlike to the middle of Wade's living room. "There isn't going to be any marriage to celebrate by November anyway."

"Would you quit? You sound like Eeyore."

Taylor balanced on one leg, the other forming a triangle against her knee. Her hands pressed together, her arms stretched toward the ceiling in a yoga tree position. "Hey, you haven't been around them lately as much as I have."

Therein lies the problem. Not that he would lay that on her, but on some level Taylor had to realize that the stupid decisions she'd been making were putting a strain on their parents' marriage. She had to know that staying with him for the school year wasn't only to get her away from the wrong friends, but to give their parents a break and time to work on a game plan for dealing with a fifteen-year-old with the common sense of a first grader.

Taylor waved toward the end of the brochure sticking out of the couch. "Even if Grandma and Grandpa pitch in, it's still gonna be a gob of money. Probably for nothing. I'm telling you, they're not going to make it to thirty years."

I'm not going to make it to thirty days. He ignored her doom and gloom. "They're just going through a rough patch."

"Yeah. Whatever. Anyway, two days ago we were talking cake and punch and a couple balloons in the basement, and now we're doing a carnivorous feast for forty people. You're either a sucker. . .or you're in love with the party planner."

Wade focused on writing a reply, but the heat at the back of his neck irked him.

"You're blushing."

22

"You're nuts."

"You like her."

"I don't even know her."

"What's that got to do with it?" Taylor pointed toward the mess on the floor with her blood-red toenails. "You gonna pick them up?"

"Not when I've got a maid."

The yoga tree bent, then straightened, and pelted him with pretzel rods. "You need a wife."

Angel leaned against the carved back of the chair, chewing slowly and savoring the last bite of her Irish sausages with homemade fries. Smiling at Bapcia and then her mother, she broke a piece of soda bread and sighed. "I've ordered bangers 'n' chips in the city, but they're never this good. Why did I ever move to Chicago?"

"Don't get me started on that one," her mother answered.

"Don't go there, Jeanie." Bapcia winked at Angel.

Gesturing to the restaurant's etched mirror and stained glass windows, Angel said, "I have this recurring dream of sitting here at Frank O'Dowd's. What do you think it means?"

"That you're supposed to move back to Galena." Her mother's eyebrows A-framed her eyes.

"And marry a tall, handsome school teacher," Bapcia added.

Her mother leaned forward, her gaze fixed on Angel, a sure sign that she was about to be the next topic of conversation. Angel smiled at her mother and headed her off. Nodding to her left, she directed her mother's and grandmother's gazes toward a table where two plump, tropical-bronzed women in their sixties with matching platinum hair and rings on every finger were carrying on an animated, giggly discussion with their college-aged waiter. Angel whispered, "That's the kind of role models I want you two to be for my kids."

Bapcia's eye's crinkled. "I'll wear leopard skin to your wedding, if I ever see the day."

Her mother patted her hand. "And I'll dye my hair red and ride a Harley to the hospital the day I'm a grandma."

"I'll hold you to it."

"Hold me to it, but I won't hold my breath."

Angel rolled her eyes. "So, how was business this week?"

"Incredible. If we'd had the Internet years ago. . ." Her mother didn't finish the thought. She didn't need to. They'd all lived through the hard times, the off seasons when no tourists stood in line at the bakery. "Mail orders are up more than fifty percent from this time last year."

"Good." Angel buttered her second slice of bread. "You have the perfect product, you know."

Bapcia raised her tea glass. "Long live chruscik and *mazurki!*"

Angel touched her glass to Bapcia's. "Polish pastry reaches the heart."

The "look" hadn't left her mother's face. Angel stared back at her, waiting.

Jeanie Cholewinski had designed and sewn the rust-and-gold print dress that complemented her coffee-colored eyes. The dark brown French braid that ended at her shoulder blades was the same style she'd worn for years. Angel noticed a few strands of silver that hadn't been there just weeks ago. Even with the smile lines that splayed out from the corners of her eyes and bracketed her mouth, Angel thought of her mother as timeless. At forty-six, she still turned heads, and why she had never married was a mystery Angel had never solved.

Using her fingertip to trace the path of a bead of water on her glass, her mother shook her head slightly. "I still struggle with the ethical dilemma of making money off of selling people something that's not healthy for them." As she said it, her eyes hooked Angel's.

Angel pressed her lips together. "That was a very creative segue, Mom."

"I thought so. Now that we're on the topic of ethical dilemmas. . .how are you doing, really?"

Angel had told her mother about Joe Hart's party, but they'd agreed to keep it from her grandmother. Her mother's disappointment in her was hard enough. She couldn't handle tarnishing Bapcia's new image of her. "I'm. . .coping."

"You fired somebody yesterday?"

"Two somebodies, actually."

"Ouch."

Angel pushed her plate away. Sliding her chair back, she stared at the tourists and local patrons sitting in high-backed chairs at round tables. "There were plenty of people telling me to ease into changes, to honor the contracts we'd already signed. But that seemed like an alcoholic making a commitment to stop drinking as soon as he finished off all the bottles in the liquor cabinet. I thought I heard God telling me what we were doing was wrong, so I stopped. . .cold turkey." *Almost.*

Her mother patted her arm. "God will honor your. . .obedience."

"Will He? I'm not seeing it yet. I called all our bachelor- and bachelorette-party clients personally and told them about the changes we. . .I. . ."

"Did you tell them why?" Bapcia's eyes sparkled with anticipation.

How Angel wished she had amazing stories of God's faithfulness to share with her grandmother. "Yes. I told them I had recently become a follower of Jesus Christ and that I wanted my business decisions to honor Him."

"And. . .?" Bapcia smiled, waiting for something other than what Angel had to report.

"And I got sworn at, hung up on, and threatened with lawsuits."

Her mother tapped her fingers on the table. "I suppose it does constitute breach of contract."

"It does. I offered to provide alternate entertainment at our cost. A few clients have taken me up on it, but most of them want their money back and say they're going to take legal action. So now I'm wondering if I heard God right. I don't think He wants my business to tank." She reached out and played with the tines of her dessert fork. "Why do I have to be so all-or-nothing? If I'd gradually made the shift away from parties centered on half-dressed entertainment I wouldn't be staring at bankruptcy."

Her mother's braid swung emphatically. "And you'd feel like a hypocrite."

Mmm. Know that feeling well. Her cheeks burned with a kind of shame she hadn't experienced until a few weeks ago. She knew she probably still didn't fully understand the humiliation she'd brought on her God-honoring mother and grandmother over the past few years. "But I made promises to my clients. . . ."

She looked from her mother to her grandmother, seeing thinning patience on both faces. "And I'm messing up the lives of my employees. I turned everything upside down overnight and expected them to just fall into step. They're not Christians. I can't expect them to 'get it' right away." As she talked, she heard a waiter two tables away giving directions to the restroom to a white-haired woman who was apparently hard of hearing. "I took off like a crazed fanatical lunatic and—" The words stuck in her throat as the white-haired woman stood and walked away from her table, giving Angel a side view of a man who was facing the front windows. A man she knew.

A man she had hoped never to see again as long as she lived.

Bapcia and Jeanie stared at Angel, swiveled in unison to stare at the man, then back at Angel. "What's wrong?" Her mother's hand clamped on her wrist.

Angel gripped the edge of the table and leaned in. "That's Matt Peterson."

"Who's that?" Bapcia asked.

Both of Jeanie's eyebrows arched. "The boy who got you fired from Célébrez?"

Angel nodded.

"Have you seen him since then?"

"No. Thankfully," Angel hissed.

Bapcia put her hand over Angel's white-tipped fingers that still gripped the table. "That was a long time ago. People change."

"Not *that* people."

"Weren't you dating him?" Bapcia whispered, as if Matt were close enough to hear.

Angel curled her top lip. "Not dat*ing*. One date. And one of the stupider things I've done in my life."

"And what did he do again?" Bapcia craned her neck so that her ear was closer to Angel. "I don't think I ever got the full story."

Jeanie looked at Angel with her brow furrowed, clearly trying to read her. "Do you want to leave?"

Slowly, Angel released her grip on the table and forced herself to sit back in her chair. "No. I'm not going to let him ruin my night." Seeing their waitress coming toward them, she added, "Not before strawberry cake, anyway."

Angel gave her full attention to the plate in front of her. Stabbing a strawberry, she tried to ignore the question that still hung in the air. *And what did he do again? He betrayed a confidence. He cost me my job. He undermined my confidence for years to come. . . .*

"I wonder what he's doing here." Bapcia's expression was eerily similar to the one she'd had sitting on the deck at noon. Angel didn't like the look at all.

"This is *not* a serendipitous moment, if that's what you're thinking."

Bapcia held up both hands, doing a poor job of acting offended.

"You do need to let it go," her mother added.

Angel folded her arms across her chest. "It's not a forgiveness thing, Mom. I just don't want to be in the same room with the guy. I'd just as soon forget it ever happened."

"Maybe you need to let him know you've forgiven him. . .if you have." Bapcia's attitude was patronizing, and Angel suddenly felt like a toddler. "That's part of the healing process."

Jeanie nodded. "Maybe God is giving you this opportunity."

"Mom!" She narrowed her eyes and looked back at Matt Peterson, who was laughing with the middle-aged woman to his right. "I really don't think God wants me to go. . .over. . .and. . ."

Her words slowed as comprehension set in. Matt was no longer laughing. The woman sitting next to him grabbed his shoulder and shook him. A man at the next table stood but didn't move. Bapcia pointed to Matt and yelled, "He's choking!"

Angel didn't think about her next move. Swerving around tables and chairs and pushing between the people who were now crowding toward Matt's table, she reached him in seconds. The man who had first stood grabbed Matt's arms and held them in the air. The middle-aged woman screamed, "Call 911!"

Stooping so she was nose-to-nose with Matt's reddening face, Angel locked eyes with his wide, panicky blue ones. "Matt! Are you choking?"

As he struggled desperately with the man holding his arms, Matt nodded frantically.

"Somebody hit him on the back!" the man yelled.

Angel stood. "Put his arms down." She shoved the man as he stumbled back, and Angel positioned herself behind Matt, wrapped her arms around his chest, and felt for the right spot below his ribs. Making a fist, she grabbed it with her other hand and thrust it upward. When nothing happened, she repeated the move with slightly more force, and a chunk of something flew out of Matt's mouth and hit the floor.

The crowd cheered, and in the distance, a siren blew. Angel stepped away, shaking and breathing hard. Someone offered her a chair and she sank into it.

Matt coughed and sucked in air. The white-haired woman who had walked away from his table earlier pushed her way through the crowd and wrapped her arms around his shoulders. Her eyes brimmed with tears.

When the trembling in Angel's legs calmed, all she wanted to do was get away. As she tried to stand, Matt looked up at her for the first time since he'd resumed breathing. His mouth opened, registering shock. In a voice much deeper than Angel remembered, he whispered, "Angel."

The man who had held Matt's arms clapped Angel hard on the back and guffawed. "She sure is, boy! She sure is! You got yourself a real gen-u-ine guardian angel!"

Chapter 4

Angel's pulse pounded in her ears. Her legs still felt like her roommate's homemade linguine. All she wanted to do was get away from O'Dowd's Pub and Matt Peterson's grateful eyes, but too many bodies blocked her way. The white-haired lady introduced herself as Matt's great-aunt Berta and tried to stick a roll of money in her hand. A boy of about ten asked her to pose for a picture. Mom and Bapcia were no help, standing around collecting kudos on her behalf.

When the paramedics arrived, the sea of bodies parted, and Angel made her break. She reached the restaurant's front door, her mother and grandmother at her heels. Bapcia grinned and pulled Angel into yet one more hug as a thin blond man with thick glasses stopped in front of them. "Are you a paramedic?"

Angel shook her head while taking her first real breath in minutes. "I'm in food service."

Jeanie put her hand on top of Angel's head. "My daughter owns her own party-planning company. She's Red Cross certified to teach CPR."

Get me out of here. Angel gave her mother a look that conveyed just that. She walked past the man with the glasses and out the door.

"He was trying to talk to you," Bapcia whispered behind her.

"He asked if I was a paramedic, and I answered him."

"Not him. Matt. He was trying to get you to stop when you ran out."

Angel didn't answer. She'd heard him.

"You just saved his life. You could at least have let the poor man thank you."

Angel stopped then pivoted, her fists clenched. "The man is anything but poor. That man cost me my job and then weaseled his way into the position I was headed for. By the grace of God alone, I didn't stop to think before I saved his life."

She spun back around and started taking long strides until she heard Bapcia whispering behind her. "What did he do again?"

Jeanie sighed. "He blew some things out of proportion to the boss and Angel got fired."

"What kind of things?"

"I don't remember all the details, but Angel said—"

Her phone rang. Angel looked at the name and then the time, and her pulse once again hammered in her ears.

"What's up, Dena?" Angel kept her voice calm, fully expecting the opposite tone from her assistant manager. If Dena was calling, something was wrong.

"You fired Chuck without telling me?" Dena's voice held not only anger but blatant fear.

"Yes."

"But Joe Hart's party starts in forty-five minutes!"

"What's that got to do with Chuck? You wanted to handle this one on your own."

There was a pause long enough for Angel's heart to skip two beats. "I couldn't get the entertainment I wanted, so Chuck said he knew a girl band that would be perfect." Her voice teetered on the edge of hysteria. "He said he'd take care of the details, but now he left a message on my voice mail saying you fired him, so he told the band not to show and said I was on my own. I don't even know the name of the band. Angel, you have to do something."

"Dena, slow down. You can do this; that's what this job is all about, learning to think on your feet. Grab a phone book. You've got five people there who can help you make calls."

"We did that. I wouldn't call you unless I was desperate. We can't find anything at the last minute. You have to do something!"

"You've got Gary, right? Just go with the deejay."

"But they're expecting live music and a show. Ange, these people have money, and they won't pay if they're not happy. We're depending on this one. We can't disappoint them."

Angel rubbed the back of her neck where the knot was building again and turned away from her mother's worried look. "I'll call Chuck. We'll work something out."

After assuring Dena, once again, that "things like this happen all the time in this business," Angel told her mother and grandmother to go on home without her and opened her phone to perform the most humiliating task she'd done in years.

Chuck answered her appeal with a mocking laugh. "Can't quite make it without me, can you? I knew you'd figure that out. I just didn't think it would be so soon."

"This is a one-time request, Chuck. You and Dena are friends. You can't leave her in the lurch like this. The band couldn't have rebooked since last night."

The laugh again. "For Dena, huh? Not to save your skin? Right. Sure, I'll have some girls there by nine. Tell Dena I've got everything under control."

"Thank you." It took every ounce of Angel's self-control to say the last two words.

☙

Some time alone. . .and chocolate. That's what she needed. Time to walk and pray and think of anything but the past hour. When she got home, she darted upstairs before the questions could start. She changed into sweats, put Sunny on his leash, and headed for the door, yelling behind her that she was going for a long walk. A *very* long walk. After only a moment's hesitation, she left her cell phone on the kitchen counter. There was nothing she could do from three hours away. Dena would sink or swim without her help. If she pulled Pleasant Surprises under with her, at least that would answer the question of Angel's future—she wouldn't have one.

She crossed the river just in time to watch the vermilion sun skim one last finger across the Galena River before slipping behind the trees. A rainbow-striped hot air balloon floated overhead, low enough that she could hear the *whoosh* of the burners. Below her, three kayaks cut ripples in the surface of the water.

With its panoramic view of the river, of red brick houses nestled into the bank, this was the spot she missed most when she was in the city. Native Americans had named this area *manitoomie*—"God's country." That's what it was to her. She'd memorized this place with all five senses and could play it back on restless nights when the sound of sirens and car horns made sleep impossible. The framed Galena sunset above her desk at work had become her escape window in the past weeks, sometimes feeling like the only source of light in the room.

When a teenage couple vacated a park bench, Angel grabbed it. Even though the sun was no longer visible, the sky was still tinged with pink and streaks of pale orange. Angel drank in the soft pastels as she took a cleansing breath, and then another, willing the bitterness ignited by her encounter with Matt to dissipate. It wasn't working.

And what did he do again? Bapcia's question hovered over her like a droning hornet, but she wasn't about to let it sting. The next few hours were hers. She needed some serious God time and a bit of self-indulgence. What she didn't need was a visitation from the ghosts of her past.

Thoughts cluttered her brain like her jam-packed office desk. "First things first," she said out loud, thankful that Sunny provided a good cover for talking to herself. "Prioritize." She grabbed thoughts as they shot through her head and assigned them spots on her to-do list.

She'd done all she could for the bachelor party that was beginning in minutes—with or without entertainment. It was a party that shouldn't be happening. She'd been on the verge of calling Joe Hart's friends to tell them about her new policies when Chuck's brand of logic had worn her resolve to nothing. All of her radical new Christian convictions vaporized in the face of the frightening red figures on Chuck's spreadsheet. At the rate they were losing clients, thanks to Angel's new policy of avoiding anything off-color, she wouldn't have enough to pay next month's rent. And so, with Chuck's numbers and Dena's repeated promise that she'd keep it "tasteful and sophisticated," Angel had let the booking stand as originally planned. *Hypocrite.*

30

She loosened her ponytail and bent over, shaking her head. Gathering the unruly mass back into her hair band, she nudged Sunny with her knee. "Come on, we have to earn our custard. Two miles is a single scoop of chocolate, four miles is hot fudge."

As she power walked, she tried a second pass at prioritizing. *Urgent things first.* On her mental list, "truck" went in the "later" box. She'd talked to the garage and learned it would be at least a week before the new fender came in. She could rent a car, of course, but she really didn't mind that her weekend "runaway" was turning into a forced vacation. If she managed her time right, she might actually be able to handle the business—what was left of it—long distance and still leave a good chunk of each day open. Open to. . ."serendipity." She said Bapcia's word out loud, loving the sound. It had a Christmas-morning kind of feel to it, and at no time in her life had she been more in need of a "fortunate accidental discovery."

Saying the word out loud brought Wade Ramsey's face clearly into focus. She gave in to serendipitous fantasy. What if he just happened to be waiting in line for ice cream or just pulling out of a side street as she and Sunny walked past? What if he asked her out, and what if she miraculously woke up skinny tomorrow morning and a first date turned into a second and a third. . . The fantasies eased her tension. Her muscles warmed, and she fell into a comfortable pace.

The easy pace lasted until she looked up and realized she was passing Frank O'Dowd's Irish Pub. The droning hornet was back.

"You do need to let it go," her mother had said. But she had, hadn't she? Months went by now without a thought of Matt Peterson. *And what did he do again?* He'd ratted on her, that's what. It was the only word that seemed to fit.

Getting hired at twenty years old by Célébrez, the largest event planner in the area, had been a dream. For the first time in her life, she had a solid hope of getting beyond the stigma of growing up *without*. The job hours dovetailed with her class schedule, and she was able to put into practice the things she was learning as she worked toward her hospitality management degree. Within two years, she'd become an integral part of the creative team, and it was no secret she was being groomed for management. And then, along came Matt Peterson and his Boy Scout conscience.

The atmosphere at Célébrez had always been relaxed. There were times Angel punched out at noon and then spent the next hour taking a phone call from a client or talking shop with someone from advertising. She didn't mind giving time to her job without getting paid once in a while, so on the rare occasion when she wanted an afternoon of shopping, it was no big deal to call the girl in the next cubicle and ask her to punch her in. It was payback, balancing the books. Everyone did it. And then along came Matt Peterson.

Angel's head was starting to hurt. She had to get her thoughts off Matt.

Putting on her headphones, she turned the music up until she couldn't hear the cars driving by or the crying baby in the stroller across the street, or the droning of her own hornetlike thoughts.

Lord, I choose to praise You right now. I choose to leave everything in Your hands. You are worthy of praise. Please help me to center my thoughts on You alone.

❦

A black Explorer. In Bapcia's driveway. An old, familiar, sinking feeling pulled at her, as if the force of gravity had suddenly increased. Her reaction had nothing to do with the reality of the moment. It had everything to do with years of being ashamed of the two-bedroom house where, for fifteen years, she'd slept on a fold-out couch in the living room. It wasn't the same house anymore, thanks to the success of Pleasant Surprises. Vinyl siding, landscaping, and an addition that doubled the square footage had changed everything. . .except the shame imbedded in her memory.

The sound of her shoes slapping the newly blacktopped drive brought her into the present. Wade. . .here. Why, in all her "what-ifs," hadn't she thought about the possibility and dressed for it?

Groaning, she looked from her too-tight lime green shirt to the ice cream splotch on her pale blue sweat pants. Why now? This was not serendipitous, this was tragic. Her hair was damp and tangled, her mascara probably running, and she most likely had hot fudge smeared on her face. And, thanks to the sweat pants and twenty-four hours of indulgence, her stomach stuck out even more than it had the first time she'd met the gorgeous man in the black Explorer. *Way to sabotage, Angel.*

When in doubt, smile. It was a line she used often on the job. At this point, that was about all she could do. Through the screen door, she heard Taylor's voice. He hadn't come alone. Hiding her disappointment behind a smile and sucking in her stomach, she walked into the living room and was met with a round of applause.

Sunny bounded over to Taylor and greeted her like an old friend. Angel felt a blush creep from her neck to her ears as she stared at the tall man in the bleached muslin shirt, who she just now noticed had espresso-colored eyes. A man who jumped to his feet and gave her a standing ovation.

"You're a hero. . .I mean heroine!" Taylor yelled.

"A gen-u-ine guardian angel we hear," Wade added.

Angel held up both hands, palms out. "Don't believe a word they're telling you."

Taylor's two-toned hair fanned her face as she shook her head. Strands of chin-length black hair peaked out beneath choppy blond layers. "You saved a guy's life!" she said, twirling the silver post in her eyebrow with one hand as she stroked Sunny's head with the other. "That's amazing!"

Angel scrambled to get the focus off herself. "So what brings you two back to Galena?"

Wade picked up an angel wing and held it up as if he were giving a toast. "I'm addicted." A slow, crooked smile deepened a dimple Angel hadn't noticed the night before. "Actually, I had a few questions about planning the anniversary party. . .and we have an invitation. My church is having a gospel music night tomorrow."

Taylor wrinkled her nose. "And even if you don't like that kind of music, there's a killer barbecue afterwards. Wade buried the pig this morning."

Wade closed his eyes and shook his head. "In a barbecue pit." He shot his sister a mind-your-manners look. "We thought all of you might like to come."

Angel looked from her mother to her grandmother. Their unspoken messages were loud enough for the neighbors to hear. "Sounds fun."

"Good." Wade nodded. "So sit down and tell us all about your—" A knock rattled the screen door. Wade's gaze shifted to a spot over Angel's head.

Angel turned. Matt Peterson stood framed in the doorway.

In her rush to get away from him earlier, she hadn't gotten—hadn't wanted—a good look at him. What she did remember was that her arms barely fit around his granite chest, and his biceps were the size of bocce balls. Now that he stood three feet in front of her, she took it all in—short-cut blond hair, frameless glasses, a tan he'd either paid for or gotten from sunning beside some body of water farther south than Lake Michigan. It was obvious the years and a ton of discipline had brought changes to his body. But she had her doubts that time had fixed the inside.

Matt's eyes roved the room, settling back on her. "I didn't get a chance to thank you."

As Angel's pulse began to pound, a familiar ringtone played in the distance. Behind her, she heard someone get up and walk to the kitchen.

Matt's discomfort hung around him like a cloud of bug spray, so palpable Angel had a split second of empathy, but it didn't last. "I'd like to talk to you," he said. "Maybe another time?"

She stared back, trying to get the word "no" out of her mouth. "I don't think that'll—"

"Angel! It's Pug." Her mother held the phone straight out as she strode into the room.

Saved. . .with a little help from her friend. For once, she wasn't irritated that her mother had answered her phone. "Pugsley!" Angel laughed into the phone out of sheer relief and stepped toward the kitchen.

"I'm praying big time, girl. What can I do?"

"About what?"

A short sigh burst in her ear. "Turn on the news, Ange."

Chapter 5

C huck. Some way, somehow, this was his fault. Angel stared at the television screen, at the huddle of hysterical girls in too-short skirts, at the flashing lights of the ambulance.

"Sit down, Angelika."

She sat.

"Pleasant Surprises. . ." Matt pointed at the newscaster. "You work for them?"

Angel didn't blink. "If only. I own it."

His eyes bugged as if the hunk of sirloin were still lodged there. He paced from the television to the giant jade plant in the corner of the living room. "Oh man, Angel, you're in deep."

The anchorwoman moved on to a house fire in Dubuque, and Bapcia changed the channel. They waited in silence through a Visa commercial. Angel folded her hands on her lap. She wouldn't add gasoline to the embers of panic burning her throat until she heard the whole story.

"Good evening." A man in a black suit with a pinstriped shirt and red tie smiled at them from behind his polished desk. He gave teasers of the upcoming sports and weather. He didn't look like a bearer of bad news. But then, on some off-camera cue, the smile left.

"A sixteen-year-old girl has been rushed to Lake Forest Hospital following a single-car accident. The girl, who was the driver and only person in the vehicle, apparently hit a utility pole just minutes after leaving a condominium complex where she was part of the entertainment at a bachelor party for Joe Hart, recently suspended linebacker for the Chicago Bears. The teen was driving a Camaro owned by Hart. She is apparently one of six state champion cheerleaders from Lakeland High School hired to perform for the all-male party attendees. Police have arrested an employee of Pleasant Surprises, coordinators of the event, for serving alcohol to minors. Just two weeks ago, Joe Hart was involved in a similar—"

"Turn it off." Angel closed her eyes and tried to pray, but words flashed then disappeared like ambulance lights.

Wade got up and turned off the news. Bapcia still stood, staring at the black screen, until Wade pointed to the rocking chair in front of the window, and she finally sat down.

Her mother stood behind the love seat where Angel had landed when told to sit. Her hands worked Angel's shoulders as if she were kneading bread. "It'll be okay, honey." Her voice didn't match her words.

Bapcia clucked, shaking her head. "I know you had nothing to do with this, Angelika. It's probably all some big mistake."

"It may be a big mistake, but Joe Hart's got big money on his side." Matt's pacing tightened to a three-step route. "I've been in the restaurant business long enough to know this won't be pretty."

Sunny left Taylor and planted his head on Angel's knee. Wade walked over and knelt on the floor beside Sunny. "Do you have a lawyer, Angel?" His fingertips touched her hand for a moment, as if he thought he needed to get her attention.

He had her attention. He was close enough to give her a clear view of the line between tanned skin and the dark stubble that swept across his jawline like a distant herd of buffalo. For the span of two breaths, she didn't own a company on the verge of disaster and wasn't responsible for a sixteen-year-old girl in the Lake Forest emergency room.

"Should I get your lawyer on the phone for you?"

Angel blinked, stepping back from the cliff where she'd teetered while tracking the buffalo herd on its way to the craggy cleft of Wade Ramsey's chin. "Yes. Um. No. I have her number in my phone. I'll call her. But how. . .how do I find out about the girl?"

"We may have to wait on that. I don't think they'll give you any information. Maybe your lawyer can find out something."

A handclap drew Angel's gaze from Wade's chin. Matt paced to Sunny's other side. His index finger sliced the air in a frenzy. "I know somebody."

"At the hospital?"

"No. A lawyer."

"I have a lawyer."

"But this one's good. Perfect for what you're going to be up against. He's done a lot of high-profile stuff, and I'm sure if I talk to him he'll—"

"I like my lawyer. She's a friend of mine." She was remembering more reasons why she'd had only one date with this man.

Angel's phone rang in her hand. She stared down at her caller ID, knowing her "Things like this happen all the time" speech just wasn't going to cut it.

☙❧

Lord, what do You want me to do here? Wade felt the floorboards press into his knees, but he didn't get up. He was pretty sure neither of the things he wanted to do right now was God's answer. Shoving a sock in the mouth of the man he'd deduced was the person Angel had saved from choking would negate her heroic efforts. And wrapping his arms around the woman he'd found on the side of the road less than twenty-four hours ago just might result in Irish setter teeth in his brachialis muscle. He settled for simply being there, praying, while she tried to calm the frantic female on the phone whose words could be heard by everyone in the room.

Taylor tiptoed over and crouched beside him. "Should we leave?" she whispered.

And let the man who should be sucking on a sock take charge? "Not yet." He looked at his sister, tapping her thigh to music that played only in her head. Taylor's ADD was showing. He nodded toward Angel's grandmother. "Why don't you ask Ruby if she wants a glass of water? She looks a little pale. And bring one for Angel, too."

"Okay."

The next to squat beside him was Sock Man. The man jerked his head toward Angel. "You two going out?"

"No."

"How well do you know her?"

I hope better than you. Wade gathered there was some connection between the two beyond the Heimlich maneuver. "Why?"

"Because I think she's going to need some guidance here."

Okay, so maybe the guy wasn't as egotistical as Wade had made him out to be. Maybe his first impression of the buzz cut with the muscles was based on irrational jealousy. He couldn't make sense of his almost primal desire to protect a woman whose last name he couldn't even pronounce yet. He nodded at the man and stuck out his hand. "Wade Ramsey. I actually just met Angel yesterday." If he were playing chess, that move would hurt him.

Sock Man took his hand and, thankfully, didn't use all the strength he clearly possessed. "Matt Peterson. Angel and I go way back."

That statement could mean just about anything. Had they dated. . .or played in the sandbox together? Wade stood at the same time Matt did. At least he had one physical advantage. He had height in his favor. "You're in the restaurant business?" He stepped toward the window and Matt followed.

"Yup. I have a little place in Chicago on East Ontario, a block off Michigan Avenue."

"How's business these days? Economy affecting you?" The taxes alone on a building near the Magnificent Mile had to be deadly.

"People still need to eat."

"Is that how you know Angel? Business connection?"

"We. . .worked together years ago." A look of doubt or something negative pinched his face then vanished in a quick smile. "What do you do?"

Taylor entered the room in time to catch that last question. Her eyes did the goofy figure-eight that had made Wade laugh since she was three. He'd heard her commentary on men engaged in "Can you top this?" He shoved the laugh back down. "I'm a teacher. High school. History."

"Hmm."

"You said something about Angel's case being in the 'big leagues,' but isn't it likely to be the girl's family that files suit and not Joe Hart?"

"Oh, he'll get involved. His reputation, what there is of it, will be at stake. His lawyers will glom onto this like killer whales."

Killer whales? A bit over the top.

"And the condo association may jump on board. . .and the families of the other minors, if indeed they were paid to be there."

It was beginning to sound like a class action suit. Wade turned to look at Angel. To her credit, she hadn't shed a tear and didn't appear to be in the kind of shock he thought he'd be experiencing in her shoes. He listened in while she tried to say good-bye to the sobbing person on the other end.

"We'll work it out Dena," he heard her say. "We'll get through this. Things like this happen all the time in this business."

⁂

Angel ended the call, Dena's wails still pealing in her ear. She looked up at two men. Two men who hadn't been in her life two days ago. *Lord, I have to believe You brought them here.* The cute one *and* the irritating one.

"What did you learn, honey?" Her mother's fingers would soon wear holes in the shoulders of her lime green shirt.

Angel patted her mother's hand and stood, surprised her legs would support her. She stepped toward the TV so she could include everyone in the room. "One of my employees. . ." It suddenly dawned on her that Matt knew him. The three of them had worked together. "Chuck Morehouse, an *ex*-employee, actually, was supposed to hire a girl band. Instead, he hired the cheerleaders to. . .cheer." The word tasted sour. "One of them was only fourteen." She rubbed both hands across her face. "And a server hired by Pleasant Surprises stupidly served them drinks without checking ID."

"*Youch.*" Matt folded his arms.

"What's next?" Wade asked. "What's your responsibility?"

All of it. All my responsibility. All my fault. "I have to call my lawyer. . .get back to the office. . .then, I suppose I'll need to talk to the police and see if they'll let me speak to the server. And somehow I'll need to avoid reporters. . .keep my assistant from jumping off the State Street Bridge. . .and strangle Chuck." She flashed a faux smile and leaned against the television console so hard it moved.

"When will your truck be done?" Wade asked.

"Your truck? What happened?" Matt's hands moved to his hips.

"I hit a deer last night. My truck's in the shop." She turned her eyes from the floor to Wade. "It won't be done until Friday at the earliest."

Bapcia looked over Angel's head in a nonverbal connection with her daughter. "You can take our car back. Leave Sunny here."

"Oh! Can I take care of Sunny for you?" Taylor looked through bicolored bangs with hopeful eyes. "Since you'll be so busy?"

"Don't you have school?"

"I'm doing alternative high school." Her head jerked toward Wade. "Makes my brother proud." Wade cleared his throat, and Taylor's eyes swiveled in a way Angel had never seen eyes swivel. "Anyway, I'm not there as long as Wade is every day, so I can take care of Sunny and then I'll have something to do so I won't get so bored. Please?"

Angel laughed. "Okay." *It'll give me another reason to connect with you. . .and your brother. . .again.* "It would really help if you'd watch him."

"Thank you, Taylor." Jeanie walked around the couch and stood beside Angel, resting her hand on the middle of her back. "Would you like me to go with you?" Her fingertips swept up then down.

Angel understood the maternal touch thing, but it was starting to aggravate already raw nerves. "No. Thank you. I'll probably end up camping out at the office. I wouldn't have any time to spend with you. I'll rent a car."

"You can't afford that."

Did her mother have to air her dirty laundry in front of the men?

"Yes I—"

"Angel." Matt crossed his arms across his chest, Mr. Clean-style. "I'll take you back to the city in the morning."

Chapter 6

Matt winked across the front seat of his dark blue Porsche Boxster as he turned onto Highway 20. "You know, in some cultures, if you save someone's life that person becomes your property. . .your slave for life."

Matt Peterson had a sense of humor? "So you'll peel my grapes and fetch my slippers?" Angel cringed. That sounded way too much like flirting.

"Your slightest wish is my command."

My wish is that you weren't the one driving me home. Angel massaged the back of her neck where a tension headache had set up residence two weeks ago. She groped for a safe subject. Instead of safe, she landed on one that needed to be tackled if she was going to spend the next three hours and twelve minutes in this car—this very nice, very cushy little leather-seated car. "Are you still with Célébrez?"

"I had a feeling that would come up."

Angel stared at him, trying to analyze his tone. Surprisingly, it wasn't defensive. She waited for him to expand his answer.

"I left not long after you did, actually."

Indignation fizzed in Angel's stomach. He'd pushed her out then never even took the place that would have been hers? She'd always been sure that was his motive. "You never got into management?"

"No."

The clock on the dash changed from 9:23 to 9:24. Angel closed her eyes and counted to ten.

"Chuck also got fired because of what I started back then, didn't he?" he asked.

"Yes. He worked for me. . .until last night."

He answered in silence that lasted several miles. "Angel, I owe you an apology."

Way too late, but she'd take it.

Matt shifted into fifth gear and whipped around a semi. "I was kind of overzealous in those days."

Overzealous. That was probably a mild version of what her employees were saying about her. "If you were in the same situation right now, what would you do?"

"Mind my own business." He glanced her way and gave a slight shrug. "Management knew what was going on, Angel. Half the company was cheating on the time clock and they knew it. They turned a blind eye to the gray areas, and it drove me nuts. I was all black-or-white back then. Had to do everything by the book." He offered an apologetic smile. "When I tattled, they had to act, had to make an example out of you. . .and Chuck, too, I guess."

"But. . .we were in the wrong." The truth of it hit like a slap. "Some things *are* black or white. The company had rules and we were breaking them."

"You were bending the rules."

"No. We were breaking them." Was she actually going to start an argument with Matt Peterson to convince him he'd been right all along? Angel put both hands over her eyes and shook her head.

Matt laughed. "Does this mean you don't hold it against me? I've figured all these years you must hate me."

She turned toward the window, staring at the sunlight glinting off a steel silo. "I did."

"But you don't now?"

"No." She didn't hate him. After six years of stuffing bitterness, the realization came with a surge of relief.

"I was an idealistic snob back then, wasn't I?" He changed lanes again, slipping smoothly around two cars and moving back into the right lane ahead of them. "I can assure you, all that self-righteousness is gone. Reality smacks you upside the head a few times, and you change. You're getting a pretty fierce dose of reality right now, aren't you?"

Angel leaned back in the leather seat with a sigh and stared out the window. "Yeah. . ."

"I gathered there's more going on with your business than what happened last night."

She painted a picture of the past few weeks. "I may lose it all."

"Maybe I can help you out. . .I am your slave for life, you know." He laughed. Angel didn't join in. "You're in a bad place right now, but things'll work out and you'll get past this speed bump and move on to better times."

Speed bump? A young girl lay in a coma, possibly dying, Angel was on the brink of losing all she'd worked for, losing her very identity, and Matt called it a speed bump?

It was going to be a long ride.

⚘

"Shrimp scampi and linguine okay?" Patti Pugelli, aka Pugsley, stood in front of the freezer compartment of the beach blue retro refrigerator. Short black curls bobbed as she looked over her shoulder. "Or tortellini? Or both?"

At the chrome-legged kitchen table, Angel slumped over her laptop, propping her head with her fists. The "Community News" page of the *Daily Herald* stared back at her. "Both. And grab the apple dumplings out of the freezer. Better to eat myself to death than let the world nibble away at me."

"Oh, come on, it's just a little speed bump." Pug's almost black eyes sparkled.

Angel bared her teeth then managed a half-hearted laugh. "Yeah, no big whoop." She pointed to the picture on her laptop of a utility pole imbedded in the front end of a red Camaro. "The girl might be in a coma for life, but hey, it's all good." Closing the computer and shoving it to the side, she stood up. "I'm going to the hospital."

"I thought Doreen told you not to."

"Doreen the lawyer has to say that. Doreen the real person would go to the hospital if she were me."

"You don't even know the girl's name yet."

"I'll find someone who does." She held up her phone. "There have to be kids talking about this on the Internet." Angel grabbed her jacket from the orange bag that still sat by the door where she'd dropped it five hours ago. "I need to do something. I can't just sit here waiting for news. I need to talk to the girl's family and let them know how sorry I am, and that I'm praying and. . ."

Pug stared at her, chewing on her lip.

"What?"

"Is that what *they* need?"

Angel groaned. In three months, Pug would have her master of arts in spiritual formation and discipleship from Moody Bible Institute. Sharing an apartment with that much knowledge was sometimes a pain. Angel dropped her jacket and flopped on the couch. "What would you do?"

Pug set a bag of frozen shrimp in the sink in the granite-topped island. "This is one of those 'Do as I say' things."

"So you'd go to the hospital?"

"Probably. But stop and pray about this, Ange. Just your presence could make things worse for them."

Angel sat up. "Come with me then. You can be a go-between and talk to—" Her phone, still in her hand, jingled its generic ring. Not family, not a close friend or a coworker. "Please be Doreen." She opened it. "Hello."

"Hi, Angel. It's Wade. Is this a bad time?"

In my life? Yes. To talk to you? Never. "I can talk." *And talk and talk and talk.*

"How are you doing? Have you heard anything about the girl?"

"She's in an induced coma. They're watching for swelling on her brain. It could be hours. . .or days. . .until they know anything."

"How are you holding up?" His voice was warm. Hot chocolate on a winter day warm. "I've been praying for you." Hot chocolate on a winter day with whipped cream warm.

"Thank you. That means a lot." Angel grabbed a pink chenille throw and snuggled into her huge round coffee-colored chair.

Pug mouthed, "Is that *him*?"

Angel nodded and tried to ignore the "*Whoot! Whoot!*" coming from the kitchen as she pressed the phone close to her ear.

"Have you talked to your lawyer?"

"Yes. She's probably at the jail as we speak, meeting with the server." Angel kicked her shoes off and punched down the pillow on the back of her three-sixty chair to make a dent for her head.

"On Sunday?"

"She's in my small group from church. A good friend."

"Must be. And what are you doing while you wait for news? Pacing? Chewing fingernails?"

"Just sitting around in sackcloth and ashes mostly."

"Self-condemnation. . .very constructive." His laugh was gentle. A sprinkle of cinnamon on the whipped cream.

"I'm finding I have quite a knack for it."

"Can I ask you a tough question before I subtly change the subject to something upbeat?"

"I guess."

"How did you get caught up in this? Why did you agree to do a bachelor party for Joe Hart? You had to know his reputation."

I did. And what if you knew mine? She didn't want to ruin what might be starting here by telling her handsome rescuer that just weeks ago she'd been the go-to girl for upscale sleazy bachelor parties. "I. . .compromised."

Silence. It hit her suddenly that this could be the end of a very short, but very sweet thing. She waited.

"I appreciate your honesty."

Seconds passed. Angel didn't know how to answer him.

"So what can we talk about to get your mind off all the yuck?"

Angel breathed a heavy sigh. *Let's talk about the tiny herd of buffalo stampeding across your chin. . .or your warm chocolate voice. . . .* "Aren't you supposed to be at the gospel service?"

"I'm waiting for Taylor to finish primping, polishing her eyebrow stud, or whatever she does."

"Good way to learn patience. Are you dressing up like Al Capone this week?"

"That's next week. This week we're studying the temperance movement in the twentieth century. Tomorrow I'm Billy Sunday, delivering highlights from his famous 'Booze' sermon."

"You can get away with that in a public school?"

Wade's laugh rumbled in the phone. "All in the name of history. As long as I'm using Billy Sunday's words and not my own, I can stand in front of a bunch of high school seniors and yell, 'I want every man to say, "God, You can count on me to protect my wife, my home, my mother, and my children, and the manhood of America." ' "

"Wow. And you've got the voice down, too. I mean, it sounds authentic. Let me hear some more."

"Okay. Wait. I have to stand up for this." A creaking sound followed, like a recliner returning to upright position. "Here goes. 'By the mercy of God, which has given to you the unshaken and unshakable confidence of her you love, I beseech you, make a fight for the women who wait until the saloons spew out their husbands and their sons, and send them home maudlin, brutish, devilish, stinking, blear-eyed, bloated-faced drunkards!' " He ended with a gasp for air.

Angel set the phone down and clapped. Pug dumped shrimp into a bowl and circled her ear with her finger.

The phone rolled down the pink blanket, and Angel caught it at her ankle. "That's amazing! Really, really amazing. But what's their reaction? Don't they laugh?"

"Sure. But they listen. We talk about why people were so opposed to alcohol, and it always seems to happen that one of the kids brings up a personal story. A family member or neighbor who's an alcoholic. I don't give opinions, I just sit and pray and let the conversation go where it will."

"So they get serious?"

"Usually. And when they do, I quote Billy again. Want to hear it?"

"Of course."

"I go to a family and it is broken up, and I say, 'What caused this?' Drink! I step up to a young man on the scaffold and say, 'What brought you here?' Drink!" Wade's voice quieted and his words slowed for impact. "Whence all the misery and sorrow and corruption? Invariably it is drink."

"Wow."

"It makes them think. Well, it makes some of them think."

"Do you go around to other schools with this stuff?"

"I have."

"Hmm. There's a bunch of kids at a high school in Lake Forest that just might listen to you about now."

Wade was silent for a moment. "Guess I didn't do such a great job of keeping your mind off it, did I?"

"Sure you did. . .for a little while."

"Angel. . .this is in God's hands. You didn't cause it and you can't fix it. I got the impression yesterday that you and I are pretty much on the same page with God—trying to let Him lead—am I right?"

"Trying, yes. Not so much succeeding. I'm new at this."

"How long have you been a believer?"

"Two months. . .almost."

He laughed. "Don't be so hard on yourself. Learning to let go and let God takes time."

"I suppose."

"You're a babe, Angel."

"*What?*"

"You heard me. You're a babe." He laughed again. "Hebrews, chapter five, in the King James Version. It's referring to people who aren't ready for heavy-duty spiritual meat. They still need spiritual milk."

"Oh."

"But you're the other kind, too."

❧

"He called you a babe?" Pug dumped thawed shrimp into a pan sizzling with garlic and melted butter, then spun around and waved both hands in true Italian form. "He called you a babe."

"Uh-huh." Angel opened her mouth to the linguine snake dangling over it. "He was just trying to cheer me up."

"Right. I remember learning about that technique in one of my biblical counseling classes."

Angel turned off the burner, lifted the pasta pot, and carried it to the sink. "I'm not under any illusions."

"Stop that."

"What?"

"Stop being down on yourself."

Steam rose from the colander. Angel tested another noodle. "I'm sure he's got tons of girls dying to go out with him. Can you imagine being in high school and having a teacher that looks like he should be on a magazine cover?"

"Those better not be the girls he's dating, or the guy's gonna get fired. . .or arrested."

"Do you have to use that word?"

"Do you have to get off track so easily? Why do you think a guy like that wouldn't be interested in you?"

Angel dumped the linguine into a red stoneware bowl and unwrapped a stick of cold butter. Cutting a chunk, she stabbed it with a knife and used it like a pointer. "Because a guy like that doesn't want a girl who eats too much of this."

Pug stirred the shrimp. "You think he'd rather have a twig who can't cook?"

"I think he'd rather have—" Her phone rang. The generic ring. She dropped the butter onto the pasta and grabbed the phone. Doreen's name appeared. "Hello?"

"Good news, Angel. The girl is awake. She has a skull fracture, but no apparent swelling. The doctors think she'll be totally okay."

Angel pulled out a chair and dropped onto it. "Thank God." Tears spilled onto the hand that held the phone.

"Amen to that."

"Do you know anything else?"

"All of the girls, including the one who was injured, have been cited for

44

illegal consumption of alcohol. Your server is still in jail, and she's denying everything. The charges will probably be lighter now that we know the girl's going to make it. You'll be getting a call to come in for questioning, but don't stress about it now. Let's just celebrate this good news and take each thing as it comes."

Angel hung up the phone and raised her hands. "Thank You, Jesus!" She told Pug about the girl.

Pug let out a massive sigh. She turned and leaned against the stove. "Let's pray and eat. Best way to celebrate good news."

"Not, however, the best way to snag a guy like that."

Chapter 7

I f you drink responsibly it's not a problem, Mr. Ramsey." The black-haired girl in the front row picked at her blue fingernail polish as she talked.

Wade looked up at the clock. Six minutes until the bell rang. He ran a hand over his slicked-back, parted-down-the-middle Billy Sunday hair. "I agree. Responsibility is the key. Raise your hand if you can think of three people—include yourself if it fits—who, in the past six months, have partaken of 'the awful malignity of strong drink.'" His chest vibrated with his deep, practiced "preacher voice."

All seventeen hands rose.

"If you know for a fact that none of the people you're thinking of have ever gotten drunk, drop your hand."

Not a single hand dropped. The few snickers died quickly as the students turned in their seats to look at all the hands.

"Sobering, isn't it?" Wade sat on the edge of his desk. "And I do mean *sobering*."

A quiet classroom was a rare thing.

"You can put your hands down." He folded his arms across the front of his 1920s suit. "How long has it been since you heard something on the news about teenage drinking?"

A dozen kids answered at once. He called on the black-haired girl in the front row. "Jennifer."

"Saturday. That cheerleader who smashed her car into a light pole."

"I heard she's paralyzed," came from the back of the room.

"They said she might be in a coma forever."

Wade held up his hand. "The latest report is that she's going to be all right." The sound of Angel's voice when she'd called him last night, crying and laughing at the same time, did funny things to his own voice. He cleared his throat. "She was one very fortunate girl. But, in preparation for your assignment, I'd like you to be thinking about the ripple effect of that girl's actions."

Seventeen groans lifted in chorus. His kids were sick of the term.

"Who else was hurt when that young girl's car hit a light pole?"

"Her family."

"Her friends."

Wade nodded. "What about Joe Hart?"

A smattering of smart remarks joined the laughter. "His reputation was trashed before this."

"What about the Chicago Bears or the other people who live where the party was held, or the person who served her, who is now in jail?"

The bell rang.

What about the red-haired woman who was beyond adorable in Disney pajamas?

His students walked out and Wade pulled out his phone.

☙

"Pleasant Surprises. This is Angel." Angel took two files off the stack on her desk as she answered the phone that was still in her hand from the last three calls.

"Hi. It's Matt."

"Oh. . .hi."

"I heard the girl's going to make it. That's good news. One less thing to worry about. What else is happening?"

I'm doing just fine, thank you. "I'm waiting to hear from my attorney."

"Keep my offer about that lawyer in mind, Angel. This could still get sticky, and my guy knows the ropes."

Even after driving across the entire state with him, she didn't know how to decipher his tone. Sincere. . .with more than a twist of ego, and totally unpredictable. "Thanks. I will."

"This is kind of. . .awkward, given our history, but. . ."

"Matt? Could you hold on a minute? My cell phone is ringing." She reached in her purse, thinking she owed the person calling her a debt of gratitude. Matt Peterson was about to ask her out and she needed a moment to rehearse a graceful "no." She opened her phone. "Hello."

"Hi, Angel. This is Billy Sunday."

Angel grinned, hoping none of her employees in the somber office walked past her open door. "Hi, Billy."

"Are you in the middle of something?"

A triangle, possibly. "Matt's on my office line. Can you hold a sec?"

"Sure." Was there just the slightest hint of jealousy in his voice? "But I've only got seven minutes until my next class."

"I'll be right back." She clicked back to Matt on her office phone. "I need to take this call, Matt." She ignored the twinge of guilt. Taking this call *was* a need.

"Okay. I really just called to say that I'm here for you. I'd be happy to offer advice anytime you need it. I've got a degree in business and a few years under my belt. Just say the word."

"Thanks. I will. Bye." She let out a shaky sigh of relief and put her cell phone to her ear. "I'm back."

"I'm glad. I was just wondering if you could use a little distraction this weekend. Are you busy Saturday night?"

"Saturday. . .let me look." Did her thudding pulse make her voice shake? She looked down at the calendar that covered half her desk. She had a surprise baby shower at Via Veneto at one. At the bottom of Saturday's square, two angry red *X*s crossed out the bachelor parties Pleasant Surprises was no longer planning. "I should be free after five."

"Wonderful. Well, wonderful if you'll consider a date with a fire-and-brimstone preacher."

"I would, actually."

"How's Ruth's Chris sound?"

Expensive. "Fantastic."

"Can I pick you up at six?"

"I'll be ready."

"I'll give you my e-mail address, and you can send me directions to your place."

Angel scribbled on a sticky note, said good-bye, and picked up her purse. She had to be at the Lake Forest police department in an hour. She had no idea if she'd be sitting at her desk by afternoon or sitting in the Lake County jail.

❧

Do you have any proof that Charles Morehouse was no longer in your employ? Have you hired underage entertainers in the past? What is your training protocol for servers? Are your servers instructed to check all IDs? The questioning hadn't been as intense as she'd anticipated, yet as Angel pulled away from the Public Safety Building on Deerpath, she felt drained.

She'd walked out with a court date. . .and a lot of unanswered questions for the server who'd just been released on bond. But one question had been inadvertently answered in the past hour. She'd overheard the name of the injured girl. Nicole Alby.

The Lake Forest Hospital was less than two miles away. She had to try.

Twenty minutes later, she walked into a hospital room with a vase of yellow roses from the gift shop. The girl lay still, staring at the ceiling. Angel shot a prayer in the same direction.

"Nicole? Hi. My name is Angel." She set a vase on the bedside table.

The girl had clear tape on her right cheekbone that didn't hide the blood-crusted stitches beneath it. She gave a weak, lopsided smile. "Hi. Sorry, I can't turn my head much. My neck hurts."

Angel stepped to the end of the bed. "Is this better?"

"Yeah. That works." She closed her eyes for several long seconds. "They moved me here from ICU awhile ago, and I'm still pretty drugged up."

"I'm sure you are." Angel stuck her hands in her jacket pocket then took them out again. "Nicole. . .I'm the owner of Pleasant Surprises, the event planners for Joe Hart's party."

Nicole gave a weak laugh. "The surprise wasn't all that pleasant, you know."

Angel let out a shaky breath. "I know. That's why I came, actually. I wanted to see you in person and—" Firm footsteps sounded on the vinyl floor.

"That's my dad." Still looking at Angel, Nicole held her hand out toward the door. "Hey, Pops."

A surprisingly young-looking man with longish dark hair walked straight to the bed and planted two kisses on his daughter's forehead. "How are you, Pipsqueak?"

"I need a neck transplant."

"I'll talk to the doctor." He smiled up at Angel.

Angel wiped her damp palms on her skirt. "I'm Angel Cholewinski." She kept her hands at her sides. "I'm the CEO of Pleasant Surprises, the—"

"I know." The man held out his hand. "Tim Alby."

Angel shook his hand. "Mr. Alby, I just came to tell you how very sorry I am about all of this. The people we hire know they have to check IDs. I haven't had a chance to talk to the server yet, but I assure you we'll do anything we can to get to the bottom of this."

The man sighed. "It's been a horrifying ordeal for all of us. And a learning opportunity for the girls." He turned back to Nicole. "Where's Mom?"

"In the cafeteria."

He nodded. "Personally, I'd like to leave this all behind and just move on with life. My daughter is all right and that's all that matters. But—" He stopped talking when a woman in a gray sweatshirt walked into the room. He put his arm around her. "Marlene, this is Angel. . .I'm sorry, I don't remember your last name."

"Angel Cholewinski. I own Pleasant Surprises, the event coordinators for Joe Hart's party." She held out her hand.

The woman didn't even look at Angel's hand. She pulled away from her husband. "We'll communicate with you through our lawyer. And don't come back here. You've caused us enough pain."

"Marlene. . ." Nicole's father looked embarrassed.

The woman shook her head. "I just got off the phone with the mother of one of the other girls. Something new came up today." She sucked in a seething breath. "Our daughter's future is destroyed." She aimed a hot, searing look at Angel. "And I'm holding *you* responsible."

❧

"She was just trying to scare you." Pug held out Angel's long white cardigan. "Put it on. We're going."

"I can't." Angel curled in the three-sixty chair, hugging a tub of Ben & Jerry's Chunky Monkey. "I'm fine. You go."

"You're not fine. You're eating banana ice cream and chow-mein noodles for supper."

"I like the crunch."

"Before that you had rice cakes with chocolate frosting."

Angel wiped her mouth with her sleeve. "Rice cakes are good for you."

"You're stuffing your emotions. You need to deal with them."

"I am dealing. Chunky Monkey is a perfectly legitimate coping mechanism."

Pug dropped the sweater on the floor and straddled a round pink footstool.

49

"You already know the girl is going to be fine. So what's the worst that could happen now?"

"We'll get sued."

"Then what?"

"My people lose their jobs and I lose everything."

"They'll sue the corporation, not you personally."

Angel dipped a spoonful of ice cream into a bowl of noodles and stuck it in her mouth. "My reputation will be ruined and I'll never work again," she garbled.

"No one will remember your name a week after it's out of the papers."

"Exactly. I'll go back to being the nothing I was my whole childhood. It'll go on my permanent record, and people will treat me like a leper. Wade will pretend he never found me on the side of the road and I'll never get to go to Ruth's Chris Steakhouse, and even if I do, I'll have to go naked because I'll have to sell all my clothes on eBay just to pay my half of the rent. . .if you let me stay here."

An unladylike scream of frustration accompanied Pug's launch from the stool. "I give up."

"This isn't just my job, it's me. It's who I am. If this falls apart, I'm back to being the dumpy poor kid with rummage sale clothes and no dad."

"Ange, you don't really believe what you're saying. Where's your faith, girl?"

"Gone. Zip. Nada."

The sweater shot at her, just missing her ice cream. "Get up. Or I'll go see a movie alone, and you can add that to your guilt list."

"Okay." Angel glanced at the clock and tossed the sweater back. She still had time to brush her teeth and change her shirt before they'd have to leave. The melodrama and sugar were lifting her spirits. Not that she'd let on to Pug until she actually walked out the door alone.

"Fine. I'm leaving."

Angel's sweater jettisoned from the end of her best friend's foot. Pug opened the apartment door. . .and a gasp sounded from the hallway.

Pug jumped back. "Doreen!"

"I need to talk to Angel."

"She's right here."

Without another word, Doreen walked in and handed a large envelope to Angel.

The pictures that fell onto Angel's lap made her retch and clamp her hand over her mouth. She recognized Nicole Alby in several. And Joe Hart.

And a swimming pool.

"These were taken with a cell phone. Every kid in that school has seen them."

Chapter 8

Tuesday morning dawned rainy and cold. It seemed right that the weather would fit her life. She hadn't slept more than two hours last night. Word about the pictures had hit the ten o'clock news. Parents and teachers were outraged. And the name Pleasant Surprises came up more than once in the story. Angel spent the night rotating between praying, crying, and punching her pillow.

She parked her rental car on the top level of the parking garage and hunted for the umbrella that was always in her glove compartment. Only today it wasn't. Not surprising.

By the time she got to the elevator, her hair was damp and twenty minutes of flat ironing completely undone. She took the skywalk to her building, got on another elevator, and ended up on the eighth floor at the exact moment Chuck Morehouse walked out of Pleasant Surprises with two large plastic bins. He glared and walked toward the elevators.

"Chuck." Angel swept wet corkscrews away from her eyes. "We need to talk."

"Maybe you need to talk, Angel. I don't." His smile was cocky.

"Have the police questioned you yet?"

He set the boxes down. "Ask my lawyer."

"Don't make this ugly."

Chuck shook his head. "You made it ugly when you fired me. No. When you decided to turn this business into something it's not supposed to be. And now you're going to lose your shirt." He eyed her with a look that made her hug her bag to her chest.

"You were supposed to hire a band."

"I don't work for you, remember? I wasn't supposed to do anything. But just for you, I hired entertainment anyway."

"They're teenagers."

"Oh, they were old enough. From what I hear, the guests were more than satisfied with my choice." He laughed, sending crawly fingers up her back. "I can't help it if your people were dumb enough not to card them."

She didn't have an answer.

"Angel, why don't you just get out of this business?" His voice lowered, sounding almost caring. "Go start something else with all your holy ideas. You don't belong here anymore." His hand swept toward the door with the Pleasant

Surprises logo. "I'll buy it from you. I'll give you a decent price and you can just walk away, free and clear. What do you say?"

Walk away. Free and clear. She could regroup, start a business that wouldn't eat at her conscience and ruin her name. She could start over from scratch. A clean slate, a new day.

She took out her keys and brushed past him. "I say no."

❧

"Angel, that was crazy." Matt stood in front of her desk, eyes wide. "I ran into Chuck on the elevator." His arms rose like a symphony conductor. "With the economy the way it is and your reputation in the tank, you won't get another offer."

"I don't want to sell it. I want to fix it." She jabbed her calendar with the end of a pen. "This is my life, my baby. I'm not interested in selling it." Why was she justifying her actions to this man?

Matt turned around and pulled a chair close to her desk. He sat down and leaned toward her. "Can I ask you something that's guaranteed to make you mad?"

For some strange reason, she laughed. "Have at it."

"Don't you think it's time for you to think about real babies? Settling down, giving this up?"

Her face warmed. Her teeth clenched. "Did you come here for a reason?" *Other than harassment?*

"I was a couple blocks away, and I really just stopped in to see how you were doing. I'm worried about you. I know you've got high ideals, but your 'cold turkey' idea isn't going to work. You owe people. You've shelled out money to hotels and catering services that you're not going to get back, and you're refunding clients at the same time. It can't work. Be reasonable, Angel. Wean away from the stuff that's your bread and butter, but don't drop it until you've got some other money coming in. I get that you're a Christian and all that, but God's not going to be glorified by bankruptcy. Either do it slow or sell it and get out before you lose everything."

Angel's pulse tripped then raced, as if she'd guzzled an energy drink and the caffeine just hit her bloodstream. Matt was reading from Chuck's script. "So I should just find me a nice man and start making babies, huh?"

Matt glanced at his watch and walked toward the door. His index finger jutted out at her. "Maybe."

❧

Wade called during his lunch. "I tried calling last night. You okay?"

Tears welled, and Angel got up and closed her office door. "No." She told him about the pictures in the envelope in front of her.

"Oh, Angel, I'm so sorry. Man, how much more can you take?"

"I. . .don't know."

52

"I wish I were there. I couldn't fix anything, but I'd loan you a shoulder and a hug."

Visualizing Wade Ramsey's arms closing around her broke the dam. Her tears were unstoppable.

"Let it out. Let God take it, Angel." And then he began to pray, softly, barely above a whisper. "Lord God, she's Your child, You know every thought, every fear. In the midst of her confusion, You are the answer. You are her rock, her shield, her fortress, her hiding place. You are the source of all comfort. . ."

His voice floated over her like a lullaby. Her tears came to an end. "Thank you," she whispered.

"Are you going to be all right? I can take a day off school if it would help."

Oh, it would help. "No. Just promise me a day when I'm fun again."

"I'll promise you more than one day."

Her heart fumbled to find its rhythm. "I'll take it."

"Angel? Don't give up. . .or in. You made one wrong decision and you're paying the consequences, but you'll see the fruits of your good decisions."

If only she'd made just one wrong decision. "Wade, there's something I need to explain." She told him about the kind of parties she was known for and the kind of entertainment she'd hired. She explained her decision and how she'd failed to stick to it. And then she held her breath.

"It must be incredibly hard to walk away from that kind of success."

That was not the answer she'd expected. "I had a lot of. . .zeal, I guess, when I started telling our clients about the changes. It's fading fast."

"But you're getting other bookings, right? Birthday parties and things like that?"

"I was working on it. But the accident and now the pictures are killing my chances of getting new business and pulling out of this nosedive." She closed her eyes and leaned back in her chair. "I thought God was in this, but I could lose everything."

"You could. And God would still be in it." His voice took on the same softness as when he prayed. "Angel, I hate to say good-bye, but I have to go."

"Thank you. . .for praying. . .and for caring."

"That's easy. Call me anytime, okay? If it's urgent, text me. I'll stop my class and pray with you if you need it. Understand?"

No. She was soaking it up, reveling in a kind of compassion she'd never experienced. But understand? Never. "Thank you. That means more than you can imagine."

≈❧

Just after seven, Angel closed the door to her private office. The phone rang at Luanne's desk. Angel let it go to voice mail. She stood in the middle of the quiet, remembering the way she'd felt the night before Pleasant Surprises opened its doors for the first time. Standing in this same spot, trying to see each detail through the eyes of a client, she had declared it good. Her vision had become reality and destiny seemed to smile down on her.

And then she became a Christ-follower. And all that changed.

But her feelings for this place hadn't. She loved the decor. Light birch-wood cabinets, tables with brushed nickel legs. Black chairs and couches in the reception area. The walls were pale sherbet colors. Raspberry behind the reception area. A soft peach in the consultation room. Honeydew melon and lemon chiffon in the reception area. Each room displayed several black and white photographs—pictures of weddings and birthday parties. In each picture, one thing had a surprising pop of color. Candles on a black and white cake stood out in lime green. One ribbon in a jumble of gifts was a splash of lavender.

No, Angel's feelings about the space hadn't changed. "Lord, I'm asking for a second chance. Let good things happen here." She prayed out loud, walking from desk to desk. Three more calls came in, but she ignored them. "Please bring the right people to fill these chairs."

Just as she reached the front door, the phone rang for the fifth time in less than ten minutes. That seemed odd for this time of night. She decided to answer it.

"Pleasant Surprises, this is Angel speaking."

"Hi. This is Taylor."

"Taylor?" A flicker of panic put an edge to Angel's voice. "Is Sunny okay?"

"Oh, yeah. Sorry. I probably scared you. He's great. We're out on a walk right now."

"Good. How are you?" *And how's your brother? Haven't talked to him in six and a half hours.*

"I'm okay."

"Have you been trying to call? The phone's been ringing off the hook."

"N–no."

Angel set her bag down on a couch and sank to the leather cushion. A dozen possible reasons for Taylor's call flitted through her mind. The most logical was that Wade had put her up to it. Wanted to know her favorite color or what she'd be wearing Saturday night. Angel smiled and leaned against the back of the couch. "So what are you up to tonight?"

"Well. . . Wade said I should keep my nose out of it, but I figured maybe you didn't know and you should know. . . ."

"Know what?"

"That there are pictures on the Internet from that party."

Angel felt her shoulders slump. "I knew there were pictures. I guess I should have figured that would happen."

"Did you know about the video?"

Angel hadn't eaten for over six hours, yet her lunch seemed in danger of reappearing. "No."

"It's on YouTube. It just got posted."

Angel closed her eyes. *Lord, how much more?* "Thanks for calling." A silent sigh slipped into the empty room. "I'm not going to look at it, but I needed to know."

"Um. . .I think you should probably watch it."

"Why?"

"Just go on YouTube. . .and type in Pleasant Surprises."

❧

Angel sat in her dark office, her knuckles pressed against her mouth. The two girls on her monitor wore bathing suits that had no business being in public. . . or anywhere.

"Hi, I'm Nicole."

"And I'm Carrie."

"And these are our friends." The two girls spoke in unison then pivoted away, showing the swimming pool behind them. Suspended above the water on the forearms of two bare-chested men, a third girl kicked her feet and giggled. The girl looked younger than Taylor.

"We work for Pleasant Surprises. We do bachelor parties and birthday parties and parties for no reason. And we do them right. If you want to plan a party like this for your friends, just call Pleasant Surprises." The girls were obviously reading their lines. "Call 555-S-U-R-P-R-I-S-E." They giggled. "And ask for Angel."

Chuck. It had to be. Angel threw a pen at the Galena sunset picture and turned off her monitor. The phone in the outer office rang again, then three more times as she stared at the dark screen. And then her cell phone rang, startling her out of her trance. Numbly, she picked it up. By now, she recognized the number. Wade. Calling to cancel. "Hello."

"Angel. Taylor just told me she called you. I'm sorry. You've got enough to deal with."

"I'm glad she called." Her voice rasped on the last syllable. "The phone hasn't stopped ringing." She heard a laugh and knew it was hers, though it had an unfamiliar tinny sound. "I guess Pleasant Surprises is going to be in the black now. We'll have business coming out of our ears."

Silence. He was the kind of guy who would try to let her down gracefully. She didn't blame him. She wouldn't want to go out with someone in her kind of mess. The least she could do was make it easy on him. "Wade. . .I think we should cancel Saturday night."

More silence. Several seconds passed, and Wade cleared his throat. "You think we should cancel because you don't want to be with me?"

"No! Of course not."

"You think we should cancel because you think I don't want to be with you?" The guy was good. He'd cornered her right into the truth. "I don't know why you would. It makes no sense to spend that kind of money on an evening with a miserable, crabby, hopeless business failure."

"Couldn't you squeeze just one more adjective in there?"

A weak smile pulled at her lips. "Tired. Depressed. Scared."

"Then being alone is the last thing you need."

"But—"

"No buts. Let me be the hero again. It's good for my ego. Let me rescue you from depression."

Warm chocolate once again. The smile took up a bit more of her tired face. "Thank you."

"That's a yes?"

"Yes."

"You going to be all right until Saturday?"

No. "I might need a rescue call or two." *Way to sound desperate and needy.*

"My pleasure. What are you going to do about this video thing?"

Throw things. Hide in the closet with a gallon of Chunky Monkey. "Change our phone number before I leave the office tonight."

"You're still at the office? Is that normal for you?"

"More normal than it should be, I suppose. My business is my baby." Matt's comment bounced against the walls of her consciousness like an October fly. *Don't you think it's time for you to think about real babies?*

"I'm thinking the event planner needs to plan some events for herself."

"Yeah. Maybe."

"We'll work on that. But about the YouTube thing—I have a thought."

"Uh-oh."

"Do you believe everything happens for a reason?"

Angel laughed. "That's Bapcia's philosophy. I guess I believe that. God is in control even in the midst of the storm." *Even if I'm not acting like He is.*

"So why not make the most of this? Are you familiar with 1 Peter 3:15?"

Familiar? The words were plastered all over her apartment, her car, and her office. "Yes. Can't say as I'm obeying it, but I know it well."

"Why don't you try living it out? Answer the phone calls and tell people the truth. Give 'em an earful. . .a little taste of what happens when God gets ahold of somebody."

Chapter 9

Angel stood with one hand on her office doorknob. The idea was absurd. Like volunteering for the lion's den. And yet, there was something in Wade's challenge that sank its teeth into her flagging spirit.

Always be prepared to give an answer to everyone who asks you to give the reason for the hope that you have. But do this with gentleness and respect.

Hope? She was running low. But that was her fault. She may be a "babe" in Christ, but there were a few things she was sure of. One was the power of prayer. Another was the need to get—and stay—connected to the source of hope. Angel tossed her purse onto her desk and walked back to her chair. Only this time, instead of sitting in it, she knelt in front of it.

The clock on her desk glowed 8:05 when she rose from her knees. She walked out to Luanne's desk and listened to the phone messages. Each one was more embarrassing than the one before. Most were pranks, but two left names and numbers. She scribbled them down and reached for the phone. "Lord, grant me courage and grace." She dialed the first one.

"This is Josh. What can I do you for?"

Angel's mouth acted like she'd just been to the dentist. A deep breath brought a moment of calm and she jumped on it. "Hi, Josh. This is Angel Cholewinski. I'm the owner of Pleasant Surprises, returning your call."

Josh answered with the kind of laugh she'd expected. "Hey. Wasn't sure this was a real deal."

"Well, Josh, that's the reason I'm calling. That video was somebody's sick idea of funny. But we're a legitimate event planning company." She dug in her purse for a water bottle and unscrewed the cap. "Did you have an event in mind or were you just. . ." She took a gulp of water. ". . .curious?"

He laughed again. "That, too, but I'm the best man for a friend of mine, and it's my job to plan the bachelor party. I don't have a wad of cash to spend, but I'd like it to be decent."

"Decent. . ." He couldn't possibly have set it up any better for her. "That's exactly the kind of parties we specialize in. We know that most men are sick and tired of the old cliché bachelor parties, and I'm guessing you're one of them." She paused to find out if she'd confused him the way she hoped.

"Yeah. . .I guess." His tone told her he had no clue what she'd just said.

"We've developed some fantastic theme parties that make for a memorable evening that won't get the groom in trouble with his future wife, if you get my drift."

"I get it. What do you mean by themes?"

"We'll plan a night around any sport—from football to fly fishing. Or pick a computer game, or a book, or movie."

"That's kind of cool. Most of us are deer hunters. Could you do something around hunting?"

"Absolutely. Complete with a camouflage cake and blaze orange candles."

"But no girls in the swimming pool, huh?"

Angel pressed the bottle of room temperature water to her forehead. "Don't you think we women deserve more respect than that?"

"Well. . ." Laughter played in his voice. "I guess I better say yes to that one. But that YouTube video was taken at the party that was on the news the other night, right? And you planned that."

"Unfortunately, that's true."

"So you're not doing that kind of thing anymore because you got busted?"

Angel's tired sigh ruffled the sticky notes on Luanne's desk. *Always be prepared to give an answer. . . .* "I've changed our policies because I recently became a Christian, and I want everything I do to reflect my love for Jesus."

Several seconds passed. Angel waited for the call to disconnect. And then she heard the click of a door, and the television noise she'd been hearing behind Josh disappeared. "I respect that. You don't find too many people with convictions they're willing to take a stand on. And I like the theme idea. 'Cause the guy I'm holding this party for? He's marrying my sister. And I don't want anything wrecking what they've got going."

"Your sister will be very grateful, Josh."

"I think she will. I'll pick a date and call you back in a couple days."

Angel pressed the OFF button and dialed another number. A number she now knew by heart. Wade answered on the second ring. "I've missed you." There was teasing in his words, but they still managed to warm her to her toes.

"It worked. I called a guy back and he didn't send out the lions."

A low whistle vibrated in her ear. "I'm proud of you."

"Thank you. And thank you. . .for the courage."

Wade laughed. Hot chocolate with a stick of peppermint. "I might have given you the idea, but God supplied the courage."

"You're right."

"Now go home."

Angel picked up her purse. "I will."

"Leave all the yuck in God's hands."

"I'll try."

"And dream about Saturday."

"That I can do."

≈❧

By Friday morning, Angel's skin had grown considerably thicker than it was on

Tuesday. She'd given Luanne instructions to answer all calls from reporters with a polite one-liner and to route all the YouTube calls to her office. Only two, three including Josh, of the dozens of people she'd talked to had a positive response. The rest laughed, hung up, or used words that raised the temperature on the thermostat in her purple-walled office. When yet one more call came through, Angel did what was becoming second nature. She prayed for strength and grace then smiled. "Angel speaking. How can I help you?"

"Angel, what's going on?"

"Matt. Hello."

"One of my employees called you about booking a party and said you preached at him for like an hour."

"Really?" Angel massaged the sore points near the bridge of her nose. "Was he the one who wanted Cat Woman to slide down the fire pole or the one who wondered what it would cost to hire just a couple of the Dallas Cowboys cheerleaders?"

"Hey, I'm not the enemy here. All the guy wanted was to plan a surprise party for somebody's thirtieth birthday and you give him a sermon? Are you *trying* to kill your business?"

"I remember the thirtieth birthday idea." Angel closed her eyes and blocked out the details. "Did he tell you where he got our number?"

"Yeah. He said he got it online. Your Web site, I imagine."

Angel sighed. Most of her breaths came out long and loud these days. "Are you near a computer?"

"I can be."

She gave him the YouTube address and waited while he watched.

"Oh, Angel. . .whoa. . . Who did this?"

"Chuck."

"You're sure?"

"Sure enough."

"What's his motive? Revenge?"

"Partly. I think he's starting his own business. He wants to ruin mine first."

Matt was quiet for a moment. "Chuck's good, Angel. You can't afford to have him competing with you."

"Tell me about it. My lawyer's looking into suing him for defamation. . .if they can get somebody in that video to say he was behind this."

"Hmm. Hey, are you free to meet for lunch?"

Free? Yes. Meet for lunch? She still didn't know how, or if, Matt Peterson was supposed to fit into her life.

Matt answered the things she hadn't asked. "Let's call it a business lunch. I want to run some ideas by you."

"O–kay."

"Good. Why don't you come to my place?"

Not a chance. Angel opened her mouth, but Matt supplied the words. "My restaurant place. I'll reserve a table for two."

Angel tipped the cab driver and stepped onto the curb and into a sliver of sunshine that sneaked between the buildings on East Ontario. She stared at the dark red awning over the doorway in front of her. Silver letters fluttering in the breeze spelled out MATT's PLACE.

Reluctantly, Angel walked out of the strip of warmth and into the chilly shadow that darkened the brown brick around the doorway. She followed two women in expensive suits into the restaurant.

The focal point of the room was the round counter and display case in the center. Rich red wood and yards of glass lit by tiny spotlights. *Very classy.*

A dark-eyed man, probably in his forties and several inches shorter than Angel, walked toward her. He wore a little black beret. "You must be Angel." He spoke with a thick French accent and bent in a slight bow.

"Yes."

"Follow me." He led her to a corner table and handed her a single parchment sheet. In seconds, Matt walked out of a door at the back, wearing black pants and a form-fitting black T-shirt. "Welcome to my place."

"It's amazing. And busy."

"I'm doing all right. Getting a little restless, though. I'm itching to expand the catering end or use my skills in something new altogether. You can never make too much money, you know." He winked at her.

"Restless. . .wish I had your problems." Angel picked up the piece of parchment paper. "What do you recommend?"

"Everything. If you like surprises, I can have Andre fix plates for us."

"I'm all about surprises."

"Cute." He motioned to the man who'd seated her and gave instructions smattered with French. "Andre will bring you a bite-by-bite tour of the wonders of Matt's."

"You're quite the wordsmith. Did you write this? She pointed to the menu. "MATT's PLACE. A FUSION OF SIMPLICITY, CONVENIENCE, AND ELEGANCE."

Matt shrugged. "I took a lot of advertising and marketing classes in school."

"Chuck was my marketing manager. Maybe I should hire you to develop a new image for Pleasant Surprises. . .and erase the old one." If only it were that simple. Change her image and stem the flood of cancellations. Just this morning she'd lost two weddings and a birthday party.

The blue of Matt's eyes suddenly darkened from summer to navy. "Creating a new image is exactly what I wanted to talk to you about." His fingers tapped a restless rhythm on the sides of a candle sconce. "I'd love to do that for you—redesign your Web site and work on marketing. If I can just get you to ease up on one thing, I think we can not only salvage your business, but make it boom."

One of the weights Angel carried on her back suddenly lifted. "I couldn't afford to hire you, but if you could give me a few pointers I'd—"

"You don't have to pay me. I owe you, remember?"

Andre approached at that moment with a large green bottle of Perrier and two frosted glasses.

"You're taking this indebtedness a little too seriously."

"You saved my life, Angel. And I very nearly ruined yours."

So he did get it.

He set a notebook on the table. "And it's not all altruistic. You and I can work together. I can handle all your catering—if you like the food, that is."

Angel gestured toward the deli island. "I can already tell I'll love your food." She played with his idea. "The 'one thing' you want me to ease up on. . .would that have anything to do with the part of my business I want to let go?"

He laughed. "It would."

Angel stretched her tightening neck muscles as unobtrusively as she could. "Matt, I have to get out of this. No more bachelor parties. The theme parties are way better than what we were doing, but. . ."

"But it's not the place for a woman with sensibilities."

"Sensibilities?" Angel laughed. "You make me sound like a prude out of a Jane Austen novel." She looked down at the ice bobbing in her glass and back at Matt. "Actually, I guess I don't mind that."

"Good." Matt pulled the cap off his pen. "I have an idea. I've been mulling something over since I talked to you this morning, and now it's crystallizing. If you want to get out of doing bachelor parties altogether, why don't I take over that part? You show me the ropes, and I'll bring in a couple people if I need to."

"But—"

"I know. You don't think I should be doing it either. But, Angel, it's a gold mine. Your whole business was built on these clients. It doesn't make sense to walk away from something that's a proven success when your business is in danger. We'll capitalize on what Pleasant Surprises is famous for, but make it wholesome this time. I promise I'll avoid all things sordid. Theme parties, just like you said."

"I don't know. The very nature of a bachelor party leans toward the dark side."

Matt covered his mouth with his fingers as he laughed. "We'll show your clients the light. We just won't do things quite as radically as you were trying. Consider this a slow and steady journey away from the da–a–ark side." His voice took on a horror film tone on the last two words.

"I don't know. . . ."

Matt's hand slid over hers. "Trust me on this, Angel."

☙

By Saturday, Angel felt like she'd spent the week in a food processor. Her thoughts spun from Matt—who'd called, text messaged, and e-mailed dozens of image ideas since their lunch—to Wade, who was picking her up in just hours for an evening at Ruth's Chris Steakhouse.

Staying present in the moment at the baby shower was a struggle. The surprise had come off flawlessly. The mother-to-be thought she was meeting her old college roommate for a late lunch at Via Veneto. Instead, she walked into a room full of friends and family. The decorations and party favors—pink rosebuds in milk-white vases, tiny pink piggy banks at each place setting, and mini gift bags filled with raspberry divinity—were a hit. Flavored coffees, finger sandwiches, and individual cheesecakes served on silver-rimmed plates turned out just as Angel had visualized.

Shower guests stood in line to say good-bye to the mother-to-be. Angel was planning her cleanup strategy when the mother of the guest of honor handed her a check. "This was everything we hoped for. I guess we made the right decision not to cancel."

Should she bite at that one? What did she have to lose? "You were. . .thinking of canceling?"

"Well. . .yes." The woman said it as though Angel should have expected her to cancel. "When I heard about Pleasant Surprises on the news, I was ready to get out of this. That's quite a mess your company is in."

"We're working it out."

The woman's laugh wasn't comforting. "My sister knows the parents of one of those girls." The woman shook brown curls. "Why did you hire them?"

"I'm not at liberty to explain how the cheerleaders—"

"Cheerleaders, my foot. They were on exhibition for a bunch of ogling men." She walked away, muttering to herself.

Angel was more tired and empty than she'd felt all week—not even close to the right frame of mind for a date with Wade.

Chapter 10

Wade knocked on the door of Angel's apartment and it flew open. Angel stood in the doorway wearing the strangest outfit he'd ever seen for a date. The first words out of her mouth were, "My truck is done!"

"Hi to you, too!"

Grinning, she motioned him into the kitchen. The stove and refrigerator were ocean blue and the walls were pink. As if those colors weren't enough to assault his male senses, a furry, lime-colored bathrobe hung, half open, over her clothes—a fact she seemed oblivious to until he raised an eyebrow at her outfit.

"Oops. Sorry. The garage called, and then I called my mom to tell her, and of course it took an hour to figure out that she's going to bring the truck here next week, and here I am doing my hair and makeup while I'm on the phone and. . ." She set the phone on a chrome-legged table and shrugged out of her robe, "and then you showed up right on time and I wasn't."

"Wasn't. . .on time?"

"Right." She pointed toward the living room side of the great room. "Why don't you have a seat?"

"Interesting place." He'd never seen anything quite like it. Along one wall sat the strangest shaped brown couch he'd ever seen. Next to it was a huge round chair. Pink and white pillows were everywhere. "What do you call this style?"

"Funky retro." Her hair swayed as she laughed. She was wearing it down. Untamed ringlets framed perfect, velvet-looking skin.

"It's. . .girlie."

"Why doesn't that sound like a compliment?" She motioned for him to find a place to sit.

He decided to try out the lopsided-kidney-bean sofa. "My sister would love it."

"Where is she, by the way?"

"She's at my parents'. My mom wants her home on weekends. That's nice for me. . ." *Especially since it brings me closer to you every weekend.* "Not so great for them."

Angel sat on the other end of the weird couch. She wore a pink sweater. Two of them, actually. One underneath and one on top with buttons. Little pearl buttons.

He gestured toward her arm. "You dressed to match your living room."

"Image is everything in the business I'm in." Her face scrunched in a grimace. "But we are *not* talking about my business tonight. Now where were we?"

"I was saying you look very pretty tonight."

"You were?" Angel tugged at the bottom of her underneath sweater.

"I was going to."

"Thank you." She stacked her arms over her belly.

Five years of teaching had taught him a few things about the mind of a female. He recognized that universal gesture and knew the two-word self-talk that went with it—*I'm fat.*

The woman sitting on the other end of the goofy couch was rounded. Curvy. Very Renaissance, actually. He didn't see it as a bad thing. Not in the least. But her body language said she did. At least she hadn't said it out loud. That was a corner no man wanted to find himself in. "You're welcome."

Angel looked toward a pink-faced clock surrounded by concentric circles of chrome. "What time do we have to leave?"

"We've got about ten minutes."

"My roommate wants to meet you. She should be here any—"

The apartment door opened and a woman with coal black hair and snappy dark eyes walked in, weighted down by an armload of books and an over-stuffed backpack.

"Hi! You're Wade." She dropped the books in the big round chair and walked over to him. "I'm Patti Pugelli, call me Pug." She held out her hand. "Glad to finally meet you."

Finally? He'd known Angel for eight days. "Nice to meet you, too." He shook her hand.

Pug perched on a round pink footstool. "When do you have to leave?"

"About ten minutes." Was she anxious to get rid of him?

"That's enough time."

He wasn't sure he liked that smile. "For. . .?"

"Interrogation." Pug looked at Angel. "You have a little thing. . ." She pointed between her own front teeth.

Angel laughed and stood up. "Guess that's my cue to finish getting ready. Go easy on him. He rescued me in my hour of need, you know."

Wade sat back down, though what he really wanted to do was claim he'd forgotten to feed the parking meter. He was about to be given the third degree about who-knows-what from a woman who looked like she really could have a godfather in the Mafia.

"So. . ." Pug sat cross-legged on the stool. She wore a hot pink sweater. Was pink mandatory for these two? Her probably designer jeans appeared about the same size as Angel's. But there was a difference. This girl seemed very comfy with who she was. "What are your intentions with my BFF?"

"Well. . . I. . ."

"Just kidding. Actually, I'm not. I have a few questions. Just tell me when I step over your comfort line. It's a checks-and-balances thing we do for each other."

Wade relaxed just enough to rest against the arm of the strange couch. "Watching each other's backs?"

"Yup. You got it, mistah." Her voice deepened with a rough-sounding Italian accent. "We watch out for each uddah, ya know?"

Goose bumps jumped up on Wade's arm. Was the woman clairvoyant? "That's good. What would you like to know?"

"Religion?"

"Christian. Put my faith in Christ when I was ten."

"Been in any trouble with the law?"

"Library fines and a few parking tickets." He rested against the back of the sofa. "Oh, and one speeding ticket. Going fifty-seven in a forty-five zone. A hundred and ninety-two dollar fine."

"Yowza. That'll learn ya." Pug folded her hands and rested her forearms on her knees. "Dating history?"

"Not much to report. I had a serious girlfriend in high school. I broke up with her when I went to college in Champagne. Had two girlfriends at the U of I. No time for dating since then."

"Still pure?"

Wade's tongue made a clicking noise as his mouth fell open and quickly closed. He was used to this kind of blatant talk from kids. It was a little disconcerting from a grown woman, and yet her frankness really wasn't offensive. He liked the fact that they watched out for "each uddah."

"Want to pass on that one?" she asked.

"No. You just—"

"Shocked the stuffing out of you?" Pug laughed and hugged her knees.

"I just wasn't prepared for it. But the answer is yes, by the grace of God."

"Amen to that. So you set clear boundaries for dating?"

"Absolutely." He waited for another question, but the girl just sat there smiling and staring. A door opened somewhere beyond the kitchen. "Do I pass?"

Pug tilted her head to the side. "What's your stand on marriage and children?"

"In favor of both." Wade laughed and let go of the remainder of his tension. "In that order."

"Then I guess you've passed round one."

"What's next? Fingerprinting? Polygraph?"

She laughed. "There will be a PI on your trail 24/7." She made binoculars with her hands. "She's pretty fragile right now, you know. Maybe you can't see it, but she's really got this awesome sense of humor." She lowered her hands to her lap.

"I can see that."

"And she's the best listener I've ever met."

"I've experienced a bit of it."

"She has a big heart. She cries when she watches the news. She has Sunny because she saw his picture at a fundraiser for the Humane Society and she just had to have him, even though we live in a third floor apartment in Oak Park. And she's really spontaneous. I mean, you could call that girl in the middle of the night and ask her to go parasailing and she'd be up for it."

"And she'd be an accident waiting to happen." Wade laughed and leaned forward. "Why the sudden gear shift? One minute I'm getting cross-examined and the next minute you're giving me a sales pitch. I don't really need to be talked into this, you know. I already asked her out."

"I know I sound like an idiot." Pug's bottom lip pooched out. "I just don't want you to get discouraged before you see what she's really like."

Before he had a chance to figure out how to answer her, he heard Angel's footsteps in the kitchen.

She had a cream-colored jacket and a huge black purse over her arm. She aimed flag blue eyes at him. "You're still here."

"You thought I'd leave?"

"Pug usually chases 'em away." A grimace stretched her lips. "Not that there have been many of them. . . . Did she grill you?"

"We were just getting to my credit score. Blood tests and hair analysis come on the second date, I hear." He stood. His gaze swept across the pile of papers on an end table. A printed e-mail sat on the top of the stack, and he caught Taylor's name. "This is from my sister."

Angel picked it up.

"What's it about?" He tried to keep his tone light, as if he weren't suspicious of Taylor's every move.

"She's applying for a job at Pleasant Surprises." Angel handed him the letter. "I didn't take it seriously because of the distance, but if she'll be in Wheaton every weekend, I might be able to work something out."

Wade's insides tightened. Angel's business was already in crisis because of employees with poor judgment. She didn't need to compound the problem. "That's not such a great idea. My sister's. . .not the most responsible. She's staying with me because she's been getting in trouble back home. "

"Maybe she needs another chance." Angel lifted her chin. "Maybe she's learned from past mistakes."

Maybe she's not capable of learning. "We'll talk on the way." He motioned toward the door.

This was not the way to start a date.

❧

"Can I make a suggestion?" Angel buckled her seat belt and stared across the front seat of the Explorer at the miniature buffalo that were almost extinct, thanks to a recent shave that had left a hint of spice in its wake.

"Sure."

"To use your word, let's get all the 'yuck' out of the way before we get there. You can tell me why Taylor shouldn't work for me and I'll tell you about my raunchy day, and then we'll pretend everything's wonderful during dinner. Okay?"

"Deal. We have fifteen minutes. Seven and a half for Taylor and seven and a half for your day. If we get stuck in traffic, we'll come up with a whole new category of yuck." He turned the key in the ignition and flashed a smile that lit the interior as the dome light dimmed.

"Sounds like a plan." Angel pulled back her sleeve and pointed to her watch. "Okay. Your turn in five-four-three-two-go!"

Wade backed up in the parallel parking space and put his left blinker on. "My sister has attention deficit disorder. She's always been a handful, but now that she's in high school, everything's magnified. Life's a party to Taylor. . .no offense, party planner."

Angel returned the smile she heard in his voice. "None taken."

"She doesn't take anything seriously and she doesn't learn from consequences. My parents can't agree on how to handle her, and it's literally wrecking their marriage. So I offered to get her away from her friends for a while and let her live with me. I can keep a close eye on her that way. That's not the total answer, but it might buy them some time to get help."

"That's a huge sacrifice."

Wade shrugged. "I couldn't think of anything else to do."

Angel's "fix-it" penchant went into overdrive. "It would be good for her to have a job, wouldn't it? It would only be Friday and Saturday nights."

"I. . .don't know. It would be good if she miraculously learned to be responsible."

"You could keep close tabs on her if she worked with someone you knew." *Someone, hopefully, you plan to get to know better.* "If you were coaching me, maybe we could work something out for her."

Slowing to a corner, Wade smiled and shook his head. "You really would parasail in the middle of the night, wouldn't you?"

᪣

Wade had been to the Ruth's Chris Steakhouse on Dearborn only once. On his first and only blind date. By the time he'd finished his salad, he'd wished he'd chosen Burger King.

He smiled at Angel across the candlelit table. "I suppose you've been here quite a few times."

She laughed. "I know I *look* like I eat out all the time. . ."

Ouch. There it was. The corner he didn't know how to get out of. *Think,*

67

Ramsey. He reached across the white tablecloth and laid his hand over hers. "Can I say something kind of. . .direct?"

"You met my loud-mouthed Italian roomie. I'm pretty used to direct."

"This is how a guy's foot finds its way to his mouth. . .so promise me you'll try to hear what I'm saying and not what you think I mean, okay?"

"O–kay."

He took a massive breath and let it out slowly. "You don't have to be skin and bones to be beautiful, Angel. A lot of guys, and I'm one of them, like a little. . . softness."

He studied her, watching for any hint that he was going to regret spending money on a dinner eaten in silence. Her eyes took on a shimmer. *Please don't let her cry.* Her hand moved under his. Not a good sign.

"So. . ." Her right eyebrow rose, her smile disappeared. Her eyes narrowed. "You think I'm fat."

In one quick, reflexive jolt, he pulled his hand off hers.

And Angel laughed. Loud and long, with that cute little snort, until her eyes watered.

"That is so cruel."

She reached across the table and, this time, took his hand in both of hers. He felt the way he'd felt when he was eight and Sally Northrup kissed him on the monkey bars. They were holding hands! Angel gave a slight squeeze. "Thank you."

A loud sigh whooshed out of him. "Don't ever do that again."

"You could get in so much trouble calling a woman soft."

"Then how in the world am I supposed to say it?"

"You already know how." Her eyes shimmered with repressed laughter. "Just say, 'Angel. . .you're a *babe*.'"

Chapter 11

T ell me something I don't know about you yet." Angel cut a slice of butter-infused filet mignon as she asked.

"Well. . .did I tell you I'm doing my doctoral dissertation on the effects of Route 66 on our country?"

"No."

"Well, I am."

The waiter filled their water glasses for the third time.

"Now that's the kind of history I could get interested in. I remember only one thing about it from school—the first McDonald's was started in San Bernardino thanks to Route 66. I'm sure there were more significant contributions to our culture than burgers and fries."

"But where would we be without Big Macs?"

Angel held up a forkful of baked potato mounded with sour cream. "For starters, heart disease wouldn't be the leading cause of death in this country. Tell me something else."

"Route 66 started here in Chicago and ended in Los Angeles. During the Depression, thousands of unemployed men got jobs on the road gangs." Wade set his fork down. His eyes glittered. "And in the forties, it helped facilitate the single greatest wartime manpower mobilization in the history of the nation."

"All because of a single road." Angel took a moment just to stare. Wade Ramsey was created from a unique recipe. Gorgeous, intelligent, and not conceited about either. Handsome, humorous history nerd. What a combo. "Are you actually writing yet?"

"I'm doing research right now. And then I'm taking a road trip after school's out."

"That sounds so adventurous. I'd love to travel, but my business doesn't make it easy."

Wade's lips pursed and twisted slightly to the right. "Are you feeling adventurous tonight?"

"Tonight?" What was he suggesting?

"Yeah. How'd you like to take a road trip back to Galena with me?"

❧

"Are you sure you should do this? On your first date?" Pug stood in the doorway pointing with her toothbrush toward the pajamas, socks, and underwear stacked on Angel's bed.

"We're going to a Sunday afternoon picnic, not eloping. Besides, I can get my truck and Sunny."

"What if he doesn't take you to your mom's tonight? What if you end up in some dark alley?"

"Then I'll be a statistic." Angel laid two blouses on the flowered spread. "Which one will impress his colleagues and hide the muffin top?" She pinched the rolls above her hips.

"That one." The toothbrush indicated the sage green faux suede instead of the swirly rose-colored print. "With your black pants. And boots."

Angel took the green blouse off the hanger and folded it.

"Can I have the other one if you end up a statistic? It looks good with my hair."

"It's all yours."

Pug sat down cross-legged on the bed. "Even for you, this is. . .impetuous."

"I know." Angel threw her makeup bag on top of her high-heeled boots. "Isn't it wonderful? The guy makes me feel. . .a little ditsy. Or dizzy. . .or something that isn't me."

"Don't check your brains at the brown eyes, girlfriend."

"I'm not. Really. I don't even know if he's my type." Did it count as a lie if she knew that Pug knew that she knew it wasn't true? "And he's too cute to be seriously interested in a chubette like me."

"Stop that." The toothbrush pointed toward the mirrored panels of Angel's closet. "Stand in front of that mirror."

"Why?"

"Because you need to see the truth. Tell me what you see."

Angel stared at the jeans and fitted button-down shirt she'd just changed into. Her ponytail swayed like a metronome as she shook her head. "I see a chunky redhead in a blouse that doesn't fit over her steak and baked potato."

Pug gave a loud sigh and shot a purple pillow at Angel's head. "Tell me again what he said."

"He said I was soft."

"He said you were pretty!"

"Shh! He said I *looked* pretty. That probably just means he likes pink."

"He doesn't really look like a pink man to me. Now, look." The toothbrush flailed. "The blouse shows off your waistline. . .and look at that hair. Look at your perfect skin. I would die for that skin."

"You'd look anemic with this skin."

"Angel Cholewinski, you're insulting God when you diss yourself like that. He knit you together in your mother's womb!"

Angel bent slowly and picked up the pillow. She held it over her stomach and turned sideways in the mirror. "Okay, I get it."

"Finally."

"But He didn't knit these thighs."

Another pillow hit her head.

"You'll drive that man away if you keep talking like that. Self-fulfilling prophecy."

Angel stuffed her bag then put her arms around Pug. "I'll work on my attitude."

"Good. Starting now. Walk out there like a daughter of the King and that's how he'll see you."

Angel stood at attention, stuck her chin in the air, and pulled her shoulders back. "Yes, ma'am."

"It'll make a difference."

"Right. See you tomorrow night. Take care of you."

"Take care of you."

Angel walked down the hall and through the kitchen as if she were balancing a book on her head, softly humming "Pomp and Circumstance."

Wade stood when she entered the living room. "You look comfy." He held out his hand for her bag. "And very pretty."

☙

Wade smiled at her across the front seat of the Explorer, as if he wanted to say something.

"What?"

"I like your spontaneity."

"Pug thinks I'm nuts." Angel fastened her seat belt. "But it feels good to be. . .impetuous. I've lost that side of me lately. I'm the party pla–a–a–nner, you know."

"All fun must be charted weeks in advance?"

"Exactly. I'm all about having a good time. . .as long as I know I've ordered enough plastic forks." She adjusted the shoulder harness until she could comfortably face Wade for the next three hours. "You're a strange influence on me." She watched his profile change as a smile spread across his face.

"Maybe it'll work both ways. I'll help you regain the joy of *un*planning, and you can show me that an anniversary celebration can be more than a Dairy Queen cake in my parents' basement."

Angel felt her own profile alter. Strange that she could laugh in the midst of the ruins of her life. "You need to become a party visionary."

"Or just know someone who is." His eyebrows rose as he darted a look her way.

The prickly sensation at the back of her neck meant her skin was doing the thing redheads do so well. She was grateful for the darkness. "Are you ready for me to book the date at the Welcome Inn?"

"Y–y–yes." Wade grinned as he turned onto South Harlem. "Sorry, but even with your generosity, it'll come to around twenty dollars a plate. That makes my skin crawl just a bit. But my grandparents are excited about the idea."

"Will their excitement translate into cash?"

"I'm planning on it. I sure hope they are. So you'll do all the decorating and talking to the restaurant about the menu and everything?"

"I'll even send out the invitations and pin on your mother's corsage."

For the briefest of moments, his hand grabbed hers and held it. "I might actually enjoy this."

This. . . .anniversary party? This working together? Or this hand-holding?
"I hope you do." She wasn't sure what she was responding to, but whatever it was, she knew *she'd* enjoy it.

Wade turned onto the interstate. "This is small potatoes for you, isn't it?"

"I love throwing parties for friends." She hoped he'd accept her sidestepping as a sufficient answer. "Besides, six weeks from now I may be lucky to have a few little potatoes to sustain me."

"I'm going to assume you're being melodramatic. Can I ask about your business now?"

"That would be breaking the rules of the night."

"Not if we declare our date officially over and we're just hanging out now."

If the date could end and she'd still be with him, he could call it anything he wanted. "Okay. Ask."

"What's God telling you about Pleasant Surprises these days?"

She should know the answer to that question. She stared at the strong jawline of the man in the driver's seat and decided to be honest. "Everyone's got advice. I'm hearing so many voices. . .how do I hear His in the midst of all the noise? I know He doesn't want me to curl into a fetal position. I have to be moving in some direction. I love the concept of giving your problems over to God and letting Him work it out, but how do I do that? How do *you* do it?"

☙❧

He couldn't see her flag blue eyes in the dark, but he felt them. The girl was a teacher's dream. . .full of questions, eager for answers. He chewed on his answer for a moment before sharing it.

"It's a combination of a lot of things, I guess. First, it's confessing that you can't figure it out on your own and praying for discernment, asking God to help you hear His voice over all the others. Then, you start listening. God speaks in a lot of ways—through scripture, through other believers, through our circumstances. Sometimes you feel the Holy Spirit nudging you with a feeling in your gut that something's not right, or a freed-up feeling that confirms you're heading in the right direction."

She was quiet for a long time. He was about to ask if she was disappointed in his answer, when she broke the silence.

"Tell me something specific—a problem you wrestled with and how you knew God was directing you."

The first thing to creep into his mind wasn't something he thought he should share, yet it wouldn't go away. He took a deep breath. "Well. . .take the subject of singleness. Mine in particular."

The atmosphere in the car altered. Air molecules seemed to rearrange in hypervigilant patterns. He had her attention.

"Dating—or the lack of it—is. . .not a problem, exactly. . .a concern, I guess. None of the unmarried female teachers at my school are anywhere close to my age. And I live in a town of seven hundred, where the main events of the year are the Hobo Hap'nin' and the Cow Pie Lottery. There are precisely eight single women around my age in Elizabeth. Two of them I've gone out with and decided they'd make great friends. One goes to my church and is about to be proposed to by the youth director. And the other five I rarely cross paths with because I don't frequent the Half Moon Saloon." Wade smiled, more at the sound of Angel's laugh than his own words. "The advice I'm getting from trusted friends is 'Wait. The right girl will come along.' I can't explain it, but that advice clicks with me." He put his hand on his chest. "I'm convinced God has a plan for my life, so I pray, and I wait. And then one night I'm driving along the highway. . ."

He let the fragment hang between them, unfinished.

"Serendipity," she whispered.

"Hmm. I like the sound of that."

Chapter 12

As she set her grandmother's table for five, Angel hummed a chorus she'd learned in church an hour ago. She set a plate of pastries on the counter and mindlessly stuck a blueberry-filled *kolaczki* in her mouth. Her mother cleared her throat.

"What?"

"You're stress stuffing."

"I'm just getting an early start on brunch!" She was sure her mother hadn't seen the two angel wings she'd downed while pouring orange juice.

Her mother's sympathetic smile made it hard to stay offended. "Brunch is what we're going to eat with tall, dark, and handsome and his little sister. What you're doing is called something else." She shrugged and smoothed her skirt with both hands. "You told me to say something when I catch you."

There were good things about growing up with a mother who sometimes wanted to be more friend than parent. This wasn't one of them. Sure, during one of her many diets in her teens, Angel had asked her mother to hold her accountable for what she put in her mouth. But at twenty-eight, she wanted the freedom to "stress stuff" without someone pointing it out—especially someone who'd maintained the same weight for thirty years in spite of spending most of her waking hours up to her elbows in pastry dough. "I'm not bingeing." *Not yet, anyway.*

"I imagine Wade's a great motivation for cutting back on calories." Her mother gave a knowing look as she turned maple-cured bacon in a massive iron frying pan.

To Angel, the moment seemed a snapshot of the mixed message she'd been fed her whole life—food is comfort/everything in moderation. Since junior high, she'd been trying to find comfort in something that couldn't give it. . .which only made her want more. Inevitably, it led to a destructive cycle of food. . .guilt. . .more food. . .more guilt. Being fully aware of what she was doing hadn't stopped it. "Moderation" hadn't entered her repertoire until Pleasant Surprises got off the ground and, for once, she didn't have a reason to stuff. For three years, she'd broken free, dropped to a size ten, and thought she'd never return to self-destruction. She was wrong.

Angel finished off the blueberry pastry without making eye contact with her mother. As she wiped her mouth with the back of her hand, the doorbell rang. Pulling at the front of the blouse that Pug had assured her flattered her figure, she went to the door.

Bapcia beat her to it and was reaching up to hug Wade when Angel walked into the living room. Taylor opened the screen door behind Wade, and Sunny leaped the threshold and jumped onto Angel, planting his front paws on her shoulders and slurping off one side of the makeup she'd so carefully applied. Angel buried her face in Sunny's neck then smiled at Taylor. "He smells good."

"I gave him a bath. I didn't have dog soap, so I used cherry blossom shower gel."

"Thank you so much for watching him."

"Hey, me and Sunny are tight now. I'll keep him anytime."

Sunny jumped down and followed Taylor and Bapcia to the kitchen. And then, only Wade stood in front of her. Since he'd only squeezed her hand when he dropped her off the night before, Angel wasn't sure what was expected. Before she had time to feel awkward, his arms slid around her in a quick hug—short enough not to be embarrassing, long enough to smell something that reminded her of a walk in the woods after a summer rain. She would have tolerated her mother's raised eyebrows for a few more whiffs. His lips came dizzyingly close to her ear as he pulled away. "Good morning," he whispered.

"Good morning." Angel motioned toward the kitchen. "Everything's ready."

"Last night I thought I'd never be hungry again."

"Me, too." *But then I consumed a day's worth of calories before ten a.m.* "Funny how that works. Did you go to church?"

"Yup. Heard a message on giving all your worries to God." He grinned at her. "I thought about getting a copy for you."

"I could use it. Ours was about integrity. I think my mother called the pastor last night and told him I was coming."

"I'm sure he changed his whole message just for you." Wade put his hand on her back as they walked into the kitchen.

With his warm hand resting on her "muffin top," the three pieces of pastry suddenly felt like cement in her stomach. The faux suede blouse seemed to grow tighter by the second. Wade pulled out a chair for her. "Thank you." Angel kept her gaze on the fruit bowl, certain that every one of the three faces at the table held a don't-they-look-cute-together smile.

Bapcia set a bowl of scrambled eggs in front of Wade and sat at his left. "It's been a long time since a man asked the blessing in this house."

"I'd be honored." Wade picked up Angel's hand then Bapcia's.

Angel reached toward her mother and got the "cute couple" smile she'd anticipated.

As Wade bowed his head, his thumb stroked the back of Angel's hand. "Almighty God, we come before You with grateful hearts. Please bless this bounty and the hands that prepared it. Guide us now in conversation that is pleasing to You. In the name of Jesus, amen."

Bowls and platters started making clockwise rounds. Each time Wade took a dish from Angel, his fingers overlapped hers and stayed there until he'd helped himself. Angel spooned fresh fruit and scrambled eggs on her plate, passing on hash browns, bacon, and shame-inducing pastry. Wade leaned toward her and whispered, "You'll insult the cooks eating like that."

If you only knew. And then, like a scrolling marquis, words from the sermon she'd just heard ran through her conscience—*Integrity is doing the right thing in the right way at the right time with the right attitude. . .even when you don't want to. Even when no one's looking.* Sitting in church, she'd thought of all the ways the definition applied to her business. But they were words she needed to apply to every facet of her life—even eating. She looked at Wade with a sheepish smile. "I snuck a few bites while I was setting the table."

"Can't blame you for that."

"But they make me soft."

Hash browns jiggled on Wade's fork. His top teeth clamped onto a widening grin. "I like soft," he mumbled.

She had to come up with a new way to describe what he did to her. All the chocolate metaphors that came to mind weren't healthy. But nothing else seemed to describe the sweet warmth he wrapped around her.

Taylor popped a grape in her mouth. "What are you two whispering about?"

"That's what I was wondering." Bapcia leaned down, looking across Wade's plate and aiming her gaze at Angel.

Slowly, Wade tore a piece of raisin bread in half. "I was just telling Angel how much I love soft. . .bread."

Taylor swept her gaze toward the ceiling and back to Wade. "Uh-huh. I thought maybe you were telling her how much you want me to work for her."

"Taylor. . ."

"Actually—"Angel inserted a silent moment for effect "—I wanted to discuss that with both of you together." She shot a quick look at Wade and didn't sense him telling her to drop the subject. "If things pick up, I may need a girl Friday."

"What's that?" Taylor's brow furrowed, tilting her eyebrow ring at a bizarre angle.

"A gofer—somebody to take notes, run and get things, maybe answer the phone or make some calls on the days we have events. Things are kind of slow right now, but I have a couple busy weekends next month. And since you're coming that way on Fridays. . ." Again, she tried to gauge Wade's reaction.

"Awesome!" Taylor bounced in her seat. Several seconds passed before Wade nodded.

"Then welcome to Pleasant Surprises."

Wade coughed into a napkin and muttered, "I'll be surprised if it's pleasant."

🙢

"That was delicious, Jeanie." Wade carried a stack of dirty plates from the table and set them on the counter next to Angel's mother. He picked up a dish towel.

"Oh no you don't!" Bapcia materialized behind him like a little wood nymph. Seconds ago, he'd heard her in the backyard with Taylor and the dog. She grabbed the towel. "That's women's work."

"Tell that to my sister. She's got this crazy notion we should be sharing chores."

Bapcia's short hair didn't move as she shook her head. "Women these days have it all wrong. It's good to be queen of your kitchen." She swept her arm across the kitchen. "Who wants a man's mess in your kingdom?"

Wade laughed. "I like how you think. You women do amazing things in your realm. I don't know how Angel and I are going to be able to eat again in a couple hours."

Jeanie looked over her shoulder. "This is a school function you're going to?"

"A staff picnic. Steven Vandenburg, the new principal, is throwing a bash to get to know the teachers. He's from Texas, but I guess he used to teach in Galena. Do you know him?"

Bapcia shrugged. "We haven't paid attention to what's going on in the schools since Angel graduated." Wade took two juice glasses off the table, and she tried to grab them from him. He laughed and held them out of her reach—not a hard feat.

"Jeanie, you don't mind a man in the kitchen, do you?" He set the glasses on the counter.

She didn't respond, her eyes focused on something that Wade had a feeling wasn't actually outside the window. He gave himself a mental lashing. The "man in the kitchen" comment was thoughtless. But how in the world should he apologize? Before he figured it out, a strained smile crossed her face. She dipped the glasses in soapy water and quickly rinsed them. "Well, looks like we're done here." She wiped her hands on a towel and left the kitchen. Moments later, he heard steps above them on the second floor.

Ruby drained the sink, and Wade wiped the counters in spite of her protests. As he rinsed the dishrag, he glanced at the clock above the window. They should be leaving for the picnic.

"I'll go see if that granddaughter of mine is ready to go. Help yourself to a soda if you want and don't forget these." Ruby pointed to a cake pan with a clear lid.

"I couldn't forget the angel wings. Thank you."

She left the room and Wade was just picking up the pan when he heard voices in the sudden quiet of the kitchen. Straight above where he stood was an old-fashioned wrought-iron grate for allowing the heat from the kitchen to reach the upstairs. The tone of the conversation above made him stand still and listen.

". . .put it off any longer, Angel. He keeps calling and asking when he can see you. Today would be the perfect time."

"I'm not changing my plans, Mom. And this really isn't a good time for me to start something with him, anyway. My life is a mess, in case you hadn't noticed. I'll call him and—"

The back door opened. Taylor tumbled in, winded and giggling and chased by Sunny—ending Wade's chances of hearing more about "him."

Angel was strangely quiet on the drive to the picnic—her mind on "him," most likely. Wade had little doubt that the "he" in question was Sock Man. He thought back to Jeanie's reaction when Matt Peterson had offered to give Angel a ride to Chicago. She'd fairly glowed with happiness. Not surprising. The man drove a Porsche. Clearly, he could take care of her daughter.

A lowly history teacher didn't offer much competition in a mother's eyes.

After several minutes, Wade decided to ask what most men were too smart or scared to ask. "Something wrong?"

The sigh that rushed out of Angel seemed too big for a girl. Where had she been storing all that air?

"My mother's being weird."

Because she wants you to talk to a rich guy who owns his own restaurant? Makes sense to me. Wade flipped the turn signal with a little more force than needed. "What about?"

Another sigh, this one accompanied by shaking the handles of her purse. "My mother's pastor wants me to help with a retreat he's putting on for college-age kids over Christmas. He's all excited about my conversion story and—"

"A pastor? That's the *him* she wanted you to talk to?" Relief spilled out in an unmanly kind of laugh. It wasn't until the look of confusion hit Angel's eyes that he realized what he'd just confessed to. "I. . .um. . ."

The confused eyes opened wider and then lit with a spark of knowing. "You were eavesdropping."

"I—"

Angel laughed. "That vent is the one thing I wouldn't allow the remodelers to touch. Too many memories. It works even better when you're lying on the floor upstairs listening to what's going on in the kitchen. Either way, it's dangerous when you only hear part of a conversation."

"I wasn't trying to eavesdrop."

"I know." She set her purse on the floor of the car. "So just what were you thinking when you heard her tell me to call *himmm*?"

Wade rubbed the back of his neck. Honesty would be good for a laugh, but would it be good for their relationship? "I thought she was trying to get you to arrange something with Sock Ma—Matt."

Just as he thought, it was good for a laugh.

"*What* did you call him?"

Chapter 13

Angel was still laughing when they pulled into a narrow gravel drive. Sock Man. It fit. She thought of all the times in the past week when a sock would have come in handy. But, to be fair, there were more times when she'd wanted to hug him for all his help. But no reflection of Matt—good, bad, or confusing—was allowed for the next five hours.

Wade pulled to the side of the drive behind two other cars. Angel got out then reached back in for the pan. By then, Wade was standing on her side of the car with a backpack slung over his shoulder. He took the pan and closed her door.

"Thank you, sir."

"My pleasure. By the way, you look very pretty in that."

"Thank you." She held out her arm. "Feel." She laughed at his wary look. "It's soft."

Wade complied. "It is." Playfulness sparkled in his eyes. "I like soft."

"I'm glad."

They came to the end of the trees, and the driveway opened into a grassy area filled with cars. "Wow. This is bigger than I expected."

"It's for the middle school, too. Probably over sixty people when you include nonteaching staff, tons more with spouses and"—he smiled at her—"friends. I'll stick to first names when I do introductions—then you only have half to remember when I quiz you."

"And you won't have to mangle mine."

His hand slid to her back as they rounded the corner of the house. "I was afraid you'd see through that."

A couple walked toward them hand in hand, and Wade introduced Angel to the algebra teacher, who in turn introduced her husband. Obedient to the slight pressure on her back, Angel let Wade steer her toward a table lined with rectangular silver chafing dishes. She searched for an empty spot for the cake pan. "Where should I put this?"

"Right in my hands." The man reaching for the pan was as big as his voice. "I'm the server in charge of all things sweet. Welcome." He held out a huge hand. "Steven Vandenburg." From his size and grip, Angel would have guessed lumberjack before school principal.

Wade's hand dropped from her back. "Steven, this is my friend Angel." The two men stood eye to eye, Wade maybe half an inch taller. But Steven was much broader.

"Nice to meet you, Angel." Steven tapped the top of the pan. "May I?"

"Of course."

He slid the cover open and inhaled loudly. "Oh my. There goes the diet."

"I'll be hurt if you don't try one." Angel opened the lid wider.

"Well, if you insist." He pulled out an angel wing and stared at it. "Chruscik. Right?"

Angel nodded. "I'm impressed."

"Haven't had one of these in years." Steven took a bite and closed his eyes. "Scrumptious. Did you make them?"

"My grandmother gets the credit for these."

Wade reached across Angel and took a pastry. "Rumor has it Angel's an accomplished baker. I just haven't seen any evidence yet."

The principal raised his sunglasses and winked at Angel with bright blue eyes filled with mischief. "Sounds like an invitation. You know what they say about the way to a man's heart, Angel. . . ." He lowered the glasses. "That is, if this guy's heart is what you're aft—"

"Steven!" A woman yelled from the back door of the house.

"Sorry. I'm being paged." He thrust the pan back at Angel and sprinted toward the house, leaving her wondering how to conceal the pink his words had brushed on her face. She kept her head down until she found a clear spot on the table to set the pastry.

Looking up, she saw Wade's tongue making a sizable lump in the side of his cheek. His eyebrows rose. "The man has a point, you know. If that's what you're after, that is."

⌒❦

"Do you realize it's four o'clock already?" Wade slipped a watch fob back in a narrow vest pocket. "We should get going."

Angel dumped a stack of Styrofoam plates in the wastebasket under Steven's kitchen sink. "My face hurts from laughing. You were incredible."

"I should have warned you." He folded a pair of wire-rimmed glasses and put them in a leather case.

"I love surprises." She reached up and touched the bald top of his Ben Franklin wig. "I almost dropped my lemonade when you came out of the bedroom in this. You could act professionally, you know."

"Probably wouldn't be fun if I had to do the same thing day after day." He pulled off the wig and ran his fingers through his hair. Angel swallowed her offer to help.

Steven walked in from the back door. Snatching the wig from Wade, he tried it on. With sunglasses and a short-cropped gray beard, it looked ridiculous. He took a plate from Angel. "I hear you have to get back to Chi-Town tonight. You don't have to help with cleanup—I've got servants for the menial tasks. Besides, you know what I always say. . . ." He stroked the fake chin-length hair.

"Guests, like fish, begin to smell after three hours."

Wade laughed. "That's three days, Benjamin. Get your quotes right."

Steve shrugged and handed the wig back. "I really enjoyed meeting you and your grandmother's chruscik, Angel." He took his sunglasses off and set them on the counter. "I've never met a real, live party planner before. It's something my Lindy would have been good at."

Angel looked past Steven to a refrigerator filled with pictures. "How long ago did you lose your wife?"

"Three years. She'd been dealing with MS since she turned thirty." A sad smile dimmed his eyes. "We had twenty-three wonderful years and two wonderful sons. We were blessed."

"Do your boys live near?"

"No. One's working in Washington state, the other's going to school in Boston. So, I thought I'd come back to my roots where I'm halfway between them." At the mention of his sons, the light returned to his eyes.

Wade picked up a platter with three pieces of wilted cheese and opened the cupboard under the sink. Angel reached for the cheese, but Steven beat her to it. He laughed. "I'll share it with you. I hate waste—as you can see."

"Me, too." Angel patted her right hip.

Steven tilted his head slightly. "You have beautiful hair." He glanced at Wade. "That doesn't constitute harassment, does it?"

"Only if she were a teacher."

Steven sighed. "Gone are the days you can compliment a woman and not be afraid of getting decked."

Angel set the platter in the sink. "I'm not stupid enough to hurt a man who gives me a genuine compliment. Thank you."

"You're welcome. It truly is an amazing shade. My mother's was just about the same color, and my wife always hoped for a little girl with red hair. Instead, she got two blond boys who grew up to have red beards like mine. Well. . . like mine *was*." The wistful look returned, but only for a moment. An easy smile took over. "I just thought of something. Does your company ever do fundraisers?"

"We haven't yet." *But I'm willing to take on just about anything under the circumstances.* Thankfully, Steven Vandenburg didn't seem to know anything about her circumstances. "What do you have in mind?"

"I'm a member of an organization called HIS—Hands in Service—and I'm in charge of organizing a fundraiser for Pacific Garden Missions in Chicago. If you'd be willing to quote us some prices for a banquet, maybe I could dig up a history teacher somewhere to put on a program for us. Is that something you'd like to tackle?"

A tingle of electricity started at the top of Angel's head and skittered all the way to her toes. She locked eyes with Wade and wondered if he'd gotten zapped.

He grinned and gave a slight nod.

"Absolutely."

❧

Wade made a Y-turn in Steven's drive. "What time do you have to get up in the morning?"

"Around six. Why?"

"I was just wondering how long I could keep you." He stepped on the brake and stared at Angel. Was it possible he'd known her for only a week and a day?

The lips she'd just touched up with something shiny and peach-smelling pressed together in a straight line. He wished he knew her well enough to read that expression. If he was right, she was holding back a smile. So maybe she'd gotten his double meaning. . .and didn't take issue with it.

"What did you have in mind?" She batted long lashes and dipped her head so two rust-red curls slid across her forehead.

Lord, I'm trying here. . .guard my thoughts. . .and my eyes. . .and my future. Did she have any idea what her coy little act could do to a man's brain? Much more of this and he'd be saying "I do" before he could even say her last name. Wade cleared his throat. "A walk." Nice and brisk. . .and public. "Let's go back to Galena and pretend we're tourists."

"Sounds fun." She narrowed her eyes. "There you go making me be spontaneous again."

"Could be habit-forming." *As could you.*

"I hope it is."

He had to talk about something that didn't scream "happily ever after." Not that he didn't like the idea. . . He turned onto Snipe Hollow Road. "I run out here."

"From your house?" Her eyes widened.

Wade laughed. "It's only four miles."

"Yeah, but you have to get back again. What's the farthest you've run?"

"Twenty-six point two miles."

"Seriously? You mentioned that you run, but you didn't say you run marathons. Are you doing Chicago?"

Wade felt his face warm in the glow of admiration. "This'll be my sixth in a row."

"Wow. I go every year—to watch. I've probably seen you cross the finish line many times. Strange to think about, isn't it?"

It is. "Will you be there this year?"

"I wouldn't miss it."

After too many minutes of visualizing Angel at the finish line, he realized he needed to say something. "So what do you think of Steven's idea?"

Angel twirled a thin silver bracelet. "Pug volunteers at Pacific Garden Mission once in a while. I'm ashamed to admit I've never gone with her. Hanging out with street people and drug addicts wasn't my thing, but I'm thinking God will probably change that while He's turning my little world upside down. Have you ever been there?"

"Many times. Volunteering and researching." He hoped that didn't sound self-righteous right after she'd just confessed her reluctance.

"So you know gobs about its history?"

"More than you would ever care to, I'm afraid."

"I figured."

"Billy Sunday came to know the Lord through their ministry."

"Really?" Blue eyes widened. "Wow. . .that's kind of—"

"Serendipitous?" He chanced another quick look, long enough to savor the glimmer in her eyes as she nodded.

"Would it take a lot of work for you to play several characters at one function?"

"The pla–a–a–nner at work." He reached out and tugged a wayward copper strand.

Angel released her seat belt and bounced, ringlets vibrating, into a position facing him. "What if you wore costumes of people who had something to do with the history of the mission. . .Billy Sunday, for instance. . .and you walked around between tables with a cordless mic, talking to people in character, telling them about the Mission and how it's helped people?" She clicked the clasp of her belt into place. "Wouldn't that bring their philosophy to life and get people excited about supporting them?"

It was actually a bit embarrassing—the way her words shot adrenaline to every nerve ending. "I can see it. . . ." His mind spun with visions of playing Mel Trotter, a suicidal drunk who became a Presbyterian minister because of the Mission.

A hand waved in front of his face, jarring him back to the twenty-first century. "Sorry. Did I glaze over?"

The redhead was laughing at him. "Welcome back."

"So. . .about your part. . .what are we going to eat?"

"I'm torn. Go all out with a fabulous meal—that's a draw, of course—or give people a taste of life in a homeless shelter. Plastic trays and instant potatoes wouldn't go over too well, but what if we did soups and bread? Really good stuff, but it would still have the feel we'd be after."

"And money goes for the Mission instead of prime rib."

"Right." Her hand landed on his arm. "This is going to be a blast to plan. . . provided I still have a business to work with."

Wade took his left hand off the wheel and slid it over hers. "Whether you do or not, we can still make soup."

She laughed. "We can, can't we?"

"We can." *Nice word. . .we.*

"What brought you to the Lord, Angel?"

She played with her bracelet then took a deep breath. "Emptiness."

Wade nodded—and waited.

"I finally had everything I'd always wanted. My career was flying, I was thinner than I'd ever been, I had great clothes and a nice apartment. I had the respect of people who a few years earlier wouldn't have talked to me. I didn't have close friends, but you can ignore that little fact when you're in charge of half a dozen parties every week. I was making people happy. . ."

"But not yourself?"

"I thought I was happy. And then Pug moved in. We'd been friends in college. She'd been a Christian back then, but I accepted her and she didn't preach at me, so it was all good. And then she did a complete one-eighty and decided to go to Bible college. We drifted apart and then ran into each other about a year ago. She was a starving student, sharing a dinky place with three other girls, so I invited her to move in with me. And that's when life started looking. . .gray."

"In comparison?"

"Yes. My life was all glitz and busyness and her life was homework and Bible studies and charity work. But she absolutely glowed." Angel fingered the lock on the glove compartment and gave a short laugh. "It made me mad."

"I get that. So you wrestled for quite a while, I take it."

"Months. I guess if I'd really understood what was going on—that I was fighting God—I might have surrendered sooner. I only knew the shine had worn off everything. I snapped at people and I. . .ate."

So much emotion wrapped in one short word. "Filling the emptiness."

"Yes."

"But you finally surrendered."

"In an Oscar-worthy scene. I woke Pug in the middle of the night, crying, and told her she wasn't going back to sleep until she told me what she was so happy about."

Wade laughed. "How did she respond?"

"Like you just did. Laughed like crazy and said she'd been praying for that moment for years. She prayed with me and I had about ten days of bliss. Devouring the Bible, asking so many questions Pug couldn't study, getting introduced to Christian music. It was awesome. And then, the truth about what I did for a living came slamming down on me."

"And life hasn't been the same since."

"You got that right."

"'Weeping may stay for the night, but rejoicing comes in the morning.'"

"Is that from the Bible?"

"Psalms." He reached over and took her hand. "Your joy is coming."

"I hope you're right."

The next few minutes passed in silence. Wade took quick glances, watching her smile fade and her mouth turn pensive. "What are you thinking?"

She resurrected the smile, but clearly, it was a struggle. "Nothing."

Now there was an answer no man ever believed. He'd come close to losing body parts when he'd challenged Taylor on that response. But letting it stand might just be worse. "Nothing about what?"

He heard the softest of snickers. "You're persistent."

"When I have reason to be. So what were you not thinking about?"

"Doubts."

"About?"

A long pause passed, in which Wade caught her worrying her bottom lip until he was sure she'd nibbled off all the shiny peach stuff. The thought did crazy things to his own lips.

Finally, she looked over at him with an expression that was part smile, part grimace. "You and me."

That wasn't what he'd been expecting. Not after a day of laughing and talking as if they'd known each other eight months instead of eight days. "Talk."

"I just. . .I don't want to sound like I'm making assumptions about where we're headed, but. . ." She let out the cutest groan. "This is hard to explain. I don't want to drag you down. No, that's not exactly what I mean. Hold you back, maybe."

"Hold me back from what?"

"My life could blow up any minute here. I could end up in jail or lose my business." Angel made a loop out of her purse strap, let it go, and looped it again.

"And?"

"Huh?"

"And if you went to jail for a spell or lost your business, how would that affect you and me?"

"Well. . ." She held her hands out, palms up. "Wouldn't it?"

"Only if we choose to let it. Anything else you're not thinking about?"

"Yes. My shady past."

Wade laughed then wished he hadn't. "Is there something more I need to know?"

"No. I mean, you already do. My business was. . .disgusting is the only word that nails it. That has to bother you. You're a teacher, a Christian, a. . ."

"Human. And far, far, far from perfect." He looked in the rearview mirror and slowly pulled to the side of the road. "Angel. . ." He took a deep breath. "Chole. . .winski?"

She laughed. "You got it!"

"Angel Cholewinski, I may just barely know you, but I'm making a pledge to you. I don't know what our relationship will look like in a week or a month, but I promise you that there is nothing I know about you right now that is going to keep me from getting to know more. Do you believe me?"

She nodded.

"Then can we stop talking about nothing and get back to having fun?"

Blue eyes, wide with trust, gave him a glimpse of her soul. "I'd like that."

⁓

Wade pulled into a parking space on North Main Street in Galena. They got out and walked along the brick sidewalk, stopping to look up at the bumpy cobblestones on Perry Street. The sun was low, and shadows painted squares on the sides of the corner café. They waited as a red trolley pulled over to the curb. Listening to the tour guide point out the jumbled bricks on the street that rose steeply up the bluff, Angel closed her eyes for a moment and took a deep breath. Sunshine on century-old clay, riverbank mud, and a hint of something delightfully deep-fried swirled together in a smell that created a collage of childhood memories.

"Napping?" Wade spoke close enough to add his woodsy, rain-washed scent to the mix.

She didn't open her eyes. "Memorizing. I have to take a little bit of this"—*and you*—"back to the city with me."

His hand closed over hers. "Okay. You memorize, I'll steer. Step down."

As if she could walk with the heat from his fingers frying the communication between her brain and her feet. She tried. One step off the curb and onto the uneven street, three steps toward the middle. . .and her toe caught on a cobblestone and sent her flying. . .into strong arms.

The entire trolley of tourists cheered.

Wade stabilized her, laughing right along with their audience. "Shall we take a bow?"

Aware that her face matched the trolley, Angel stared up at him. "What if they want an encore?"

His lips brushed across her forehead, leaving a streak of tingles. "Guess we'll have to comply."

Chapter 14

On the last Friday of September, Angel sat in her lavender-walled office, tapping her fingernails on the desk calendar. In five days, she could rip off the page and start fresh. Even though October was littered with red Xs, just this morning she'd penciled in two new bookings. If she survived the square labeled COURT in permanent marker, she'd have a glimmer of hope for the future. She slid a business card from Matt's Place over that square.

As if on cue, a rap on her door frame announced Matt. "Well, what do you think?" Was it her imagination, or did Matt's already broad chest add several inches?

"I love it. . .most of it anyway. We've had fifteen hits just this morning." She motioned for him to pull up a chair next to her so they could look at her computer together. She clicked to the Pleasant Surprises home page he'd just redesigned.

"What is it you don't like?"

"You know." She pointed to the tab for BACHELOR/BACHELORETTE PARTIES.

"Just ignore that. When a customer e-mails for info, it'll go to me, just like we talked about. Essentially, I'm working for you now. Just turn all your files over to me, even the clients that canceled. I have a feeling talking to another man may change some of their minds, and we may be able to salvage some. I'll do all the work, but it's your company generating the business, so you'll still be making money off the bookings." His index finger shook at her. "You can never make too much money, you know." Just as he had at Matt's Place, he winked. "That will buy you time to build up the clientele you really want. It's a win-win."

"I have a few theme parties booked that I really need to do myself. I've changed things enough for these people, I can't step out of the picture now."

"That's fine. Get everything else together and send it to me." He pointed to her calendar. "You do have all this in the computer, right?"

"Of course. This is just always at my fingertips. I'm old-fashioned."

Matt laughed and Angel had the feeling he wasn't just laughing at her calendar. "Good. 'Cause a spilled cup of coffee could obliterate your business. So, back to the Web site. . ."

"If the bachelor party page were at least in the new colors instead of the old ones it would give the impression we're trying. . . ."

"So you like the colors?" Matt set one elbow on the desk, inches from hers.

He'd used the sherbet colors of her office suite as backgrounds. She'd spent hours looking at her Web site last night. She'd sent the new pages to Wade and was waiting for his opinion. "They're delicious."

"Delicious?" Matt picked up a 100-calorie bag of trail mix from her desk and dropped it back on her calendar. "You start calling colors delicious, it's a sure sign you need real food. I'll have to do something about that soon. Dulce de leche cheesecake maybe. Or maybe something new. . . "

"I'm dieting, Matt."

"Diet the rest of the week. You have to live." He pointed at the computer. "Everything else good?"

"I want to change our tagline. I should have mentioned that before. I've been brainstorming and getting ideas from Pug and Wade. I haven't found anything I like, but the old one has to go. It's too suggestive."

"'Pleasant Surprises—we stop at *nothing* to *pull off* the surprise.'" Matt read with a grin. "It's not the least bit suggestive now that we changed your logo. Without the girl jumping out of the cake it—"

"Just change it."

"How about 'where the surprises are always pleasant.'"

"Cliché, trite. . .I want something fresh and original. Just take off the old one and we'll keep brainstorming. And I want to cut out a few of the testimonials. They're too—"

"I know. . .suggestive." Matt sighed and pulled a notebook out of his pocket.

"I can make the changes myself. You've done so much already. Oh! The flyers came in this morning. Look." She lifted the corner of a file and pushed a stack of papers aside until she found the half-sheet postcard. The black-and-white birthday cake with colored candles that hung in the reception area was the picture on the front. "This might just be enough to overcome all the attacks on our image. You should go into the planning-a-party-planning-business business."

Matt leaned to the side, bumping her shoulder with his. "It wouldn't fit in a yellow pages ad."

Luanne popped in the doorway. In her hands was a fruit basket wrapped in yellow cellophane. Dena hovered over her right shoulder.

"What's that? I mean, I know *what* it is. . . ." Gifts from clients and companies wanting their business weren't uncommon. The reaction of her employees was.

"It's yours." Luanne walked in and set it on the desk with a thud.

Apples, oranges, bananas, kiwis, and a cluster of red grapes took on weird colors through the yellow paper.

Dena pointed to a card tucked under a raffia bow. There was no envelope. Which meant the two women in front of her were already privy to the name on the card.

Angel casually lifted it. *Congrats on your new image. Happy snacking. See you tomorrow. Love, Wade.*

"Aren't you going to share?" Dena tapped her fingers on the cellophane, making a crinkly ticking sound.

Angel cut the raffia. "Help yourself."

The top layer of fruit was quickly dismantled. Dena picked up a Granny Smith apple and an orange then pointed into the middle of the basket. "What's that?"

Angel stood up and looked down into the shadow. . .and began to laugh in a way she hadn't laughed in months.

Beneath the fruit was a layer of white. Round, white, rolled-up socks.

◈

Two hours after Matt left, Dena stood in front of Angel's desk. "Come on, tell me."

"No." Angel tempered her grin as she stared at the sock pyramid on the corner of her desk.

"Fine." Dena sighed dramatically. "For now. But I'll bug you till you spill the. . .socks." She laughed at her joke. "So what are you doing with this guy tomorrow?"

Angel glanced down at the red slashes over the party once scheduled for Saturday night. Over the top of the *X* she'd written "Wade." "I don't know. He sent a text this morning saying he's picking me up at ten in the morning, and I should wear comfy shoes." She picked up a receipt.

"Mystery. . .love it." Dena stuck her pinkie in her mouth and chewed the nail. "How's it look? Are we in the black?"

"Not yet." Angel tallied numbers and stared at the end-of-week balance. Although she'd returned more deposits to disgruntled clients than she'd taken in over the past two weeks, there hadn't been a request for a refund in twenty-four hours. "But we got three new bookings this week, and the Wilson party decided to go with a sci-fi theme instead of canceling."

"Good."

"Did you talk to Gary about deejaying on the"—she looked down at the chicken scratchings on her calendar—"twentieth?"

"Yeah. He agreed, but he had a few choice words I don't think I'll repeat. Basically thinks you're wacky. Oh, and he hates being muzzled."

"Muzzled?" Angel shook her head.

"He says you're cramping his style. He's Chuck's little buddy, you know."

"I know. But he's cute and good at what he does and people love him. As long as he's willing to stick to my playlist and lay off the trashy jokes, I'll put up with his drama."

"Okay. I'll humor his tantrums." Dena picked up a tangerine and walked out of the room.

Angel touched the handwritten card balancing on top of the sock pile. Wade's message was subtle, funny, but made a point. He was drawing some lines and it made her feel wanted.

୨ৎ

At five o'clock, Angel was deep into frustrating phone calls when Dena walked in and set a bag on her desk. A bag the same color as the awning at Matt's Place. "The guy who brought it said it's for all of us."

"The guy?" Angel looked around Dena's elbow, expecting to find Matt for the second time today.

"Just a delivery guy. Open it."

Angel stood up and opened the bag. Reaching in, she touched plastic. "It's cold." She pulled out a clear plastic box. "Mmm. . ." Meringue on the bottom, whipped cream on the top, and garnished with a twist of candied lemon rind. "Wonder what's in the middle."

"Only one way to find out." Dena reached in the bag and brought out a handful of forks and a piece of paper.

Angel unfolded the parchment and read it out loud. " 'This is Angel Pie. It's a new recipe that just might become one of our signature desserts, if. . .' "

"If what?" Dena craned her neck to see the other side. "Is the rest of it too personal?"

"No. . ." Angel turned the letter over, then back again. "There is no 'rest of it.' "

୨ৎ

Angel took one bite of her namesake delicacy and purred. Dena's opinion was more of an ecstatic yelp. As the lemon chiffon filling slid down her throat, Angel slapped the cover back on the container. She swallowed, took a deep breath for strength, and threw her fork away. "Take this. Share it with Luanne and who-ever walks through the front door, but do not get it anywhere near me."

Smiling like a feather-spitting cat, Dena hugged the plastic box to her chest. "Yes, ma'am." She nodded toward the note. "Whatever 'if' is, you gotta go along with it. Promise?"

"We'll see."

"If you don't, I'm defecting. I'm going to work for Deli Dude." She pointed at the phone. "Call him. Say yes. To letting him use your name or taking his. Whatever." Cuddling her bounty, she scurried into the hallway.

Angel reached for the phone. When she got through to Matt, his first words were, "What do you think?"

"Incredible, amazing, delectable, decadent. . .light, feathery, like a lemon-flavored cloud."

Matt's laugh rumbled in her ear. "So you like it?"

"I have never tasted anything so delicious. Seriously." Angel glanced down at the note, felt her pulse shift to high velocity, and asked, " 'If what?' "

"If. . .we merge."

Angel's lips parted—
"Our businesses."

&

Angel flopped into bed after three on Saturday morning and didn't move until her alarm went off at nine. In spite of the short night, she felt more rested than she had in weeks. With only four more bachelor parties that she was in charge of, the end was in sight. She walked into the bathroom and turned on the shower, then stepped on the scale. She'd lost two pounds. If emotions carried actual weight, it would have been much more. As soon as she organized her files and turned them over to Matt, she'd probably feel weightless.

When she stood beneath the spray of hot water, the smell of last night's cigarette smoke rose in a steamy cloud then vanished in the suds of the crème brûlèe shampoo she reserved for special occasions. The sweet scent seemed symbolic of what she hoped her life would become when she no longer had to deal with the "dark side."

At five to ten, dressed in jeans and a kelly green shirt, she padded lightly out to the kitchen. Pug's bedroom door was open, her bed unmade, and Angel wasn't surprised to find her sprawled on the couch, hugging a textbook, in the exact position she'd been in when Angel tiptoed in the door at two thirty.

Pug opened one eye and closed it again. "Morning."

"Good morning. It's a beautiful day in the neighborhood."

"What're you so chipper about?"

"Well, I. . ." The explanation evaporated on her tongue. Why, she wasn't sure. Maybe it would be better to wait and tell Pug about her business merge with Matt when she had more time. Wade would be here any minute. She opened a box of granola and took out a handful.

"I—what?"

"I'm. . .just in a good mood." Angel kept her back to Pug. She had two reasons for being "chipper." She didn't have to share them both. "I'm spending the day with"—there was a knock at the door—"Wade."

Chapter 15

At the corner of Wells and Locust in downtown Chicago, Wade turned into a parking lot. After pulling into a space and putting the Explorer in PARK, he smiled at Angel's ridged forehead. "We're here."

"Moody Bible Institute. I bet you take all your dates here."

Wade winked at her. "Leave all those other women out of it. I'm going to show you just how thrilling history can be." He got out and ran around to Angel's door. Offering his hand, he bent low and pulled her up. As naturally as if he'd done it a hundred times, his arms went around her and he rested his cheek against the top of her head. "You smell like a bakery. It must be in your blood."

"Or in my shampoo."

"Whatever it is, I like it." He lowered his arms and looked in her eyes. "And I like you in green—it goes with the hair. You must have some Irish in you."

Angel gave a slight shrug. "Maybe I do."

Once again, he'd stumbled onto that missing piece of her life. "You know, if you ever decide you want to pursue it, I've got some research skills you could take advantage of." He took her hand and they started walking.

"I think you're more curious than I am."

"It intrigues me. It's half of your heritage, your history."

Angel nodded, her loose curls shimmering in the sunlight. "I've thought about sidestepping my mother, but I'd feel like I was betraying her. Besides, my father's name isn't on my birth certificate, and she claims she's never told a single soul."

"Except your father."

"Yes. I assume, anyway."

❧

Angel's hand rested in Wade's as the lights dimmed and the video began. Piano music played as a quote from D. L. Moody appeared on the screen. "I do not know anything America needs more today than men and women on fire with the fire of heaven."

On fire with the fire of heaven. Angel pressed her lips together. She'd felt that fire for only a matter of days after giving her life to the Lord.

The narrator began telling of Moody's humble beginnings. Fatherless at the age of four, Moody's early memories were clouded with hardship. And yet, he claimed his family's lack of resources strengthened their faith in a God who was "faithful to widows and a father to the fatherless."

Wade's hand tightened around hers. The narrator talked of Moody's early success in business. "Earning money soon became the most important goal in Moody's life. But God had other plans."

An unfamiliar heaviness settled on Angel's chest as the narrator told about Dwight L. Moody's conversion to Christ. "Though his heart still burned with ambition for business. . .he brought the same relentless energy to his spiritual pursuits."

In less than ten minutes, it was over and the lights came up again. She walked with Wade through an exhibit on American evangelists. Wade talked and she listened, awed by tales of sacrifice and passion for God's people. Would the "fire of heaven" ever land on her again? Wade put his arm around her shoulders and gave her a gentle squeeze. "You're awful quiet. Bored?"

"No. Not at all." She didn't quite know how to explain the feelings the stories were generating.

"Maybe you need to eat. Let's go grab some lunch and come back to finish the tour."

Food. The universal answer to all of life's problems. She glanced at her watch. It was ten to twelve. Lunchtime, a legitimate time to fuel your body. Would she ever be able to look at food that way? Not comfort, not punishment or escape, but necessary fuel meant to be enjoyed? "Lunch sounds good."

❧

They walked the half mile to Bistro 110. After they were seated, Wade glanced over the menu. "I thought about the Cheesecake Factory, but I know you don't want to be tempted, and I need to be eating right these next two weeks before the marathon."

"Thank you." *For not putting decadent desserts right under my nose.* "Aren't you supposed to carb load?"

"The night before. Which reminds me, how'd you like to go out for Italian two weeks from tonight?"

"I have a party that night."

"How about lunch then?"

"My mother and grandmother will be here."

"Are you making up excuses to get out of going out with me?"

"No." Angel grew suddenly serious. "Never." *Ever.*

"Good. I'm kind of liking you across the table from me."

Angel stared into deep chocolate eyes. Her throat tightened. "Me, too."

"I'll take all three of you out. Maybe my sister, too. As much as my mom says she wants her home on weekends, I'm not sure she can handle it."

"It's so hard to imagine Taylor being such a problem. She's a sweet kid."

"You need to tell her that. She doesn't hear a lot of positives."

Their waiter came to take their orders. Angel ordered the spinach and asparagus salad then handed the menu back to the waiter. "I have an engagement party next Friday night she could help with. If it would work for you to get her to my office by six thirty, I'll spend the whole night showering her with positives."

"We have a half day at school. That will be perfect. I thank you. My mother thanks you."

Angel smiled. "Most guys wouldn't even think of taking on the responsibility you have."

Wade tapped one finger on the handle of his butter knife. The waiter brought a bread basket and left again. Wade continued to stare at the tablecloth. Finally he looked up, a wistful expression on his face. "When I was ten, my best friend's mom had a baby. I wanted a baby sister, too. My mother couldn't have any more kids because of health problems, but they finally gave in to my begging and started looking into adoption. The process took two years. Taylor was a year old when they adopted her from Russia. I was almost a teenager by then, not nearly as interested in babies as I was at ten, and not much help. To make a long story short, it wasn't the wonderful experience we'd all dreamed of. Taylor's all about extremes. She can be wonderful, or she can be your worst nightmare. It's taken a huge toll on my mother's health."

"And you feel responsible."

His eyes rose quickly to meet hers. "Yes."

She thought about telling him he wasn't responsible for his parents' decision or his sister's problems. The defensiveness in his eyes told her that was what he expected. But it wasn't what he needed to hear. "There's a Bible verse about sharing each other's burdens, isn't there?"

"Yes."

"Then tell me how I can help."

The look in his eyes made her forget to breathe. "I can't think of anyone in the world I'd rather share my burden with."

⁂

It was dark by the time they walked out of Pacific Garden Mission. Wade put his arm around Angel but didn't try to start a conversation. He'd give her a little more time to process the past few hours. They'd watched a production session for *Unshackled!* the radio drama that had been produced at the Mission since 1950. Through at least half of the story of the alcoholic who'd reconciled with his wife after turning to the Lord, Angel had cried. And then they'd eaten a meal with other visitors, staff, and Mission converts and joined in their praise and testimony service. Wade wrapped his other arm around Angel as they walked to the car, encircling her.

With the sweet scent of her shampoo filling his senses, there were things he wanted to say to her, things that had jelled with her comment about sharing his burden. But would it only confuse her right now? And were there rules about how long you had to know a girl before you laid your feelings out on the table? They were both just a couple of years from thirty. At the moment, he couldn't think of a single reason not to tell her soon.

They got in the car and were reaching the city limits when she finally spoke. "Thank you." Her voice was still tight from tears. "It's been an unbelievable day."

Wade lifted her hand to his lips and kissed her fingertips. "Thank *you*. It was another thing I wouldn't have wanted to share with anyone else."

In the glow of a streetlight, he caught her smile. "So what's God telling you the last couple days?" It wasn't the specific question he really wanted to ask, but it was a way to ease toward "What's God telling you about us?"

"Well. . ." She pulled her hand away from his and wiped her face with a tissue. "I've made a huge decision about the business. I'm going into partnership with Matt."

Alarm bells clanged in Wade's head. He didn't like the sound of this. Not for Angel, and not for him. "Why?"

She rattled off something about catering and marketing. Wade was having a hard time hearing the details over the alarm bells. "So Matt's catering business increases because of your business." He looked over at her, but she was facing the side window. "What's in this for you, Angel?"

"Well. . ." She took an audible breath. "Matt's got marketing experience. . . and. . .he's offered to take over all the bachelor parties."

A little light went on in Wade's head. "So that way you won't keep losing business, but you won't have to deal with anything. . .distasteful."

"Well, it's not quite like that. He's going to steer away from anything 'distasteful.' Just not quite as radically as I was."

"Steer away slowly, huh?" Wade's grip on the steering wheel tightened. He'd had a bit too much experience dealing with that kind of rationalization.

He sensed her looking at him then away again. "What are you thinking?" she asked.

That you sound just like my sister. "It's none of my business."

"I'm making it your business." There was a jagged edge to her voice.

Wade took a deep breath, feeling the intimacy they'd shared all day vaporizing. And the only way he could get it back was to avoid the truth—something he wouldn't even consider. "I think you're not giving God a chance. You were taking a tough stand, Angel, ready to lose it all to stand up for what's right." He swallowed hard. "I think you're taking the easy way out."

Out of the corner of his eye, he saw curls flying as she whipped around to face him. "Maybe it's not the easy way out, but the right way out." He felt the heat of her gaze in the darkness. "What if Matt Peterson is God's answer to my questions?"

Jaw clenched, fingers tightening, Wade pressed down on the accelerator, disengaging the cruise control. He passed a semi, and then another, before realizing the speedometer needle had left eighty behind. Everything in him wanted to push the pedal to the floor. But he pulled back.

95

Silence filled the space between them like a lead wall until he pulled up in front of her apartment. He turned then and stared straight into defiant eyes. "I wouldn't dream of getting in the way of God's answer to your questions."

Angel had no sooner set foot on the sidewalk than he was speeding away.

Chapter 16

Wade sat on the edge of the bed in the room that hadn't changed since he left for college ten years ago. A Michael Jordan poster was still tacked to the ceiling, and a Nerf basketball hoop hung on the back of the door. At the moment, he didn't feel any older than the kid who'd decorated the room. He'd acted like a jealous teenager tonight. Picking up his phone, he rehearsed his apology. Then set it down again.

There was no denying that he needed to say he was sorry for his attitude. But his mistake paled in comparison to hers. Not only was Angel taking the easy way out, she was also enabling Matt to continue doing what she was convicted was wrong. How, in her mind, could that be right? She didn't really believe Matt would "steer away" from such a moneymaker, did she?

No, he'd wait for her to call him. And he'd pray for God to open her eyes.

He lay back on the bed and turned off the lamp. In the blackness, he heard Angel's voice again. "What if Matt Peterson is God's answer. . ."

Lord, show her the truth.

❧

By Tuesday morning, Angel felt like she had the flu. Her head ached; she couldn't look at food. She sat at her desk sucking on an antacid and staring at a text message from Pug.

Worried about u. Talk.

If only she could. But she knew what she'd hear from her roommate. Or her mother or grandmother—do the right thing, leave it in God's hands, not Matt's. But what if leaving it in God's hands meant bankruptcy?

What if? She thought back to her pity party with Ben and Jerry's, when she'd whined to Pug about losing her apartment and selling her clothes on eBay. But she hadn't once had the courage to ask herself what would really happen. She'd lose the business, her apartment, her credit score would plummet. No one would want to hire her. And then what would she do?

She'd move back in with her mother and work at the bakery.

The burning in her stomach suddenly intensified. She saw herself at Taylor's age. Stuck behind the counter at Angel Wing's every afternoon, every Saturday morning. Waiting on the kids who wouldn't talk to her in school. Staring at their clothes, their hairstyles. Listening to them laugh. . .

Chubette.

97

As they laughed, she'd vowed that someday money wouldn't be an issue. Someday, she'd be rich. And thin. Someday, she wouldn't sleep on a couch. She'd have her own place, a new car, money to burn. And no one would laugh.

Angel took another antacid out of the roll. And a tear dropped onto her calendar.

"Oh, God," she whispered. "I'm scared. I'm so afraid of going back to who I was."

Angel swiped at another tear. A thin ray of sunlight sliced between the buildings across the street and landed on her hand.

You are a new creature in Christ. The voice wasn't audible, yet more than a thought. Her lips parted. *Lord, it's true. Even if I have to go without, I don't have to respond like I did back then.* She thought of Dwight L. Moody's family. Poverty strengthened their faith in a God who was faithful to widows and a father to the fatherless.

"Father to the fatherless." She said the words out loud. *I've waited all my life for my father to rescue me. You are the father to the fatherless. You are my rescuer.* Why, then, was she turning to Matt for answers?

Her hand closed into a fist in the patch of sunlight on her desk. "No more." Even if it meant losing everything, she was finally going to do the right thing. She dried her face and cleared her throat. But before she had a chance to reach for her cell, her desk phone rang.

"Angel speaking."

"Ms. Angel, this is Andre from Matt's Place. I am not able to reach Matt, and I thought maybe you could help me."

"I'll try."

"A prospective client just called about a bachelor party. He is meeting with Matt and Mr. Morehouse in an hour, but before he comes in, he wants to be sure that the Plaza Hotel has a—"

"He's meeting with Matt and *who*?" Angel groped for her roll of antacids.

"Mr. Morehouse."

With shaking fingers, Angel grabbed two pink tablets. It couldn't be. . . . "*Chuck* Morehouse?"

"Yes. He is coordinating the bachelor parties for us. Hasn't Matt talked—"

Angel slammed the phone into its base.

⌘

Fifteen minutes into his third class, Wade's phone vibrated in his vest pocket. He turned toward the blackboard and wrote, WOODROW WILSON'S FOURTEEN POINTS while sliding his phone out and looking at the caller ID through his pince-nez glasses.

Angel.

The rest of the hour crawled by. When the last student filed out, he sank into his desk chair and closed his eyes as he waited for the voicemail message.

"Wade. It's Angel." She was crying. "I know you're in class, but I couldn't wait till the end of the day. I had to tell you"—her voice cracked—"I was wrong. So wrong. I was too scared to let God be in control. But no more. I'm done with Matt. I'm cutting all ties. I'll explain everything when you call back." She blew her nose. "*If* you call back. Wade, I'm so sorry. I ruined Saturday. But if it weren't for Saturday, I wouldn't have figured this out. Please call. I know you can't talk, but I just want to hear your voice. Oh, man, I sound needy." She laughed. "I have to leave for a meeting, so if you do call and I don't answer, I'll talk to you tonight. Just please call."

He looked at the clock. Not enough time to say even a fraction of what he wanted to. He got her voice mail. "Angel, I just want to hear your voice, too. You didn't ruin Saturday, and I miss you, and I'm sorry, too. I'll call you after school."

❧

"Is Matt back yet?" Angel interrupted Andre as he spoke to a customer at the deli counter.

"He is in his office with—"

Angel brushed past them. Without knocking, she pushed open the door to Matt's private office. Shock registered on the two men's faces. Matt stood up, knocking over his chair. "Angel. . ."

"Sit down, Matt."

"I can explain. . ."

"I've had enough of your explanations, Matt. I'm through."

A triumphant grin replaced Chuck's shock. "So you're finally ready to sell."

Angel laughed. "Do you really think I came here to tell you your cowardly little schemes worked, Chuck?" She gripped the handle of her purse with both hands. She narrowed her eyes at Matt. "I'm here to tell you there is no way on earth I'm going into business with you. I was ready to do this nicely, to sever our business relationship, but not our friendship. . .until I heard about your new partner. But I'm afraid I just can't find the nice in me at the moment."

"Angel. . ." Matt's hand turned over in a pleading gesture.

"I'm not giving you my files, Matt. And at this very moment, Dena is working on changing our server so you won't have access to our Web site. The dark page no longer exists. So anything you boys intend to do in your little partnership, you'll have to start from scratch." She pivoted on her heel, then stopped and turned slowly back. "You know, I feel sorry for both of you. Take it from somebody who's been there—when you make money the wrong way, you never really get to enjoy it." She slammed the door as she left.

❧

Angel looked up at her office clock for the hundredth time. Wade would be done with school soon. To keep her mind off the slow-moving minute hand, she pulled her Bible across her desk. It fell open where a church bulletin marked her place in Matthew. The bookmark had been in the same spot for over a week. She began to read where she'd left off, at chapter 14, under the heading "Jesus Walks on the Water." As she pictured the disciple Peter, standing in a boat and calling to Jesus, "Lord, if it's You, tell me to come to you on the water," she suddenly saw herself. In all her untested zeal, she'd declared, "Lord, if you tell me to stop doing things that don't honor You, I will." She'd stepped out in faith, her eyes on Jesus, and for a few days she'd felt like she was walking on water. But the cancellations came, the threats of lawsuits. Like Peter, she took her eyes off the Lord and focused on the rising waves. And she sank. *Lord, forgive me. . . .*

She was still praying at three fifteen when "Rescue Me" trilled from her phone.

"Hello."

"Did I mention I missed your voice?"

Angel pushed the last two antacids into the wastebasket and sat back in her chair, smiling in spite of her tears.

❧

Taylor scampered through the empty rooms of Pleasant Surprises like a five-year-old on a treasure hunt. Wade stood in the reception area, turning slowly around. "It reminds me of those little mints they always have at weddings."

"Is that a positive?"

He laughed. "Yes. It makes you want balloons and streamers and confetti and ice cream. But you haven't redecorated in the past two months?"

"No. This is essentially what it looked like the day we opened."

"Really. . ."

"What are you thinking?"

"None of this reflects what you've told me about your old image. I walk in here and I think weddings, birthday parties, make-a-happy-memory stuff—not sleazy, boozy, smoke-filled bachelor parties. Why is that?"

Angel stopped her absentminded magazine straightening. "I. . .don't know." For some inexplicable reason, tears stung her eyes.

"I think I do." He crossed two yards of carpet to stand in front of her. His fingertips touched the bottom of her chin and lifted it.

She had no choice but to stare into the coffee-colored eyes that beckoned from above the line of bison crossing his cheek. No choice but to breathe in the intoxicating scent of spring rain.

"I think"—he whispered just inches from her mouth—"that the real you is what I see on these walls."

The unexplainable tear found its way to her chin.

Wade crooked his finger and scooped it up. "What about that makes you cry? Because it's true?"

"Because I never realized it before." *And because you did.*

"I think the real Angel. . ." his lips closed the distance to hers, "is the color

100

of wedding mints, and I think—"

The phone rang.

Eyes closed, Angel murmured, "It'll go to voice mail."

"Good." His breath feathered her cheek.

"Can I answer it?" Taylor careened into the room. "Oh! Were you guys going to k—"

"Yes! Answer it! It'll be good practice." Angel took a step back and pointed to the reception desk Taylor lunged for. "Say, 'Pleasant Surprises. Taylor speaking. How may I help you?' and write down the message."

Taylor lifted the phone. "Hi! It's Pleasant Surprises. What can I do for you? Oh. . .this is Taylor."

Angel cringed and hoped it wasn't obvious. Wade's hand rested on her shoulder. "I told you this was a bad idea." He gave a slight squeeze. "Hiring my sister, I mean."

"I'm willing to give it a try."

Wade's mouth tipped up, sending buffalo into deep valleys. "So am I."

Angel smiled back, sure his answer had nothing to do with his sister. Wade walked over to a black-and-white picture of a little girl holding a bouquet with trailing pink ribbons.

Angel studied his expressions. "Did you take psychology in school?"

"A little. Why do you ask? Because I figured out you're really all pastel inside?"

Angel bent and picked a piece of lint off the carpeting. "Yes. You're right. If deep down I'd really wanted to attract the market I ended up with, I should have painted the walls black and had neon lights and a smoke machine."

Wade turned to look at her. "So how did the mint-colored person lose her way?"

"Desperation. Before I even found this office space, I knew the competition was too stiff. I had to do something to stand out. A friend asked me to plan a surprise bachelor party for his buddy. It was a success and I got two referrals from it. . .and that's how I found my niche."

"And still you designed this place all light and airy."

"Yeah. Interesting. . . You know, I never did feel good about what we were doing. I just never let myself feel bad. Does that make sense?"

"Sure. You had happy customers, you were making good money and getting recognized for—"

"Um. . . .Angel? I think you should come here." Taylor covered the phone with her hand.

Angel walked over to the desk. In the times she'd been around Taylor, she'd never seen such a somber look. "Who is it?"

"He didn't say," she whispered. "He's asking all sorts of personal questions."

"Questions about me?"

101

"A reporter?" Wade asked.

"No. About me. Here." She shoved the phone into Angel's hand.

Angel's fingers closed around the receiver. She'd dealt with enough prank calls to write a book about it. She steeled herself and got ready to slam the phone down or give the guy a piece of her mind big enough to choke on. "Hello?"

"Hey. . .about that little talk we had at Matt's Place. . ." The voice was thick and muffled. He'd been drinking.

Through gritted teeth, Angel let out a snakelike hiss. "I have nothing more to say to you, Chuck."

"Well, that's the thing. . . See, I have something to say to you. Let's just make this quick and painless, okay?"

Angel tried to swallow, but her throat muscles constricted. "What are you talking about?"

"Just sell it to me. Save your rep and your money and get out before you go under."

Her quivering insides suddenly hardened. "Sorry, Chuck. You've tried to pull us down, but it's not working. Business is picking up, thank you."

The laugh that followed stopped her breath. "You're going under, Angel." Again the laugh. "You got my number."

Icy fingers squeezed her heart. The phone went dead.

Chapter 17

Something Taylor had said pierced through Angel's anger. She stared at the pale-faced girl who'd sunk into the chair behind the desk. "He asked things about *you*?"

Taylor nodded. Her cheeks stained pink. "He asked how old I was and how long I'd been working for you and if I had a boyfriend and. . .other stuff I don't want to repeat. I should have hung up, but I couldn't think."

"You did the right thing." Angel handed the phone to Wade and watched as he smacked it back into its cradle. "He's still trying to scare me into selling him the business."

Bending down to stare into Taylor's eyes, Wade put both hands on her shoulders. "Did you tell him anything?"

"Just my age and that today was the first day I was working here. He said he was a friend of Angel's, so I thought he was just being friendly. But when he started asking creepy stuff I shut up."

"Good girl."

Angel pounded a fist on the counter.

Wade gestured toward the phone. "You need to get a restraining order."

Fatigue swept over Angel. She nodded. "I'll call my lawyer." She looked at the clock. "I have to be at the Marriott in half an hour. If you don't want her coming with me, I'll understand."

"No! I want to go." Taylor aimed pleading eyes at Wade.

"Is this guy all talk?"

"I don't know." Angel leaned both elbows on the counter and rested her forehead in her hands. "I've known him for years, but I never saw this side of him until I changed. He was always sarcastic, always critical, but it never bothered me when we had the same goals. But from the moment I told him I wanted to shift directions, he got weird. Way more angry than a rational person should." She looked up and tapped her temple. "When I saw him at Matt's it was like he was. . .possessed. I think something snapped when I fired him. I have no idea what he's capable of."

"Do you think you're in danger? Do you want me to go with you tonight?"

Yes. "No. I'll be fine. But I'll respect your decision on her."

Taylor waved a hand in front of Wade's face. "Don't talk about me like I'm not here. If she's safe, then I'm safe."

"Will she be with you the whole time?"

"Yes. I want her to shadow me tonight. Tomorrow morning, I'll show her the ropes here, and she can help me pack my car for the bachelor party at the Hilton."

"Can't I work at the bachelor party?"

Wade rolled his eyes.

Angel rubbed her hand on the back of her neck. "I wish you could, kiddo. We're doing a computer geek theme—everyone gets a pair of horn-rimmed glasses and a pocket protector when they walk in. The entertainment is G-rated, but I can't vouch for what comes out of the mouths of the guests. It's why I'm getting out of this, and I wouldn't feel comfortable bringing you into it. But tonight is a surprise engagement party. Should be all good."

"And Mom and Dad want to see you sometime this weekend."

Taylor pouted at her brother, an adorable gesture that had probably made her parents give in to things they shouldn't have. She turned to Angel. "But in between, we party at your place, right?"

"Hah. In between, we sleep. But we can probably get my roommate to make strawberry pancakes for breakfast." The thought made her stomach growl. One bite of strawberry pancakes and she'd be off the wagon and into the whipped cream. "For you."

"Cool." Taylor jumped out of the chair. "I'm going to try on my uniform."

As she ran off, Wade pointed at Angel. "By the way, your willpower is showing. You look great."

"Less soft?"

"I am not going to touch that one." He walked around the corner of the counter until he stood only inches away. "Can I say something direct?"

"Always."

He looked down at the counter, then into her eyes. "I'm impressed that you're sticking to your diet, and I know you're feeling good about it. But I want to be absolutely sure you understand something." His shoulders rose, then slowly lowered. "I like you for you."

"Really?" The word came out slightly strangled.

"Really. Don't get me wrong, I like the wrapping. . .a lot." His fingers threaded through the ends of her curls. "But what I really like"—The backs of his fingers brushed her cheek—"is all the pretty-colored stuff inside."

☙❧

"What if somebody asks me something I don't know?" Taylor clicked the switch on a long, silver candle lighter and lit a hurricane lamp.

"Smile and nod and act like you don't speak English."

"Seriously?"

"No." Angel sprinkled diamond-ring-shaped confetti around the base of the lamp. "Just say, 'I'll find out,' and come and ask me. The most important thing is to be friendly and polite. People overlook a lot if you're respectful."

"What if I drop cake on somebody's head?"

"Run for your life." Angel walked to another table as Taylor's giggle bounced in the empty banquet hall. "You won't have to do anything tonight other than help me supervise. Once we get things set up, the servers will take over, and we just have to be available to make sure everything runs without a—" The squeal of a microphone covered her words. She looked toward the corner of the room where the deejay was arranging speakers.

"Sorry!" Gary Hahn ran a hand through his chin-length hair as he walked toward her. "I'll have all the bugs worked out of the system by the time we start." He glanced toward Taylor. "New help?"

"Gary, this is Taylor Ramsey. She's my official gofer tonight. Taylor, meet Gary Hahn, best deejay money can buy." Angel held back a laugh at the look on Taylor's face. Her eyes reflected the candlelight as she self-consciously fingered the Pleasant Surprises logo on her uniform.

In a black tux, the deejay would have stopped Angel's pulse if she were ten years younger. He might throw his tantrums behind the scenes, but on the job, he was pure charm. Gary held out a hand. "Nice to meet you, Taylor. So you get to stand around with Angel all night and look important, huh?" He reached behind Angel and took a handful of mints out of a bowl. Tossing one in the air and catching it in his mouth, he aimed a twenty-four-carat smile at the girl. "Come visit me when you get bored." Waving the cordless mic, he walked back to his table.

Angel turned around and picked up the candy bowl, shaking it to cover the dent Gary had made. Staring at the mints brought a smile. Looking up, she saw the same look on Taylor's face. The look was followed by a sigh. "He's gorgeous."

Picking up a mint—only seven calories—and letting it dissolve on her tongue, Angel nodded. But not about Gary. "That he is."

⇌❧

All fifty-six guests were seated at round tables. Angel stood in the hallway, gripping the handle of one of the five-foot-wide doors. Taylor manned the other one. "I think I hear them," she whispered.

A split second later, a young couple came around the corner, flanked by the bride-to-be's parents. Angel smiled but avoided eye contact with the MOB. She didn't trust Mrs. Davis, the mother of the bride, not to dissolve into giggles as she had several times in the past hour. Mr. Davis played his role to the hilt. His hand rested on his future son-in-law's shoulder. "Glad we have a chance for a nice quiet dinner before the wedding hulabaloo starts. You and I are just going to be kicked to the curb for the next eight months, son." Two yards from the door, he nodded to Angel and Taylor, and the doors swung open.

"SURPRISE!" The room erupted in applause. Gary started "Stand by Me." And the newly engaged Cassie Davis fainted into her fiancé's arms.

As Cassie was lowered to the floor, Angel winked at Taylor. "Off to a beautiful beginning." Pulling an ammonia capsule out of her purse, Angel bent down over Cassie, snapped the capsule, and waved it under her nose. A gasp, a shudder, and startled eyes fluttered open. Angel patted the prospective groom on the arm, motioned to Taylor, and led the way around the growing huddle of gawkers. Approaching the headwaiter, she said, "Let's get the salads started. Give people something to do instead of gape."

Motioning for Taylor to follow, Angel found a place in the shadows along the wall. "And now, as Gary said, you stand around and be bored with me."

Taylor's eyes gleamed as the bride-to-be was raised to her feet and the guests applauded. "This is so awesome. There's nothing boring about it. Cute guys, fainting girls. . ." While tapping her foot to the music, Taylor's fingers beat out the rhythm on her thighs. "I'm going to be a party planner, too. I'm going to learn everything you know. Give me something to do." Though she stayed in a one-foot-square space, Taylor's restless energy stirred the air around her.

"Go over and tell Mr. Bridges that he can give his toast as soon as Marty and Cassie are seated. And let Gary know so he can get the mic to him."

Taylor nodded. "Got it. And then can I hang out over by Gary?"

"Just stay out of his way."

"I will." Like a power walker pushing off her starting block, Taylor made a beeline for the head table.

Angel laughed and whispered at her back, "Just don't OD on the charm."

Angel leaned against the wall and checked her watch. 9:45 and the dance floor was still crowded. She'd heard nothing but positive exclamations over the food and the ambience. Just as she allowed her first relaxed sigh of the evening, Taylor's laughter rose above the music from the other side of the room. Angel sighed again, this one borne of frustration. Taylor's hand caressed Gary's arm and she gazed at him with nothing short of reverence. Another laugh brought Angel to attention. Wade would not like this one bit.

She'd walked halfway across the room when she spotted the headwaiter marching in her direction.

"We have a problem." He leaned close to Angel's ear to be heard over "Unchained Melody."

Were there four words in the English language she dreaded more? "What's wrong?"

"The groom's mother says the coffee tastes like the bottom of Lake Michigan. We brewed a fresh pot, but she's still complaining."

Having watched the icy interaction between MOG and MOB, Angel had a feeling the complaints had nothing to do with lake water. "I'll handle it. Thank you."

Apologizing profusely to Mrs. Bridges, April promised to put a perfect cup of coffee in her hands *stat*. Which meant half-running to the Starbucks on the main floor. When she returned, Gary was announcing the final dance. Angel darted into the kitchen, grabbed a coffee carafe, emptied two black grande coffees into it, and presented it, with a smile and a flurry of apologies, to the mother of the groom.

And then she went to extract her apprentice from Gary's charm.

&

"She was hanging on your arm fifteen minutes ago. The girl didn't dissolve into thin air!"

"Maybe she went to the bathroom or something." Gary shrugged and stuck his MP3 player in his jacket pocket.

"I checked the bathrooms. Twice."

"Maybe she went out for a cigarette. You got my check?"

Angel pulled an envelope from her pocket, threw it on the table, and ran toward the kitchen. Maybe Taylor had gone in to see things behind the scenes.

She wasn't there.

Panic, like quick-setting cement, started at the bottom of her rib cage and moved up to her throat. Steering around guests ambling toward the exit, Angel shot into the hallway. At every alcove and doorway she tried door handles, looked behind potted plants. At the elevator she stopped. She had three choices. Elevator, stairs, or through the lobby to the front entrance. Gary's suggestion came back to her. Maybe she'd gone out for a cigarette. She had no idea if Taylor smoked.

As she dodged men with briefcases and women in evening gowns, her eyes locked onto a circle of people just outside the front door. A camera flash, and then another. Laughter.

Her breath coming in ragged drags, Angel reached the sidewalk. Her eyes followed the gazes of a dozen people to the spectacle that swayed beneath a green awning. A spectacle in a Pleasant Surprises uniform.

Wobbling on one leg, Taylor bent the other to create a number 4. Her hands stretched over her head. A helium-filled diamond-ring-shaped balloon bobbed against the awning, anchored to a string tied around her neck. As she teetered, she sang an off-key version of "I Got You Babe."

Taylor was drunk.

Chapter 18

I'm calling Wade." Angel stretched the seat belt across Taylor and snapped it, then slammed the car door. The sound reverberated off the concrete walls of the parking garage. Seconds later, she shoved her bag behind the driver's seat and repeated the slam.

"He's ashlllleep." Taylor's finger weaved like a pendulum in the general direction of the dashboard clock. "He gets really, really cranky if you wake him u–up." The last word was a mesh of hiccup and laugh. "And he's at my house. You'll wake up my dad." Her head oscillated at the same speed as her finger. "Not a good idea."

Perspiration dampened Angel's blouse. The nerves in her hands prickled when they clamped onto the steering wheel. Her eyes felt like glowing coals. She squinted at the girl slouched against the passenger-side door. "Not a good idea?" Her chest vibrated as she tried to draw a full breath. "Not a good idea is you getting smashed while you're working for me! Not a good idea is you posing for pictures with a balloon around your neck—in *my* uniform!"

Taylor sunk into the seat and closed her eyes.

"Look at me! Maybe you're used to people protecting you from consequences, but it's not going to happen this time. If those pictures show up anywhere, I might as well lock my doors and go work at Burger King."

Half-mast, expressionless eyes rotated toward her.

"If you didn't think about me, did it maybe once cross your mind that Gary is going to lose his job for this?"

"He didn't do anything wrong."

Angel banged the wheel with the side of her hand. "He got you plastered."

"No, he didn't." Taylor pressed farther into the corner. "He just told me where it was. He had a couple soda bottles under the table. Only it wasn't soda." She rubbed her fingertips up and down her forehead. "I didn't drink that much."

Right. No remorse, no apology. And the girl had the nerve to defend Gary. Angel exhaled, part sigh, part growl. Reaching behind the seat, she tossed things out of her bag until she found her phone. *Lord, I don't want to do this.*

"He doesn't have to know." The quiet voice was much more sober than moments before. "Let's just go to your place."

Angel played with the thought. She could take Taylor home, put her to bed, and tell Wade tomorrow. If he didn't have to talk to her like this he'd probably handle it much better. She slid the phone into her pocket and stuck the key in the ignition. But she couldn't turn the key. "Your parents need to know. Do you want to tell Wade or should I?"

The heels of Taylor's hands pressed against her eyes. Her fingers curled. "I. . .don't want. . .them to know." With a convulsive sob, she sat up straight. Her hands slid down to cover her face. "I promise I'll never do anything this stupid again. Just let me prove it to you. I'll work really hard tomorrow. Just give me a chance."

The pleas didn't move Angel. She really didn't care what awaited Taylor. Her hesitation had come from her fear of facing Wade's disappointment. Not in Taylor, but in her. Tears fuzzed the outline of the car next to hers as she opened her phone.

❧

Wade heard the phone, but it rang twice before he was coherent enough to get out of bed and hunt for it. By the time he found it, "1 MISSED CALL" flashed on the screen. *Angel.* His pulse tripped and his brain started a litany of worst-case scenarios until he glanced at the clock. It felt like the middle of the night, but it wasn't even eleven. He smiled. Had he asked her to call when they got home? He couldn't remember. *Calling to say good night, my Angel?* He pushed the button to return her call.

"Wade?"

He didn't like the sound of her voice. "What's wrong? Where are you?"

"We're safe. We're just leaving the Marriott." A ragged breath ended her sentence. "But something. . .happened tonight."

Wade turned on the overhead light and closed the bedroom door. His pulse gained speed as he waited for her to continue. "What?"

"Taylor got. . .she had. . .a drink." It sounded as though she was covering her mouth with her hand. "She. . .she's drunk."

"*What?* How. . . You said she was going to be with you the whole time." His free hand balled into a fist.

"She was. I'm so sorry. I didn't know—"

"You didn't know she was getting wasted? What kind of—"

"She'll explain it all tomorrow."

Wade picked his jeans off the floor and threw them on the bed. "She'll explain tonight. Put her on."

Angel didn't answer. After a moment, he heard her talking to Taylor, telling her to wake up. Finally, he heard a sound he thought was his name. "What did you do, Taylor?"

"I just had a—oh, man, I'm gonna be—"

He heard a car door open and the next sound made him hold the phone away from his ear.

"Wade?" Fear coated Angel's voice. "I'll get her home and I'll call you in the morning."

Sticking one leg into his jeans, Wade stumbled, kicking the bed frame with his bare foot and spitting out a word he hadn't used in years. "She's not staying with you. I'll meet you at your place."

❧

The black Explorer was parked in front of Angel's building when she pulled up. She didn't want to imagine how fast he must have been driving to beat her there.

Wade paced the sidewalk beneath a street lamp, running both hands through his hair. He stopped pacing when she pulled up to the curb. In three long strides, he was at the passenger door. Angel grabbed Taylor's arm as Wade whipped the door open. If she hadn't, the girl would have landed on the ground. Wade reached in and lifted his sister as effortlessly as plucking a shirt off a clothesline.

Angel still hadn't seen his face. Hands shaking, she scrambled in the backseat for the things she'd thrown out of her bag, and got out of the car. Wade was putting Taylor in the Explorer. He slammed the door. She knew that feeling. With a quick prayer for strength, Angel stepped onto the sidewalk and walked toward him. "I'm so sorry. I was watching her all night, and I thought she—" She stopped midsentence when he turned his back and walked around the front of the car. "Wade, please. . ."

He halted and looked slowly over his left shoulder. "I'll talk to you later." With that, he got in the car, gunned the engine, and screeched away from the curb.

❧

Pug was still awake. Awake and exercising to her *Sweating in the Spirit* video. She jumped when Angel's bag dropped to the floor. She turned and looked, then paused the DVD. "What now?"

Angel dissolved into the three-sixty chair. Rolling the chenille throw into a lumpy ball, she hugged it. Sunny jumped up beside her. "Taylor got drunk. There were cameras. . . . Wade took her home. I don't think I'll see him again." She stared, not blinking, at a single broken chow-mein noodle on the footstool. "I'm going to bed." She didn't move.

The footstool did. Pug pushed it with her foot until it sat just inches away from Angel's chair. Plopping onto it, Pug leaned forward, panting like an Olympic sprinter. "How'd she get ahold of alcohol? Not one of the servers again?"

"No." Angel picked up the chow-mein noodle and stuck it in her mouth. "This time it was my deejay."

"Are you kidding?" Pug wiped her forehead with the sleeve of her shirt. "Ange, this is starting to sound like a conspiracy."

Angel's squeaky laugh came from high in her chest. "I wish. If I could blame anyone else for this, I'd jump on it. This was all my doing. I hired a kid I don't know anything about, after her brother warned me not to, and I kept my deejay even after he came right out and said he had no respect for my new way of doing things." She buried her face in the blanket and shook her head. "Stupid. Stupid. Stupid."

"How old is Wade's sister? She's not a four-year-old. You can't—" Angel's generic ring tone jangled from her bag. "That has to be Wade, right?" Pug jumped up and dug through the bag as she brought it to Angel.

Angel shook her head "Wade is 'Rescue Me.'" Angel took the phone and glared at the screen. "Gary. Unless he's groveling, he's going to be sorry he called." Her parting shot at him as she'd half-carried Taylor to the parking garage had been, "Just wait." She opened the phone and said his name with a voice as flat as her mood.

"Don't think for a minute you can pin this on me, Angel. I didn't have anything to do with it."

"You brought the bottles."

"Prove it."

Angel opened her mouth, but she had no idea how to respond. He was right. She couldn't prove a thing. "You'll hear from my lawyer."

"I'd better not hear anything from anyone or this is all going to come smashing right back in your face. But, hey, that's gonna happen no matter what, isn't it? You hired a minor *again* and let her get drunk on the job. Dumb business strategy, Angel. And by the way, I can't work for somebody that irresponsible. The rest of the gigs you booked with me. . .look for another deejay."

☙❧

This time, Angel changed the phone number. By Saturday afternoon, a cellphone video clip of Taylor's dance debut titled "We Got *You*, Babe" had appeared on the Internet with a voice-over message: "At Pleasant Surprises, we believe in joining the fun. If you want servers who get sauced right along with you, call 555-S-U-R-P-R-I-S-E."

In the middle of her fourth night of waking up somewhere between three and five, taunted by Sonny and Cher and Wade and Taylor, Angel whipped off her quilt, startling Sunny, and stomped into the kitchen. She turned on the light over the stove and opened the refrigerator. Pug had made tiramisu for her study group and the leftovers beckoned. Angel took it out, grabbed a package of graham crackers from the cupboard, and crawled onto her round chair. Sunny followed her and rested his head on the footstool. "Don't look at me like that. I deserve every bite of this."

Hugging the huge glass bowl, she tucked her feet beneath her and scooped an espresso-infused escape onto a graham cracker spoon. Sugar. . .her drug of choice. For a moment, she was lost in the textures. The sweet cream surrounding her tongue, the spongy lady fingers, the crunch of the crackers. Her eyes closed.

Chubette.

Angel's eyes jarred open. It wasn't an actual voice, just a memory ghost whispering through the tiramisu. But the word still held the power it had on her thirteenth birthday. She jabbed the point of a broken cracker through the cocoa

111

sprinkled over the tiramisu and shoveled a mound into her mouth. But it only turned up the volume on the memories.

Chubette.

She remembered the new outfit as clearly as if it still hung in her closet. Her mother had said no—said it wasn't modest and wasn't right for her "body type." But Angel had birthday money, and what did her mother know about style, anyway? So she bought the black tube skirt and the crop top and wore it to a friend's party. . .a party she was sure would turn out to be a surprise for her. The surprise had turned out to be overhearing two of her best friends: "Hey, Tara, I finally get to talk to you without Chubette around. You gotta tell that girl she's got way too much belly for a belly top." In the midst of their giggles, she'd left, walking home in platform shoes that killed her feet. Home to a half-eaten birthday cake that she finished off in her room and lied about the next day. It was only a small lie. She really *had* dropped it. . .right into her mouth.

Staring at the gob of coffee-laced fluff headed toward her lips, Angel froze. "What am I doing?" Stuffing her face hadn't filled the gnawing emptiness when she was thirteen. Nor had it satisfied her emotional hunger any time since then. It wasn't going to work now. Tomorrow she would still have a business on the verge of destruction. And there would still be a gaping hole in the place Wade Ramsey had started to occupy. Wiping her mouth with the back of her hand, Angel got out of the chair and dumped the rest of the dessert into the trash.

Lord, fill me. Show me how to find what I need in You alone.

≈❧

Wade threw his pillow against the wall and glared at the clock. 2:47. He'd gotten a good three hours in before waking, for the fourth night, to the argument in his head. *Stop blaming her.* But she should have been watching. *It was Taylor's fault.* No, it was Angel's. *Call her.* She's the one who needs to apologize. *She tried. . . .*

Giving up on sleep, he got out of bed and put on his running clothes. He'd been hoping to get in a long run after school. *Might as well do it now.* He dug a headlamp and reflective vest out of his bottom drawer, filled two water bottles, scribbled a note to Taylor in case she happened to get up and find him gone, and walked out into fall air tinged with the scent of apples from the Red Delicious tree behind the house. He stretched on the porch, then ran down the sidewalk and stepped off the curb onto North Ash. This would be his last long run before the Chicago Marathon. The thought, like most of his thoughts, led straight to Angel. She'd be there. He glanced at his watch. With all he was running from, eight-minute miles would be a piece of cake.

After two miles, he fell into a blissfully mindless state where ideas and impressions flitted out of his mind as quickly as they entered. He'd just passed his thirteen-mile mark—an abandoned corn planter turning to rust at the edge of a field—when his phone rang. Home. He flipped it open, trying not to slow his pace. "Taylor?"

"Are you nuts?"

"Couldn't. . .sleep."

"Duh. Of course you can't sleep."

"What. . .do you mean by that?" His lungs burned. He didn't have the stamina for that many words.

"Think about it."

The phone went silent, and Wade kept running. He got home at five to six and headed down the hall to the bathroom. As he passed his office, where Taylor shared space with his bookshelves, he heard a giggle. He stopped and looked in. In the glow of a night-light, he saw his sister sitting on the floor in the corner.

In her hand was a dark brown bottle.

"Hey. Have a nishe run?" She waved the bottle at him. "Wan' some? I'll sh–h–hare." She hiccuped.

Wade stared, mouth open. Taylor giggled again. The sound pushed a button, igniting unfamiliar rage. "How. . .*dare*. . .you!" He breathed it out like a curse and took a step toward her. "What is wrong with you? Didn't you learn anything—" He reached for the bottle.

Taylor jumped up and backed into the corner, holding the bottle over her head. "Why sh–h–houldn't I? Huh? Nobody was watsh–h–hing me." She took a swig and laughed.

Wade took another step and yanked the bottle out of her hand. "You ungrateful little—" He stopped. A faint smell wafted from the bottle. He turned it around and held it toward the dim light, then lifted it to his nose.

Root beer.

Taylor dissolved in a different kind of giggle. "Gotcha."

"I ought to club you with this." His grip on the bottle was viselike. "You think that's funny?"

Pulling her hair away from her face with both hands, Taylor shook her head slowly. "What would you have done if it was real? Stop talking to yourself because I got drunk right under your nose?"

"What?" Wade slammed the bottle onto a shelf.

"Well, that's obviously working with Angel."

The comment thumped his midsection like a close-range basketball, making the next breath a struggle. "My relationship with Angel is none of your business."

"Fine. But my brother being an idiot *is* my business. The reason you can't sleep is because you're taking this out on the wrong person. You're blaming Angel for not watching me because you're really mad at yourself and you don't want to admit it. But it's not her fault, and it's not your fault. I'm the one who decided to drink. If you're going to be mad at anybody you should be mad at me."

"Don't you think for one second that I'm not mad at you!"

"But you're grounding Angel. . .and yourself. . .right along with me." Her gaze swooped toward the ceiling and back at him. "I may be the one with ADD, but I think way better than you. You're in love with Angel, and you're too dumb to know it."

Chapter 19

Oatmeal?" Pug looked at Angel's bowl and made the international sign for gagging. "What are you doing penance for?"

"Tiramisu at four a.m."

"Ah." Pug stuffed a book in her school bag and padded in her bunny slippers to the coffeepot. "Save a little for an oatmeal mask. It might get rid of the stuffing-anger-and-false-guilt-and-haven't-slept-in-days bags under your eyes."

"How about the should-I-miss-him-or-hate-him pout lines?"

"Should help those, too." Pug sat down across from Angel, dropping a handful of sugar packets that slid across the table. "Did you call him yet?"

"Twice. I left an 'I know I'm pond scum' message on Sunday and yesterday I tried 'Ple–e–e–ease just listen to my side of it.'" She took a bite of oatmeal and grabbed a sugar packet. Opening it, she swirled a *W* on the gray mass. "If I decide to humiliate myself even further, I'm going for 'You've got the maturity of unhatched fly larvae.'"

"That's mature."

Angel groaned. "I didn't let myself have crushes in high school because the cool guys wouldn't look twice at me. Most of the guys I dated after I got rich, skinny, and confident treated me great, but I saw how they were to the girls who looked like I used to. And now, here I am bulging at the seams again, and I find what I've wanted all my life. . .a guy who accepts me for who I am. . .and then *zap!* he's gone."

"Maybe not forever."

"But maybe forever. Why'd I go and fall like a ton of bricks. . .or lard?" Stabbing her spoon into the center of the *W*, Angel narrowed her eyes. "I ought to—" A text message beep sounded from her phone. She slid her hand toward her phone until her whole arm rested on the table. The phone beeped again from two inches beyond her fingertips. She laid her head on her arm. "Whatever it is, it can't be good this early in the morning."

"What if it's him?"

Angel craned her neck to look at the clock. It was seven forty. "He's teaching."

She sat up and finished her cereal, then picked up her bowl and phone. On the way to the sink, she opened her phone.

Got something 2 tell u. Can I call at noon? Taylor

With fumbling fingers, Angel replied.

Of course.

At times during the rest of the morning, Angel wondered if the battery in her office clock was dying. The second hand jerked, stopped, and hung there in limbo, as if deciding whether another tick was worth the effort. But every time she checked, the time on her computer screen matched the lazy clock.

At eleven thirty she shut her door, set her phone on the desk, and bowed her head over it. *Lord, I need Your peace. Whatever this is about, give me the grace to handle it. Help me to tell her I forgive her and mean it. And whatever she says about Wade, let me accept it.*

When her office phone rang at ten to twelve, she was pacing. "Hello?"

"Hi, Angel. It's Steven Vandenburg. Have you got a minute?"

Angel looked at the frozen second hand. "I'm expecting a call at noon, but I've got a few minutes. How are you, Steven?"

"Couldn't be better. Wade's kept me up to speed on your ideas for the fundraiser. I'm impressed, and so is the rest of the committee."

"I'm. . .glad."

"You two make a good team."

Angel blinked. Her mind went blank.

"Angel? I'm not being totally forthright here. I talked to Wade last night. He told me what happened with his sister."

"Oh." Again, she couldn't think of what to say next.

"Would you mind an old man sticking his nose in your business?"

Something about his tone made her smile. "I'll take advice from you—not so sure I want an old man's opinion."

Steven's laugh was deep and easy. He struck her as a man who laughed often, in spite of all he'd lost. "In three years I'll be fifty-five and getting senior discounts at the Welcome Inn. That's old." He chuckled again. "Wade's beating himself up over this. You're not the real target, and he's figuring that out. Guys are a little slow most of the time. Are you willing to give him some time?"

"Yes." It came out as a whisper.

"Good. Then, I think there's something I have to do for my buddy Wade."

"I don't like the sound of that."

Again, the laugh. "He told me about the interrogation your roommate gave him."

"Uh-oh."

"So. . .how old are you, Angel?"

Laughter felt foreign, but freeing. "You should never ask a lady that. But I'm not much of a lady. I'll be twenty-nine in January."

He was silent for a moment. "You're just enough of a lady. Where were you born?"

"California." She had no idea why. It was one of the few entries in the blank pages of her history. "Sacramento." Close enough to Hollywood to feed fantasies of her father's name in lights. "I've only got ten minutes, Steven."

"Okay. So let's cut to the pertinent stuff." She could hear his smile. "What's the best way for a guy to say he's sorry? Pick one: candy, flowers, dinner, jewelry—"

"Just words. Tell him that's all I need."

"I'll do that, Angel. I'll let you go now."

"Thank you, Steven. You made me smile."

"I'm glad. We'll have to get together soon to flesh out some details. . .the three of us."

"I hope."

"It'll happen."

ॐ

Her cell phone rang at 12:06.

"Hey." Taylor sounded breathless. "I'm really sorry about Friday. I know you're mad at me, but I gotta tell you this. After what happened with that cheerleader, I checked out her and her friends on Facebook. I've been exchanging messages with some of them, just seeing if I could learn anything that might help you out when you go to court. Anyway, my picture's on my page, so when that stupid YouTube thing came out the other day, they recognized me. So one of them e-mails me and asks if I got the booze from Gary"—she paused, clearly for dramatic effect—"like they did."

Angel's knees buckled. "What?"

"Weird, huh? I've got the whole story—all the evidence you need. He picked them up and gave them pizza and soda on the way. Evidently, it was the same brand of soda he gave me. Anyway, they knew the stuff was spiked, but that didn't stop them. Those girls didn't get served anything by your people."

Angel crumpled into her desk chair. Tears spilled onto her calendar. "Taylor. . .you just saved my life. Thank you."

"Hey. I gotta know how to do this stuff if I'm gonna be a party planner. I gotta run. I'll send this to you as soon as I get home."

"Thank you. More than you can possibly know." Angel closed the phone and sobbed, then opened it and called her lawyer.

ॐ

By midmorning on Wednesday, the *Alby v. Pleasant Surprises* case was dropped and Gary was in jail. Angel hung up the phone that she'd hardly put down all morning. She'd just received a call from Nicole Alby's father, apologizing for whatever effect his daughter's lying, and her part in the YouTube video, had on Pleasant Surprises. As Angel stared at the phone, still numbed by what had happened in the past twenty-four hours, the phone rang again.

"Hi, Doreen."

"Great news, Angel. Gary Hahn fingered Chuck Morehouse. We've got proof now that he was behind everything. It's all over, girl."

117

An hour before noon, Angel walked back into her lilac-walled office after a meeting with her minuscule staff and stood by the window. A light rain began softly tapping at the window, muting her view. She watched the drops gathering dust and rolling it away, leaving clean streaks behind. A perfect illustration of how she felt. Fresh, clean, rain-washed. . .like the smell of Wade's cologne. The uninvited thought clouded over the moment, and she went back to her desk.

In hopes of avoiding thoughts of Wade, she tackled the most unsavory item on her to-do list first. Her decision to change the Pleasant Surprises phone number meant someone needed to call each of their past, current, and undecided clients and give them the new number. Angel had taken on that job herself and had only made a small dent in the list. After twenty more minutes of calls, she drew a fresh red *X* across a December birthday party. The words of the man she'd just spoken to still stung her ears: "The way things are going with you guys, you'll probably abscond with my deposit and split the country before Christmas. I'll plan my own party."

Opening her e-mail, Angel read a message from her mother. *So, so relieved and happy for you. Looks like the weather will be nice this weekend. Still up for some company for watching the marathon?*

Angel clicked REPLY then hesitated. With forty-five thousand runners and over a million spectators, she wasn't too worried about bumping into Wade, but she might get a glimpse of him crossing the finish line. And just knowing he was in the city and purposely not looking her up would feel strange. But she didn't have the heart to break the tradition.

Hi, Mom—Thanks for all your prayers. I can't tell you how good it feels to have this behind me. I'm still planning on you two for the weekend. I'll be out late Friday night, so make yourselves at home. Pug and I are having a slumber party in the living room, so the older generations can have the beds. I have a party on Saturday night, but we'll do something fun during the day and Sunday's free for Marathon watching. Love you.

She pushed SEND and stared at the screen until her out-box cleared. As it did, the tape she had stuck to her monitor two months ago suddenly gave out, sending the Bible verse attached to it sailing onto her scarred desk calendar.

Always be prepared to give an answer to everyone who asks you to give the reason for the hope that you have. Angel got a new piece of tape and stuck it back on. *Lord, thank You. But I'm still in need of hope.*

Chapter 20

I'm looking into taking out a loan until things pick up again. I'm sure I could pay it back in six months and. . ." Angel stared at her mother. Clearly, she'd lost her audience. They'd left Bapcia at Barnes and Noble and were walking toward the *Cloud Gate* sculpture in Millennium Park, and the thirty-foot-high seamless blob of polished steel was taking precedence over the future of Angel's career.

"It's so serene." Her mother walked closer. The sculpture reflected the coral in her shirt like a silver-tinted sunrise. "A still pool in the middle of chaos."

"My mother, the poet." Angel stared at the skyline mirrored in the sculpture, at the clear blue dome that copied the sky. "It looks like a melting metal jelly bean to me."

"My daughter, *not* the poet." Her mother walked into the shadow of the arch beneath the sculpture, and Angel followed.

British artist Anish Kapoor claimed a blob of mercury was the inspiration for his shimmery masterpiece. Angel agreed with her mother about its calming presence in the midst of the noise and busyness, but she was having a hard time syncing her quicksilver thoughts to the peacefulness of the park. While an underlying sense of relief formed the backdrop of her mindset, her brain still fizzed with anxiety over Pleasant Surprises and Wade Ramsey.

Her mother walked back into the sunlight. "What an amazing day." She held out her arms, closed her eyes, and lifted her face to the cloudless span above them. She was the embodiment of serenity.

Angel envied the smile on her mother's face, the ability to embrace the moment. It wasn't a trait she'd inherited. "If you want to stop at the fountain. . ." They'd promised to meet Bapcia for lunch at noon. The lunch they should have been having with Wade. "We need to step it up a bit." She hated being the nag, but it had always been that way. Her mother had an aversion to clocks.

Her mother nodded, face still to the sun. "Let's go." She put her arm around Angel's shoulders and started walking. "It's good to see you hopeful again."

"Yeah. About some things."

They stepped out of a treelined walkway and got their first glimpse of the *Crown Fountain*. Two fifty-foot towers made of translucent glass blocks rose out of a reflecting pool. Her mother gasped as if this were the first time she'd seen it. As they watched, the image of a man's face appeared behind the clear sheet of water cascading down the side of one of the monoliths. After a moment, she turned her attention back to Angel. "Your thing with Wade was exciting—what woman doesn't want to be rescued by a handsome stranger?—but that doesn't mean anything solid would have come out of it." Her mother slipped out of her sandals and stood barefoot on the black granite surrounding the pool. "If he's still mad at you because of his sister's immaturity, you know other things like this would come up in the future. You need a man who's going to be consistent."

As close as she was to her mom, she'd never had an easy time talking to her about relationships. To her knowledge, the only one her mother had ever been involved in had ended with heartbreak. . .and her.

"You'll get over him, honey."

"I'm not so sure."

"You never forget your first real love." She smoothed the end of her braid. "But you do get past the pain."

Angel set her bag down and watched two little boys splash through the inch-deep pool and turn their backsides into a stream of water shooting from the massive lips of the face on the tower. "There's just something about Wade that's—"

"*Here!*" Her mother's fingers bit into her arm just above the elbow.

"Ouch. What in the—" She followed the line of her mother's gaze to its end point.

On the opposite side of the fountain stood two men. One, looking like a lumberjack wearing a lime green polo shirt, the other in shorts that showcased a runner's legs. . .and eyes that, even behind sunglasses, seared Angel's skin.

☙

In a movie, it would have been the perfect setup for a slow-motion reuniting scene. Eyes meet, lips part in shock, tears spring to her eyes, his. . .and then, in graceful, gliding strokes they run across the water. Droplets sparkling in the sun, fountain spray forming a misty cloud, the star-crossed lovers melt in a passionate kiss. . . .

In real life, nothing happened. Wade froze. Beside him, Steven Vandenberg did the same. Then slowly, sunglasses lowered.

But not Wade's.

It was Steven who took off his glasses while Wade remained as unmoved as the statue of Ulysses S. Grant atop his horse.

"This is ridiculous," Angel whispered over her thundering pulse. "If that man doesn't—"

Her mother pivoted on her heel as she said, "Let's get out of here." She took a step away from Angel. "If it takes him that long to react, he's not ready to apologize. Come on."

Angel shook her head. "I'm standing my ground."

"Call me when he's gone."

By the time Angel started to protest, her mother was too far away to be heard without yelling. "What is wrong with that wom—"

"Rescue Me" piped from her purse.

Like a guided missile, her hand dove around the contents of her bag and made a direct hit on her phone. She fumbled it open then remembered he was watching. But she'd already lost her opportunity to look nonchalant. "Hi."

Steven walked away. Wade stood alone, facing her and the morning sun. "Hi." Three preschoolers scampered in the pool between them. "I was wondering. . .if I came over there, is there a chance you'd stick around long enough to hear me say I was stupid and prideful and sorry for blaming you for something that wasn't your fault?"

Angel tipped her phone away from her mouth as a week's worth of torment escaped in a single sigh. "There's a chance."

He didn't answer.

He ran. Through the water. Not in graceful, gliding strokes surrounded by sun-kissed droplets, but in a loud, splashing, finish-line sprint.

He didn't hug her. She'd expected strong arms to engulf her. Instead, he stopped two inches from her, close enough that she felt his words grace her cheek. "Can you forgive me?"

"Of course," she breathed.

His hands slid into her hair and cupped the back of her head. And there, before Saturday shoppers, little children, foreign tourists, a fifty-foot-tall face spewing water, and quite possibly in front of her mother, he kissed her. Once.

And then again.

≈❦

Wade pulled his hands slowly from her hair. For a moment, he simply stared. "You're very good at forgiving."

"Maybe it's my turn to apologize, so you can forgive me."

"You have nothing to be sorry for, but I won't stop you."

"I'm sorry I didn't watch Taylor closer."

"I don't blame you. But I forgive you." He grazed his lips across hers. "And I'd forgive you even better if there weren't thousands of people staring."

"There won't be thousands of people staring until tomorrow when I kiss you at the finish line."

≈❦

Approaching the twenty-one-mile marker, Wade breathed a prayer. *Thank You.* He wasn't hitting the wall like the poor souls he passed, bent over, hands on knees, or slowly walking. *Too hot.* His thoughts came in disjointed fragments. He took two cups of water from a volunteer, downed one, dumped the other over his head, and threw the cups on the ground. Reaching the marker, he pressed a button on his watch. *Splits are good. Averaging two seconds under.* He passed familiar restaurants. Yee Heung Seafood House, Hong Min, Emerald City. China Town. *Does Angel like Chinese? Five more miles. . .She'll be there. . . . My feet hurt. . . . One step at a time. . .Angel's there. . . . I can tell her. . . . My back hurts. . . .*

Thoughts faded. He was just a machine. *Stride. Stride. Relax hands.* Sweat stung his eyes. Wentworth Avenue. Thirty-third Street. State. Thirty-fifth. Finally, he turned north on Michigan Avenue. *Straight shot. . . Two more miles. . . Angel's there. . . . I can tell her.* The crowd of spectators grew denser and louder. Air horns, neon signs, cab whistles, shouts. "Almost there!" "You can make it!" The support felt almost physical, buoying him up. He stared at a guy about five yards ahead. Blue shorts, white singlet. *Pass him.* His lungs hurt. From deep inside he dredged a drop of energy, glued his gaze to the white shirt, and passed him. *Now the woman with the red bandana. . .*

எை

The finish line clock read 2:43. Angel's voice was already hoarse, and her arms hurt from hanging over the fence, clapping and waving as the names were announced.

"Congratulations, everyone! You have run Chicago!" The loudspeakers blared over the music. "And it's a hot one. Thermometer's just hit eighty-two."

Lord, that's dangerous. Take care of him. . .all of them. Each runner that approached the clock appeared increasingly exhausted. Volunteers ran wheelchair relays to the first-aid tent.

Sandwiched between her mother and grandmother, Angel feigned deafness as the older generations discussed Wade.

Bapcia clicked her tongue. "If I were thirty years younger, those eyes of his would—"

"Mother!" The exclamation shot across Angel. "Act your age. Looks aren't everything."

"Well they sure do—"

The announcer's voice covered her words. "Shawn O'Brian from Lexington, Kentucky, just crossed the finish line, followed by Butch Polaski from right here in the Windy City. Hope you're all planning on the postrace party."

Angel wiped the sweat from her temple. "Any idea where we should go for lunch? Wade's treating."

Her mother shook her head. "We need to get back."

"But I thought you were planning—"

"I think I'm getting a migraine. The heat. . ." Her mother blew away her bangs.

Angel wasn't buying it. "What's going on, Mom? When I first met Wade you thought he was wonderful."

Bapcia patted Angel's hand. "Your mom's just being a mom. But God's got things figured out. I'm thinking He's going to announce your destiny from the heavens any min—"

"There he is!"

"Wade Ramsey from Elizabeth, Illinois! Right behind him is Sydney McKay from Pine Bluff, Minnesota."

"I'm going to run ahead and try to catch him. I'll see you at the *R*." Angel pushed her way through the crowd and joined the river of spectators heading toward the yellow MEET AND GREET signs, keeping her eyes on the swarm of runners draped in silver Mylar sheets on the other side of the fence. She spotted him once, balancing two bananas and a water bottle while trying to hold onto his space blanket. She wasn't close enough to be heard over the music.

She could feel the hair around her face springing into rebellious corkscrews in the heat. Her pale pink T-shirt was damp with sweat, and her Shalimar perfume had evaporated hours ago. She wasn't going to be the cool pink vision she'd hoped to be for him.

Breaking through a knot of people, she saw him standing under a spray of water. His tired face broke into a grin, and it was Angel's turn to run. Water dripped from his hair onto her face as her arms closed around his chest. "You did it!"

"You kept me going. I had to finish. . .because. . .I had something to tell you." His chest still heaved and Angel could feel his heart pounding.

"I'm listening," she whispered against his shoulder.

His fingers trembled as he lifted her chin and touched his lips to hers. "I ran. . . twenty-six miles. . .to tell you. . .I'm in love with you."

Chapter 21

The banquet hall was empty except for four people. The soup bowls had been cleared, the baskets of hard rolls made by Angel Wings Bakery cleared away. Angel took the last stack of donation envelopes from Taylor and handed them to Steven.

Steven put his arm around her shoulders. "Thank you, Angel. This whole night was perfect, thanks to you."

"It was an amazing experience."

"Could you see yourself doing more of these? A lot more of these?"

"What do you mean?"

"I'm on the national board of Hands in Service. I've been talking you up. I think you could be as busy as you wanted to be with fundraisers."

Angel's throat tightened. From bachelor parties to Christian fundraisers in less than a year. *Lord, sometimes You make my head spin.* "Thank you." She pointed at the envelopes in his hand. "Now go. Count." She laughed at the sparkle of anticipation in his eyes before he turned away.

Angel pulled Taylor into a hug. "And we couldn't have done it without you. You did great tonight."

"Thank you." Taylor looked down at her long apron and brushed away a bread crumb. "I think we should only do fundraisers. I mean, I know business is really good now, and I like doing birthdays and showers, but this. . .this helps people. I think maybe it's like our purpose, you know?"

Angel's arms tightened and then released her. Taylor didn't know yet what she believed, but she was a self-proclaimed "seeker of truth." God would get ahold of her. Angel had no doubt that, someday, all of that restless energy would be harnessed for good. "If this is what God wants us to do, I could see doing this full-time."

"And besides, we get to wear costumes."

"I don't know about that part." Angel ran her finger under the high lace collar of her costume. She was dressed as Sarah Dunn Clarke, cofounder of Pacific Garden Mission. "Maybe if—"

"Testing one-two-three." Wade's voice boomed through the speakers on either side of the stage. "Will the party planner please come up on stage?"

Angel did Taylor's figure-eight eye roll. "Your brother likes that microphone way too much."

Taylor giggled. "Get up there. It might be something important."

Walking up the steps to the simple set where, two hours ago, they had acted out a scene between Mr. and Mrs. Clarke, Angel's pulse suddenly picked up tempo. There was something strange about the lopsided grin on the man with the fake goatee. "What are you up to?"

Wade set the microphone down. "Come here." He pointed to a high-backed Victorian chair and she sat down. "Just a minute." He turned his back, and Angel heard a muffled gasp. When he turned around, the goatee was gone.

For several moments, he stood just inches in front of her, staring down at her with a look that made her heart pound so fast Angel wondered if it would give out altogether.

And then, without warning, he knelt.

He took her hands and held them to his lips. "Angel Chole. . .winski"—the stammer was clearly put on—"I love you more than I can ever express. I want to spend the rest of my life making history with you. Will you marry me?" He opened a small square box.

As Steven clapped and Taylor screamed, Angel held her left hand steady with her right. "Yes. Yes—yes—yes."

ঔ

Angel got out of her truck at Grant City Park, and Sunny jumped out after her, a white bow tied to his collar. Pug walked toward her, carrying a huge gift bag and raising bare arms toward the cloudless June sky. "Gorgeous, huh?"

Angel lifted her face and closed her eyes. "Please let it be like this tomorrow." Reaching through the open car window, she pulled out two paper plates burgeoning with bridal shower ribbons. "Catch practice!" She tossed one toward her maid of honor.

Pug caught it in one hand. "Cinch." She held out the gift bag. "For you two. Open it."

Pulling back layers of tissue paper, Angel pulled out two black satin jackets. Emblazoned across the back were the words, ROUTE 66 HONEYMOON. MILE AFTER MAGNIFICENT MILE TOGETHER. Angel slipped on the smaller one and twirled around. "I love it." She put her arms around Pug. "I'm gonna miss you, roomie."

"Don't get me started. I won't stop crying till after the wedding."

Arm in arm, they started walking. They hadn't gotten far when Pug pointed toward the Civil War cannon beneath the flagpole. "That's an odd sight."

Angel's mother sat on the cannon, her face in her hands. Wade sat beside her, his arm around her. Angel's stomach tightened. Her mother had been nursing a migraine for days and had even hinted she might not make it to the rehearsal. "Maybe she's finally making peace with this."

"What's she got against him?"

"Nothing. She loves him. It's the wedding that's the problem. I don't get it. The finality of it all, maybe." They walked slower, waiting for a signal from one of them. After a few minutes, Wade saw her and smiled.

Pug squeezed Angel's shoulders. "I'll go entertain everyone. You take as long as you need."

Her mother looked up, eyes rimmed in red. "Angel. Baby." She stretched out her hand.

"Mom?" Angel kneeled in front of her. Wade cupped the side of her face then walked away.

"I. . .have something to tell you." She stared over Angel's head. Several silent moments passed. "I guess it's time. . ."

Footsteps approached, and Angel turned to see Wade walking toward them with Steven. As they got closer, Steven walked ahead of Wade and dropped to his knees beside Angel. "Jeanie." He reached for her mother's hand.

Angel's lips parted, but nothing came out.

"Steven." Her mother swiped at her tears and smiled. She put her other hand on Angel's shoulder. "Angel, there's a question you've asked me a million times since you were old enough to talk."

The ground beneath Angel seemed to tilt. "About my father," she whispered.

Her mother nodded, took a deep, shaky breath. "When I was seventeen, I fell in love with my English teacher. No one knew about it. We met secretly." She smiled sadly at Steven. "I was out west when I found out I was pregnant, and I stayed there until you were three. I never told anyone who your father was because I had to protect him." Tears streamed down her face. "And I never told *him* about you." She pulled her hand from Steven's and touched his face. "Until now."

A quiet moan came from Steven. Angel's vision dimmed. Sparks danced before her eyes. Finally, she forced a shuddering breath. And then she cried.

In her father's arms.

And when her tears were spent, amid the questions and apologies that swirled above her, she laughed. "Will you walk me down the aisle?"

❧

Angel stood behind a tree, hidden from Wade's view, and took one last look in the mirror Pug held up for her. A layer of French net fell over the satin of her strapless A-line gown. Venice lace adorned with hand-sewn seed pearls covered the bodice. It was everything she'd ever wanted, except for one thing. She'd needed a size fourteen instead of the ten she'd dreamed of. But thanks to a man who loved all the pretty-colored stuff inside her, that really didn't matter anymore.

Beneath her veil, she wore her hair in two long braids plaited by her mother and grandmother, following an old Polish custom. She smoothed a few wayward strands and shifted her bouquet of red and white roses to her right hand. With her left, she took Steven's arm.

He smiled at her, eyes misting over. "Ready, daughter?"

Blinking back tears, she nodded.

"I've wondered from the moment I heard your last name. But it's so surreal. So amazing." He pulled a white handkerchief out of his pocket. "I'm a wreck."

Angel leaned over and kissed him on the cheek. "You're a wreck, but you're mine. I could never have dreamed of a better wedding gift."

Violin music floated on the faint summer breeze, and they walked up the gazebo steps to Wade and the pastor.

"Who gives this woman to be married to this man?"

"Her mother"—Steven cleared his throat—"and I do."

The next few moments passed in a haze of wonder as she stared into Wade's rich chocolate eyes. And then, it was time for their vows. Wade held both of her hands. "Angel, I am so in awe that God has chosen to bless me with you. I give myself to you, not holding anything back, for the rest of my days. I promise to cherish and protect you, to pick you up when you're stranded, and to share every burden with you. I will pray for you daily and strive to grow in Christ with you. I will love you and only you through rich times and poor, and I want nothing more than to grow old, and soft, with you."

Angel laughed and squeezed his hands. "Wade, you are my friend who points me to what is right and true. My love, who gives me reason to smile every day. And my rescuer, who saves me—often from myself. I promise to be faithful to you in every way, to never let work or things come before you. I promise to pray for you, to comfort and encourage you, to share your joys and your burdens. I will spend the rest of my life trying to love history as much as you do, and I can't wait to begin making our own."

❧

They stood outside the door to the reception hall, alone for the first time all day. Angel held her wedding ring up to the light. "Pinch me," she whispered.

Wade kissed her forehead. His lips trailed down and brushed across her eyelids. "Never." He leaned down and kissed her with more intensity than he'd ever allowed before. "I love you, Mrs. Ramsey."

"I love you. And thank you."

"For loving you?"

"For giving me a name that everyone can pronounce." Reluctantly, she reached out for the door handle. "Are you sure you're ready for my big fat Polish reception?"

"Shh!" Wade's fingertips closed her lips. "Never, ever say that word. Your big *soft* Polish reception."

They were still laughing when they walked into a room filled with people and the smells of roast beef and turkey, stuffed dumplings and sausage. "Ladies and gentlemen," the deejay announced, "it is my pleasure to present to you Mr. and Mrs. Wade Ramsey."

They were met in front of the head table by Wade's parents, Angel's mother. . . and father. Next to Steven stood Bapcia, in a full-length leopard-print gown. She

127

held out a loaf of bread. "Bread—so you will never go hungry." Wade's father handed his son a crystal saltshaker. "Salt—to remind you to work through the hard times."

Bapcia reached up and put her hand on Angel's head. "Following Polish tradition, we are going to remove the bride's veil and replace it with something more fitting for her current status." Angel's mother pulled out the combs that held the veil. From behind her back, Bapcia produced a lace-covered apron. The room burst into laughter.

"This morning," Bapcia continued, "Angel's mother and I braided her hair in two braids, symbolizing that it is no longer just herself she has to think of. She must now always be mindful of her groom as well. Now we are going to undo her braids, signaling she has fulfilled her destiny as a bride."

Her mother removed the hair bands, but just as Angel started to shake out her braids, Wade reached out and grabbed her hand. "That's my job," he whispered. As his fingers ran through coppery curls that fell to just below her shoulders, their guests began to clap and whistle and clang spoons on glasses. Leaning down, Wade's cheek brushed Angel's.

She smiled as his lips drew close to hers. "What if they want an encore?"

His hand pressed against her back, and he dipped her until her hair touched the floor. "Then I guess we'll have to comply."

Angel Wings (Chruscik)

Deep-fried bow-shaped pastries dusted with powdered sugar.

  9 egg yolks
  3 tablespoons white sugar
  3 tablespoons sour cream
  1 tablespoon rum
  1 teaspoon vanilla extract
  3 cups all-purpose flour
  ½ teaspoon baking powder
  ½ teaspoon salt
  1 cup vegetable oil for frying
  1 cup powdered sugar

In medium bowl, beat egg yolks with sugar until well blended. Add sour cream, rum, and vanilla; mix until smooth. Sift together flour, baking powder, and salt; stir into egg yolk mixture a little at a time. Turn dough out onto heavily floured surface and knead vigorously for about ½ hour. Allow dough to absorb as much of the flour as it can so it is no longer sticky.

Separate dough into 4 or 5 portions and roll out very thin. Dough should be almost as thin as paper and slightly transparent. Cut dough into strips about 1½ inches wide and 4 inches long. Make a 1½ inch slit in the strip closer to one end. Pull long end of strip through the slit.

Heat oil to 375 degrees F (190 degrees C). Fry cookies quickly, turning once. They should be golden but not brown. Drain on paper towels and dust with powdered sugar when cool.

PARTING SECRETS

Dedication

In loving memory of my mom, Dorothy Archer Schwenn, for what was, what is, and what I longed for. . . . "I can only imagine. . ."

Cathy

To our newest blessings: Keira Soleil, Oliver Liam, Lillyanne Alice Lola, and Caden Luke Melby.

Love you with all my heart,
Grandma Becky

Chapter 1

Jeanie Cholewinski leaned against the reception hall door and waved one last time at the Ford Explorer covered in white paper bells. Evading the blue eyes of the man beside her, she bent down and forced trembling fingers to detach a satin bow from the collar of her daughter's Irish setter. She pressed her cheek to a copper-colored ear. "They'll be back in two months, Sunny."

When the silence grew heavy, she stood, raised her chin, and faced the man who'd haunted her dreams for thirty years.

Running a hand across his graying beard, Steven Vandenburg cleared his throat. "I imagined a million reasons why you disappeared." His gruff tenor cut the summer air as he nodded toward the fading taillights. "*She* wasn't one of them."

Jeanie stared at his profile, not trusting her instincts to gauge his tone. Too many years had passed since she'd prided herself on reading Mr. Vandenburg like a book. "I know."

Broad shoulders rose and fell in a jagged sigh. "You owe me some answers. Can we go get some coffee?" His gaze fixed on the spot where the headlights had vanished.

Jeanie repositioned a hairpin, willing her fingers to cooperate. Coffee with Steven sounded both tantalizing and terrifying. If he didn't ask too many questions, if he didn't push too hard for answers, coffee with Steven would be more than she'd let herself hope for.

The door behind them squeaked on its hinges. Jeanie turned and smiled at the maid of honor. "Hi, Pug."

In shorts and bare feet, Patti Pugelli dangled white sandals from her fingertips. Slinging a lavender gown in a filmy bag over one shoulder, she put her arms around Jeanie and sighed. "Happily ever after."

Jeanie nodded. "Keep praying for them."

"I will." Pug's hold tightened. "Wade's a prince. He'll treat Angel like gold." She lowered her arms. "I have to get on the road."

"Did you take leftovers?"

"My backseat is as stuffed with pastry as I am. I've got *kluskies* and *kolacz* to last all week. And that was absolutely the most beautiful and scrumptious wedding cake I've ever tasted."

"Thank you." Jeanie kissed her daughter's roommate on the cheek. "Drive careful, honey."

133

"I will."

Pug walked down the steps, and Jeanie turned back to Steven. Her eyes gravitated again to wide shoulders and traveled down to muscled arms. Uninvited, an image of those arms surrounding her took up residence. She blinked and took a deep breath for courage. "I want to change first. Would you like to come over to the house?"

"I don't want to upset your mother."

"How old are you now, Steven?" she teased, trying to lighten the moment. "Fifty-two and you're still scared of my mother?"

A hint of the smile she once knew tipped his mouth. "How about the Log Cabin?"

Jeanie bit the corner of her bottom lip as memories turned like faded pages of a yearbook. Coded messages across a crowded room. . .letting their eyes speak for them because they couldn't be seen together in public. "They've totally remodeled it since. . .recently."

"Is that a yes?"

She nodded. It had to be a yes. No matter how tired she was after the craziness of her only daughter's wedding, she owed him the next hour.

No, she owed him the past twenty-nine years. . .with Angel. With *his* only daughter.

"I'll go put my jeans on and—"

Screeching tires, rubber scraping the curb, and the slam of a car door ended her sentence.

"Jeanie! Jeanie!" Her mother slid from behind the steering wheel and jumped out of the car. Flowing leopard print cascading over purple slippers, she charged toward them, short legs taking the steps two at a time.

"What happened? What's wrong?" A fire at the bakery, a break-in at home. . . dozens of scenarios flooded Jeanie's imagination before Ruby Cholewinski caught her breath enough to explain.

A legal-sized envelope materialized from the folds of her dress. "Open it."

Jeanie grabbed the envelope. A stylized French chef in the upper left corner cranked the tempo on her pulse. "Grégoire Pâtisserie!" The envelope fluttered in her hands like a moth anxious for escape. When she finally got it open, she read the words silently, tears springing to already tender eyes. "I'm in! I'm going to New York!"

Her mother squealed. As Jeanie wiped her eyes she caught Steven's confusion and handed him the letter. "It's a national pastry competition. I've been chosen to compete at Grégoire Pâtisserie in New York City. First prize is a year of study in Paris."

"That's wonderful. Exciting. Congratulations." Steven's expression conflicted with his words.

His lack of excitement disappointed her. He had, after all, been the one to paint the first broad brushstrokes of this thirty-year-old dream. She answered with a sad smile. She couldn't expect him to rejoice with her. He was still staggering from the news she'd given him yesterday. How long would it take him to embrace the knowledge that he had a daughter? "I'll go change clothes."

"What for?" Her mother's piercing gray gaze dashed from her to Steven and back again.

"We're going to get coffee. Will you take Sunny home?"

"*Hmph*." Her mother turned on her soft purple heels, patted her thigh for the dog to follow, and stomped back to the car.

Jeanie grabbed the door handle. "I'll be right back." *And then I'll give you answers. But only some of them.*

✑

The woman who sat in front of him was a stranger.

Steven hugged his coffee mug as Jeanie, across the table from him, chatted with the bald, black-suited maître d'. . .in English smattered with Greek. Where had she learned Greek? All these years of wondering about her and feeling guilty for wondering, and maybe the person he'd once thought he couldn't breathe without no longer existed. The girl he knew—the girl he shouldn't have known the way he did—possessed the heart of a poet and the curiosity of a child. This confident woman prattling on about a French chef whose name sounded like "Gray Gwah" reflected so little of that innocence. She'd had only one ambition back then. . .to love him.

He studied her profile, noticed the fine lines that branched from the outside corners of her eyes and deepened when she smiled. Her face was thinner than the last time he'd touched it, and time, like a skilled sculptor, had added angles and curves to the rest of her. He'd once told her she was the cutest girl in school. At forty-six, the word that fit her was stunning.

One thing hadn't changed. Deep brown eyes transported him to a time of furtive glances and moonlight trysts—a time best left in the shadows of the past. Regret, a familiar companion, made its presence known in the tightening in his chest. *If only. . .*

The maître d' held out a manicured hand. "I know you just ate wedding cake, but I must bring you *saganaki* on the house. Okay?"

Steven's stomach roiled at the thought of the deep-fried cheese he'd loved with a passion so many years ago, but he shook the man's hand and thanked him. "We wouldn't dream of turning that down."

Jeanie thanked the man and turned coffee-colored eyes back on him. "You knew before I told you, didn't you? That Angel was yours?"

Pressing his finger onto the tines of his fork, Steven felt the sharp edges of the question that had taunted him for nine months, since he first met the girl with blue eyes like his sons' and his mother's red hair. "I did the math. But there was no way I could be sure she was mine."

Jeanie flinched. His insinuation had to hurt. Her eyes closed for a moment, then followed a waiter with sizzling plates. She turned back. "I understand."

Her head tipped slightly to the right, making a silent groan rise from his belly. He remembered that look. *I can read you like the Sunday comics, Mr. Vandenburg.* Could she still?

Her arms crossed. "I thought if you'd put two and two together you'd call."

"It wasn't my place. I have a little pride, Jeanie. I wasn't about to pick up the phone and ask if I'd fathered your daughter." He rocked the fork, letting the handle bang the wood planks on the table. "When I saw you in Chicago last fall and you ran. . ." The ache of loss came back with a rush. He'd gotten only a glimpse of her across the reflecting pool at Millennium Park. A glimpse, and then she'd turned and run. "I knew you didn't want anything to do with me, and I didn't want to do anything to hurt Angel."

"Steven." Her fingertips grazed his sleeve. "I'm sorry." Her eyes searched his for a long, wordless moment. "How *are* you, Steven?" Her question flickered the flame in the amber glass holder between them.

How are you? Did she really want him to answer that? Did she really not know that her decision to stay in California without a single word had scarred every inch of his psyche? That her selfishness had insured a life that always felt second-best? He swallowed every angry retort and finally managed "God is good." In truth, in spite of his shattered hopes, it summed up his life to date.

"He is."

"And how are *you*?" The way the words left his tongue showed he hadn't really forgiven her the way he'd once convinced himself he had.

"I'm good. Hitting my stride a bit late in life, but I finally know what I want to do when I grow up."

"And what is that?"

"I want to teach. At a pastry school."

"Hmm." Why did her announcement put his chest in a vice?

"I started taking classes in St. Louis when Angel was in grade school, but my father died and I gave it up. I tried a few more times, but something always came up—car repairs, Angel's tuition—and I'd have to go back to the bakery full time. It's taken me awhile to recapture my dream, but a chance at this contest is another step toward my goal."

"Where would you have to go to teach?"

Her eyes sparkled. "Realistically, Chicago."

He took a gulp of ice water.

"But my dream goal is Paris."

An ice cube lodged in his throat. He coughed and gasped.

Her hand rested on his arm. "Are you okay?"

"I'm f–fine," he rasped. His breathing finally calmed, and he gave her an embarrassed smile. He wasn't ready to lay his feelings on the table, but choking on her words probably accomplished just that.

She pulled her hand away. "Angel says you have two sons."

He nodded. "Griffin is twenty-five. He's still single and working in Tacoma. Toby's nineteen. He's going to school in Boston. They're good guys."

"I'm so sorry about your wife. How long ago did you lose her?"

"It's been almost four years. We had a good life together." Well-worn guilt surfaced. They had built a good life. But he'd given Lindy second-best.

The casual catch-up talk suddenly irked him. They weren't old school buddies touching base after thirty years. He wasn't ready to share the details of his life. And he couldn't feign interest in what she was doing now until he understood what she'd done then. "Did you know you were pregnant when you left?"

She drew back as if his hand, instead of his words, had slapped her. She looked down, tucking a stray strand of hair into the lacquered braids and purple jewels that crowned her head. Did she still hate hair spray? Why, in the midst of his anger, did he suddenly want nothing more than to yank out the hairpins and watch her hair fall to her shoulders?

"I found out I was pregnant two weeks after I got to Aunt Freda's. I should have realized it sooner, but I di—"

"Why didn't you call me?" *Did you really love me? Is Angel really mine?*

Her eyes shimmered as she raised her head. "It would have been the end of your career, Steven."

"So?" His fist hit the table. "Jeanie. . ." His voice strangled on her name. "You knew that wouldn't have mattered. I would have flipped burgers or cleaned toilets to be with you. I thought we had honesty. I thought. . .you knew me." A sigh ripped from his throat.

"Steven, I was seventeen. You were my teacher." She leaned forward, her gaze latched onto his. "You would have been charged with statutory rape."

❧

Jeanie watched as the truth found its target. The muscles on his jaw slackened. His lips parted, but he didn't say a word.

"I would never have let that happen to you." Her voice sounded odd to her ears—soft and hushed. She wrapped her hands around her coffee mug to steady them.

Slowly, he nodded, giving her time to study the way the years had altered him. He'd changed, but not in the ways she'd expected. His dark blond hair had thinned and whitened at the temples. She guessed he'd added a good fifty pounds, but he carried it well. The weight made him seem strong, protective, though his expression at the moment was just the opposite.

Those eyes. . .hurt, transparent. . .and the same shade as Angel's. Her daughter's eyes had been a constant reminder of Steven. His voice hadn't changed either, and that unnerved her. "Staying away from you was the hardest thing I ever did," she whispered. He'd never know what that decision had cost her.

"You should have told me."

"I didn't tell you because I *did* know you. You would have done the noble thing. And you would have been fired and humiliated and probably gone to jail." Her hand loosened its grip on her mug and she reached out to him, touching his sleeve. "Your family would have disowned you."

His hand clamped over hers with an intensity that scared her. "Jeanie—"

A waiter rounded a corner with a red tray. A waitress approached and poured brandy over the square of cheese on the tray. A click, a tiny light, and suddenly the dish erupted in orange flames that shot three feet in the air. "Opaaa!" The waiters yelled and doused the flames in lemon. "Cheers!" Gingerly, she slid the black plate of browned cheese onto the table.

"Thank you." Jeanie smiled apologetically at Steven. "Life goes on, doesn't it?"

"Never the way you plan."

"Never."

Steven ran a hand over his beard. "It's going to take me awhile to sort this out. Eventually, we need to move past this, but I can't until I'm sure you understand something."

With her hand still covered by his, all she could do was nod.

"I would have gone to jail, Jeanie. I would have given up my career and faced whatever humiliation the school district or my family would have thrown at me. If you'd come back on your birthday the way we planned, we could have figured it out together. Do you understand?" Blue eyes stabbed her. "I would have done anything for you. . .if you'd given me the chance."

Turning away from the honesty in his eyes, Jeanie blinked back tears.

But not if you'd known what I did to survive.

Chapter 2

Hairpins mounded on the bathroom counter as stiff curls sprang free. Jeanie yawned and dropped two more pins. With her free hand, she turned a page in a cloth-covered book and read the ending of a poem she'd just written.

> *I returned the gift he gave,*
> *Though she wasn't his to keep,*
> *And as he gave his child away,*
> *God returned a gift to me.*

Closing her eyes along with the book, she wiped a stray tear. *Lord, I am in awe of You. In Your time, You have answered my prayers. Whatever happens from here on is also in Your hands.*

She stared out the window of her apartment above her mother's garage. Lights turned out on the porch next door, leaving the miniature lilacs blooming between the houses bathed in moonlight. It was a peaceful scene. She scooped hairpins into a plastic bag and turned on the shower. She didn't want the smell of hair spray invading her sleep. And tonight she would sleep.

Maybe better than she had in thirty years.

The wedding was over. She was going to New York. And finally, Steven knew the truth. The only secrets she harbored now were the ones she never needed to share.

Steven knew. Tonight, she would sleep.

Why, after what she'd done, had he protected her? Protected her from the emotions that brought him out on the deck at two in the morning.

Steven sat on the edge of his hammock, but the sway of his usual sanctuary nauseated him. He stood and walked down the deck steps. Motion sensor lights flicked on. He bent and picked up a cold and damp steel horseshoe. The stakes were lost in darkness, but that didn't matter. He drew his arm back and let it fly. It hit the fence with a *thud*. He picked up three more and let them fly. *Thud. Thud. Ding.* A little self-restraint on the last one earned him a ringer. He congratulated himself with a fist in the air. A momentary victory over bitterness.

She should have told him. Whatever she claimed as her reasons, it boiled down to one thing. Selfishness. She'd done what was best for herself. Not what was right. . .for him, or for Angel.

He could easily picture Angel as a little girl, red curls bouncing, chubby little legs running. To him. That little girl needed a daddy. And he'd needed a daughter.

How many times had he and Lindy picked out girls' names? How many pink paint swatches had his wife collected over the years? But after two uncomplicated pregnancies and births, she'd suffered three miscarriages in a row. The first sign that something wasn't right.

Even if Jeanie had told him about Angel years after he was married, he would have been there for his daughter. Lindy would have been there for his daughter. She would have accepted his past and accepted the consequences with him. That's just the kind of woman she was.

At some point, he was going to have to confront Jeanie with the truth of his feelings. For now, he just needed sleep.

His eyes swept the darkness, envisioning his backyard in Texas. A tree house, a fort. . .yet there would have been room for a pink and white playhouse.

It wasn't likely he'd sleep tonight.

🐝

Jeanie rubbed tired eyes. The Monday after your only daughter marries should be an official day of rest.

As she turned on the bakery's OPEN sign at six thirty, the phone rang.

"Angel Wings Bakery. This is Jeanie."

"Jeanie, I can't come in this morning." The voice of their only full-time employee shook.

"Sue? What's wrong?"

"We had to take Bradley into the ER. He's been up all night with stomach pains. Hey, I gotta run. I'm so sorry. Can you cover till your mom comes in?"

"Of course. I'll be praying. Call me when you know something."

She set the phone in its cradle as the door opened and more than a dozen silver-haired tourists in matching blue jackets swarmed the bakery.

"Morning everyone. Welcome to Angel Wings, where Polish pastry touches the heart." She handed a Morning Glory muffin to the first woman in line and counted out change. Tour busses paid the bills.

She emptied two pots of coffee and made two more. The chairs filled and customers stood outside. Three men took the only stools at the counter. A man in a faded yellow shirt and red bow tie pointed to his name tag. "Name's Joe Crow, sweetheart. Can't forget a moniker like that now, can you?"

Furrowed cheeks puffed on the man beside Joe. "Ah, don't pay him no never—"

A coffee cup clunked on the front counter. Jeanie reached out and took it. "Can I h—" Her breath caught as she stared at the man's garish parrot tattoo. *Just like the one. . .* Her pulse hammered. The cup crashed to the floor.

Just a flashback. Refocus. Relax. She turned away, then back to the man who held out his cup for a refill. *Just an illusion.*

"Well, well. All the way from Reno. . .and after all these years. . . Small world, isn't it? You haven't changed a bit." Apelike fingers reached out and ran along her arm.

Jeanie stumbled back, knocking the phone off its hook. Her arms crossed her chest; her fingers bit into her shoulders.

"What a nice surprise." The man was far too old for his bluish-black hair. A black moustache, so thin it could have been penciled, curved in a sneer. "I've been sitting over there staring, and I finally figured out why you look so familiar." An evil laugh rumbled across the counter. "You're a long way from home, Misty."

"I'm not. . .who you think I am." Her back pushed against the phone. *There's nowhere to run.*

He laughed and reached into the pocket of his short-sleeved black shirt. Red letters below the pocket spelled out *Diamond Jo Casino, Dubuque.*

Jeanie's heart squeezed as though the man held it in his thick hands. *Oh, God, why is he here?*

The man pulled out a pair of glasses and squinted at her name tag. "Jeanie, huh? Doesn't suit you. Call yourself whatever you want—it doesn't change who you are."

"Denny?" A blond, maybe in her late thirties—the one who'd ordered two cups of coffee and a single *chruscik*—laid a hand on the man's arm. "Let's go."

"Anything you say." He took off his glasses. Black eyes smoldered. "We'll be back. Gotta have some more of that pastry." His gaze crept from the top of Jeanie's head to her name tag. "*Misty.*" He turned on his heel.

The blond took two steps toward the door, then turned and eyed Jeanie with blatant suspicion. "Do you know her?"

Another evil laugh. "Not nearly as well as I'd like to."

Jeanie dropped to her knees, the pieces of the broken cup blurring before her eyes.

"Are you all right? Miss?"

A shard stabbed her finger. Blood dripped as prickles skittered across her arms. Voices blurred. She was back in that room, Angel in her arms. And just outside was the man with the parrot on his arm, talking to her through the door, making promises she prayed he'd never keep. In the distance, she heard the men at the counter asking if she was all right. She stared at the bottom shelf below the cash register. *We could hide there. We'd both fit. Don't cry, baby. Angel, please don't cry.*

"Miss? Did you get cut?"

Refocus. Breathe. Be somewhere else. She blinked, nodded, and looked up. "I'm fine. Just fine."

141

Summer break used to be the best part about working for the school system. Until Lindy died.

When he was teaching, he'd had two and a half months free and it had never seemed long enough. Now that he was a principal, his contract gave him only two weeks. . .and it seemed to last forever.

Turning up his iPod, Steven rode his year-old John Deere mower out of the shed. He'd bought it at the same time as the house when he'd moved up here from Dallas.

As he cut the first swath, he tried to focus on the week ahead and not the Saturday behind him. Mondays, the first of five long days he'd have to fill with something, were hard enough. Thoughts of unsaid words to Jeanie would only make them seem longer.

He'd only made one sweep around the backyard when his phone vibrated in his shirt pocket. He put the mower in neutral and checked his caller ID. Jim Hansen, calling from his daughter's place in Maryland. Thank God for Monday morning friends. He turned off the mower. "Hey, Jim."

"Steven. You won't believe this. I met someone." Jim's staccato voice beat faster than usual.

"Someone. . .like a woman, you mean?"

"Of course a woman. Cindy set me up. Didn't want any part of it. But she's amazing."

Steven laughed. "Jim, you can't leave the Sorry Widowers! We have a pact."

"Ha. Just wanted to beat you to it."

" 'Ha' to you, too. So what's she like?"

"Her name's Amanda. She's pretty and nice. And she can cook. Kind of like your Texas woman."

Steven pushed his Cubs cap back on his forehead. "I don't have a woman."

"Yeah. Okay. So what've I missed?"

Leaning against the backrest, Steven sifted through the weekend events he was in the mood to share. "Another exciting weekend. Burt and I mowed Mrs. Simpson's lawn on Saturday and went to see Oren Willmar in the nursing home. Burt took Emma to Fried Green Tomatoes after church and I had dinner at the Larsen's."

"Wow. Lucky you. Turkey lasagna?"

"Of course."

A high, raspy laugh came through the phone. "So sorry I wasn't there. Anyway, gotta run. Going to brunch with Amanda. Just wanted you guys to pray. Need to be wise about this. Any requests?"

If he gave even the condensed version of the news he'd had confirmed on Friday, the lawn would never get mowed and Jim would miss his date. "Pray for wisdom for me, too. Got a lot going on. I'll explain when you have time."

"Will do. See ya."

Steven tucked his phone back in his pocket and prayed for Jim as he started the mower again. The smell of freshly cut grass and the song filtering into his ears elevated his Monday frame of mind. *Let me fight through the nothingness of this life.* Matthew West sang "The Motions," and the lyrics pumped conviction into his veins. Though at times, especially at the beginning of a long, lonely week, it felt as though his heart had stopped when Lindy's did, he knew he still had purpose. *Lord, let passion for You consume my thoughts and my days.*

As he cranked the wheel to the left, his pocket vibrated once again. He stopped the mower and pulled out his phone.

Gretchen. Interesting timing, considering Jim's comments. "Hello?"

"Steven. I'm in Houston this morning. I've only got a minute between meetings. Guess what?" Her breathless question sent nervous tingles down his arms.

"What?" *Lord, I'm confused enough right now. . .*

"I just heard they want me to do photo shoots in Iowa this week. I'll be in Dubuque on Thursday." Her voice rose like a child opening a birthday present. "And I'm taking Friday off."

"Wonderful." It was. Really. "Should I book you a room?"

"There are no other options, are there?" Her soft tease fed his confusion.

He didn't bite on the bait she'd dangled. "I'll call and see if the Sunshine Room is open. What time will you be here?"

"I'll come over and make you breakfast on Friday morning. How's that sound?" *A bit too cozy.* His palm felt damp against the phone. "See you then."

"Can't wait. Love you."

He tried to swallow but couldn't. He looked longingly at the glass of iced tea sitting on the deck railing. "You, too. Bye."

❧

"Go home. I'll stay." Jeanie pointed Sue toward the back door. "You have a sick boy. That's all you need to be thinking about."

"You took over for me yesterday. I can't do this to you two days in a row." Sue's weary eyes welled with tears. "You've been here since four."

"And you've been here since five. Get. I have nothing else to do today and I hardly ever get to work the front. Go."

"I just hate to do this to you, and I'm afraid it's going to happen a lot." A tear slid down her pale face. "Now that we know it's Crohn's disease. . ."

"I've been thinking about hiring someone part-time for summer anyway. Now that the wedding's over I can concentrate on that. But that's my problem. Go home and take care of Bradley. And sleep."

Sue walked out. The side door closed and silence pressed against Jeanie's ears. She didn't usually mind being alone. But the nightmares spawned by the man in black infused her consciousness as though he still leered at her over the counter. As though he still had power over her. She locked the door. "Whatever is true, whatever is noble, whatever is right, whatever is pure, whatever is lovely, whatever is admirable—if anything is excellent or praiseworthy—think about such things." The verse from Philippians slowed her heart rate.

The buzzer on the front door sounded and she jumped. "Be still, and know that I am God," she whispered. She tried to check her reflection in the window of the deck oven, but the yellowed glass made her look jaundiced. If she won the contest in New York, the ancient appliance would disappear. And so would she for a while.

But, by then, would she still want to? She smoothed back a few wayward tendrils and tried to do the same with the question. With a deep breath, she left thoughts of Steven in the kitchen and walked to the front of the store. "Morning, Lucas." She smiled, the remnants of her nightmares evaporating in the presence of the friend she'd known all her life.

"Mornin', sweet pea."

"How's business?" Jeanie poured a cup of coffee for the man who owned the jewelry store across the street. Though he'd been born in Galena, Lucas Zemken's accent was as thick as his Welsh-born father's. Finger tracks showed in silver-streaked hair. More lines marked the corner of his right eye than the left—earned by forty years of squinting into a jeweler's loupe.

"Ah. . .love is in the air." He pointed at a cherry-filled *kolaczki* in the display case.

"Lucas, you're a unique breed. You're in love with love, but too chicken to try it yourself." Jeanie handed him a medium coffee with two spoons of sugar. She pulled a piece of bakery tissue from a blue dispenser box and put two pastries on a paper plate.

Lowering his glasses, he looked at her over the top rim. "One could maybe say the same of you, sweet pea."

"Sooo. . ." Jeanie scrunched her nose at him and side-stepped the jab. "Selling lots of engagement rings?"

"Not lots. I *wish*. But enough to pay the bills." He sat on a stool, then swiveled to face the front window. They'd had very few face-to-face conversations since Lucas was always facing his store, watching over the tops of parked cars for his door to open.

Lucas raised his cup in a toast. "To the best wedding cake baker this side of France."

"Oh, Lucas, I know you say that to all the girls."

"It was a beautiful wedding."

"Wade's ring is amazing."

Smile lines crinkled on Lucas's right eye. "It is, isn't it? And do you know what is engraved inside?"

"No. Should you be telling me this? Isn't there a jeweler-client privacy act or something?"

"Nah." His fingers formed an imaginary loupe. "It said. . .are you ready for this? It said 'She loves you, yeah, yeah, yeah.'" He took a swig of coffee then appeared ready to spray it all over the bakery.

"Seriously? All that fit on a ring?"

Lucas patted his chest. "Takes a real craftsman. And as long as we're speaking of 'She loves you,' I've been waiting to get the scoop. I nearly fell off my chair when I saw this strange man walking Angel down the aisle."

Jeanie sighed. "You and everyone else."

"Makes me wonder what other secrets you're hiding. He's a nice guy."

"He is."

"And. . . ?"

"And. . .God alone knows the future. I'm glad it's out in the open and Angel can get to know him."

"Where was he all these years?" One fist lodged at his hip.

"Put your shotgun away, Mr. Dillon. It wasn't his fault he wasn't around. Let's just say I was in a bad place and I couldn't see any point in bringing Steven in with me."

Lucas pressed his lips in a firm, hard line. "So what now? He's single, you're single."

"We'll see. We're not the same people we were back then."

"What was your visceral response the first time you saw him after all these years?"

"Visceral response? Any other guy would say 'gut reaction,' but you—"

"Just answer the question."

Jeanie lined up boxes of herbal tea as the answer brought her back to the moment. Last October, at the Crowne Fountain in Chicago, she'd looked across the reflecting pool and there he was. "Visceral response" didn't come close. "Lightning bolt" would almost describe it. Heart slamming her ribs, painful sting in her eyes, the whisper in her head—*Steven. . .it's you.* It was as close to an out-of-body experience as she was likely to encounter. Her imagination ran to him, dropped her to her knees in front of him. And then rational thought swept in and she ran. Away from him.

She threw an empty tea box at the wastebasket. Short of breath, as though she'd just turned her back on Steven and fled into the trees, she took two quick inhales. "No violins or fireworks. I was just scared about his reaction—"

Lucas slid off the stool. "I'm sorry. I've got a customer." He pushed his breakfast to her side of the counter and patted her hand. "I'll be bock"—his Arnold Schwarzenegger impression fell flat—"because I'm not really buying the nonchalance, sweet pea." He took several steps but stopped when a man walked in front of the window and reached for the door handle. "Ho ho. Look who's here." Lucas turned and winked. "Definitely not buying the nonchalance." He laughed, greeted the man, and waved.

And Steven walked in.

Chapter 3

He glanced away from the fat little baker on the wall with a clock for a stomach, but Steven was sure the hands started spinning backward at the speed of light. He was twenty-two again, days away from beginning his first year of student teaching. Alone and not in the mood to fix his own breakfast, he'd wandered into town. It was a growling stomach that first introduced him to the girl who now stood, older and more beautiful than ever, behind the pastry case.

Jeanie smiled as he took a stool at the counter.

"Coffee and *chruscik* please."

Another customer walked in. As Jeanie filled a bag with long johns and bismarcks, Steven poured in the cream and sugar she'd set in front of him. He hadn't used cream and sugar in twenty years. Taking a bite of the "angel wing" he closed his eyes. The smell alone reversed the hands of the clock. The first time he'd met Angel, at a picnic with Wade, the man who was now her husband, she'd brought *chruscik*. It was his first clue, though it hadn't registered until she'd left. Red hair like his mother's, and a sweet taste that could only come from one bakery. . .

"Steven?" Jeanie stared at him, her smile now wary, from the other side of the counter. The other customer was gone. Had the door buzzer sounded when he left?

He hadn't even said hello. It seemed too late now. "I was wondering if we could get together to talk sometime."

"I. . .we could talk now. The morning rush is over. My mother will be here in a few minutes to work the counter." She nodded toward the back. "Let's go in my office."

He followed her into a tiny green-walled room. It couldn't have measured more than eight feet square. A desk, two chairs, and shelves on all three walls were piled with books and papers—neat, clean, but cluttered. He took the chair across from hers.

She cleared a spot for his coffee. Her braid swung over her shoulder. She'd worn her hair loose when they first met, but braided it every day in the weeks before she'd left for California. Had she really worn the same style ever since? No woman he'd ever known did that.

Jeanie sat in a scuffed leather chair. "Not very often you're on that side of a desk, I imagine."

His thoughts flew back to the first time Jeanie Cholewinski sat on the other side of a desk from him. The first of many private, literary magazine meetings. In the first thirty seconds he'd slaughtered her name. "*Janka Chow-link-ski?*" She'd tossed long brown hair and jutted her chin. "*Janka is Polish for the feminine version John. I prefer Jeanie—that's French. And it's Co-leh-win-ski.*"

He smiled. "Feels kind of strange." Something about the swing of that braid took the muscle out of his emotions. "Jeanie. . ." He leaned forward, set his elbows on the arms of the chair, then changed his mind and crossed his arms over his chest. He had no idea where to start. The Mr. Vandenburg who normally sat on the other side of the desk and had the power to make smack-talking teenage boys quiver in their Nikes suddenly felt like a freshman caught smoking in the restroom.

Jeanie leaned against the back of her chair. Her eyes dimmed.

"This is all history for you, Jeanie. For me, it's like opening an old wound. I know we can't change anything." He ran his fingertips up and down the middle of his forehead. "I just need to understand. I've thought through what you said about me going to jail. That would have been bad, but it wouldn't have been forever. It wasn't an insurmountable problem. The girl I thought I knew would have called, would have wanted to work it out together." He leaned forward. "Make me understand, Jeanie."

❧

Dampness prickled beneath her arms. She hadn't perspired like this since junior high. She had barely enough saliva to moisten her tongue. "I was young and scared and alone." *If you knew how scared and why. . .and how alone. . .* "I maybe wasn't thinking as clearly as I should have been."

"But you had nine months to think. You had twenty-nine years to think. Didn't you once, in all that time, come to the conclusion that I should know?"

"You were married. . . ."

"I got married *three years* after you left." Bright blue eyes drilled into her. "Not even a phone call before that?"

"You moved to Texas."

"You could have found me. The school had my parents' address. I made sure your friends knew I was going to Dallas. I was in the phone book."

Her breathing became shallow. *Refocus. Pray.* But even the words that used to bring moments of clarity triggered shuttered, hidden images. She needed to pull away. *Into the corner where it's dark and he can't see. Angel, don't cry. Please don't cry, baby.* The buzzer announced a customer and dispelled the memory. "I'll be right back."

A woman with two small boys stood at the counter. Fingerprints multiplied on the display case as the boys pointed out sprinkle-covered doughnuts and frosted cookies. The mother apologized for their indecision. "Take your time." *Please.* A thud and the jingle of keys sounded in the kitchen. Her mother was here. And the office door was wide open.

The children finally made up their minds. Jeanie bagged two cookies and threw a third in for free for a frazzled mom who looked like she was counting her pennies. "Enjoy."

"Thank you. You didn't have to do that." She waved as she walked out. "This is the brightest spot in my day so far."

A hand touched Jeanie's back. "What's *he* doing here?" Her mother's voice seemed more worried than harsh.

"He just stopped in to talk. There's still a lot he needs to know."

"There's still a lot *I* need to know. About him and his intentions."

"I know. We'll talk." Something her mother had seemed unwilling to do since Friday. She gave her mother a quick hug and walked back to the office.

Steven sat with his fingertips together, tapping his lip. "So you had a great job out there, huh?" His eyes narrowed.

Her throat tightened. What did he know? "Y–yes."

He nodded, then stood. "You really don't want to talk about this, do you?"

"It was a hard time. I thought I'd made the best decision for you. You have to believe that."

"Yeah. You said that." He walked toward the door. "One last question and I'll try to leave it alone. Was there someone else? Did you meet someone before your birthday? Is that the real reason you didn't come home?"

The answer screamed in her brain. *Yes. But not like you think. Not a boyfriend. I met someone. And I couldn't get away.* "No. There wasn't anyone else."

He nodded. "You know, there is one more question." Blue eyes scanned her face. "When did you stop loving me, Jeanie?"

"I nev—" She gasped. That wasn't what she'd meant to say.

He smiled. Gentle. Sweet. He walked over to her. The backs of his fingers brushed her face. "That's all I need to know."

And he walked out, closing the office door behind him.

Jeanie's mother glared at him as he walked out of the office. He sent a sheepish smile her way and crossed the hardwood floor between her and the front door in as few steps as possible. Outside, the air had warmed considerably. The shade from the awning felt good. He looked up the sidewalk at the redbrick buildings lining the cobblestone street. He loved this town, though he'd avoided it this past year. His address might say Elizabeth, but Galena felt like home.

And now that he felt free to come to Galena, he couldn't very well be at war with one of its residents. *If it is possible, as far as it depends on you, live at peace with everyone.* He turned the corner onto Perry Street, arguing with the butterflies break-dancing in his belly. After three steps he stopped, turned around, and walked back into the bakery.

The office door was ajar. Jeanie wasn't in sight. *Good.* He waited for her mother to count out change into a young boy's hand then stepped to the counter. Her name was Ruby, right? It didn't matter, first names were too familiar. He needed the element of respect. "Mrs. Cholewinski, could I talk to you for a minute?"

"Hmm." Gray eyes sparked. "You may not like what you hear if you do."

He fought a smile, shoved it down again when it pushed to the surface. "I can't imagine what you must think of me."

"No, you can't."

"I can't defend myself, but I'd like to explain. I want you to know I wasn't a. . ." Wasn't a what? A letch? A child molester? "I wasn't a predator."

Ruby Cholewinski ripped a paper towel in half and began cleaning around the knobs on the cappuccino machine. "What were you, Mr. Vandenburg? An upstanding role model for the children in your care?"

Children? "Jeanie was only five years younger than I was. I was a *student* teacher."

"I don't think the law would have made that distinction. You were a legal adult. She wasn't."

"I loved your daughter. More than I could ever put into words. I was the advisor for a school magazine. We spent a lot of time working together. We had a relationship. It was wrong, I know. I spent hours. . .weeks. . .on my knees over that. But you have to understand that I wasn't taking advantage of her. We were in love. I wanted to spend the rest of my life with Jeanie. She doesn't know it, but I had a ring." *Still have a ring.* "I was going to propose to her on her birthday. I know we were young, but. . ." The faraway look on the woman's face made him stop.

She set the paper towel on the counter and faced him, bracing her hands on the counter. For a long, uncomfortable moment, she simply stared. He felt as though he was undergoing a wordless interrogation. Did she, like her daughter once did, have the ability to read his thoughts? If so, she'd find nothing deceptive in what he'd claimed.

Finally, she nodded, ever so slowly. A faint smile smoothed her lips.

"I believe you, Mr. Vandenburg."

≈❧

Jeanie dropped onto the only clear spot on the couch. It was after nine on Wednesday night, and she'd been up since four. The pillow-top mattress in the next room called to her, but two plastic bins on either side of her called louder.

She yawned. Nightmares had turned to night terrors that stalked her waking hours. The energy it took to push them back was taking a toll. She'd had years to work on forgiveness, more sleepless nights than she could ever count to wrestle with God and barrage Him with "Why?" and God had not failed her. Peace had been her companion for many years. Until one Sunday in September—an uneventful brunch with Angel and her new friend, Wade Ramsey. She'd been minding her own business, humming a praise song while she washed dishes, when Wade dropped a name that stole her peace. *Steven Vandenburg*—the new principal of the school where he taught.

She didn't believe in coincidence. God had brought Steven back into her life for a reason. But that reason might not include rekindling their relationship. *"That's all I need to know,"* Steven had said yesterday. She could still feel the warmth of his hand brushing her face. He'd read the truth in her eyes. . . . Would it end up hurting him?

God was in control. That conviction had brought her through much worse. But if her theology was accurate, it meant He'd not only brought Steven, he'd also brought the man in the black shirt. The man who'd stood guard outside her room for three years, who was once again imprisoning her with vestiges of a fear she thought she'd left behind forever.

God knew all things, but all she was sure of at the moment was confusion. Running both hands over her face, she sighed.

The box to her right overflowed with cookbooks and cake decorating magazines. The one on her left held fifteen years worth of mementos—Angel's life, all but the first three years, in photographs, crayon drawings, and school papers. She pulled out a faded report card and smiled at a comment on the back. *Angel is very polite and kind. I would like to see her participate in class more.*

In Tuesday's restless predawn hours, she'd decided to make a scrapbook for Steven. Tangible evidence of all he'd missed would be painful, but maybe glimpses of Angel's past would fill in some blanks and keep him from asking more questions.

Kicking off her shoes, she scooted back on the couch. A battered purple notebook, the spiral binding kinked and stretched, slid off the pile of Angel's keepsakes. "My Diary" scrolled across the cover in silver glitter. Jeanie opened it and stared at the date on the first page. Angel's thirteenth birthday.

Dear Diary,

I know I'm too old for pretending, but birthdays are different. I think every year on my birthday, even when I'm an old, old lady, I will always pretend that the doorbell rings and there is my father. He says "Surprise!" and then he hugs me and tells me why he had to stay away. Sometimes he is a spy for the CIA and sometimes he is a movie star. But always, when he hugs me, it doesn't matter anymore that he missed all my other birthdays.

The clack of Sunny's nails on the outside step announced a visitor. A knock followed.

"Come on in."

Her mother walked in and set a covered dish on the small kitchen table. "What's wrong?"

Closing the notebook, Jeanie looked up. "Nothing."

"You're crying."

A single tear dropped off her chin and onto the silver glitter. "I'm fine." She took a deep breath, willing unruly emotions back between the pages of the notebook.

"Mm-hmm." Her mother walked across the kitchen, pushed aside a stack of travel magazines, and sat on the trunk that served as a coffee table. Her very presence spoke volumes. "The tuna casserole is a peace offering."

"Thank you."

"It was silly, but I reacted the same way I would have if I'd found out the truth at the time you got pregnant. All I could think about was that man taking advantage of my little girl and wonder how I could have been so blind."

"You weren't blind." Jeanie rubbed a kink at the base of her neck. "I was deceitful. I worked very hard at making sure no one knew. And Steven didn't take advantage of me. I knew what I was doing."

Her mother nodded. "I know. And I'm ready to leave it all in the past. God and I had a little talk and I think I'm done wanting to take you over my knee."

"Thank you. And Steven?"

A ghost of a smile tipped her mother's lips. "I think he's suffered enough for his sins."

"He'd be happy to hear that."

"He already has."

"You talked to him? When?"

"I have my ways. Maybe it's time I started keeping a few secrets from *you*." The quick smile she'd kept hidden for days loosened a few of Jeanie's tight muscles. "So where does he fit in? Is he part of the family now? Do we invite him for Christmas? Sunday dinner?"

Jeanie laughed. "If Angel wants to include him, I'm fine with it."

"Angel, huh?" Her tone was anything but subtle. "It's pure serendipity that man is back in your life. A Godcidental discovery. Not a coincidence." Her eyes narrowed. "You still care about him."

"Of course I care. He gave me Angel. But we're totally different people now." There was no sense in stirring her mother's probably dormant hopes that her daughter would someday marry. There was nothing she could do about her own hopes. She slid Angel's bin onto the floor. "They say you have a complete cell turnover every seven years. That means I've been four whole new people since high school."

With a shake of her head, her mother stood. "With that logic, I've been three whole new people since I became a widow. Every one of those three new people was in love with your father." She walked toward the door, then turned around and smiled. "I'm not so sure all your cells are out of love, *Janka*."

151

Chapter 4

Steven picked up the kitchen phone and set it down again. He'd lost track of how many times now. He dumped the burnt-edged crust from his pizza into the trash under the sink and glanced at the clock. It was nine fifteen in Boston, three hours earlier in Tacoma, Washington.

His boys were probably busy on a Thursday night. Toby would be scarfing pizza—most likely as burnt as his—with his study group. He could easily picture Griff schmoozing a client over dinner.

But just when was a good time to tell your grown sons they had a sister? He didn't quite know how to word it. *Hey, Griff, you sitting down? Tobe, you'll never believe this. . . .*

Maybe he'd wait until his own astonishment had worn off a bit. He brushed crumbs off the pizza pan and was sticking it back in the cupboard when the doorbell rang. After a quick scan of the kitchen—not too messy—he opened the back door. "Burt! Come on in."

"Put your shoes on. We have a mission." Burt's communication skills were a product of his years in the Navy.

"Yes, sir."

Steven dug his shoes out from under his recliner, grabbed the drugstore bag that contained what he'd bought for Jim and Burt just this afternoon, and joined Burt on the back step. At sixty-three, Burt still ran three miles a day and lifted weights. Rock-hard arms, resting on his knees, boasted tattoos that told stories of what he referred to as his "brain-fried years."

Burt nodded toward his 1971 Warbonnet Yellow Corvette convertible. "Emma's sump pump quit working. Supposed to rain before midnight."

Staring at the sleek slope of the front of the car, already imagining the wind in his thinning hair, Steven finished tying his shoes and stood up. "I love doing ministry with you."

"We'll get extra jewels in our crown for these sacrifices. Ready?"

Steven followed Burt to the car and leaped, far less gracefully than Burt, over the door and into the seat. As he fastened his seat belt, he looked up into a cloudless sky. "Emma's pulling your leg."

"Yeah, I know."

"Bet she busted her own sump pump."

"Probably."

"When are you going to propose?"

Burt laughed and put the car in second, spitting gravel all the way to the end of Steven's drive. "I'll shave my head in mourning when you take the plunge, but I won't be following you. When you going to put a ring on Gretchen's finger?"

"Look! A fox." Steven pointed toward a white-tipped tail disappearing into the woods.

Burt laughed. "That's not the fox you're supposed to be talking about." He turned onto the highway and had the machine doing sixty in seconds.

Steven ran his hand along the sleek gold finish on the outside of the door. Corvette Therapy. It worked every time. The rush of wind in his ears, the hum of tires on pavement, melted Steven's tension. "Burt, I need to talk to you about something."

Easing on the brake, Burt nodded. "Spill it."

"There's something I haven't told you about my past."

"Hey, we all got bones in our closets." Burt pulled to a stop sign and turned to face him. "What is it?"

Pressing his lips together, Steven reached in his pocket and pulled out something pink. He handed Burt a bubble gum cigar.

"It's a girl."

≈❦

Emma Winter eased down her basement steps with two glasses of lemonade. Setting the tray on the floor beside Burt, she turned to Steven. "Tongues are wagging about you, Steven."

"About me?"

"Didn't you see how people stared on Sunday?"

"He's a man, Em." Burt picked up a glass with a greasy hand. "We don't have that sixth sense thing you women got going on."

Emma pushed pale silver bangs to the side and sighed. "No more accurate statement was ever spoken. So is it true?"

Steven handed a wrench to Burt. "That I'm oblivious to gossip? Pretty much."

"Is it true you have a daughter that you didn't know about until she asked you to be in her wedding?"

Steven wasn't generally a blusher, but the warmth creeping up the back of his neck probably glowed in the dim basement light. "That's pretty close to the truth."

Emma turned over an old galvanized metal bucket and sat on it. "Her mother owns Angel Wings in Galena, right?"

"Yes." Steven cringed inwardly as Burt set down his glass and crossed one arm over his chest. The knuckles of his other hand supported his chin and his eyes widened with the rapt expression of a child settling in for a bedtime story. Steven took a long, slow draught of lemonade. "Angel Cholewinski is my daughter."

"I know her grandmother. Used to be friends of sorts. I remember when Ruby's daughter went to California. I thought something was fishy. So it was all because you—"

153

"Let's just say I made some unwise decisions when I was young and leave it at that."

Emma's hand oscillated in time with her head. "Your past is just that. We've all got skeletons, and I know God's dealt with your closet like He's dealt with mine."

Steven cocked an eyebrow at Burt.

"It's your present that counts. Was the news really a shock?"

With a quick glance at Burt's knowing smile, Steven nodded. In spite of what she'd just said, by the time the new sump pump was installed, Emma would have wrangled a book's worth of details about the past she claimed didn't interest her. "I first met Angel back in September. Her new husband taught at my school. In my gut, I knew she was mine the first time I heard her last name. She has my mother's hair color and the same eyes as my boys. But denial is a handy thing. Hearing it put into words when her mother confirmed it was still a shock."

Wrapping a navy cardigan tighter over her middle, Emma leaned forward. "I'm sure it was. So you've stayed friends with her mother this whole time?"

Excellent work, Emma. "No. We lost touch before Angel was born. I never knew her mother was pregnant."

"Oh my. . ." Emma's prayer chain wheels were almost visibly turning. *Please pray for Steven Vandenburg as he adjusts to the shocking news that he fathered a child out of wedlock. . . .* "So how does it stand between you and the girl's mother now? Are you angry? Or was it your fault you never knew?"

Burt's hands shot into the air. "Whoa. . .slow down, Emma. Give your victim a breather."

"You're right. Steven, I just want you to know I care. Is there anything the church can do to reach out to your daughter? If they don't go to Ruby's church I could invite them to ours."

Steven patted her on the shoulder. "Thank you for your concern, but they're both solid believers, involved in their churches."

"Well. . .isn't God good? In spite of all the dark spots in your past, He saw fit to draw every one of you to Him. What a testimony. That's what you need to tell people to shut them up, you know. God's plan is perfect in spite of us. You just ignore those busybodies at church. Like I said, your past is your past."

It may be my past, but I'm guessing it's about to be everybody's business.

⁂

Travel mug in hand, Jeanie stepped into the halo of lamplight on the sidewalk in front of the house. There was a time she'd hated waking before the birds, but now she relished the quiet. The smell of dew-drenched grass mingled with the scent of the neighbors' hybrid tea roses. For a moment, the only sound was the padding of her work shoes on cement and the faint clanging of wind chimes in the distance. Lights glowed from upstairs windows in the house across the street. Her walk to work was like strolling through a Thomas Kincaid painting. Today, it was her window of peace before the Saturday morning craziness took over.

With one last look at canopies fluttering in the shadows of redbrick buildings, she turned onto Perry Street and took out her keys. Entering through the side entrance, she flipped on the lights and, in a motion that had become automatic, opened the cupboard for a clean apron and hairnet.

As she opened flour bins, cracked eggs, and measured sugar, she imagined the announcer's voice as he handed her the first place trophy. *"And Jeanie Cholewinski is going on to Paris!"*

Lost in thought, she jumped when Sue opened the back door.

"Happy Saturday." Jeanie held up the plastic-sheathed list of orders and her weekend help groaned. "How's Bradley?"

"Back to normal for now." Tying her apron, Sue walked to the sink. As she scrubbed her hands she glanced over her shoulder. "Now that my life is back to somewhat normal, any chance you're going to fill me in on the details?"

"About the contest?"

"No. Congratulations, by the way. That's so cool." Sue turned around as she dried her hands. "But it kind of takes a backseat to the humongous secret you've kept from everyone."

She'd known Sue for more than twenty years. She'd been Angel's babysitter in her early teens and started working at the bakery in high school. "It was a necessary secret."

Sue sighed. "Your life is like a Hallmark movie."

Jeanie scooped dough out of a bowl, flattened it with her hands on the floured table, and folded it into thirds. Walking over to the sheeter, she plopped the dough down and shook her head. "I've got a good life, but it doesn't qualify for happily ever after."

"Hey, you don't know what the last scene's gonna look like. So. . .what's next? He's a widower, right?"

"Yes, but. . .we're not the same people we were way back then." How many more times would she have to say that?

"You don't really believe that, do you? Was he your first love?"

First. And only. "Yes."

"And you were his?"

"Yes. But he was happily married for a lot of years in between."

"There's nothing like your first love. Something magical about it, something you never really get over."

Jeanie pushed the button on the sheeter and listened to the low-pitched whine as the machine flattened the dough and cut it into perfect strips.

"When will you see him again?"

Bending over her work, she hid a smile. "When I'm done here, actually."

If I don't chicken out.

Chapter 5

Her pulse thumped in her throat as she maneuvered the winding, tree-lined driveway. Why hadn't she listened to her doubts? Showing up on his doorstep at ten o'clock on a Saturday morning might convey the wrong message. But she'd gotten this far. . . .

She'd found his address in the phone book and debated calling first, but any way she phrased it in her head sounded awkward. If she just showed up, the reason for her visit would be obvious.

What is the reason for my visit? It would make more sense for Angel to give him the scrapbook. Was she being less than honest about her motives? If she could control the scene that waited for her at Steven's house, what would it look like? The picture that came to mind—Steven opening up his arms to her—belonged in the Hallmark movie Sue had brought up, not in her life.

She slowed the car and pulled to the side, then picked up the book. It wasn't anything fancy. She didn't have time for stencils and templates and colored pens, but in spite of its simplicity, she felt good about the finished product. Twenty pages capturing Angel's childhood. . .in Galena.

The thought of actually putting the book in his hands suddenly terrified her. *The mailbox.* She'd write a note and leave the book in the mailbox she'd passed out by the road. The lane opened into a clearing. A large gravel circle would allow plenty of room to turn around. Hopefully Steven wasn't looking out. As she eased to the right, she stared at the house. Mediterranean-style, with massive carved double doors and an asymmetrical roofline. The colors—several shades of brown, windows trimmed in olive green—blended into the trees. On the side, a brick chimney rose above the second story. A fireplace. She'd always wanted a fireplace.

Curiosity suddenly shoved aside anxiety. He'd only lived here a little over a year. What drew him to this place? What did it look like inside? She put the car in park, picked up the scrapbook, and got out. The air was cooler here. She reached back in for a sweater.

A car with an Iowa license plate sat in front of the garage. A rental car. One of Steven's sons, maybe. Did they know about her yet?

Clutching the book like a shield, she walked up to the door and searched for a doorbell. All she found was a heavy medieval-looking iron ring. She knocked it twice against the wood, deciding she'd give him to the count of ten.

"One. . .two. . .three—"

Footsteps. Then laughter. The door opened.

"Jeanie!" Surprise lifted Steven's brows. "Come. . .in."

Two seconds of hesitation—the space between "come" and "in" were all she needed to change her mind. "Actually, I can't stay. I just came to bring you this." She held out the book. "I thought you might like some pictures of Angel."

As he took the scrapbook a strange expression crossed his face. Fear? He seemed to draw back.

"Have a good day, Steven." She started to turn.

Almost imperceptibly, the door opened wider. "Come in. Please."

She wavered, not at all sure she was ready for whatever waited inside— meeting his children or being alone with him. "Just. . .for a minute." She stepped past him. He smelled of soap and something spicy.

Her eyes adjusted to the dim light from a black chandelier with flame-shaped bulbs. They stood in a split foyer. Carpeted stairs led up. Slate-tiled stairs that matched the floor beneath their feet led down. To her right was a bookcase. Amid rows of dusty carved and cast metal animal heads that appeared to come from all over the world, one thing stood out—totally incongruous with its bright colors. . .and googly eyes. "You *kept* it?"

Reaching across her, Steven picked up the mug by one of its handle-ears, dusting it with his sleeve. Bulging, yellow, crossed eyes stared from the aqua-blue face. Purplish, cyanotic lips puckered in a kiss. She'd made it in ceramics class.

"I found it in a box when I moved. Couldn't very well leave it there."

Jeanie touched the lips with the tip of her finger. "It goes so well with your collection."

Setting it back, Steven smiled. "I think so. These are all souvenirs of times I want to remember." His gaze fastened on hers.

Attempting a smile and a swallow, Jeanie wrenched her attention from him and directed it toward a tall, blue-and-white urn at the top of the stairs. "You've traveled a lot." She'd intended to phrase it as a question, but the wording evaporated under his stare. "You have a lot of souvenirs."

He nodded. And his hand slid behind her, just barely touching the back of her sweater. "Come and see the rest of them."

From the third step she could see a grandfather clock and a bust of Shakespeare on a dust-covered stand. From the fifth step she could see the floor-to-ceiling stone fireplace. A huge brass-framed picture hung above it. In front of the fireplace was an Oriental rug.

And a woman.

Wearing a man's flannel shirt.

☙❧

"Jeanie, I'd like you to meet Gretchen Newman. She's a friend from Texas, up here on business. Gretchen, this is Jeanie Cholewinski."

The woman offered her hand and Jeanie shook it. "Glad to meet you."

"Jeanie. . .and how do you two know each other?"

Gretchen's tone was warm, her smile genuine, but her question had the power to give Jeanie momentary brain freeze. Who was this woman? Jeanie appraised the chin-length, slightly curled hair, professionally done brows and nails. Gretchen had to be about the same age as Steven. She appeared rounded, but not really overweight. At least from what she could tell with the baggy shirt hanging to the knees of her jeans. Steven's baggy shirt, most likely.

How did she fit into Steven's life, and what answer was appropriate? Jeanie smiled back, doing all she could to match the warmth. "We're old friends. We met years ago at the bakery my family owns." It was all true. Nothing else needed to be said.

"You own a bakery? Do you. . .bake?" Gretchen gave a becoming little giggle.

"Six days a week from four to nine a.m."

"Oh my." Gretchen laid a hand on Steven's arm. "She's a sister foodie."

Steven laughed. Nervously. "Jeanie's a sixth generation baker."

Jeanie did a double take. He remembered that? She would have had to stop and think before figuring out if she was fifth or sixth generation.

Gretchen brought her hands together and pressed the sides of her index fingers to her bottom lip. "You're going to help with HIS pizza sale, right?"

"Whose pizza sale?"

Steven shifted from his right foot to his left. "I. . .haven't talked to her about it."

"You're having a pizza sale?"

Gretchen laughed. "It's a fundraiser. Steven is one of the directors of Hands in Service. They do bake sales to raise money for food pantries and the homeless." Her face brightened with a wider smile. "They're doing a pizza sale on Fourth of July weekend in Chicago. He works with the kids to make the pizzas. I just assumed, since you're a baker. . ."

"I just"—Steven cleared his throat—"haven't had the opportunity to ask Jeanie if she'd like to help." He turned his blue eyes on her, his expression far too intense for a man asking only for help making pizza. "It would be great if you could come along. I can use as many experienced hands as I can get."

Something about the project resonated in her soul. "I'd love to help." The look of surprise and gratitude Steven shot her upped her pulse to a dangerous level.

Gretchen clapped. "Wonderful. This will be so fun."

"So you're helping, too?" It came out with a slight edge. The last thing she wanted was for this woman to think she was in competition. Even if she was.

"I'll be taking pictures."

"Gretchen is a professional photographer." Steven put his hand on Gretchen's shoulder, then removed it. "She takes pictures for. . .what do you call them? Cookbooks?"

"Sometimes cookbooks. Right now we're doing a series of books on famous American barbeque restaurants."

"Seriously?" A faint current of electricity zipped from the top of Jeanie's head to the bottoms of her feet. A professional food photographer stood two feet in front of her. Her mother would label this serendipity. "So you'll be here for the next two weeks?"

"Oh no. I have to be in Dubuque at four. I'm doing a shoot at Sugar Ray's Barbeque. I'll fly back for the fundraiser."

"How long will you be around then?"

"Just for the weekend. Why?"

"I'm in the Grégoire Pâtisserie contest and—"

"Say no more. You need amazing photos of your entry."

"A friend of mine's an amateur, but he never gets the lighting quite right." How would Lucas feel about being pushed aside?

Gretchen reached out and laid her hand on Jeanie's arm. "I'll do it. I'll work my schedule around it whenever you need me."

Jeanie blinked twice, then again. "I wouldn't ask you to come back just for that and I'd need to know what you charge before—"

"We'll figure it out. Come—you have to taste the caramel rolls I made this morning." She pointed toward what Jeanie assumed was the direction of the kitchen.

"Good idea." Steven set the scrapbook on a low table.

"What's this? Pictures?" Gretchen picked up the book and opened it.

Jeanie shot a quick look at Steven. His eyes appeared riveted to the book.

"Look at that red hair. . .and curls. What a sweet little girl."

"Thank you." Jeanie offered a tight smile. "She's my daughter."

Steven cleared his throat and took an audible breath. "Actually, she's *our* daughter."

Chapter 6

Steven gripped the shelf behind Jeanie as if his hold on it could somehow stabilize the teetering emotions around him. "How about those caramel rolls?"

The looks he got in return told him humor was the wrong choice. "Let's go sit in the kitchen. I'll make coffee."

Jeanie was the first to move. "Coffee sounds good." She walked around the corner, leaving him alone with a woman with a polite smile stitched to her face.

"I just found out, Gretchen. I've only known for a week."

She closed the book and looked up at him. The question in her eyes didn't need to be asked. She was leaving this afternoon and he hadn't told her yet.

"It's just all so. . .new." Did he have to be totally honest? Did he have to admit he had decided not to tell her yet? "I haven't even talked to the boys."

To her credit, Gretchen managed a smile. "I don't need to know any more, Steven. I never expected you to tell me every detail of your past."

"Let's go sit down."

She led the way. Jeanie looked up as she stacked two empty juice glasses on top of the two dirty plates in her hand. The sight rocked him. What must she be thinking? He walked over to the sink and dumped the coffeepot. "I made this when Gretchen came this morning, but I'll make a fresh pot." Was that too obvious? Probably, but he was more concerned about Jeanie knowing he hadn't entertained an overnight guest than looking silly.

"I'll warm up the rolls in the oven. The microwave doesn't do them justice." Gretchen opened a drawer and pulled out a box of aluminum foil. It was all too clear she knew her way around his kitchen.

Jeanie wiped off the table. "They look delicious. Where did you get the recipe?"

"It's one my grandmother was famous for. I made a few alterations, but it's essentially hers."

Measuring coffee into a filter, Steven fought a weird urge to laugh. All this nicey-nice chitchat had him strung tighter than a stuck fly reel.

"She used to just sprinkle the sugar on the bottom of the pan and heat it in the oven, but I find if I add a little corn syrup to the brown sugar it makes a much smoother consistency." Gretchen's words picked up speed as she slid the pan into the oven. "I set the oven a little higher, too. Sometimes her rolls weren't quite done. I guess my grandpa liked them doughy, but I—"

"Gretchen. . ." Jeanie motioned toward a kitchen chair and took the one across from it.

Thank you. It might get ugly, but at least the inane chatter and strained politeness would come to an end.

Wiping her hands on her jeans, Gretchen nodded, stared at the chair, then sat down. "Like I just told Steven. . .please don't feel like you have to explain anything. Lindy was my best friend for a long time, but we lived two counties apart." The fingers of one hand patted the table as if she were tapping out Morse code in quadruplicate. "Steven and I. . .we've really just been in each other's lives on a regular basis for a few years so I certainly don't expect—"

Jeanie reached across the table and stopped the table tapping with a hand over Gretchen's. Once again, Steven fought laughter. His first love reassuring his. . .what was Gretchen, anyway? He went back to filling the pot with water. Would they notice if he filled it one meticulous tablespoon at a time? Anything to stay out of the middle of the drama.

"I. . .*we*. . .want you to understand."

We do? Where did Jeanie get the idea she was the spokesperson for both of them?

"I was seventeen when I got pregnant."

"Oh my. So young."

"Young and immature. I wasn't ready to be a mother, but I was even less ready to be a wife. So I never told Steven I was pregnant. It was a selfish thing to do, but, looking back, I know it was for the best."

Really? Says who? And was that really your reason, Jeanie? You weren't ready to spend the rest of your life with me?

"I understand."

I don't.

"But God orchestrated things this past year that were totally out of our hands. My daughter—her name is Angel—fell in love with a man who teaches at Steven's school."

"That wasn't a coincidence." Gretchen's eyes grew watery.

"I know."

Please don't let them both start crying. He stared at the back deck through the window above the sink. In the corner, his hammock beckoned from beneath a limb of a century-old oak. *Beam me up, Scotty.*

"Being a single mother isn't easy. But I think you made a wise decision. Two kids right out of high school would have had a tough time making a go of it."

Water flowed over the top of the glass pot. Steven set it down and shut off the faucet. He walked to the table and put his hands on the back of a chair. "It wasn't exactly like that, Gretchen. The story's a little more complicated than that."

"Steven, like I said, you don't—"

"I was Jeanie's teacher."

"Oh." Gretchen looked down at her empty cup, then back at him. "Oh." She repeated the cup inspection. "You could. . .you could have been charged with. . ."

Jeanie nodded. "That's why I never told anyone."

Gretchen's eyes suddenly flashed wide. "Could you still be charged? Now that people know?"

Steven laughed. Again, he knew immediately it was the wrong choice. "There are statutes of limitations."

"Actually, until about eight years ago it could have been possible." Jeanie folded her hands in her lap. "The laws would have been much harsher if I'd been under seventeen, but still, in some cases they can prosecute up to twenty years after the victim turns eighteen."

Victim? Is that how she saw herself? He pulled out the chair and sank into it.

"Victim is a legal term, Steven. I don't. . .I didn't ever. . .think of myself. . ." Jeanie looked toward the sink. "I'll finish the coffee." She jumped up and went to the sink.

Gretchen shook off her shock like a dog flinging water after a bath. She looked at him and smiled. "Your daughter is so blessed to get to know you."

"I'm the one who's blessed." His eyes suddenly stung. "She's an amazing young woman. It's just beginning to sink in. I have a daughter. . . ."

For all his fears that the women would make a scene, it was just his embarrassing luck to be the first to shed a tear.

&

As he closed the door after Jeanie, the bug-eyed cup caught his attention. It could have been yesterday he'd torn neon yellow wrapping paper from a lumpy ball of bubble wrap—sitting on a blanket in the center of a grove of aspen saplings behind the fairgrounds, Jeanie's braid bouncing as she laughed at him fighting with an entire roll of tape.

He headed up the steps. As he walked through the living room, he looked over at the leather-bound volume of Shakespeare sonnets sitting next to his recliner. Had Jeanie seen it? Would she be surprised to know an aspen leaf still held their place?

Sonnet 116 was branded in his head, not only from years of teaching English. Emotion, experts claimed, enhances memory.

Love's not Time's fool, though rosy lips and cheeks
*   Within his bending sickle's compass come:*
Love alters not with his brief hours and weeks,
*   But bears it out even to the edge of doom.*

He walked slowly into the kitchen, picked up the empty cake pan, and ran his finger along the bottom. Brown sugar and butter coated his fingertip. "Jeanie sure loved your rolls." Licking the sticky decadence, he walked over to Gretchen and slid the pan in the suds-filled sink.

She didn't answer. Even before he looked at her, he knew what he'd see. Tears streamed onto the bubbles. His gut knotted and he walked back to the table, pretending he hadn't noticed and hating himself for it. He picked up the sea turtle trivet Lindy had bought in Hawaii and braced himself for the lashing he deserved. "I'm sorry I didn't tell you sooner. I should—"

"No, I don't care about that." She turned around and leaned against the sink, drying her hands on a towel. "I was just thinking about your daughter. What I would have given to have known my father. Promise me you'll get involved. Be her daddy even if she's almost thirty and married."

Gretchen Newman, you're one fine lady. "I will."

"You have no idea what a difference you can make in her sense of security. And her image of God." She turned back to the sink and began scrubbing at the caramel that would have melted in the warm water if she'd given it a little time. "Maybe it's none of my business, but I need to know. . ."

Steven set the cover on the butter dish and nodded to her back. "About Jeanie?"

"Those old feelings aren't really gone, are they?" Reddened eyes turned to him.

He picked up the dish and carried it to the cupboard above the toaster. He moved the saltshaker to make room, slid in the dish, and closed the door.

"I. . .need some time to figure things out." He didn't turn around.

Behind him, the sink drained, the sprayer rinsed it. A drawer opened and closed.

Footsteps headed toward the table. From the corner of his eye he saw her unbutton the flannel shirt and lay it over the back of the chair.

"I think I'll get an early start."

≈≈

It was time. The boys needed to know. Steven stuck the clean cake pan in the cupboard next to the stove and pulled out his phone. As he did, he glanced under the kitchen table. Sandals. Gretchen's sandals. She'd left in bare feet.

Lord, I handled that so wrong. He stared down at his phone and pushed a number that didn't belong to either of his sons. His friend's voice eased a bit of tension. "Burt, I need a dose of wisdom."

A low rumble met his ear. "Just happened to have read a few chapters in Proverbs this morning. What's up?"

"Gretchen."

"Oh. You didn't mention you wanted woman wisdom. Fresh out of that. Ask my daughters—I've never had much of that."

"You and me both." Steven opened the back door and walked out on the deck. The air smelled of warm damp earth. "Jeanie showed up this morning while Gretchen was here."

"And you hadn't breathed a word of this to Gretchen yet, right?"

"Right. It was all very civil until Jeanie left."

"And the questions started."

Steven stretched out on the green and tan striped hammock. "She asked me if I still had feelings for Jeanie."

"Please tell me you didn't say yes."

"I didn't say yes."

"Good."

"But I didn't say no."

In spite of his predicament, Burt's sputtering laugh made him smile. "Smooth shave, Gillette. Well, you've been looking for a way out. Looks like you found it."

"I didn't want a way out. I wanted a reprieve, a break. I just wish she'd give me enough time to figure out if I'd miss her. She's been up here at least once a month since I moved."

"Funny she didn't get that hint. Moving to Elizabeth, Illinois, wasn't exactly an upgrade from the Dallas public school system."

"I told her I wanted to get back to my roots and lead a simpler, slower lifestyle. That was the truth. I just didn't mention I wanted a quieter life, too." He pushed against the deck rail and the hammock swung. "She can be a little intense."

"And now you've got two women and you're not sure how you feel about either one. Nice, quiet life. You need to call Gretchen. Let her know it's not over, unless you want it to be. Spell it out. Women always figure they know what we're thinking. I'd bet money she thinks it's over between you two."

"Why does there have to be a 'thing' to be over? Why couldn't we just be friends and wait and see how things progress?"

"Because you're a man and she's a woman."

"I knew I could count on you for profundity."

"You don't have to thank me. Any other problems I can solve on this fine morning?"

"Yeah. You want to call my boys and let them know they've got a sister?"

The sputtering laugh resounded. "Wouldn't touch that with an eighty-foot telephone pole. But I'll pray."

❧

"I knew you'd call. I was sure I'd hear your voice before I crossed the Mississippi. I understand your need for space."

"Thank you, Gretchen. I'm just in a bit of shock right now. I need to figure out how all this new information fits into my world."

"Everything in its place." He could hear her smile. "Now if you could just learn to dust."

He didn't even want to know if there was hidden meaning in her comment. Knowing Gretchen, it was most likely literal. He laughed. "Never. Thanks again for understanding. I'm going to go call my kids now."

"Steven?"

"Yes?"

"Can I still help with the pizza sale?"

His eyes closed. So much for space. "Of course." He didn't sigh until she hung up.

As long as the phone was in his hand, he might as well get all of his calls over and done with. Positive kid first, or negative? He'd always held to the philosophy that it was better to get the bad out of the way so you could thoroughly enjoy the good. Eat the lima beans out of the succotash first, delete the spam before reading personal e-mails.

So he'd call the half-empty son first. He punched "3" and waited for Griffin's voice. "Hello?"

"Griff. Are you in the middle of something?"

"Always. But I've got a minute. Actually, I was going to call you at lunch. Do you have plans for next weekend?"

Next weekend? Father's Day. Irrational hope sprouted and he squashed it. "Nothing special." *Why?*

"Well you do now. How'd you like a couple bums hanging out at your house?"

"A couple? You bringing a friend?" *Or. . .please God. . .a brother?*

"Toby and I are flying in Friday night."

He'd prided himself, especially in the last few years, on having mastered the art of reining in emotion. But it wasn't even noon and this was the second time he'd mopped at tears. *Softy.* "That will be"—*better than any gift money could buy*—"wonderful."

"I'll e-mail details. Hey, I have to go. Boss got up on the wrong side of the world this morning. Did you call about something in particular?"

"Nothing that can't wait until the weekend. Love you."

"Love you, too."

Happy Father's Day. . .times three.

Chapter 7

"Taste." Jeanie held out two numbered paper plates. On each was a slice of yellow cake cut in half. "Tell me which one you like the best."

"My pleasure." Lucas occupied his usual spot at the counter, staring, out of habit, at the CLOSED sign across the street.

"Wait till I lock up." Her mother walked past Lucas, locked the door, and turned off the signs, then came back to the counter and tasted both cakes.

Lucas's eyebrows huddled together in overstated concentration. "Hmm. Number one is light, buttery. Two has a stronger hint of vanilla, but could be a smidgeon sweeter. I think. . .one. Ruby? What do you—" His eyes narrowed. "Who's that?"

A knock sounded on the glass. Jeanie looked up. "What in the world is she doing here?"

Her mother unlocked the door and a girl walked in. Sixteen years old, brown hair in short pigtails covered by a triangle scarf tied at the back of her neck. She wore khaki overalls and a tan T-shirt and carried a backpack.

Jeanie ran around the end of the counter. "Taylor." She hugged her daughter's new and very bedraggled-looking sister-in-law. "Do your parents know you're here?"

Taylor shrugged out of her backpack and set it on the floor. Hazel eyes looked down at the bulging pack. "Wade's rent is paid up until the end of the month. I'm staying there."

Having met Wade's parents several times, Jeanie knew they hadn't given their blessing. "How did you get here?"

"I got a ride."

Taylor's evasiveness was all too recognizable to someone who'd once made an art form out of skirting truth. A ribbon of fear looped around her chest, making her suddenly light-headed. "With someone you know?"

"Of course." Taylor's sandaled toe jabbed her pack.

Jeanie didn't buy it. "Taylor?"

The toe began kicking faster. "They were nice people."

Chills skittered along the backs of her arms. Memory ghosts whispered. "You could have been. . .hurt." She took a deep breath. "Sit down. When's the last time you ate?"

"This morning."

"I'll get you something." *And then I'll call your parents and then I'll make you*

166

talk. She pointed to the stool two down from Lucas. "Lucas, I'd like you to meet my new son-in-law's sister, Taylor Ramsey, a fugitive from Wheaton."

"I'm not a fugitive. I'm going to take care of Wade's plants and stuff."

"Mm-hmm. Taylor, this is Lucas Zemken. He owns the jewelry store across the street."

Lucas held out his hand. "Glad to meet you, Taylor. Seems you and I have something in common."

Don't you dare tell her some yarn glorifying hitchhiking.

"What's that?"

"I was a fugitive once."

Rolling her eyes, Jeanie walked around the end of the counter. Lucas was a storyteller. Only a fraction of the tales he spun were true.

"Really?"

"Had an APB out on my sorry hide—half the sheriffs in Jo Daviess County plus a search party combing the woods and checking every abandoned building for miles around."

"What did you do? Why were you running?" Taylor's eyes widened with what appeared to be admiration. Not a good sign.

"I absconded with the contents of my mother's purse."

Jeanie glanced at her mother and both shook their heads. Her mother leaned across the counter and put her chin in her hand. "How old were you, Lucas?"

A small bump appeared in his cheek. "I was four."

Taylor burst into giggles.

"I stole a pack of gum and knew there was a wooden spoon with my name on it, so I ran. Cops found me in my grandma's garage. Never did get that spoon. Slick, huh?" He held his hand out, palm up.

Taylor slapped his hand. "Slick."

"So what are you doing here, Taylor? Problems at home? You're honor bound to tell me since I confessed my crimes to you."

A sigh as big as she was whistled out of Taylor. "My parents are forcing me to go to church camp."

Good work, Lucas. Jeanie reached across the counter and rested her hand on Taylor's shoulder. In a no-nonsense yet gentle tone she asked, "Will you call your parents or should I?"

The girl's shoulders slumped. "I will. But first can I tell you why I came here?"

"Of course."

"I don't want to go to church camp because some of my friends are going and they're the ones that pulled me down before when I was drinking and stuff. I can't tell my parents 'cause they figure they're all good kids. And besides, I don't want to be forced to sing songs about how I believe in Jesus 'cause I don't really yet and I just want to figure it out myself on my own. Anyway, I was working for

Angel on the weekends, you know, and I don't have a job until they get back and move to Chicago, so I was wondering if maybe I could work for you if you need somebody to clean the bakery or something or I could get a job somewhere else here and I was wondering if maybe I could stay with you and help you take care of Sunny until they get back." She finally stopped to breathe.

Jeanie reached into a box on the counter and pulled out a filled doughnut. "Mom, can you get a glass of milk?" It was an excuse to make eye contact.

Her mother nodded and the lines around her eyes compressed in a smile. "I'm good with it if you are." Her answer had nothing to do with a glass of milk.

Jeanie set the doughnut in front of Taylor. "As a matter of fact, we're looking for part-time help. But I warn you, I might not be as soft a boss as Angel."

Taylor grinned. "I don't think you can be too tough with a name like Dreamy." Her nose crinkled and she laughed.

Heat rose from the base of Jeanie's neck to the tips of her ears. "How did you—"

"Mr. Vandenburg was showing a high school picture of you to Angel at the wedding. It said, 'All my love forever. Dreamy' on the back. It's the coolest story in the world how you two found each other after all this time. It's like destiny, you know, like you were meant to be together and now—"

"We're not together, Taylor."

"Not yet maybe. But if I have anything to say about it. . ."

"You don't—"

A laugh popped from Lucas like a punctured balloon. He held his hand out to Taylor for another high five. "Count me in, girl." Their hands smacked. "Love is in the air."

"For sure."

❧

Steven ran a damp cloth along the top of the nightstand, stared at the ridge of gray he'd collected, and tucked the cloth in his back pocket. He picked up the alarm clock. Twelve o' clock blinked in red. The clock hadn't been set since a storm had knocked out the power for an hour three weeks ago. Griff would bring his own alarm, no doubt. Satellite radio most likely—voice activated, with a built-in GPS, if such a thing existed. Griff was doing all right for himself. Steven smoothed the plaid spread on the twin bed and walked across the hall to the other guest room.

Toby, on the other hand, would show up with the Army duffel bag he'd bought at a surplus store in Dallas six years ago when he went on a high school mission trip. In the bag would be a few of the shirts he'd taken on that trip and a couple pairs of faded jeans. And that would be just fine by him. Steven dusted the dresser, picking up the tattered Bible Promise Book Toby had been awarded in fourth grade for memorizing the Beatitudes. The book wouldn't stay on the dresser while Toby was here. He'd find it on the bedside table when his youngest son left.

He looked at another clock radio flashing twelve and glanced at his watch.

The boys should be here any minute. They were meeting at the Quad City International Airport and renting a car. Which meant that this had been Griff's idea, because Griff would be paying for all of it. Which meant that he and Toby were on speaking terms and something had softened in his oldest son. Steven went downstairs and turned on the oven. Lindy's pizza crust recipe hadn't been all that tricky after all.

The front door flew open and the first sound that met his ears threatened to start those ridiculous sappy tears again. Arguing. His sons arguing. . .

Celtics versus Sonics.

Thank You, Lord.

❧

Toby pushed aside his paper plate. Sun-streaked and carefree, chin-length brown hair tumbled over the collar of his faded shirt when he shook his head. "I'm stuffed. That was good, Dad. Mom woulda been proud. Or shocked, maybe." He laughed and folded the plate in half.

On the opposite end of the table, Griffin tapped his upper and lower front teeth together. It was an unconscious gesture accompanied by a slow, steady inhale and used primarily for his brother. It meant Griff was merely tolerating the moment. Steven knew the root of his impatience. Though it had been almost four years since his mother died, he seemed to think it irreverent to speak of her in anything but somber tones. Lindy would have hated that. Steven felt an obligation to loosen the boy up.

"I think Mom would be shocked at a lot of things I'm capable of these days. I cleaned the oven a few weeks ago and—" Griff slid his chair back, but Steven didn't let it alter what he was going to say. "Wait till you see the impatiens I planted in the backyard."

"Cool."

Griff walked toward the living room, running his hand through short, gelled dark hair. When he got to the back door he stopped and bent over. "Think Mom would be proud to know you had some woman's shoes in your kitchen?" Gretchen's sandals dangled from his finger when he stood. What could so easily have been an opportunity for humor was anything but with Griff. "Whose are they?"

First of all, I'm your father and I don't need to explain. Second of all, if you don't know me well enough to know it's not what it might look like. . . "They're Gretchen's."

"I thought you moved to break it off with her." Griff's disgust was almost tangible.

Never, ever, had he breathed a word of that to his boys. Had it been that obvious that part of his motivation for changing jobs was to disentangle? "There was nothing to break off. She's an old friend."

"Of Mom's." He walked into the living room, footsteps ricocheting off the vaulted ceiling.

Toby swiveled around in his chair. "Drop it, Griff," he yelled. "Dad's a big boy. Let him have a life."

The footsteps continued up the stairs, followed by a bedroom door shutting with too much force.

So maybe tonight wasn't the best time to tell them the news.

Steven woke on Saturday morning to the sound of his weed trimmer. Griffin. Why couldn't that boy ever relax? The next sound he heard was Toby's plaster-rattling snores. How could two offspring be so night-and-day different? Same parents, same rules and advantages. Not for the first time, he reassured himself that God was in control, even when it came to his boys. The Creator of the Universe had, after all, designed Cain and Abel, Esau and Jacob, and Joseph and his brothers. And the world had survived.

Steven got up and walked into the bathroom. He turned on the shower then looked in the mirror. He'd put on some weight since Lindy died. Stress eating. He turned sideways and stared at his profile. His frame could carry a bit extra, but maybe it was time to stop with the comfort food. And exercise. Grimacing at his reflection, he pulled his T-shirt off. Definitely time to make some changes.

After breakfast.

Maybe someday his boys would join him for the Saturday morning men's prayer breakfasts at church. Toby had joined him several times, Griff never. This morning he'd be cooking for his boys—something he'd surprisingly come to enjoy when he had someone to cook for. Lindy would indeed be proud. And shocked.

After his shower he threw on khaki shorts and a polo shirt and went down to the kitchen. Six slices of French toast were browning on the electric griddle when Toby sauntered in. Flannel boxers and a T-shirt with a hole under one arm and hair sticking out every which way made him look about six instead of nineteen.

"Morning, son."

"Hey." Toby opened the refrigerator and pulled out a carton of orange juice. He swirled the contents and downed it straight from the carton. Some things never change. At least at this age he threw the empty container away instead of sticking it back in the fridge.

"You and Griff get anything settled after I went to bed?"

"I don't know. He's a mess."

"Tobe. . ." Steven warned with a look that didn't work when Toby was six and would probably have little effect now.

"Seriously. You know it, too. He needs to figure out God's the good guy in all this and quit being mad at the world."

"You realize it's always been harder for him because he remembers Mom before she got sick. Six years makes a huge difference—you grew up accepting

170

her illness because you never knew anything else." Steven picked two eggs out of the carton and cracked them simultaneously onto the griddle, earning a thumbs-up from his son.

Toby opened three cupboards before he found the syrup bottle. "I get that. But that doesn't change the fact that he should have worked past his anger by now. Look at you. . .you're moving on with life." He nodded toward the infamous sandals. "Got a woman, even." His laugh filled the kitchen.

It wasn't exactly a conscious thought that flipped a barely warmed egg from the griddle onto his son's holey shirt. But it felt mighty good.

Toby's yelp was rewarding. But only until a slow drizzle of syrup trickled down the back of Steven's head. This time he grabbed an egg right out of the carton.

Moving at light speed, Toby found a can of whipped cream in the refrigerator. Steven's only recourse was a plate of soft butter. "You're going down, boy." He was laughing so hard he could barely utter the threat. He scooped a handful of butter just as sweet cream foamed across one eye and filled his ear.

It was at that moment Griffin walked in carrying a fruit basket. "What the. . ." His foot hit butter and Toby, thanks to years of basketball, caught the basket as Griff grabbed the edge of the table and managed to plant his backside on a chair instead of the floor.

"Smooth shave, Gillette," Steven wheezed. Burt's favorite phrase seemed the only fitting comment.

Griff glared and pulled off his shoe. Toby set the basket on the table and pulled off the cellophane. "Yum."

It wasn't an ordinary fruit basket. Cut fruit on sticks was arranged in a bowl that looked like a basketball. The bowl overflowed with grapes, cantaloupe, honeydew, daisies cut out of pineapple, and chocolate-dipped strawberries. Amid the fruit was a small Mylar balloon that said "Happy Father's Day."

Steven wiped whipped cream on his pants. "Aw, you guys. That's so cool."

"I didn't send it."

"Me neither."

Oh no.

Toby turned the balloon around. There were words scrawled on the silver back.

Oh no.

"Who's Angel?"

Chapter 8

D id Mom know?"

"Griff, *I* didn't know."

"But did Mom know you were. . .intimate with another woman before her?"

The answer is no, but it's none of your business.

Toby's hands met to form a T. "Time out. That's Dad's business."

Thank you.

"I think we should just look at the cool part of this." Toby, raw egg still gooped on his shirt, slid two pieces of French toast onto a plate and handed it to Griffin. "We've got a big sister, bro."

"Thrilling. I suppose she's going to join us for Christmas. Maybe we can take her hunting with us at Thanksgiving."

"Maybe we should. We can do sibling bonding in a tree stand."

Griff snarled.

Lord, help. Steven refilled his coffee cup for the second time in ten minutes.

"Can we meet her?" Toby's hopeful smile once again made him look like a little kid.

"She's on her honeymoon."

"Let's call her."

"I only have her office number." *But I could get her cell number from her mother.* And then it dawned on him—he had Wade's cell number. But what kind of guy would interrupt his buddy on his honeymoon? "Are you serious?"

"As a heart attack." Toby smirked at his brother. "I want to officially welcome her to the family."

Steven had locked horns with his oldest son almost since his birth. His reaction to Griff's scowl probably wasn't what a God-honoring man should be feeling. But the boy needed some shaking up. "Okay. I'll get her number."

Saturday morning. . .would Jeanie be at the bakery? He'd start there. He reached for the phone.

"You can eat first." Toby held a plate out to him.

"Yeah, I suppose I can."

Since when did making a phone call sound better than French toast?

❧

Jeanie opened the door to her apartment and set her purse on the table with a *thud*. She had forty-five minutes to shower and change. . .everything. Her clothes, her attitude, everything.

Why had she just said yes to something guaranteed to make her feel like a butterfly on a pinning block? Steven had asked for Angel's number, she'd given it, and the next thing she knew she was agreeing to lunch at Fried Green Tomatoes with him and his sons.

Awkward.

He'd said his boys wanted to learn more about Angel. She'd tried to get out of it. She'd suggested they wait and talk to Angel herself. But Steven had countered that the boys wouldn't be back until Thanksgiving. The man had been downright pushy. And she'd caved.

As she peeled off flour-dusted clothes, unbraided her hair, and let the shower massage pound her head, she prayed. Fighting God was senseless. She knew that from way too much experience. But what was He doing? Why now, when she was on the verge of finally figuring out what she wanted from life, had He brought Steven back into it? If the Divine plan for her had included Steven, why hadn't it worked out years ago?

Because you didn't let it.

She squeezed the shampoo too hard. A clear green pool filled the palm of her hand. She rubbed it in, scrubbing hard until suds fell to her feet in globs.

What's this all about, Lord? What are You trying to show me? The shower massaged her scalp, foam slid down her shoulders and back. *And why am I having lunch with Steven?* She didn't believe for a minute his sons were all that anxious to meet his old girlfriend. . .the mother of their half sister.

In spite of the steam rising around her, she shivered. Half sister. Her pulse did a tiny skip. Angel had brothers. What if they wanted an ongoing relationship with her? Angel would have the siblings she'd always longed for, the father she'd written about in her journal. *That's a good thing.* But if things didn't work out between her and Steven. . .and if Steven ever remarried. . .

She cranked the faucet. The water turned icy. Good for closing pores. . .and freezing thoughts.

☙

"What are you going to school for, Toby?"

Blue eyes that looked eerily like Angel's sparkled. "I have absolutely no idea."

Jeanie laughed. She felt immediately comfortable with Steven's younger son. "I love your honesty. Don't rush it." She took a piece of bread from the basket Steven held out to her. "And I practice what I preach—I'm actually just now figuring out what I want to be when I grow up."

"What do you want to do?"

"Like your father, I want to teach."

"Awesome." Blond highlights danced in his hair as he nodded. "It's a good calling."

"It is. What makes you passionate, Toby?"

"God. People. God changing people. I'm wondering if I should just drop out of school and go on the mission field."

"What?" Steven scrunched his napkin in a ball. "Where did this come from? You are not dropping out of school."

"He might as well." Griffin, who had been sitting like a stone statue to her left, shrugged. "His grades aren't good enough to get him into graduate school."

Steven's eyes closed and opened in a slow blink. Jeanie sensed that tension between his sons was something he was used to, and that things might escalate quickly if someone didn't do something. As if on cue, the waitress set a plate of the restaurant's signature dish in the center of the table—breaded and sautéed sliced green tomatoes, sprinkled with mozzarella and parmesan cheese. Jeanie breathed a sigh for Steven. "Have you ever had these, Griffin?"

"No."

Conversation with this guy wasn't going to be easy. But a woman who could cover a cake with a hundred and forty-six handmade frosting roses, as she'd done just this morning, had the patience to make a stubborn man talk. "Your dad says you work in Tacoma. . .for a paper company?"

Ouch. If looks could wound, she'd be bleeding. So evidently he didn't work for a paper company.

After the laser look, Griffin blinked at exactly the same speed his father had moments ago. "I work for Richlite Company. We manufacture paper-based fiber composites used for architectural, recreational, and industrial applications. All of our materials are manufactured out of environmentally sustainable resources harvested from certified managed forests." The last three words were articulated as if Jeanie were just off the boat from a non-English-speaking country.

Okay then. She could feel Steven's embarrassment radiating across the table. But God was so clearly at work in this moment, it took all her willpower to restrain the smile tempting her lips. She copied Griffin's posture, folding her hands and leaning forward. "Was it difficult getting the NSF certification for using your product in the food service industry? I can't imagine the trial and error that went into creating a tabletop surface that's water, temperature, and bacteria resistant *and* satisfies the growing demand for green products. How long did it take to perfect that?"

Surprise registered ever so slightly, but Griffin covered it smoothly. "You're familiar with our product."

"Familiar would be an understatement. I *dream* of your product." Was she slathering it a little thick? A quick glance at Steven confirmed his approval. "I'm competing in a contest in which a bakers table with a Richlite top is part of the grand prize." She pointed a piece of garlic bread at him. "I intend to win."

Griffin Vandenburg actually smiled. Jeanie felt like she'd just swung a hammer and rung the bell at the county fair. *Bong!*

"Let's pray." Steven's eyes glistened with mirth as he bent his head. "Father, thank You for gathering us together and for the food You have provided. We acknowledge Your presence. Help us glorify You in all that we say and do. Amen."

"Amen." Jeanie automatically looked straight at Steven as he ended the prayer. The look he returned unraveled her.

Turning away, she looked at Griff and then Toby. "I imagine it was quite a shock for you two to learn you had a. . .that your father has a daughter." In the space between pulse beats where she'd almost said "sister," a floodlight flashed on. Her breath caught in her throat. "I. . .owe you both an apology. I was so sure"—all her excuses seemed suddenly empty, worthless—"I was doing the right thing by not upsetting your father's life all these years. I never thought about him having other children and what it would mean to them to have a. . ."

Sister. A fresh wave of realization and regret slammed into her. The blow felt physical. *Oh, Lord, what did I do to these boys? To Angel? They should have known each other all these years. . . .* Her next breath shuttered in her chest. "I'm sorry." Her hand closed around the handle of her purse. "Excuse me." She ran to the bathroom. The stall door closed as a sob pushed against the hand she held over her mouth.

This wasn't like her. She wasn't an unstable person. *Stop this.* She ripped a piece of toilet paper and blew her nose. *Get a grip. You can't change the past. What's done is done.* Her cheeks welcomed a splash of cold water as she rehearsed a return to the table without the drama of her exit. Steven said the boys wanted to hear about Angel. That's what she was here for.

Fresh lipstick did little to enhance her blotchy face, but it was all she had to work with. *What's done is done. You can't change the past.* Reciting her mantra, she stepped into the hall. . .and almost into Steven.

The compassion in his eyes brought the tears precariously near the surface again. *Breathe. Again.* She smiled, sure her casual act wasn't convincing. "Sorry about that." She kept her voice light, her tone implying she was just having one of those female moments men laugh about.

"Let's walk outside for a minute."

"I'm fine, really." The last thing that would help her lack of composure was a minute alone with those eyes.

"Come on." He held out his hand as a waiter walked by. She'd look foolish if she didn't take it. She put her hand in his.

He'd put on weight, grown a beard, his hair had grayed and thinned, but the feel of his hand hadn't changed. Strange that she could remember the sensation so clearly. Her thumb found the scar on his index finger. The scar she'd caused.

Steven winked and reached for the door handle. "It's still there. Reminds me of you."

The air was too warm to take the heat from her face. *Keep it light.* "Did it ever remind you to forgive me?" She cringed. Her mouth tasted suddenly sour. *What a stupid thing to say.*

He turned to her as they walked past the window where Toby and Griffin could easily see them. "That's what I want to talk to you about." His eyes seemed shadowed, darkened by the furrow between his eyebrows.

Not here, Steven. Let's talk about how you straightened the picture in my paper cutter. . .too late. And how I wrapped your finger in my scarf and you teased you'd never forgive me. . .right before you kissed me the first time.

She tried to extract her hand, but he didn't let go. "Steven. . ."

They passed Durty Gurt's, and Steven pulled her into an empty lot between two buildings. Letting go of her hand, he faced her. "I owe you an apology. I don't even know how to say it. But I need you to know. . ." He took her hand and pressed it against his chest. His heart hammered against her palm. "I need you to believe how sorry I am for what I put you through. I should have been the strong one. I should have had enough self-control for both of us. I've been angry the past two weeks, putting all this on you, but it's my fault you got pregnant, my fault you had to raise Angel alone."

Don't do this, Steven. Tears wouldn't listen to her commands to retreat. She looked up the street, wanting desperately to run. "Steven. . ."

"Can you forgive me?"

"I never blamed you. Never. We were both"—*so much in love*—"so young."

"I know," he whispered.

"Life goes on."

The hint of a smile graced his lips. "Can *we*?"

"If we leave the past behind."

"Okay." He released her hand. "Let's start the future with lasagna." The end of the finger with the scar touched the tip of her nose.

And made leaving the past behind impossible.

Chapter 9

"Mom? You'll never believe who called me."

"Just a minute, honey." Jeanie slipped the open phone in her apron pocket, set a ball of blue fondant on the dented stainless-steel table, and covered it with a towel. Brushing her hands on her apron, she took a shaky breath, smiled, and picked up the phone again. "I bet I can guess. Toby Vandenburg?"

"Yes! Mom, he's so sweet and funny and. . ." Angel sniffed and blew her nose in Jeanie's ear. "I feel like I've known him all my life. He's going to fly to Chicago to meet us as soon as we get home."

"That's won—"

Taylor walked in from the bakery, waving at her. "You've got company," she whispered.

"Just a minute, Ange." She held the phone against her chest. "Can't my mother handle it?"

Pigtails jiggled as the girl laughed. "Not hardly. It's your long-lost love."

"Tell him to wait in my office."

She lifted the phone to her ear. "That's wonderful. Wade and Toby will get along great."

"I hope so. Can't you just picture Christmas with all of us together?"

"Yes." *But I can also picture you with your new family. . .and me alone.* "Honey, I need to get going. Someone's waiting in my office."

"Okay. Room service will be here with our breakfast in a minute anyway. I love you and I'll e-mail pictures soon. Send us pictures of your cake when it's done. Hey, tell Taylor to call sometime, okay?"

"Sure."

"I want to tell her all about her brother's new brother-in-law."

And how fun it will be when we're all together for Christmas.

Jeanie swiped at a tear, said good-bye to her daughter, and slammed the phone onto the table.

❧

His beard was gone.

Jeanie grabbed onto the handle of her office door. He looked so much younger. "You. . .you shaved."

"Thought it was time for a change. Are you busy?"

"A little. I'm working with fondant. It's not very forgiving."

"Unlike me."

Why, oh why, had she chosen that word? Steven grinned. Dimples materialized.

Oh, those dimples. . . "I'm. . ." She swallowed. Her throat felt dusted with cake flour. "I'm working on the cake for the contest. I'm almost done."

"Can I see?"

Anything to get out of the room that seemed to shrink around them. She led him to the kitchen and pointed toward a two-foot-high cake with five layers in graduating sizes. Two layers were Wedgwood blue, three were white. She'd been working since before dawn on the painstaking task of forming tiny flowers and ribbons to cover it.

Steven gasped. "Wow. It's unbelievable. It looks like my grandmother's dishes."

"I got the idea from the china Angel and Wade picked out. The pattern is called Harmony."

"Nice name." The dimples came into view again.

"The one for the contest will have a lot more flowers and ribbons. I'm donating this one to the Veteran's home. I'll make another in a few weeks. The judges want pictures before the contest so Lucas is going to photograph."

"You never heard from Gretchen?"

"No. I didn't really expect. . ."

Steven nodded.

"And then I should be able to make the whole thing by heart. We can't use a recipe or pictures for the contest."

"Impressive. Can I watch you work?"

How could she possibly steady her hand to place miniature ribbons in exactly the right places with him watching? She shrugged, embarrassed in a way she hadn't been in years. She walked over to the sink and began washing her hands. "I'll have to ask you to wear a hairnet." That would make any guy run.

"It'll enhance my new look."

She dried her hands and took a hairnet and apron out of the cupboard and handed them to him. He tied the apron and stretched the net over his hair. Scarred finger pressed against his chin, he did a Shirley Temple–style curtsy.

Jeanie laughed and sat down. She motioned toward a wheeled stool on the opposite side of the table. What was he doing here anyway? "I just talked to Angel. She and Toby really clicked." She fought the image that popped in her head—Angel and her brothers and father posing in front of a Christmas tree. Without her.

"It sounds that way. Toby's planning a trip to see them next month. I imagine he's assuming his spineless father will kick in the cost of a ticket."

"And will he?"

"Of course."

She looked up from the fondant warming in her hand and forgot what she was about to say. Wedgwood. Steven's eyes were Wedgwood blue. She cleared her throat and picked up a rolling pin. "You're a good father."

"Thank you. It hasn't been easy. As you saw, I have one child who brings sunlight into a room and one who sucks it out."

She set the rolling pin on the fondant and began flattening it. "And a third who is all or nothing. . .sometimes black, sometimes white." Her voice came out as hushed as her thoughts.

"Does it bother you that we want to be part of Angel's life?"

"No." She picked up a cutting tool and cut a thin, wavy strip.

"If I were you I'd be hurting right now."

He could still see through her. She used to love the feeling, now it made her nervous. "I'm happy for her."

The room filled with silence until a timer buzzed. Taylor walked in, smiled her smirky smile, and put on oven mitts.

Steven waved. "How are you, Taylor? Has this lady got you working hard?"

Taylor pulled a pan of twenty lemon poppy seed muffins out of an oven. "I love the work. I was sure I wanted to be a party planner like Angel, but now I think I want to own my own bakery."

Steven laughed. "First get yourself through high school."

A sputter answered him. Taylor took out a pan of Morning Glory muffins and set them on a rack. "What I really need is a tutor for English." She walked toward Steven. "Do you ever tutor, Mr. Vandenburg?"

You little sneak. "Mr. Vandenburg is the school principal, Taylor. He doesn't tutor."

"You would, wouldn't you, Mr. Vandenburg, if it included a home-cooked meal? Ruby's going to teach me how to make Polish food and I need someone to practice on."

The dimples did an encore. "I don't really see how I could turn that down."

"Cool. Thursday night then. Six o'clock." The oven mitts flew onto a counter and the girl with the pigtails bounced out of the room.

Steven's lips pressed together. "A baking, party-planning, little matchmaker is what that girl's going to be."

"Not the subtle type, is she?"

"No. But I like the way she operates. She just gave me a segue."

"Into what?" A swarm of grasshoppers took up residence in Jeanie's stomach.

"Into asking you out. My teachers gave me a gift certificate for *Mark Twain and the Laughing River*. Have you seen it?"

"No. I've heard it's fun." A date with Steven. Could she? Should she? Could the demons of three years of her life stay sealed in her memory and never escape to undo what seemed to be starting all over again? Would Steven keep his eyes on their present and future and leave the past behind? She'd never know unless she said yes. "I'd love to see it. . .with you."

179

Steven drove into the driveway of the little white cottage feeling like a trespasser. He'd been here just once, and then only to throw pebbles at an upstairs window. To wake the girl who'd fallen asleep when she'd promised to meet him.

He parked, wiped his hands on his pant legs, and picked up the spray of white carnations and small pink roses wrapped in waxy green paper. He got out and stared up at the dormer window, wondering if little stones still lingered on the window frame. Transported, he hummed the theme song from *I Dream of Jeannie*, just like he'd done when she'd snuck out the back door in bare feet that night, hair tousled from sleep. . .and rushed into his arms.

Ruby opened the door for him, interrogating him with her gaze as if he'd arrived in a souped-up car to whisk her daughter to the prom. After a nervous moment, she smiled, mischief sparking in gray eyes. "Come in."

"Thank you." He handed her the flowers. *I come in peace.*

"You should give these to the cook. . .or the person you really came to see." The spark brightened.

He shook his head. "These are for my lovely hostess."

The tiny woman laughed. "Smart man. You have to get by me to get to my daughter. This time." She winked and ushered him into a steamy, heavenly scented kitchen.

Jeanie stood with her back to him, chopping vegetables. She turned, smiled shyly, and nudged Taylor. "Your tutor's here."

The girl turned around and waved at him with a butcher knife. "Hey, Mr. Vandenburg. Wanna help?"

Slipping out of his sport jacket, he unbuttoned one sleeve. "If it will help us get to your tutoring quicker."

Taylor's mouth opened. "That was just a joke." She gave a nervous laugh. "You knew that."

Rolling up his sleeve, Steven stepped next to Jeanie. For the briefest moment he let his hand rest on her elbow. "Hi."

"Hi." Her shyness was becoming.

He picked up a carrot peeler and aimed it at Taylor. "Maybe to you it was a joke. Teaching's serious business to me." He pointed to a stained recipe card. "*Golabki.* Sounds delicious." He wrinkled his nose.

Jeanie laughed. "Cabbage rolls."

"Is that what I smell?" *And what's that other smell?* Sweet, with a hint of vanilla. The woman beside him smelled like warm vanilla custard.

Taylor nodded. "It's in the oven."

He picked up another card. "*Adass.* What's that?"

"Vegetable salad."

He nodded. "So, Taylor, what if I wanted to make this recipe plus half again as much, how much mayo—"

"Huh-uh. You're not a math teacher anyway, and you know why I said the tutoring thing." A gleam lit her eyes. "The only math you guys should be doing is you-plus-you-equals-two!" With that, she hightailed it out the back door with the dog, giggling as she ran.

Jeanie sucked in her cheeks, widened her eyes, then released her cheeks with a popping sound—a face she'd once used just to make him laugh. Her shyness seemed to fade without the prying teenage eyes.

Without thinking, his arm slid around her waist. She didn't resist. "How can I help?" He whispered.

She lifted her face to him, the silly look gone. "It helps. . .just that you're here."

His knees felt suddenly wobbly. Leaning down, he brushed his lips across her hair. "It helps me, too."

☙

It was after ten on Friday night when *Mark Twain and the Laughing River* ended. As they walked out of the Trolley Depot Theater, Steven hummed a tune from the show and tucked her hand in his. They walked between two red and green trolleys. As Jeanie looked up at the green and gold Trolley Times clock, Steven grabbed her hands and swung her around. "Oh. . .the rhythm of the river is the rhythm of life," he sang. "And dum-de-dum-de something. . .the Mighty Mississippi is the heartbeat of the land. . . ."

Jeanie laughed and joined in, conscious that a stream of tourists heading toward their bus stared at them. When Steven stopped, she impulsively hugged him. "Thank you. That was wonderful."

"My singing or dancing?"

"The show." She laughed again and reluctantly pulled her arms away.

On the way home, they talked about their favorite parts of Jim Post's portrayal of Mark Twain. The drive took only minutes, making her wish they'd decided to walk. She put her hand on the handle of the car door. "Thank you. . .again."

Steven reached across the seat and held out his hand, palm up. She slid her left hand into it. His eyes held hers. The years, the separation, all she'd done to survive, faded in the intensity of his gaze. Leaning toward her, he touched his lips to hers.

She closed her eyes, felt the warmth of his lips, and kissed him back. Too soon, he pulled away, brushed his knuckles across her cheek, and reached for the door handle. His eyes stayed on hers. "Thank *you*."

Chapter 10

I could watch you all day." Steven leaned on one elbow, a white hairnet sitting at a rakish angle on his head. His smile warmed her more than the heat rising from the fryer.

He'd been watching her for almost an hour as she mixed dough for angel wings and ran it through the sheeter. With hands that moved with practiced speed, she took one end of a flat, rectangular piece of dough and pulled it through the slit near the opposite end. She reached for a box of latex gloves. "See? Easy." She pulled out a pair of gloves. "It's time to put you to—"

Taylor swung into the room, one hand hanging on to the door frame by the fingertips. "There's a man here to see you, Jeanie, and we're almost out of"—she took a huge breath—"*okregly chleb kartoflany.*"

Laughing, Jeanie stood, grabbed a towel, and wiped her hands as she walked toward the doorway. "I'll be right back."

Taylor shadowed her like a lost puppy. "Did I get it right? Did I say Polish potato bread?"

"It was perfect." She set the towel on the end of the counter. "I can't say it that good mysel—"

The man at the counter wore a black shirt. His black eyes zeroed in on her. "Misty. I was just passing through."

From behind, Taylor gripped her sleeve. "Who's Misty? The guy's creepy," she whispered.

With icy fingers, Jeanie patted the girl's hand. "Go keep Mr. Vandenburg company."

"But—"

"*Now.*" She stared at the man and tried to block out his name. The name she'd known him by wasn't Denny. "What do you want?"

"I'm managing the Mississippi Moon Bar at Diamond Jo's. Starting a little business on the side, and I just happen to have a job opening for someone with your. . .experience. Val always said you were the best. 'Persuasive girl,' he used to say." He fingered the pencil mustache. "Pay's way better than it was back in the day."

"I'm not interested." She pulled her shoulders back and forced herself to engage the evil black eyes.

"Then maybe I'll settle for just a little of your time."

"Get out of here, Damon. Get out and don't come back, or I'll get a restraining order."

"For what? For walking in here and offering you a job?" Ape hands landed flat on the counter and he leaned forward. "You know, Misty girl, everybody that's important to me knows what I did in Reno, and it's way too late for me to pay for it." One eyebrow rose into his dyed hair. "Can you say the same? How old's that daughter of yours now?" He laughed and walked to the door. "Think about it. . .*Jeanie.*"

The door closed behind him. He walked across the street to a black car with the top down. Jeanie's legs buckled and she grabbed the counter. Her breath came in ragged gasps. Her vision narrowed. Bending over, she willed herself not to faint. She couldn't let Steven see her like—*Steven.*

Everybody that's important to me knows what I did in Reno, and it's way too late for me to pay for it. Can you say the same?

Picking up the towel, she twisted it until her knuckles whitened. Pulling her shoulders back, she forced her trembling legs to carry her into the back room.

Steven looked up, Wedgwood eyes crinkling at the corners. "Everything okay? You look kind of—"

"Taylor, go watch the front."

Eyes fixed on the towel in her hands, she waited for Taylor to leave. "I'm. . . getting a migraine. I think I'll call Sue and see if she can come in." She couldn't look at him, couldn't hold up under the concern in his eyes. "Maybe you should go home." *Please.*

He stood and walked to her. His hands took her elbows. "What just happened out there?"

"Nothing. . .it's just. . ." She pulled away, but he didn't let go. "Life is complicated for both of us right now. I've got the contest coming up and you've got Gretchen and—"

"How in the world, after the time we've spent together this week, can you think for a moment—"

"She's in love with you."

His hands dropped. "Who was the man out there? Is there someone else?"

It was her only chance to turn him away. If he thought there was someone else. . . She started to nod, but couldn't follow through. "No. There's no one else. It's just. . .not working. We have fun together, but it's like we're trying to re-create the past. We're not the same people we used to be, Steven. Life goes on. I want to travel and teach and see the world. This just isn't a good time for me right now."

"You're not making any sense. Something happened out there." He reached toward her. "Talk to me, Jeanie. Whatever it is—"

"It's me. That's all. I shouldn't have led you on. It just suddenly came clear— I have to focus on the contest. I can't have any distractions right now."

Ripping off the hairnet, he stood. "You're honestly telling me your long shot at Paris is more important than us? You'd give up any possibility of us being together, being a family, just to see the Eiffel Tower?" He threw the net at her. "I could afford to take you to Paris every year. . .several times a year." He walked toward the door. "Or is it Paris with *me* that's the problem? Maybe you've got someone else in mind—"

"Stop it, Steven."

He brushed past her, bumping her shoulder, then turned. "I'm not a groveler, Jeanie. I just want to be sure I'm clear on what you're saying. When you say 'right now,' does that mean things might change in the future?"

The towel slipped from her fingers and hit the table. "Let's just be content with things the way they were, Steven."

≈❧

Content? Not a chance.

Steven threw a steak on the grill with all the finesse of a farm boy tossing a hay bale. A second slab of meat joined it with the same snap of his wrist. He'd already tenderized the chunks to within a half inch of their lives.

"Anybody home?" Burt's voice came from somewhere near the back door.

"Out here. Help yourself to a soda."

Through the screen, he heard the refrigerator open and close, then the freezer. Burt stepped onto the deck with a glass in one hand and his Bible in the other. "Smells good."

"You should probably take over. Your supper is taking the brunt of my frustration."

"Sit down and relax then. Only have to take the moo out of it for me. You want yours hot pink, right?"

Steven did half of what he was told, sitting on the edge of the picnic table bench like a hawk ready for flight. "Relax" wasn't in his repertoire tonight. "You know me well. Why can't I find a woman just like you, Burt?"

"You like 'em mean, ugly, and tattooed, huh?"

"I'd take mean and ugly if I found one who made sense."

"So you think it's a no go, huh?"

The bottom of Steven's glass thunked on the bench. "A week ago she came this close to saying she'd never fallen out of love with me." His scarred index finger paralleled his thumb. "I know she's feeling something—it's written all over her."

"But you gotta take her at her word. Can't force it."

"I don't know if I've got what it takes to wait around."

"So don't."

"Don't what?"

Burt stabbed a steak and flipped it over. Juices spit into the coals. "Don't wait. She's not the only trout in the sea. All you gotta do is get down on one knee and you got a good woman ready to wash your socks and warm your bed. If you keep waiting on the bird in the tree, you're going to lose the goose in your hand."

Steven's chest rose. An exhale billowed his cheeks. "Maybe you're right. It doesn't feel right, but that doesn't mean it isn't." Just because he didn't believe the finality of Jeanie's answer didn't make it any less true to her. "Gretchen's a good woman. A wonderful person. We have fun together."

Burt nodded. "Life ain't perfect. If you wait around for perfect, you miss the whole shebang. You don't want to spend the rest of your life. . ."

As Burt lectured, Steven rocked—the hammock. . .and his little corner of the world. "Guess it doesn't pay to sit around and mope until she comes up with an answer that makes sense."

"Now you're talkin'."

"Better to move in the wrong direction than not move at all."

Burt stopped, steak suspended in midair. "Now you're scaring me."

"Well. . .not necessarily wrong direction. . .but if I can't have the best, it's better to have something." Once again.

Burt nodded. "And a little competition can bring a woman to her senses faster 'n a bucket o' Gatorade."

ॐ

Hush, baby, hush. Shh. . .Angel. Just take this like a good girl. It's sweet, like a grape sucker. Please, baby. Take it and we'll go bye-bye. This time we'll do it—

A single knock. The door creaked. A silver tray. *Bread and water today, Misty girl. Bread and water for girls who break the rules. But I can get you something more. Anything you want. Ice cream? French fries? All you have to do. . .*

Angel tugged. *Stay here by Mommy.* Weak hands grasped nothing but air. *Come here, Angel. Now. Please.*

Fre-fries? Wide blue eyes pleaded, red-gold curls bounced as she ran to the man with the evil laugh.

Come to Damon, Angel baby. Damon has treats. The parrot arm stretched out. . .

"Angel! Stop!"

Sweat soaked, heart banging her chest wall, Jeanie sat up, fumbled for the light that would banish the dream. The clock read 2:52.

Throwing off damp covers, she swung her legs over the edge of the bed and stood. Skin cold and clammy, she struggled into her robe and walked through the living room to the kitchen, flipping on lights as she passed.

She opened the fridge, took out a carton of milk, and filled a cup. As she set it in the microwave, chills shook her. *God, what should I do?*

He couldn't hurt her anymore. Not physically. She would get a restraining order if he showed up again. But any legal action would require explanation, would loose the specters of her past. *Everybody that's important to me knows what I did in Reno, and it's way too late for me to pay for it. Can you say the same?*

Her mother, Angel. . .the truth would shatter their image of her, would hurt the bakery's reputation. Steven. . .a school principal couldn't be associated with someone like her. Once again, she had to hide the truth to protect his future.

Doubts hummed like the drone of the microwave. If they knew the truth, her past would have no hold on her. Damon would have no power over her. But she could lose her daughter.

The microwave beeped. She took out her cup and slammed the door so hard it bounced open. Telling Angel was not an option.

The truth will set you free.

Not this time.

Turning on the television for background noise, she dragged herself to the shower and went through her morning routine robotlike. When she bent over to blow-dry her hair, her arms ached from tension. The weight of the past two days exerted a physical pull. *Lord, be my strength, my guide. Show me what to do. I've lost Steven. . . .* Her chest shuddered with the next breath. *I can't lose Angel.* Over the rush of warm air, she heard the phone.

Only her mother would call at twenty to four in the morning. She flipped open her phone. "Morning."

"Jeanie? It's Steven."

The heat drained from her shower-warmed body. "Hi." Her voice was barely understandable.

"I couldn't sleep. I knew you'd be up." A long sigh followed. "I said I wouldn't grovel, but I guess I'm not a man of my word. I haven't got anything to lose, have I?"

He waited, as if wanting an answer to his rhetorical question. She couldn't speak.

"I promise I won't make a habit of this. Just hear me out."

"Steven. . ." Her eyes smarted with hot tears. "Please. . ."

He took a sharp inhale. "I know you're afraid. I'm not exactly sure why. You keep talking about how much we've changed. Of course we have, but what if we'd be even better together because we're older and wiser? What would it hurt to give it a try?"

Each word slashed like a blade. She couldn't listen to any more. "You have Gretchen. You have a good li—"

"I don't believe for a minute you have no feelings for me. I've seen it in your eyes. What are you so afrai—"

Her phone slammed shut.

Telling Steven was not an option.

Chapter 11

Lucas locked the jewelry store door from the inside and turned over the CLOSED sign. He pulled tinted shades over the windows and gestured toward a stool in front of the diamond case. "I charge two Morning Glory muffins and a turnover for each counseling session."

"Deal." Jeanie eased her tired body onto the seat and rested her arms on cool glass. Beneath tiny lights, the gems in the showcase shot brilliant prismatic flashes. "Diamonds are depressing."

His mouth twisted to one side. One white-tinged eyebrow tented. "Only for those who wish they had one."

"For this I'm forking over muffins?"

"You're here for pearls of wisdom. No guarantee they'll be pain-free." He opened a small half door and walked behind the counter. Taking a stool across from her, he folded his arms across his chest. "I won't push you for details, sweet pea, but I'm having a hard time believing you're capable of doing anything so bad he couldn't forgive you." His voice grew as soft as the velvet under the diamonds. "It's just not in you to do anything unforgivable."

Muscles in her belly contracted, pulling away from her blouse. "I did things. . ." She stared at a huge square-cut diamond. "You said you had something to tell me."

He rubbed the end-of-day stubble on his chin. "I. . .ran into Steven."

Her hands laced together on the counter. "Where? What did he say?"

Lucas simply looked at her, as if deciding whether or not to answer. After a moment he reached toward his back pocket and pulled out his wallet. "You accused me awhile back of being too chicken to try love."

"I was only—"

"I know. I wasn't offended, but I want to set the record straight." He took out a picture—a young woman, blond hair tumbling over her shoulders.

"She's beautiful."

"Her father was a multimillionaire. We met at a gem show and had a wild, romantic summer. And then *she* proposed and ruined everything. I couldn't see myself fitting into her world and I knew she'd be miserable in this little town, so I skipped the country. Spent a year with my grandparents in Wales to get over her." His eyes glistened with a faraway look. "About ten years ago I ran into her. She was married. . .to a very wealthy, very well-known man. Just like I thought she should be." Lucas shook his head and stared over her shoulder. "He was also a workaholic and an alcoholic who changed mistresses like most men change socks." His eyes bored into hers. "You know what she said to me? She said, 'I had one chance at happiness in my life and you took it away.'"

"Lucas. . ."

"If I'd believed her when she said she'd be happy here for the rest of her life, both our lives would have turned out so different." A sad smile bent his lips. "This little talk isn't about me. It's about you giving up your chance. . .and Steven's." He patted her hand. "Let him be the one to decide if he can accept whatever it is you did. Talk to him. . .and I mean *soon*."

≈

Holding the popcorn bag by one corner, Jeanie walked to the couch and picked up the remote. She'd rented *Australia*—a long, engrossing movie to get lost in. A drama to help her forget her own.

For three weeks she'd thrown herself into preparations for the contest, coming home only to sleep, leaving no unstructured time to dwell on "what ifs." If practice truly made perfect, she had the cake trophy in her pocket already. She'd tweaked her recipe and perfected her techniques until she could pipe petals and twist curlicues in her sleep.

If she actually ever slept. Stifling a yawn, she clicked PLAY. She hadn't slept more than three hours at a stretch since Damon showed up. He hadn't returned, but she had no illusions he was gone for good. The knowledge floated through every nightmare.

And Steven visited her few good dreams.

He hadn't called again. She knew him well enough to know he wouldn't, but that knowledge hadn't brought closure to her thoughts. How was he handling things? Did he have friends, a support system? *Let it go.* How Steven dealt with it wasn't her responsibility. For the both of them, life was back to the way it was before Angel's wedding. They'd both dealt with loss and loneliness. They could do it again.

Below her, the garage door opened. She walked to the window, parted the burgundy drape, and watched her mother roll the garbage can down to the curb. An unexpected sadness tightened her throat. Her mother had been widowed for twenty-one years. She had a daughter and granddaughter and dozens of friends who would be there for her as she grew older. But it wasn't the same as a husband who could share your memories, recognize your needs before you spoke them. Growing old would be lonely without—

Stop it! She closed the curtain and opened the popcorn bag, but the smell that wafted out only darkened her mood. Movie theaters, circuses, trips to the zoo—popcorn should be shared.

She shoved a handful into her mouth. She'd go nuts with thoughts like that. She pulled a cake decorating magazine from a basket next to the recliner and leafed through it. *I have things to do, places to go.*

What about after those things? After the contest, the teaching, the trips to New York and Paris. What about being her mother's age, pushing the garbage to the curb and returning to an empty house? She pictured Lucas, living alone, running a business alone, all because he hadn't taken a chance at happiness.

Steven. . . A surge of longing weakened her knees. His eyes. . .the way he'd looked at her when they stood in the empty lot. . .the way he'd touched her cheek. . . She couldn't think of anyone else she'd rather grow old with.

She reached toward the phone for the millionth time in three weeks. *Let him be the one to decide if he can accept whatever it is you did. Talk to him. . .and I mean* soon.

What if he *could* understand she'd had no choice? What if he could move beyond the horror of the truth? Steven's words nestled into her thoughts—*I haven't got anything to lose, have I?* She picked up the phone.

But what if he couldn't? She set it down. What if she told him everything and he walked away? It wouldn't be any worse than it was now. A groan of frustration echoed off the walls. This was the kind of behavior that sent people to padded cells.

Let him be the one to decide. Her hand inched toward it again. "Okay! I'll call hi—"

It rang.

She lurched away from it. Then, with jittery fingers, snatched it off the trunk. Maybe it was Steven. Maybe God was getting rid of her "what ifs" for good, taking the decision out of her hands. "Hello?"

"Jeanie? This is Gretchen Newman."

Gretchen? "Hi." Her brain bogged. "G–good to hear from you."

"Do you have a minute?"

"Yes. I was just going to sit down to watch a movie." *Or call Steven and tell him everything.* "It can wait." She rubbed her hand over her eyes and tried to focus her thoughts.

"Good. I just got off the phone with a chef friend from Indianapolis. Cookbook stuff, you know. Anyway, he mentioned he was entered in the Grégoire Pâtisserie contest and of course I thought of you and how I'd offered to take pictures. So I was wondering. . .you're still helping with the pizza sale next weekend, right?"

Maybe. If I find the guts to make that call. "No. I won't be able to after all."

"That's what Steven thought. But I've made up my mind to persuade you. I'd really love it if you'd come and help, and I have an idea. It turns out I'll be in the Midwest all week, taking puddle jumpers all over the place. If the timing works out for you, I could spend a couple of days with you and then we could drive to Chicago together and I'll book a flight out of O'Hare on Sunday night."

Jeanie let out a quiet sigh. "That's so nice of you, but"—*but being around Steven would kill me*—"I really don't think I could affor—"

"I wouldn't charge you, silly! Photography isn't work for me, it's passion. It would be fun."

It would be free. For professional pictures at no charge she could spend two days avoiding Steven, couldn't she? She had to get used to being in the same room with him. Once Angel and Wade got home there would be times they'd have to be together. Maybe going to Chicago would give her a natural opportunity to talk to him, to give him a chance to decide. . . "Thank you." She said it before she could come up with an excuse to refuse. "You have no idea how much this means to me. And the timing would be perfect."

"Great. I'll be there on Wednesday afternoon, and we can head to Chicago with Steven on Friday."

With Steven? Her hand clenched around the phone.

"I'm staying at the Hilton and Towers. You can bunk with me. Do you have room for me at your place? A couch would be great. If not, I'll get my usual room at the. . ." Gretchen rattled on, oblivious to Jeanie's panic.

"We have room." Taylor wouldn't mind two nights on the couch.

"Wonderful. You know, I just had this feeling about you when we met. Like we were soul sisters, you know. I can't wait till we can see each other all the time. I won't have to work, so once I get that house clean and organized I'll have tons of free time. We'll have to plan a weekly thing—we can take turns having lunch at each other's houses when I'm up there for good."

Weekly? Jeanie sank onto the couch. "For good? What do you mean?"

"Oh. I just assumed you knew. . . . Steven and I are getting married."

Chapter 12

T hat's w–wonderful. Congratulations." Popcorn rained onto the couch and tumbled to the floor.

"Thank you. It's crazy. Me, Miss Independent, giving up my career for a man. But Lindy was a full-time homemaker, and she set the bar high. She always had supper on the table exactly at six, and she ironed his shirts and even did the yard work. If that's what Steven wants in a wife, that's what he'll get. It's a small price to pay, don't you think?"

Jeanie's mouth parted. Her lips wouldn't cooperate. "Wh–when are you getting married?"

The giggle rattled her eardrum. "We don't have a date set yet—you know how Steven is. . . ."

Evidently I don't have a clue. "Uh-huh."

"But I'd love you to make our cake."

Eyes focused on nothing, Jeanie nodded.

"Jeanie?"

"Oh. . .yes, of course. I'd be. . .honored."

Gretchen made a funny little gasp that Jeanie couldn't decipher. "Jeanie?"

Please, please don't ask if I'm okay with this. "Yes?"

"Are you okay with this?"

Lord, forgive me, I'm about to lie. She sucked in a ragged breath. "Of course! Yes, of course. Congratulations."

"Thank you. I just don't want anything straining our friendship." She gave a jittery laugh. "After all, I'm going to be your daughter's stepmother."

The popcorn bag let out a *whoosh* as Jeanie crushed it into the couch cushion. Lifting it, she crunched it again before firing it at the TV. It dropped to the floor, leaving behind a greasy mark on the screen. Jeanie looked down at the matching stain on the cushion. "Gretchen, my mother just got home." *From taking the trash to the curb.* The statement was irrelevant, but at least it was true. "Congratulations again. Bye."

"Okay, bye. See you on Wednesday."

Not a chance. I'm going to be so sick by Wednesday.

&

". . .and how would you feel about green and gold for our colors?"

Steven switched the phone to his other hand, rubbed his sore earlobe, and took a glass out of the cupboard. He knew he'd be in trouble if he said "feel" and "color" didn't belong in the same sentence. "I don't think that would go over so well up here. How about blue and orange instead?"

"Steven. . ." Was that a gag on the other end?

He couldn't resist pushing it. "Let's reconsider. If we get married in Dallas we can do blue and silver."

"Oh. . .I get it, silly. We are absolutely not doing football colors."

"That's what people will think." He poured a glass of grape juice. "I know a few Bears fans who'll boycott the wedding if we do green and gold."

"Steven. . ." His name stretched out on an exhale. "There are a lot of shades of green and gold that won't make anyone think of the Green Bay Packers. You'll see. We are talking fall, right? October, maybe?"

"Sure." He opened cupboards, searching for something to sustain him until he could fix a real dinner. Gretchen had called at ten minutes to five. It was now five to six and Burt would be here any minute. On the bright side, she was speeding his weight loss. "I'll have four days during teacher's convention. I can tack on a couple more. I'll talk to the boys and see if that weekend works for them."

"Have you thought about a honeymoon destination?"

A box of Fiddle Faddle tumbled from the cupboard. Thankfully, the top was closed. He opened the waxy paper inside and poured a pile of caramel-coated popcorn on the counter. *Honeymoon.* The word painted images. . . . Laughing, whispering, sharing secrets. . . "You've ne—" He cleared his throat, coughed. What was wrong with his voice? "You've never been to the Black Hills, have you?"

Silence.

What did I do now? "Or. . .something else. Maybe something. . .resorty. Cancun?"

Gretchen giggled. "That sounds delightful. I actually just ordered you a Hawaiian shirt. I had a feeling you'd be thinking tropical."

Sand, sweat, and a flowered shirt. Steven threw a kernel of popcorn up toward the ceiling fan and caught it in his mouth. "I love those cute little paper umbrellas they put in your orange juice every morning."

"I know. Me, too. I'll get online and book something so we're all set."

But. . . He squelched the doubts with a toss of a glazed pecan.

"And Jeanie's going to make our cake."

The pecan hit his nose, bounced off the Garfield cookie jar, and hit the floor.

"I just talked to her. Not only that, but she's going to Chicago with us."

The Fiddle Faddle box tipped. Hard-shelled popcorn cascaded onto the tile. "You know. . ." His throat muscles contracted, but there was nothing there to swallow. "I really need to change into work clothes. Burt and I are mowing Emma's lawn and trimming her bushes this evening."

"Is Burt ever going to propose to that poor woman?"

"I don't think so. He's got it too good the way things are. He's got his independence and a woman to take to dinner whenever he gets a little lonely. He's happy."

"Well, I'm certainly glad you don't think that way."

"Yeah. Me—" His voice faked out again. He ran to the sink, turned on the faucet, and slurped water out of his hand.

"Are you okay?"

"Yeah, fine. Have a good night. I'll talk to you tomorrow."

"Okay. Bye. Love you." She ended the connection before he had to reply.

☙

Jeanie reread the e-mail from her daughter, plopped her laptop on the grease-stained couch cushion, and stomped into the kitchen. She stared down at the plate of spaghetti on the counter. The reheated supper that had made her stomach growl before the "You've got mail" *ding* now made her stomach twist in knots that wouldn't allow for food. Retracing her steps to the living room, she narrowed her eyes at the computer, wondering if it would cost more to replace the glass on the picture behind the couch or the window over the garage. If she had the money to replace the laptop, it would have sailed into one or the other seconds ago.

> *Hi from the Grand Canyon—*
> *Just got a call from Steven's (still not sure I can ever call him Dad) fiancée. She said you're going to Chicago with her. How are you doing with the news of their engagement? I wish I was there to see for myself that you're okay. As awkward as it is, we are all going to be family soon.*
> *Love you,*
> *A*

Jeanie strode back into the kitchen, pivoted, and walked into the bedroom. She had no idea what she was after when she got there. *We're all going to be family soon.* The mocking voice in her head wouldn't stop. The gall of that woman! Getting Angel involved was nothing short of manipulative. What was Gretchen's angle? Was she hoping to get a free wedding cake out of their "friendship"?

The bedroom mirror reflected a woman with both hands curled in fists and her jaw set in a tight straight line. *This isn't me, Lord. I don't do bitterness. I'm not an angry person. Help me move past this.*

Her walking shoes lay on the floor beside the bed. She kicked out of the Garfield slippers she'd bought on a crazy whim at a 70-percent-off sale. A good, fast walk could do wonders.

She covered the spaghetti and stuck it in the refrigerator. Maybe when her head cleared her stomach would be willing to accept supper.

Seconds into her therapy session, she heard her name shouted from across the street.

"Lucas! Hi!"

Carrying his sport coat over his shoulder, he crossed the quiet street and met her at the corner of Broadway and Meeker. "Trying out for the Olympics, sweet pea?" Deep lines framed his eyes.

"Working off a little steam."

"You? You're the epitome of calm and serenity."

"That was the old me."

Lucas's laugh rumbled across the cobblestones. "Had supper yet?"

She kicked a stone, sending it rolling into the bushes. "I fixed supper. Does that count?"

"Let me treat you to a carnivorous meal at the Log Cabin. Eating like a caveman is good for frustration."

Her eyes closed and she let out another in a long line of sighs. "Supper sounds wonderful, but could we go somewhere else?"

"Old memories?"

She nodded.

"Fried Green Tomatoes?"

"New memories."

"Girl, you can't escape memories in a historic town."

The laugh that bubbled up from some deep-down place surprised her. "Guess I should stop trying."

❧

Staring up at a little stone troll perched on a brick ledge at The Market House Restaurant, Jeanie finally felt her irritation ebb away. She looked across the table. "You're a good listener, Lucas."

"It's part of my job description." He laid his fork on his salad plate and pushed it to the edge of the table. "The more I know about a person, the more chance they're going to love what I design for them." He pulled a pen out of his shirt pocket and lifted his water glass from a cocktail napkin. "Here, I'll design a piece for you—as if I'd only met you tonight, based on what I've just heard."

"No! It'll be ugly. A black dagger piercing a heart or something Goth like that. Design something for the old me."

"Calm and serene?"

"Yes." She leaned forward and watched his pen arc across the napkin.

"A swirl of silver curves embracing a round diamond. . ."

Jeanie groaned.

"I mean sapphire." He looked up at her. "A round, ice-blue sapph—"

"Hi, Jeanie."

Steven stood three feet away. He was with a large man with tattoos on both arms.

Her brain misfired. For a moment she only stared. "Steven. Hello." She gestured across the table. "You know Lucas."

Steven nodded and some kind of silent communication passed between his eyes and Lucas's. "This is Burt Jacobs. Maybe you've met—he's older than most of the buildings around here."

The taller man held out a large, calloused hand, first to Jeanie. "Steven gets *wise* confused with *old* sometimes. I've been in your bakery a time or two."

"You look a bit familiar."

"I'm the 'two chocolate-covered donuts and a bismarck' guy." He shook Lucas's hand. "Don't think we've met."

"We could have. I'm the jeweler across the street from Angel Wings."

"Never had reason to darken the door of a jewelry store."

Lucas smiled at the men. "Why don't you join us for dinner? By the time we get to dessert I'll have a ring designed to match that skull and crossbones." He pointed to Burt's arm and pushed two chairs out with his feet.

Lucas Zemken, you'll pay for this.

Burt sat. "Thank you. I'm not into death symbols anymore, but we'd love to join you for dinner." He looked up at Steven with what could only be labeled triumph. "Take a load off, Vandenburg."

Steven seemed beyond reluctant as he took the only empty chair, to her right.

Act normal. She pushed aside her half-eaten salad. *We're all going to be family soon.* The unwelcome echo in her head caused her fingers to tangle on her fork. Metal clanged against glass, displacing a piece of lettuce and a grape tomato. "We've. . .already ordered."

"No problem." Burt waved down the waiter. "We'll have whatever they're having. Unless it's more rabbit food." He pointed at the tomato rolling toward him.

The waiter scribbled on his pad. "Two half-pound tavern burgers with fries. How would you like them prepared?"

"Just past the moo for me, medium for this guy."

"I'll get that right in. What can I bring you to drink while. . ."

The man's voice faded in the distance as Jeanie aimed her glare at the vines spilling over the stone wall. . .to keep from burning Lucas with it.

". . .since I became a Christian. Maybe you could design me one of those Celtic crosses. My family's from Wales—"

"Seriously? My father grew up in. . ."

Again, the sounds grew faint. Steven was looking at her. She put on her best smile. "Congratulations on your engagement."

"Thank you." He played with a button on his polo shirt. "Did Gretchen give you details on the pizza sale?"

This was not good. All that work to come up with a plausible excuse— she had to cook for her mother's Red Hat Society meeting that weekend—and Gretchen hadn't even told him about the message she'd left. "I. . .as it turns out, I won't be able to make it after all. I have to. . .cater. . .lunch for. . .a local organization next Saturday." *The local organization consisting of my mother and five of her friends.*

"Oh." Like a polygraph, his expression told her she hadn't pulled it off. But he seemed relieved.

"You have plenty of help, don't you?" The question came from her heart, not her brain, and slipped out of her mouth before she had time to override it.

A subtle shift transformed Steven's expression. "To be honest, we really don't. If you change your mind, I'd really appreciate it."

The blue gaze that had milked more volunteer hours out of Jeanie Cholewinski than any high school student had ever sacrificed for the literary digest was working its dangerous wonder once again. "Well. . ."

Their waiter approached, bringing burgers. . .and common sense. She suddenly knew what the subtle change had been: hope. And not because he needed more hands making pizza. Jeanie shook her head, not enough for Steven to see, but enough to clear it momentarily. If for no other reason, she had to say no for Gretchen's sake.

Lucas thanked the waiter. "Could we have a couple of extra plates? We'll share ours until theirs is ready."

Burt held up his hand. "I'll wait. Nobody wants to share mine."

Steven looked at Jeanie's plate. "Still medium-rare with tomato, lettuce, and mayo?"

Dumbly, she nodded. They'd never once eaten out together. "How could you remember that?"

"I remember ev—" He stopped and stared, first at Burt, then at Lucas. His face colored. The two men were silent and gawking.

With identically smug smiles on their Welsh faces.

≈❧

As Jeanie walked in the kitchen door, the *ding* sounded from her computer. She put her phone on the table, walked to the bedroom door, then turned around. Maybe this time it wasn't an e-mail from her daughter reminding her they'd all be family soon. Maybe it was from someone in her Bible study group. . .something newsy or encouraging that would get her mind off how easy the evening had been. Too easy, after the first few awkward moments. Too much finishing each other's sentences, and way, way too much familiarity from a man who was engaged to be married in three months.

She walked back to the couch and sat down.

Angel. Again. The subject line read *one more thing.*

Just thought of something. Why don't you bring Taylor to Chicago with you? That would save Wade's parents a trip. Maybe she'd even like to help with the pizza sale. Wouldn't her jabbering make a great buffer?

196

Buffer. Would a buffer be enough when what she really needed was a draw-bridge, a mote, and an iron shield?

But she had to learn to do this, to be around Steven and not just act okay, but actually *be* okay. With one last sigh for the day, she pulled her phone out of her pocket and went to the text message screen. She found Taylor's number in her Contacts list.

TELL YOUR PARENTS I'LL GIVE YOU A RIDE HOME ON FRIDAY.

That would buffer one day.

HAVE PLANS FOR SATURDAY? WANT TO HELP WITH A PIZZA SALE IN THE CITY?

She pushed SEND, closed the phone, then opened it again.

YOU CAN RIDE BACK HERE WITH ME—AND STEVEN—ON SUNDAY.

Chapter 13

"That was so thoughtful of you to make that scrapbook for Steven." Gretchen snapped a picture as Jeanie stuck a spoon in a Ball jar of home-made raspberry filling.

Ladling the filling into a sieve to strain out the seeds, Jeanie shrugged. "I thought it would help him"—*Help him what? See everything he'd missed?* She spread a circle of filling onto the last cake layer—"get to know her."

"I looked at the book last night. Angel is a beautiful young woman. Did something happen to her baby pictures or was it that you just couldn't afford them?"

Jeanie picked up another cake layer. "It was. . .a difficult time." *But I took pictures. So many pictures. . .*

Gretchen moved her reflective umbrella to the other side of the cake and took another shot. The last of the natural light through the high windows was quickly fading. "I can identify with some of what you went through."

I don't think that's possible. "How is that?"

"My husband was in the Navy. He was killed when his ship was struck by Iraqi missiles in the Persian Gulf. I was pregnant at the time."

The cake layer tipped precariously. Jeanie righted it and set it firmly in place. "I didn't realize. . .you have a child?"

Short dark hair brushed against large pearl earrings. "He was stillborn. The doctors thought the stress of my husband's death. . ." Soft smile lines appeared. "It wasn't meant to be. But I can understand the difficulty of going through a pregnancy alone."

Heaviness pushed against Jeanie's chest. "I'm so sorry, Gretchen."

"Thank you. That was a long time ago. And God uses everything for good, doesn't He? Like it says in second Corinthians, He gives us opportunities to comfort others in the way we have been comforted."

Steven. Gretchen had a bond with him she could never fully understand. "I'm sure Steven was very grateful to have you there when he lost his wife."

"We held each other up." Gretchen looked down and fiddled with the lens on her camera. "He and Lindy were there for me when Andrew died."

"How long have you known each other?"

"Lindy and I became friends at Texas State. I remember when she first started talking about this tall blond guy she met." The camera flashed again. "They were so happy together. But I wonder, now that I've met you. . ." She shook her head and removed the lens.

"Wonder what?"

"Lindy always said she could never have all of him."

Jeanie swallowed hard, picked up a new jar of raspberry filling, and set it down again. "What did she mean by that?"

"She knew he'd left a little part of himself somewhere in his past. I don't think he ever told her about you."

Picking up the jar again, Jeanie nodded. "I'm sure he was ashamed of our decisions and just wanted to forget."

Gretchen's lips pressed together. Small puckers formed at the corners of her mouth. "I don't—"

A knock at the front door rescued Jeanie from the end of Gretchen's statement. "Excuse me." Wiping her hands, she walked through the dimly lit shop and waved through the window at Lucas. She unlocked the door and opened it wide. "Come in."

"Can I watch the photo shoot?"

"Absolutely." *Thank you, thank you.* She led him into the back and introduced the jeweler to the photographer.

Lucas took Gretchen's hand in both of his. "So you're the woman stealing my chance at fame."

"Oh, I—"

Lucas laughed and pumped her hand. "Just kidding. I'm a very amateur amateur and Jeanie deserves the best." He let go of her hand and pointed to the camera on the table next to the cake. "Nikon F6. Nice." He picked it up, squinting as if he were looking at a diamond. "I've wanted a micro lens like this for years. I want to take my own pictures for my Web site. Do you like it?"

"Love it. It would be perfect for jewelry. . .if you have the right lighting." Gretchen pulled another lens out of her bag and handed it to him. "I'd be more than happy to take pictures for you."

"Well, next time you're up here, let me know. I'll see if I can afford you."

A laugh and a bounce of curls on pearls accompanied Gretchen's emphatic head shake. "No charge for a friend of Jeanie's. We're almost done here for tonight. I'd be happy to bring my equipment over when we finish."

"Tonight? Well. . .sure. I'd better go get things ready then." Lucas set down the lenses and took two steps toward the door to the shop. "But I will pay you somehow. Everyone needs the services of a jeweler from time to time."

Gretchen grinned. "Actually, I am in need of just such service." She waved. "We'll talk." She turned back to Jeanie, a wistful smile tilting her mouth. "I was going to say that I agree with Lindy." She turned and snapped a lens into its case.

≈❧

"You were up mighty early this morning." Her mother pulled a new box of bakery tissue out of the closet. "I heard you leave at three. Someone on your mind?"

"Some*thing*. Things." Jeanie set a fondant ribbon on the cake and stretched her neck. A headache was inevitable. "We're leaving at one. I have to have this done by ten so Gretchen can do the final shoot and then run home and shower and pack and—"

The door buzzer sounded. Her mother left to wait on the customer. Jeanie rested her hands on the table and closed her eyes. *Lord, calm me.* Anxiety over the next two days and stress from the past two had rubbed her nerves raw. Gretchen had been helpful, kind, and so transparent. The proofs she'd developed were stunning, and Jeanie was more grateful than she could put into words. But the constant chatter had worn her patience thinner than phyllo dough. *Help me to be gracious to her. . .and cautious with Steven. Let me be—*

"Jeanie." Her mother's voice reached the room before she did. "There's a man asking for you." Tiny creases rutted her mother's forehead. She turned around and walked back.

Jeanie's pulse skipped, then raced. *Damon.* By the look on her mother's face it had to be. She couldn't send her mother away like she had Taylor. What should she do if Damon called her Misty? Laugh? Pretend the man was crazy? Pretend. . . Her legs trembled from fear and exhaustion. She'd spent twenty-five years pretending three years of her life had never happened.

The truth will set you free.

At what cost?

Weighted legs carried her to the front where Damon stood with a white bag in his hand and two paper cups with lids.

Jeanie stepped to her mother's left. "What do you want?" She kept her tone flat, devoid of emotion.

Damon flashed false teeth in a smile that bowed his mustache and sent icy fingers down her back. "I was just chatting with your mom about this quaint little town and I got to thinking about that opportunity I told you about. It occurred to me that we could run a satellite business right here in Galena—lots of traffic running through here during tourist season. You could be our talent scout, so to speak." His laugh brought acid to her throat. Black, beady eyes chilled her. "Have you told your mom about the job I offered you?"

Her hand rose, closed over the wall phone. Her eyes narrowed, never leaving the evil face.

Damon lifted the bakery bag. "Sorry, *Jeanie.* Got to run. I'll talk to you. . . soon."

The door buzzed as the man in black walked out to the bleached blond waiting in his convertible.

Her mother grabbed her arm. "Who was that? How do you know him?"

Jeanie's head felt light. She couldn't think straight. "He. . .used to work with me. . .in California." *And Reno.* "He's thinking of starting a. . .business."

"What kind of business? There's something frightening about him. I don't think you should get involved with—"

"I have no intention of working with that man." She took a shuddering breath and gave a pretend smile. "I need. . .to finish."

On legs that felt like lead, she walked to the back.

❧

A shrill scream burst from the living room. Jeanie's pulse skipped. Her mother's favorite mug banged against the side of the suds-filled sink. She turned around. "Taylor? What happened?"

"I wish my mother would quit going all multiball on me!" Wearing tan shorts and a white T-shirt, Taylor appeared in the kitchen doorway, cell phone in hand. Sunny trailed close behind. "She isn't consistent on anything. First she's okay with me living here, then she thinks it would be better if I came home for good, then she says I should be home for the summer and maybe I can go to school here again in the fall. . .she's schizo."

"You just gave me a heart attack because your mother wants you home?" Jeanie made a noose with her thumbs and index fingers. "I oughta. . ."

"Hey, cool it. You're wound really tight today."

"I'm just a little. . .stressed." Her attempt at a laugh missed. She walked over and tugged on a pigtail as she opened the closet and took out a broom. "Did you ever stop to think that you might be the cause of your mother being a schizo? Maybe she's a little nuts because she's having trouble keeping up with you. Look at you. . . . When we first met you, your hair was two different colors and everything was pierced. A few months later and you're all earthy and back-to-nature girl. . . . You make *my* head spin."

"I'm working on myself. My changes are good. Hers aren't. We used to get along." Taylor stretched her arms over her head and touched the frame over the doorway. "Now it's just always. . .ugly. Maybe I should do her a big favor and just disappear."

The broom stopped mid-sweep. "You don't mean that."

Taylor lowered her arms and shrugged. "Did you and your mother ever fight?"

A laugh sounded from above the kitchen. "Still do!" echoed through the old iron grate.

"And mothers never stop sticking their noses in your business!" Jeanie tapped the ceiling with the end of the broom.

Taylor's nose wrinkled. "You guys have such a cool relationship. I could never goof around with my mom like that."

This time, the laugh was a duet between Jeanie and the voice through the vent. "Do you have any idea how 'cool' our relationship was when I was your age?"

"When you were sneaking out to see Mr. Vandenburg? Shouldn't he be here by now?"

"Any minute. Are you all ready?"

"Yeah. Can't we take Sunny?" Taylor kneeled down and wrapped her arms around the dog.

"Only if he can sit on your lap for three hours."

"Cool!"

"I was kidding."

"So did Mr. Vandenburg have hair like MacGyver?"

"No, he had a neon pink Mohawk and he wore leather pants with chains."

"For real?"

"No." Jeanie ignored the tongue sticking out at her as she swept under the table. "He was a student teacher. He dressed very respectably." *Except for the jeans and sleeveless Ocean Pacific shirts he wore after school. . .after dark. . .*

"I heard a car door. I don't have to sit in back with Gretchen, do I?"

"Of course not, she'll sit in front with Steven. She's his fiancée." *Keep saying it, maybe it'll seem real.*

"Good. That lady's loony. I mean, she's nice, but she's loony. I was so glad when she left this morning. She talks like nonstop. My head was spinning."

Oh, how I know the feeling. "She means well. Her metabolism's just set at a higher notch than some of—"

The screen door squeaked open. "Sorry we're late." Gretchen stepped in wearing white walking shorts and a yellow blouse trimmed in rhinestones. "We were looking at rings. Practically had to drag that man into the jewelry store. Men! Lucas was so accommodating. I'd love to just sit and watch him sometime. He asked so many questions. I think he should teach classes to men, don't you? Most men don't know how to ask the kind of questions that make a woman think he's genuinely interested. Taylor"—Gretchen pointed at her—"look for a man who asks questions. Not that you should be looking yet, but when you're older. Maybe you should look for a jeweler! I know more about diamonds now than I ever dreamed of. I'm leaning toward a princess cut. Something different, you know. Everybody ready?"

Jeanie shot a warning at Taylor as the girl's eyes rolled toward the ceiling, down to the left, and back to the ceiling.

As ready as we'll ever be.

❧

"Have these kids had any kitchen experience?" Jeanie directed the question to the middle of the front seat between Steven and Gretchen.

"Some." Steven looked at her in the rearview mirror. Did he have to do that? "They're all at least sixteen, and the shelter is teaching them basic job skills for working in restaurants, hotels, school kitchens, things like that. They're all kids who've expressed an interest in that kind of work, so they should be cooperative and teachable. But they come from dysfunctional backgrounds. You may find some who won't say a word and some who won't shut up."

Taylor's index finger jabbed into Jeanie's forearm, then pointed toward Gretchen.

"Shush," Jeanie breathed.

Gretchen turned and looked over her seat. "They make me uncomfortable. I got the feeling last year that they didn't trust us. They know we've never experienced anything close to the kind of life they have."

If only that were true. "I went on a couple of inner-city ministry trips to Mexico with our church years ago. I've never done anything like that in the States, but I think kids must be kind of the same all over."

"Mexico City?" Steven's eyes rose to the rearview mirror.

"Yes."

Gretchen reached back and touched Jeanie's knee. "*Ciudad de México*. Isn't it an amazing place? The National Palace, Morelia Cathedral, Teotihuacán—The City of the Gods. And the food. . .what was your favorite?—"

"Well, actually. . ."

"She was there on a mission trip," Steven said. "She probably didn't get much chance to sightsee or taste the cuisine."

"Oh. . .I suppose that's true." Gretchen pulled her arm back and turned around.

Taylor's hand slid over her mouth. "Awkward," she whispered.

Jeanie looked down at her watch. Two hours and thirty minutes left.

Lord, help.

Chapter 14

I love squishing it with my hands." A'isha, an eighteen-year-old who was seven months pregnant, held up a ball of dough in her latex-gloved hand.

"It's called kneading," Gretchen corrected.

"Whatever. I *knead* to squish this stuff!" A'isha took a clumsy bow when her friends standing around the table laughed. A boy with black dreadlocks stuffed into a white hairnet threw his dough to a gangly kid with pants in danger of ending up around his ankles. Three more dough balls took flight.

Jeanie glanced at the next table. Steven's group worked like a well-trained assembly line, spreading pizza sauce and sprinkling cheese. Her thumb and fingers went to her mouth and a commotion-freezing whistle split the air. She had their attention. Shaping her hands into a catcher's mitt, she called across the table, "Throw it to me, A'isha."

The ball flew. She caught it and held it up. "Okay, we got rules here. No throwing dough unless you can *throw* dough. Everybody watching?" She dumped a cup of flour on the table, smoothed it out, and set the dough on it. Quick motions pressed it down and formed an edge. With a rolling pin, she flattened it and shaped a new edge. Picking it up, she stretched it over upturned fingers, her hands vibrating.

"You can't really do what I think you're gonna do!" Blue eyes wide, a skinny girl in a hot pink shirt gaped.

"Everybody watching?"

Taylor covered her face with her arms.

The thin, wiggly sheet flew into the air. The dough circle spun three feet above her head and landed over the backs of her hands. The table exploded in applause and whistles.

"Show me!" "Do it again!" "I wanna do that!"

"Me, too!" This was not the voice of a teenager. Steven stood just inches from her left elbow.

Jeanie took a step back. "O. . .kay. Turn your hands over and alternate them with mine."

His hands slid into place under the dough, touching hers. Blue eyes glimmered. "Make me look good, Dreamy."

This was not the time for vibrating hands. But she couldn't control it. "Twist one arm to the outside, just a little, like this. The other arm pulls back slightly. Feel it?"

"Mm-hmm." Dimples indented his cheeks and warmed hers.

"Then throw up your hands. . .and stop. The fast stop is what tosses it in the air. Up and stop, and catch it with the backs of your hands. Got it?"

"I think so."

She dipped her hands from under the dough. Steven's arms flew up and halted. The dough sailed off his hands, across the table. . .and hit the little blond girl squarely in the face.

Cheers filled the kitchen. Jeanie doubled over laughing and Steven bent with her. His arm slid around her shoulders, pulling her into a quick hug.

She knew she should push him away, but for the moment she couldn't remember why.

≈❧

Taylor slipped two unbaked pizzas into the commercial freezer and took two more pans from Nevin, a basketball player-sized boy who seemed to be taking a liking to her. Taylor smiled at him, and Jeanie's fingers tightened around the package of cheese she was sealing. She'd have to keep an eye on those two.

Nevin pushed an empty roller cart toward the wall and Taylor nudged Jeanie. "So why does he call you Dreamy?"

Jeanie glanced across the room where Steven and Gretchen were washing dishes with a group of kids. At that moment, Steven turned around and smiled. Just the way he used to back when he'd told her he had radar that detected her every move in class. "'I Dream of Jeannie' kind of got shortened."

Taylor batted starry eyes. "That's so romantic."

"That's so corny. Get your head on straight, kid." She nodded toward Nevin.

Taylor shrugged off the warning. "It's romantic and you know it. That man's still crazy nuts about you and his woman's figuring it out."

"Hush. What do you mean?"

"Didn't you see her when we were making pizzas? She was eyeing you two up one side and down the other. Didn't you see her walk out?"

"No. Was she. . .mad?"

"More sad, I think."

"I have to talk to her."

Taylor's nose crinkled. "Why? Won't change the truth."

Nevin handed two more pizza trays to Taylor. "We're done. Let's get a soda."

"Okay." Taylor looked up, and up, until her eyes locked on his.

Just stay in plain view. Jeanie tried to catch the girl's attention for another warning glance, but to no avail. She watched them grab sodas from an ice-filled tub and sit on the floor, their backs to an open shelf, their feet against the wall. *I'm watching you.* She picked up four unused bags of cheese and hugged them to her chest, wrapping her arms around them. As she opened the door of the walk-in cooler with full arms, she knocked a massive padlock from its shelf. It skittered like a hockey puck into the cooler. She shelved the bags, and as she got down on all fours to retrieve the lock, her own radar picked up Steven's scent. Not cologne, not deodorant, but the scent of *him*. She steadied her breathing and stood up.

"We need to talk."

Her arms folded against the chill. "About what?"

"I can't do this, Jeanie. I can't. . .be around you. What happened earlier. . . hugging you. . .it's too automatic, too easy to fall back into what we used to be. I can't do this."

I can't either. But with Gretchen within earshot, this wasn't the time to talk. "We're adults, Steven. We can do this. Someday we're going to have grandkids, and we'll both be there for birthdays and dedications. We have to be able to be in the same room with each other. We need to move on. I'm going to Paris to finally start living my life." The tear that slid down her cheek startled her. "You're getting married, starting a whole new—"

His hand slammed against a metal shelf. "I'm getting married because you won't admit you're still in love with me."

She froze. Like a key with just the right notches, tumblers turned, unlocking the truth. *Lord. . .* She stared into penetrating blue eyes. *It's time.* Even if Gretchen was around the corner. She closed her eyes. "Steven. . ."

"I can't do this friends thing, Jeanie. I don't want to go to Angel's house and see you there. I don't want to do holidays together like some big happy family. I don't want to be around you. Do you understand?"

Muffled laughter from the kitchen made the moment surreal. Steven stared, as if memorizing every inch of her face in the light of the single bulb hanging above them. Slowly, he shook his head.

"Steven. I have to tell—"

He held up his hand. "Don't say anything." He turned and walked out, his steps echoing across the tile.

"Steven! Wait!" She followed him into the kitchen. "Let me—"

Gretchen walked out between two rows of shelves. Her hand reached out and slid into his and they walked together up the stairs.

❧

"Are we ever gonna get done with this?" Tess, Steven's dough target, threw an empty pizza sauce can in the trash. "I'm too tired to breathe and I gotta come back and work all day tomorrow sellin' this stuff."

"Take off. I'll finish this." Jeanie formed her lips into a smile. "See you in the morning, Tess." *If I'm here.*

The girl waved and Jeanie picked up a plastic tub of olive oil. Thoughts ricocheted as she walked toward the shelves. She had to decide, once and for all—walk away from Steven, protect her pride and Gretchen's happiness, and never look back, or force Steven to listen as she poured out every last little detail and leave the decision to him.

Walking between two ceiling-high open shelves, she found the marked spot. As she slid the tub of oil into place, she heard Taylor's laugh. She leaned toward the voices.

". . .serious. You got the perfect look—tall and thin with great skin and beautiful features. The right hair and makeup and you'll be a goddess. You'll be making a hundred grand by Christmas, no lie. And think what this could lead to. Clothes, cars, jewelry, and all you gotta do is smile and pose and sometimes be somebody's arm candy. Rich guys pay big just to have some gorgeous model to show off at a party."

Jeanie clamped both hands on the shelf. She had to hear more before she acted. No, she had to do more than hear. She opened her phone, dialed her home number, and set it on a salt box on a low shelf. At that moment, Steven walked past the end of the shelf. In two quick steps, she grabbed his shirtsleeve and put her fingers to his lips. Cupping her hand around his ear, she pointed and whispered, "Listen."

". . .sixteen. My parents wouldn't allow it. Maybe after high sch—"

"You just said you're sick of your mom freaking out on you and changing her mind all the time. You gonna do what your parents say forever? Think about all that jewelry and stuff. Think about how proud your parents will be when you send 'em megachecks. There might not be an opening in two years and besides, you got the look now. It'll change when you. . .you know, mature. Right now you got what my boss is looking for."

"I don't know. . ." A sigh was followed by a tapping sound, like fingernails on tile.

"Gimme a week, okay? Come with me and give it a try. See if you don't love bein' a rich girl."

Jeanie's stomach muscles spasmed. She put both hands over her mouth.

"I came here with Jeanie. What do I say to her?"

"Nothin'. She'll figure you're with me. You know, like you and me got a thing for each other. . .which we do, right?"

The shelves towering over her seemed to tilt. The space between them grew narrower. *Hide. Find a place where he can't find us.* Her hands slid to her eyes, to stop the black spots. Steven stepped closer. He pulled her hands away from her face, his eyes searching hers. She looked down, found his phone clipped to his belt, and pulled it off. She turned off the sound and dialed 911, then set his phone beside hers. Pointing to the end of the shelves, she motioned for him to go around one end while she went the other way. "Act casual," she whispered against his ear.

She waited until she heard him say, "Hi, guys." Nice and calm. Did he have the slightest clue what was happening?

She squeezed between the wall and the end of the shelf. "I heard you offering Taylor a job, Nevin."

The boy squirmed, drew his long legs up to his chest. "Yeah. I think she'd be a great model. . .when she grows up."

"But you said—"

Nevin shot Taylor a silencing look.

Jeanie smiled. Nice and casual. "Modeling job. . . Your boss sends you out on the street looking for pretty young girls, huh?" She raised her voice, hoping she'd be heard on the other end of the phone on the shelf.

The boy's eyes darted toward the door leading up to the street.

Jeanie crossed her arms, leaned down close, raking him with her eyes. "It's a prostitution ring, isn't it, Nevin? Recruitin' right here out of the kitchen at the Twenty-Fourth Street Mission. Clever."

邊

Steven's pulse hammered in his ears. He stared at the woman he once knew, interrogating a man a foot taller than her like a seasoned cop.

"Don't get all fidgety. I'm not ratting on you, Nevin." She laughed, leaned against the wall, and folded her arms. "Your name isn't Nevin, is it?"

The boy didn't move.

"Yeah, I didn't think so. I used to go by Misty. Seems we're in the same line of work."

What?

"What?" Taylor's eyes popped wide.

Jeanie flung her braid over her shoulder. "Well, I'm retired, but I used to do just what you're doing. They call you a recruiter?"

Nevin shook his head. "I'm a scout."

Taylor gasped. Steven crouched down and pulled her to him, never taking his eyes off Jeanie. She was amazing, playing the part as realistically as any Hollywood actress.

"They gave you some pretty good training. You're smooth. Me, I had to learn on the job." Her eyes turned to steel. Fingernails pressed into her arm. "So what got you into this line of work, Nevin? Hey, what's your real name? You know mine."

"Craig." His voice was barely audible.

"Craig. Now that fits you. Sounds like a basketball player. So what was it got you into this?"

"My brother. He's making good money."

"I bet he is. What's your brother's name?"

"Wil. . ." He stopped, looked from Jeanie to Steven. "I gotta get out of here." He jumped to his feet.

Steven stood, pulling Taylor with him. He was at eye-level to the boy's Adam's apple, but he put his hand on his arm. It was his turn to take part in Jeanie's charade to stall him. "We're kind of like Taylor's guardians right now,

Craig. I imagine we could get a pretty kickback if we let her work for you. What guarantee do we have that she won't get hurt?" Taylor tried to wrench away, but he held her tight. *Play along, kid.*

"I don't. . .I don't know. I just find 'em. It's not my business what happens after that."

Jeanie took a step toward him. "Really? They should give you a promotion, Craig. When I was in the business I wasn't just a recruiter, I was a chauffeur."

Transfixed by her skill, Steven almost smiled. The woman was good.

"Got to transport the girls, see them settled into a nice, cushy mansion. Had my own room there, too. Gold faucets. You got gold faucets, *Nevin*?"

"No. *No.*" He pulled his arm from Steven. Jeanie grabbed his elbow. The boy raised his arm and swung, slamming Jeanie into a metal grate covering a window, and took off at a run.

Another set of footsteps echoed in the hallway, then more. "Police! Stop!"

Steven held his breath, waiting for a gunshot, but silence followed. He dropped to his knees and wrapped his arms around Jeanie. "Taylor, reach through there and grab my phone." As she did, he pressed Jeanie's head to his chest. "Are you okay?"

She nodded against his shirt and wrapped her arms around him.

"Everything I said before, forget it," he whispered against her hair. "I can't *not* be around you."

Chapter 15

She hadn't been held like this in so long. Again, the voice that said she shouldn't be allowing this clamored too distantly to obey. All that mattered was the moment. Steven's voice reverberating in his chest as he spoke to the dispatcher. . .the smell of him, musky, earthy. . .muscles forming ridges on his forearms. . .his fingertips brushing a rhythm on her shoulder.

If, after all he'd just heard, he could still hold her like he never wanted to let her go, maybe she'd been wrong. Maybe she didn't need to keep her guard up. Maybe, for the first time in thirty years, she could stop pretending. Her ugly secret was exposed. . .to the one person who had the most right to judge her. . . and he hadn't pushed her away.

Her hip throbbed, her elbow stung. Her leg tingled from the awkward position. Yet she felt more at peace than she had in years. As if she could finally take a full breath. She closed her eyes, letting the stroke of his fingertips push away the pain, the fear, and anger that had coursed through her veins moments earlier. She pressed her cheek into his shirt and let out the breath, long and slow.

She was safe.

Steven closed his phone. His left arm completed her circle of safety. "Paramedics are on their way."

She nodded. Words might break the spell.

"You were amazing," he whispered.

"Yeah. That was wild." Taylor's cold hand slid over hers. "Was all that stuff really true?"

"Of course it wasn't!" Steven's laugh echoed beneath his ribs.

Her diaphragm locked, lungs half full. Her chest shook with the thudding of her heart. Sparks of silver light pricked her eyes. Numb, as if she were watching someone else's body stiffen, she pulled back, looked up into cobalt eyes. "It. . .it is true. All of it." She moved away, opening the circle.

An airy whistle blew through Taylor's pursed lips.

Steven's hands tightened on her arms. "I don't. . .understand."

Could she possibly make him see? Make him feel the fear? Taste the hopelessness? A siren wailed. She lifted her hand, laid it against his cheek. "I couldn't—"

Taylor jabbed her leg.

Eyes red, fingers covering her mouth, Gretchen stood at the end of the shelf. "Are you all right?"

As if touching live coals, Jeanie's hand drew back. Steven dropped his hands to his thighs. "We're fine. Taylor was in trouble and we—"

"Good. Good." Gretchen nodded, eyes now glassy, and ran out of the kitchen.

୧୫

Jeanie woke on Saturday morning surrounded by purple pillows. Angel's apartment. Angel's *old* apartment. She closed her eyes again as a strange heaviness pulled her into the mattress. Why was she so tired? She turned toward the clock and gasped. Hot needles shot from elbow to shoulder.

Stitches. The ER. They'd given her a sleeping pill.

Nevin. As of midnight, they hadn't caught him. He'd be far from the city by now.

The apartment was quiet. Pug had told her to sleep as late as she could. She'd offered to take Taylor to the pizza sale.

The pizza sale! She should be there. She opened one eye, searching for the clock. Almost nine. The sale had started. But she was going home today, taking a bus, wasn't she? Wasn't that what she'd decided? Her thoughts slowed. No, she was going to talk to Steven. Her eyes closed; once again she was circled in his arms. So warm, so safe. . .

He knew! Her eyes shot open. Steven knew. He'd disappeared when the paramedics arrived. She had to explain. No matter what—even if he refused to ever look at her again—he had to know she hadn't chosen that life, had to know she'd tried to escape, tried to get back. . .to him.

But would he even listen?

Ignoring the pain that taunted her whole right side, she pulled on her clothes and called a cab.

୧୫

The sidewalk in front of the Twenty-Fourth Street Mission swarmed with people carrying pizza boxes or shouting orders at the harried teens behind the table.

"Jeanie!" A'isha waved her toward the cash register table. "Hey, come here a sec."

Her hopes of quietly talking to Steven evaporated. "How's it going A'isha?"

"Fine, but. . ." The girl shifted her pregnant weight from one foot to the other. "Could you take over for a minute? Everybody's busy and I gotta. . .you know."

"Sure." Jeanie laughed and shooed her on her way as a dark-skinned woman with graying hair held up two frozen pizzas and a twenty. Jeanie shoved aside A'isha's pile of soda cans and candy wrappers, uncovering the price list. "That'll be eighteen dollars." Jeanie entered the amount and reached in the drawer for two singles.

"Keep the change." The woman waved at the money Jeanie held out to her. "I lived here once. Wish I could do more."

As she waited on three more customers, a man stood at the edge of the crowd watching her. A Cubs hat sat low over mirrored sunglasses. He wore a long navy tank top over shiny white shorts that ended mid-calf. To a person without any street sense, the man would just blend with the crowd.

To a person who'd spent three years of her life watching her back, a stationary man in a milling crowd triggered alarms. The man moved into line, the only person empty-handed. His head turned with her every move, his mirrored eyes trained on her. *Hurry, A'isha.*

Two people stood between her and the man. Who was he? Nevin's boss? His brother? What did he want with her? He was too late to stop her from talking. She'd already given a statement. So had Taylor. Taylor. . .where was she? She whirled around, but couldn't spot her. . .or Steven. She counted out change with trembling hands. *Run.* She fought against instinct. She wouldn't leave the money unguarded. The man wouldn't do anything in public. *Where's Taylor?* Something nudged her arm. She jumped.

"I'm back." A'isha rubbed the sides of her belly. "Hey, that was wild about Nevin, huh? Were you really. . ."

The man moved to the head of the line. A'isha's voice faded in the thick air. *Run.*

This time she did. Through the maze of portable freezers and darting kids, over the roadblock that fenced out customers, up the steps, into the cool shadow of the crumbling brick building.

The door stood open. She flew in, down the steps, into the kitchen. "Taylor!" Where was she? "Taylor!"

Tess ran out from between the shelves. "What's wrong?" Her pale faced grew instantly paler.

"Where's Taylor?"

"She went to the store with that lady. . .Gretchen."

"Thank God."

"Why? What's. . ."

Footsteps slapped the stairs. Jeanie's gaze swept the room. *Hide. Find a place.* The cooler. She ran to it, heaved the door open, and darted in. Grabbing the inside handle with both hands, she braced her feet. On the other side of the door, someone yelled. A man's voice. The handle moved. She strained against it. It wrenched out of her hands. She opened her mouth to scream.

Steven stood in the open doorway.

Her gasp froze in her throat and air rushed from her lungs.

He took a step toward her. "What hap—"

The door slammed behind him. Something clanged against it. He turned and pushed against the handle.

It wouldn't budge.

☙

"No signal." Steven stuck his phone back on his belt and pounded on the door.

As he yelled and pounded, Jeanie turned in a slow circle, hunting for anything to cover her bare arms.

"We're trapped!" Steven's voice strained on the second word.

A dim memory floated through the chill air. She'd snuck out after midnight. They'd met in a field. It started to rain, and she'd pulled him into an old rusty horse trailer. But he wouldn't let her close the door.

Steven was claustrophobic.

Maybe it was the residual effects of the sleeping pills, or maybe it was the layers of irony—that she, who felt snug and secure in small, dark places, was locked in a cooler with a man who was terrified of them. Whatever the reason, Jeanie began to laugh. So hard she had to grip the metal shelves on either side of her.

Steven turned and gaped at her. "Are you out of your mind?"

"Maybe," she gasped. "Probably. I'm s—sorry."

His back pushed against the door, his finger ran under the collar of his polo shirt. His face flushed and his chest shuddered. If she didn't distract him, she'd be locked in a cooler with a man in a full-blown panic attack. The vision sent the muscles on her sides into spasms again. She spun around. A plastic milk crate full of apples sat in the far corner. She dumped it, sending apples rolling across the floor like pool balls. "Sit down."

He complied. She turned around again. Another crate sat on a low shelf, this one filled with cottage cheese containers. As she emptied the crate, she said, "Well, at least we won't go hungry. Are you hungry?" She overturned the empty crate and stood on it, eyeing the top shelves. "If I ran a shelter with a ton of kids around, I'd hide the good stuff up high, wouldn't you? Ah! Chocolate!" She reached between two boxes and pulled out a basket teaming with candy bars. She jumped down and sat on the crate with the basket on her knees. "Three Musketeers? No, wait, do you still like Snickers?" Still digging through the basket, she held it out.

He didn't take it. She looked up. His eyes were closed; his head shook. The tip of his tongue was held firmly with his teeth. She waited. His eyes finally opened. A faint smile took the fear from his eyes. "I'd forgotten just how crazy you made me," he whispered. A drawn-out sigh lowered his shoulders. "You always knew how to make me smile."

But this isn't me. I haven't felt silly like this since. . .you. "Steven. . ." She set the basket on the floor. "I need to explain about yesterday."

"One crisis at a time. First explain about today. Was that guy following you?" He described the man with the mirrored glasses.

"Yes. I'm guessing he's Nevin's brother."

"Then it's no accident we're locked in."

She shook her head. "There's a padlock." An involuntary shiver shook her.

"You're freezing." He stood up, walked to the back, and held up two huge flour sack towels that had been covering pans of bread dough. Next he found two mesh bags of oranges. Pulling out a jackknife, he opened the ends and dumped the oranges on the floor. "Hold out your arms." He worked for several minutes, fashioning towel-lined sleeves. "Should help a little. They'll find us soon."

"Thank you." She folded her red mesh-covered arms across her middle. "You're very resourceful."

"It's nothing compared to what you pulled off yesterday." His eyes didn't reflect the touch of humor in his voice. "You've got a captive audience, might as well put the time to good use and talk. I could say it's none of my business, but I just can't quite bring myself to say that. How old was Angel at the time you had that. . .job?"

She turned away from the interrogating eyes, willing the door to open. "I was pregnant when I started."

A ring of white outlined Steven's lips.

"I'd been at Aunt Freda's for two weeks when I found out I was pregnant. I knew I had to get out of there before she found out. I couldn't take a chance on her telling my mother. I told a waitress at this coffee shop that I needed a job. She introduced me to a guy who was looking for someone to care for his handicapped mother. His name was Val. He said he'd pay for my food, clothes, give me a room of my own."

Steven's fingers curled in toward his palms.

"The job was exactly like he said. He took me to a very classy-looking building in Reno. I had a beautiful room, an unbelievable paycheck, and a charge card for anything I needed. All I had to do was clean his mother's apartment and fix her meals. She was a sweet lady. The only drawback was I had to be with her 24/7. But I figured I'd have enough money to leave long before the baby was born. It was all wonderful, until the end of the first month. That's when Val suddenly turned on me. He accused me of using the charge card on things he hadn't authorized and said I was getting fat from eating his mother's food. He said I had to work for him until I paid off my debt. And if I didn't, they'd do something to my mother." A shudder shook her shoulders.

"So he made you. . ."

"No." Her eyes blurred. "Angel saved me. When I told Val I was pregnant he hit me. Said he'd 'fix' that problem himself if he had to. Then one of his guys quit. Val decided a pregnant woman would look trustworthy, so he trained me as a recruiter instead of putting me on the street." She stared at Steven, knowing full well that if she kept watching his reactions she wouldn't be able to finish. "I learned to spot runaways and girls who looked like they came from bad homes." She turned away, reading the label on a gallon jar of catsup as if the words mattered. "I used the 'taking care of grandma' routine on some. Sometimes I told them I lived in a shelter run by rich people and they could have a room and three meals a day. . ."

A guttural sound from Steven pierced through her. "Why didn't you run? All you had to do was call me. I would have gotten your mother in victim protection. I would have come after you. Maybe I really didn't know you at all. The girl I knew wouldn't have been capable of—"

"Steven. The girl you knew vanished the day they threatened your baby."

Chapter 16

Steven felt the cold seeping through his shirt as her words entangled him, pulling him into the desperate web that had trapped her—in a locked, windowless room at night, with the threat of losing her child by day. She hadn't once been allowed to leave the building with Angel.

"I got rewarded for following the rules. Toys, baby clothes, a camera, and access to the kitchen. I made cookies for the girls. I know it sounds crazy, but in my head it was a way of making amends. They all knew what Val was holding over me. They all said they would have done the same thing to save their baby. Even though I was the one who'd brought them there, they'd hide Angel and me when Val went into his suspicious rampages. We were like family—we didn't have anything but each other."

When she'd fought against the bondage, she was beaten. Twice she'd given Angel cold medicine and tried to smuggle her out in a backpack. Both times she'd been caught, tied to a chair. . .

"They took my pictures. I had so many pictures of Angel. . .for you."

Steven's fingernails dug into his hands. He wanted to hit something, break something. He pictured the kind of sick, evil men who would snare innocent girls and trample their bodies and spirits until they were nothing. *God. . .why?* "Jeanie. . ." He breathed her name. And something flashed in his conscience. "I'm so, so sorry." *If I hadn't touched you, if I'd walked away when everything in me knew it was wrong. . .* "If I'd been the man I should have been, none of that would have happened."

"Don't. I meant what I said—I've never blamed you." The bags rustled as she raised her hand and rested it on his cheek.

The last vestiges of anger against her evaporated in the warmth of her touch. His hand slid over hers.

She blinked, dislodging tears. "You and Angel were what kept me going, kept me fighting. I begged God to protect us and bring us back home to you." She pulled her hand away and swiped at her cheek. "He did protect us, sometimes miraculously. And He brought us home. . .just not to you."

His chest shuddered with each breath. "How old was Angel when you came home?"

"It was two months after her third birthday."

His throat contracted. He'd married Lindy five days before Jeanie turned twenty-one. He remembered the August morning in Hawaii he'd slid out of bed and walked alone on the beach. *Happy Birthday, Dreamy. Do you know I still love you? God forgive me, but I always will. Be happy, girl. Wherever you are, be happy.* "I talked to your mother. . .twice. I called once, pretended I was a friend from school. She said you'd decided to stay in California and go to Stanford. I called and sent letters, but they had no record of you. Then before I asked Lindy to marry me I flew back here and worked up the courage to walk into the bakery and ask your mother where you were and how you were doing. She said you had a successful career in California as a buyer for a department store."

Jeanie raised her shoulder, using it to wipe her cheek. "I called her whenever I was out recruiting. Everything I told her was a lie. I couldn't take the chance that she'd call the police. If they went after Val, he might do something to Angel. So I made up a life. I told her about my job and my friends. I pretended the girls I lived with all worked with me at Saks. The lies came so easy as time went on."

"How did you escape?"

"Somebody finally did what we all wanted to. Val took a bullet and died on the way to the hospital. I was pretty sure which one of the girls did it—I think we all were—but even the police didn't ask too many questions. They were rid of him and we were free. I bought a bus ticket and came home. I showed up at the bakery at closing on a Friday night. Until that moment my mother didn't know she had a grandchild."

Without conscious thought, Steven reached out and touched her damp cheek.

She pulled away, her eyes fastened on something beyond him. "I talked to your mother, too."

"*What?*"

"I called the high school, pretended I'd loaned something to you and wanted it back. It wasn't a lie—I wanted you back." A sad smile bent her lips. "They gave me the only number they had—your parents' house in Dallas. So I called and talked to your mother and said I'd been your student. She told me you'd been married for seven months."

He'd spent three years consumed with hurt and anger, trying to find her, then hoping he'd never see her face again. He'd spent a year getting drunk, acting like a crazed man. And then he met Lindy. . .and the Lord. . .and everything changed.

And all the while Jeanie and Angel were fighting to get back to him. *Lord God, I don't understand. . . . Why?* "Jeanie. . ."

She fiddled with the mesh at her wrist. "We can't change the past. I try so hard to never think about how things could have been, but sometimes the regrets just swallow me up. I believe with all my heart that God has forgiven me. But it doesn't change what I did. I look back and I think there must have been something I could have done. Maybe I should have run and left Angel behind." She looked up, eyes raw and searching. "If I'd taken my own life I could have spared a life of slavery for those girls."

"Jeanie. . .hush." His arms went around her. This time she didn't fight him. "Don't talk like that. If you hadn't done it, they would have found someone else. You were protecting Angel. You had to cooperate. You had no choice."

Cold fingers clutched his shirt. She pressed her face to his chest. "Is that what I was supposed to do? Look what God asked of Abraham. So many people got hurt because I wasn't willing"—her shoulders heaved—"to sacrifice my child."

A deep, mournful sound ripped from his throat. His fingers dug into her hair. He pulled her away so he could see her face. His conviction came from his gut, not his theology. "Questions like that will drive you insane. God was there, through all of it. He could have intervened. He could have stopped that man. We may never know why He didn't. But He did answer your prayers. In His time. He protected you." He lifted her chin. "And He brought you back home. . .to me."

Tears ran, her head shook. "But I figured it out too late."

"It's not too late." He lowered his head, his lips finding hers.

Two hands pushed against his chest. "You can't. You're engaged."

"Not for long."

"What?"

"I'm breaking it off."

Her hands stiffened against his chest. "I won't be the cause of you hurting that woman."

He smiled, feeling a twinge of guilt for the peace he felt. "Like it or not, you are the cause. But I decided yesterday—right after I told you I couldn't be around you—that I had to tell her. I would have broken it off even if there was no hope for you and me."

Grooves rippled Jeanie's forehead. "I'm so sorry."

"Sorry? That's not the reaction I expected."

"Sorry for her, I guess."

"It was my fault. I wasn't being honest with her or myself. I should have admitted weeks ago that I was using her to get back at you. I should have called off the engagement because I can't do to her what I did to Lindy—I can't give only part of me. And I can't go another day pretending I don't love you when the truth is I never stopped."

He leaned in, wanting nothing more than to kiss her. But the hint of fear in her eyes stopped him. All the times she'd said they weren't the same people anymore—now it all made sense. He couldn't wrap his brain around everything she'd just told him, couldn't put himself in her place and imagine the fears her captivity must have spawned. His lips skimmed her forehead. "Where do we go from here, Dreamy?"

❧

As naturally as if they hadn't skipped a beat of thirty years, she closed her eyes and lifted her mouth to his. "Right here," she whispered, losing herself in his response. The room was no longer cold. Her arms circled his chest. Too soon, he pulled away. The tip of his nose touched hers. "I love you."

She shivered. *I love you.* Why couldn't she say it? Why, now that she was in his arms, hearing the words she'd longed to hear, couldn't she say them back to him?

Reasons cascaded like rainwater. Because the words resounded like the clink of the padlock on the other side of the door. Because they were supposed to be followed with promises like *forever, unconditionally, no matter what*, and she suddenly felt like George Bailey in *It's a Wonderful Life.*

It's crazy. Me, Miss Independent, giving up my career for a man. Supper on the table. . .ironed shirts. . .yard work. If that's what Steven wants in a wife. . .

Misty, just do as you're told, follow the rules. Be a good girl and Val will treat you right. Don't I always treat you right, Misty girl?

Jeanie ran her hand across her eyes, dispelling the voices. Freedom. It was hers—and Steven wouldn't ask her to give it up. She could have him *and* the future she could almost taste.

He smiled down at her. "And where do we go from *here*?"

"Someplace warm." She shed the irrational fears like she would a sweater, if only she had one to shed.

He took her hands in his. "Let's stop for soup on the way home."

She soaked up the warmth of his skin. "Think we can get hot chocolate in July?"

"We'll have fun trying."

She nodded, teeth chattering. This she could do, this easy banter. "Fun is what we need. Let's start over the right way—getting to know each other, doing fun things. Fun *warm* things."

He laughed then abruptly stopped. "Do you like beach vacations?"

His serious expression made her want to laugh. Was this a test? If she didn't like the beach he'd ditch her? She thought back to the mansion, crowded on the veranda with the other girls, Angel at her feet, out of earshot from Val or Damon, waiting for the sun to lower and desert cool to take over. They'd talked for hours about dream vacations. "Well. . .I love the water. . .but I hate heat. An Alaskan cruise, the fjords in Norway. . .I'm afraid I'm not a tropics kind of girl."

"I'm so glad to hear that." A grin split his face. "Do you remember all the places we said we'd visit when we were free?"

Free. She'd forgotten that one. *When we're free to be seen in public together. When we're free to date. When we're married and free to do what we want.* If only she'd known at the time how free they'd really been. Free to talk on the phone, free to walk barefoot in the grass. Those were things she didn't take for granted now. "I remember all those books you checked out. . .the pyramids and Mexico City and Neuschwanstein Castle." What she really remembered was planning a

219

European honeymoon they knew they'd never be able to afford. "But I used to dream about simple things. . .going to the Farmers' Market together, renting a canoe, walking down Main Street holding hands, or just having a picnic."

"So next weekend we'll go to the Farmers' Market and buy food and rent a canoe and paddle to a picnic spot. And the week after that we'll go to Germany. . . or Egypt."

"Right." She smiled at the sparkle that lit his eyes. "The week after that I'll be in New York for the contest." *And then, if my dreams come true, Paris for a year . . .or more. Will you wait for me, Steven?*

"Oh. . .yeah."

"Will you come with me?" She touched her fingertips to his cheek.

He copied her gesture, his fingers warming her face. "Whither thou goest I will go."

"I'll need a cheering sec—"

"Jeanie! Are you in there?" Taylor's muffled yell, pounding, and the rattle of keys ended with a *clunk* as the door swung open.

Taylor stood in front of the janitor, a uniformed policeman, and A'isha. Her eyes opened wide. "Mr. Vandenburg!" Her right hand "high-fived" the air. "Yesss. Sah-weet. I knew you guys would figure it out."

Behind them, another face joined the picture framed in the doorway.

Gretchen.

Chapter 17

"Cool outfit." Taylor pointed to the mesh bags on Jeanie's arms. "Guess what. They got the guy who locked you in here. He ran off with the key and when the cops caught him, he said he was planning to come back and mess your face up for snitchin' on his brother."

Jeanie listened with one ear as she peeled off the sleeves. The rest of her senses concentrated on the nonverbal conversation between Steven and Gretchen.

"And because you called 911, the police have a record of Nevin saying his brother was involved in the ring so the guy is toast. Man, I can't believe I didn't read that creep Nevin, or whatever his name is, with all his flatterization. But you were on to him like. . ." Taylor's words slid under Jeanie's radar as Steven maneuvered around the crowd at the door. He reached toward Gretchen with one hand, but she shook her head and stepped back.

The officer motioned for Jeanie to walk out. Still shivering, she stood in the kitchen and answered his questions. When he finished, he turned a page in his notebook and walked over to Steven. Leaving Jeanie to face Gretchen. Alone.

Lord, what do I say? Gretchen, I'm sorry I just ruined your future. She took a step toward her. A sad, half smile told her Steven had already told her they were through.

"Gretchen. . ."

Gretchen lifted one hand, fingers splayed. It bounced slightly as her face crumpled and a sob shook her.

Jeanie did what seemed the right thing and totally wrong all at the same time. She walked over and wrapped her arms around Gretchen's heaving shoulders. "I'm sorry. So sorry."

Strangely, Gretchen returned the hug. "I cou–couldn't."

Jeanie patted her back. "Couldn't what?"

Gretchen pulled away, mopping her face with a tissue. "I can't go on like this." Red eyes blazed. "I love him. . ."

"I know."

"But I'm just not *in* love with him."

"What?"

Gretchen blew her nose. "We have so much in common. I thought that was enough. We have good times together. You know how he is. . .he's wonderful, but there's no passion, no sparks. He's just not an emotional man. I had to drag him to look at rings and planning a honeymoon was like pulling teeth. It all came to a head yesterday when I saw him playing with those kids. That's who he is. . . he's a teacher. He's happy doing stuff like this and that's great. But it's not me." She pulled another tissue out of her purse. "I want adventure—somebody who wants to see the world and be spontaneous. I'm not Lindy. I've tried, but I just can't imagine being happy as a housewife. Am I being selfish, Jeanie? Ohh. . ."A whine accompanied a stamp of one green tennis shoe. "I know I am. My timing is so awful—breaking up with him right after you two were locked in there. . .that must have been terrifying."

"We. . .managed."

"I hated to hurt him, but I had to tell him. I just. . .want more out of life." She sniffed and hiccupped. "Is that wrong?"

Jeanie covered her mouth with her fingers. "No. It's not wrong. Not wrong at all. Steven will respect you for being honest."

"What will I do?" The voice approaching her from behind didn't sound like a man who'd just been jilted.

Gretchen reached out and touched his arm. "Jeanie says you'll respect my honesty. I hope you can. . .someday."

A tempered smile lifted Steven's lips. "I can. . .if you promise we can stay friends."

"Oh!" Fresh tears sprang. "Of course." Her damp cheeks rose in a smile. "Can we just rewind? Back before things got. . .complicated?"

Steven nodded. "I'd like that."

"And Jeanie, I meant what I said about being friends. You'll probably move off to Paris after you win the contest and meet some cute French guy, but I hope we can stay in touch no matter what happens."

Jeanie allowed a quick look at Steven's dancing eyes. "I promise, Gretchen. We'll stay in touch. No matter what happens."

⁊❀

The studio lights were hotter, the live audience and competitors far more intimidating than she'd imagined. Her back hurt, her ankles were puffy from hours on her feet. But the creation next in line for judging was the most exquisite she'd ever fashioned: six alternating layers. . .four reflecting the Harmony china pattern, two in stark white with panels of scalloped lace.

Yesterday, the judges had rated the taste and texture of the cakes but kept the results a secret. All day today they'd wandered between the contestants, asking questions, tasting frosting. Their expressions had given nothing away.

The emcee handed her a microphone, and Jeanie prayed her tired voice wouldn't give out. She cleared her throat. "The original inspiration for 'Wedgwood and Lace' was a trip to the Neiman Marcus china department with my daughter before her wedding." She smiled and made eye contact with each of the seven judges as she spoke. "As the idea evolved in my mind, I pictured high tea at Neuschwanstein Castle, the palace that inspired the creators of Disney's

Magic Kingdom. I wanted something elegant, timeless—Wedgwood china and eyelet lace—with just a hint of whimsy, which I added with the spun sugar teacups on top." Discreetly, she wiped a damp palm on her white coat. "Embedded LED tea lights in the top layer make the glasslike strands glisten. . ." She hated her artificial, tour guide voice, but it was all part of the process.

As she talked, the judges nodded, jotting notes on stainless-steel clipboards. After she finished, silence reigned for several torturous minutes. The emcee told her to sit down. She took the empty seat next to Steven. His hand engulfed hers and bounced on his jiggling leg. He was as apprehensive as she was.

She watched the stony faces of the men and women who held a part of her future in the scores on their clipboards. Two more chefs with cakes, each unique and delicate, underwent the judges' scrutiny.

The emcee stepped in front of the audience. "We'll take a break while the judges tally scores and come to a decision. When their deliberation is complete, I'll ask our chefs to join me here for the results."

"Let's go outside." Steven pulled her on weak legs to a side door where they walked out into a courtyard with umbrella tables. Tiny white lights sparkled in the trees around the perimeter. Lilies floated in a lit fountain.

As exhausted as she was, she couldn't sit. "What's your gut feeling?" She nibbled on the corner of a fingernail.

"That you're beautiful." He gently pulled her finger away from her lips.

"Steven." She laughed in spite of the band of petrified muscles surrounding her rib cage.

"My gut feeling is yours is by far the most magnificent, clever, and awe-inspiring creation in the whole place. Before you know it you'll be off to meet some cute guy in Paris and that"—he wiped her damp finger on his shirt—"will be that."

She stared up into blue eyes that made her dissolve like the sugar she'd melted and spun. "The only cute guy I want to meet in Paris is you."

His smile faded. "I'd be able to visit once if I'm lucky." His lips skimmed her cheek, his breath tickled her ear. "We don't have to talk about that now. I want you to enjoy this moment."

"But you're secretly hoping I won't win, aren't you?" She said it teasingly, but there was more than a smidgeon of truth in her question.

Steven's shoulders rose and he let out a long sigh. "You know where I stand. I want the best for you. But the best for you is going to cost—"

A bell chimed and the emcee stepped in front of the fountain. "The judges have made their decision. Please join us for the awards ceremony."

ॐ

Steven took a seat, held his breath, and tried to pray for God's will. In truth, he wanted his own. A year in Paris would change her. She might actually meet the cute Frenchman Gretchen had laughed about. If she did come home after a year—and he had no assurance she would—she wouldn't belong in Galena anymore. She'd be overqualified for just about any position in the whole state of Illinois. Steven rubbed a hand over his face and confessed to the real bottom line—he'd lived without her for almost thirty years, but this next one could be the hardest of all.

The emcee opened the first envelope in slow motion. Holding the card in his hand, he stopped for a melodramatic pause then announced the third-prize winner. It wasn't Jeanie. Nor was she the second.

Steven tried to breathe but only managed a few nervous gulps of air.

"As you know, tonight's winner of the Grégoire Pâtisserie contest will receive—thanks to our sponsors—an Ideal Revolving Oven, a Richlite table, and. . .a year in Paris, which includes three months at Bellouet Conseil and a nine-month apprenticeship under renowned pastry chef Michel Moreau."

The breath he'd been holding increased in volume.

"And the first place winner of this year's Grégoire Pâtisserie contest is. . . representing Angel Wings Bakery in Galena, Illinois. . .Jeanie Cholewinski!"

Cameras flashed; the audience clapped.

Steven copied the man two seats down. He stood, he clapped, he smiled. He pretended to breathe.

⁂

"I can't believe it. I still can't believe it." Jeanie took her boarding pass from the attendant and talked to Steven over her shoulder. "Can you believe it?" Under-rested and over-coffeed, she felt like a speedboat out of control. She'd been jabbering since she'd met Steven in the hotel lobby at five thirty this morning. *Paris! I'm going to Paris!*

"I told you you'd win." His voice sounded more tired than hers.

After they were settled in their seats, she turned to him. "You didn't really sleep much, did you?"

"Not much. All the. . .excitement." He pulled a magazine from the seat pocket in front of him.

"Steven." She took the magazine out of his hands. "Tell me what you're thinking."

Loosening his seat belt, he turned to face her. "I'm thinking that I love you, Jeanie." His voice was strained. "I'm thinking that you leaving for Paris in a month is going to put a major kink in our relationship." He picked up her hand. "I am *so* proud of you. You're gifted and determined, and I think you can do just about anything you set your mind to. But even though I'm happy for you, I'm having my own little pity party here." He squeezed her hand, sat back against his seat, then back up again. "Okay, here's gut honesty. It's not so much that you *are* leaving me that's hard to take, it's that you *can* leave me. Does that make sense?"

She stared out the window at the boxy ground vehicle pulling two baggage trailers. "I need to do this, Steven." She turned back to him. "I know it's selfish to ask you to wait for me, but it's a chance of a lifetime, and if I give it up I'll—"

His lips stopped her and for a moment she wondered if she had it all wrong. If Steven were the only chance of a lifetime that mattered.

He pulled away and rested against the back of his seat. "We'll get through this. I promise I won't be a pain. I won't guilt you or mope around or make your life miserable. I'll adjust and I'll be genuinely happy for you."

"Thank you."

"And until you leave, I'll take up every minute of free time you're willing to share."

Free time. She rested her head on his shoulder, closed her eyes, and smiled.

❧

She belonged in Paris. Steven stood back and let Jeanie walk on ahead. Market Square swarmed with tourists, locals, artists, and venders selling produce and baked goods. But, like a smitten teenager, he had eyes only for the woman in the woven straw hat.

Though he'd begged her to wear it loose, her hair hung in a soft braid that caught the sunlight. A red-orange dress covered in blue swirls and tiny flowers floated around her ankles like poppies in the wind. Skinny straps showed off the tan she'd gotten just in the past two weeks. She could easily pass for someone half her age.

And she was his. Well, almost. Between LaGuardia and the Quad City Airport, in the midst of his traveling pity party, he'd made a decision. He needed to support her dream like he'd promised, but in the time he had left, he'd do everything in his power to make her want to come back, to make leaving him absolutely miserable. And if she changed her mind about leaving altogether, well, he might have influenced her decision, but she'd have to admit for the rest of their lives that it had been her choice to stay.

They'd brought Angel's dog to the Farmers' Market. Jeanie looped the leather end of Sunny's leash over her wrist as she held a jar of honey up to the sunlight. As Steven chastised himself for not bringing a camera, a woman walked past with a plastic-wrapped canvas.

"Where did you get that?"

The startled woman pointed toward a table set up next to an old buckboard wagon with red wheels.

"Thank you." He strode toward Jeanie, pulling a ten-dollar bill out of his wallet as he reached her. He paid for the honey and grabbed her by the arm. "This way. Trust me." He took the leash from her.

Her laugh was anything but trusting. He led her to a booth where a man with a leathery face sat in front of an easel. On three sides of him were trays of charcoal, chalk, and a rainbow of pastels.

"I want a sixteen by twenty portrait of her."

"Steven!"

225

He ignored her protest. "Just sit there and be beautiful."

The man extended his arm toward a chair. "I agree. I promise it will be painless."

Jeanie made a face but sat down. Her cheeks colored in a very flattering way. "Hat off or on?"

"On." *I love that look.* He turned away. Keeping a respectable distance was getting more and more difficult. In need of frequent pep talks to refresh his convictions, he'd called Burt three times this week. *Lord, be my strength, my shield.* He turned back. Smile lines formed soft brackets around her mouth. He stood in silence for the next few minutes as her likeness materialized on the canvas. The portrait captured every nuance, right down to the perfect shade of brown for her eyes. "This is going to hang over the fireplace."

"Isn't there something there already?" She spoke stiffly, her expression not changing.

"My great-grandmother. I'll stick her in a crate and ship her to Griff."

The soft smile morphed into a grin. "He'll be so hap—" Her smile froze. Eyes widened.

"What's wrong?" He looked past the artist. A man in a black shirt stood behind a white pillar on the porch of the Old Market House, smoking a cigarette. Staring at Jeanie. "Who is he?"

Perspiration glistened on her top lip. A vein pulsed on her neck. "Someone. . ." Both hands closed into white-knuckled fists. "Someone I want you to meet." She looked at the man with the easel. "Excuse us. We'll be right back." She stood, her shoulders squared with the same kind of confidence he'd seen in her Friday when she confronted the boy at the mission. She held out her hand, and Steven took it.

As they walked toward the man, he shifted his weight to the opposite foot and seemed to visibly shrink. He wiped his forehead with the back of his hand. "We meet again, *Misty.*" He leered at her.

Sunny growled.

"For the last time, Damon." She raised their linked hands. "Steven, this is Damon. He's the man I told you about—the one who stood outside my door for three years, who fed Angel bread and water if I broke the rules."

Steven felt his grip tighten on her hand. His heart hammered his chest, his eyes burned as an unfamiliar rage boiled to the surface. Sunny strained against his leash. Hair bristled below his collar. Steven wrapped the handle twice around his hand.

"Damon's the reason I slept with a spiked shoe under my pillow and—"

"You're delusional." Muscles raised under tattooed feathers on his arm. A parrot. It looked somehow evil. "You got me confused with somebody el—"

"Shut up, Damon. You've got nothing to hold over me now. I don't care who knows what you and Val forced me to do."

The man glared, threw his cigarette at the ground, mashed it with the sole of his shoe. "I have no idea what you're talking about."

Dropping the leash, Steven took two steps.

The man ignored him. "You know, Misty girl, I'm g—"

Steven's fist shot out and smashed the leering smile.

Chapter 18

Won't ask any questions." The portrait artist reached into a cooler and filled a plastic bag with ice. As he handed it to Steven a smile roughened his craggy face. "Guy sure looked like he needed more 'n a sock in the jaw. Nobody called the cops, so must be everyone thought the same." He gave the plastic-wrapped picture to Jeanie. "Take care of your tough guy here."

"I will." She tucked the picture under her arm. "Thank you. You do amazing work."

"Amazing subject makes it easy." He pointed at her face. "'Course you had a sight more color to work with before that scuzzbucket showed up." He tipped an imaginary hat. "Hope the rest of your day is uneventful."

As they walked toward Perry Street, Jeanie leaned on Steven's arm. She closed her eyes for a moment, wishing she could banish the echoes of Damon's laugh as he stumbled off the porch, covering his chin with his hand. She shivered.

Steven put his arm across her shoulders. "You okay?"

"No."

His arm tightened around her. She felt his chest rise. A long, slow exhale followed. "I hate to bring this up. But do you think there's a connection between this guy and the kid in Chicago?"

"No." She'd turned it over in her head so many times since talking to the police about Nevin. "I think it's just a coincidence. Or a Godcidence, as my mother would say. I keep wondering what God's trying to show me."

"Maybe that you have the power to do something about it." He stopped next to a trash can and threw away the ice bag. He ran his fingers along her cheek. "You should report him."

The cold from his hand coursed through her. She hadn't really meant what she'd said to Damon. She did care who knew about her past. If she reported him her testimony would be public record. Her statement would comprise more than Damon's present. It would also include her past. "He's just starting his. . .business. There might not be enough evidence yet."

"Let the police figure out the details. If you give them a heads-up, they can be watching him. Jeanie, who knows but that you have come to this position 'for such a time as this'? If you remain silent. . ."

She turned from his searching eyes, leaving his paraphrase of the verse from the book of Esther hanging between them in the heavy August air. They turned north at the corner of Commerce and Perry. "Let's leave the picture at the bakery and go get some ice cream."

"In other words, let's change the subject."

"Yes." She slipped the handle of the leash onto her wrist and reached in her purse for her keys. When they reached Angel Wings' side door, she turned to Steven. "I can't even think about talking to the police until I've talked to Angel. She'll be home in a week."

"And then?"

And then. . .nothing. Telling Angel would be hard enough. . .and maybe something she'd avoid altogether if the three people who already knew would agree to leave the past where it belonged. Making her story public record was not an option.

She unlocked the door. The sweet, yeasty smells that had backdropped her life greeted her. "Then, we'll see."

∂❦

His hand hurt, but it wasn't altogether a bad feeling. He'd never in his life punched a person in the face. Wanted to a few times, but cool-headed reason had always taken over. This time, something primal and straight from the gut had triumphed. The man needed to be stopped. Permanently. He needed to be behind bars.

Jeanie's attitude miffed him. How could she not feel the same urgency after what the guy had done to her and what he was about to do to other girls? It made Steven literally sick. And here Jeanie was jabbering on about what she should order at the Old Fashioned Ice Cream Parlor.

He ran a hand over his face. He had to shake this attitude or he'd sabotage his own plan. A plan which, up until an hour ago, had been purring along smoother than Burt's Corvette on new blacktop. He gave a smile he didn't feel as they stepped under a green-and-white striped awning. She was leaving in less than two weeks. He couldn't waste time being in a lousy mood. "I'll wait with Sunny. Get me a Green River." His stomach burned as raw as his knuckles.

"Just a soda? No ice cream?" She patted his midriff. "Don't think I'm not noticing." Dark eyes shimmered from beneath the straw hat. "You look good."

His raw stomach did summersaults to the tune of her compliment. "Thank you."

He gave her hat brim a playful tug. "Get two spoons." He handed her ten dollars.

Wisps of hair danced on her cheeks when she opened the door. The air-conditioned breeze cooled more than his face. He ruffled Sunny's ears. "She's hard to stay mad at, isn't she?"

A string of slow-moving motorcycles rumbled by on the one-way street, followed by a purplish blue Hudson. With its sloping black and white walls, he guessed it to be a '50 or '51. The town was abuzz for the annual Antique Town and Rod Show. The Hudson passed. The car behind it made Steven's hands ball

229

into fists, his pulse drum a battle call on his eardrums. Parrot man. Driving a black Galaxie convertible. The man looked straight ahead through wraparound sunglasses. Smoke drifted over both shoulders as he exhaled, as if he'd just driven straight out of The Pit.

If the guy was in town for the show, there was a chance Burt knew him or could find a way to meet him.

And Burt, in his own words, could talk a tiger into giving up his spots.

The Galaxie cruised out of sight, but Steven's knuckles were still white when Jeanie walked out with a waffle bowl mounded with whipped cream and topped with a cherry. She handed him a cold and slippery bottle of green soda and tucked several folded bills in his pocket then plunged a plastic spoon into the concoction. "It's a Grant Sundae. Chocolate, strawberry, and butter pecan with hot fudge and peanut butter."

He stared cross-eyed at the dripping spoon headed in his direction. Opening his mouth just in time, he nodded. "Yum." Under other circumstances it would have been delicious.

"You have a little whipped cream. . ." She pointed at his cheek. "Here. I'll just"—she lifted up on tiptoes and pressed her lips to the spot—"kiss it off."

Steven took a long swig of sweet green soda, wondering how he'd talk himself into walking away from her long enough to call Burt.

≈❊

Hand in hand, they walked through the floodgates at the far end of town on Sunday night. The air had cooled enough for a light jacket. A full moon hung over the Westminster Presbyterian steeple. Jeanie sighed contentedly and snuggled closer to Steven as they angled onto the path leading to the bridge. His arm tightened around her. "Warm enough?"

"Mm-hmm." She closed her eyes, letting him guide her, imagining, instead of the skinny Galena River below them, crossing the Seine on the Pont Alexandre III. "Have you looked at what it would cost to come see me at Christmas?"

Silence spanned the river. After a moment he cleared his throat. "I was thinking maybe you'd want to be home for Christmas. It will be our first. . ." His sentence trailed off.

For Jeanie to finish.

Our first Christmas as a family. Angel's first Christmas with her father. And brothers. How could she explain to Steven how that scenario shredded her insides? By her own choice, she wouldn't be there.

They walked in silence until they'd crossed Decatur and stood on Park Street in front of the Belvedere Mansion. In the glow of spotlights, milk-white scrolling trim and pillared porches stood out against red brick. Jeanie feigned absorption in architecture that had been part of her life since childhood.

His fingertips trailed across her arm. "What are you thinking?"

"Did you know the green curtains from *Gone with the Wind* are in there?"

"Yes." Steven's arm fell away from her shoulders. He turned her to face him. "Talk to me. I mention Christmas and you freeze up. What are you thinking?"

"I'm thinking the timing is all wrong. I keep picturing you and Angel and the boys. . .spending holidays together and becoming a family and it's everything I've always dreamed of and more. But so is Paris. You're the one who put that idea in my head. Remember? You said someday we'd go to Paris and I'd be a famous pastry chef. I dreamed of that in Reno and when I came back and found out you were married, I made up my mind I'd do it anyway. And I'm afraid if I don't do this I'll always regret it and resent you and—"

His fingertip sealed her lips. "Your dreams and our relationship don't have to be mutually exclusive." His voice was low, wrapping around her like his arm had done minutes ago.

"I know we could still go to Paris together, but it wouldn't be the same to go as a tourist." She thought of Gretchen stamping her green shoes. "And it's not just Paris. I'm scared I can't give you enough of me or I'm not the woman you need me to be. I can bake and clean, but I hate ironing and I want a career and some people are just designed to be single. What if I'm one of them?"

The dimple on his right cheek made a quick appearance and disappeared. "How in the world did ironing get in on this conversation?"

"Gretchen said that Lindy—"

His laughter bounced off the bricks of Belvedere Mansion. "Lindy did what she did because it was who she was. Not because it's what I required." His arms encircled her. His smile brought the dimple back. "I don't need Suzy Homemaker. And I don't think you were designed to be single."

"But Reno changed me, Steven." She whispered against the softness of his shirt. "Forever. I'm terrified of anyone controlling me. You wouldn't purposely, I know, but sometimes even being in business with my mother is too hard. It's an irrational fear—like your phobia of small places—but it's so ingrained. What if I can't adjust? What if I commit to you and then I get. . .claustrophobic? I can't do that to you."

"I'm willing to take that chance. This time around I'd like to decide for myself."

"But—"

"I don't want you worrying about what's best for me. Okay?" The backs of his fingers brushed her cheek. "I understand you not wanting to be controlled and needing to fulfill your dreams. Of course I don't want you to go, but I won't ever be happy if you're not happy, so your dreams have to be mine, too. I won't hold you back and I won't resent you." He lowered his hand, then stuck both hands in his pockets. "Is that really what's bothering you? Are you worried about hurting me. . .or is this. . .*us*. . .not what you want at all?" With his hands in his pockets and the toe of his shoe scuffing the sidewalk, he looked about forty years younger than fifty-two.

Her eyes stung, an almost-silent moan echoed in her chest. "Steven. . ." Her hands framed his face. Her eyes locked on his. "I want you. I want us. I love you. I never stopped loving you. I never will."

Rising on tiptoes, she lifted her mouth to his. As his arms engulfed her, the charm of seeing Paris alone faded like mist on the river. How crazy could she be to think that, now that she'd finally found him, she could be happy away from him for a whole year? Her fingers sank into his hair.

"If I promise"—his breathless words tickled her ear—"not to hold you down or control you or mess with your dreams, would you consider spending the rest of—"

Her phone, in the breast pocket of her jacket, rang at full volume in their ears.

"Sorry." She took it out, silenced the ring, and looked down at the caller ID. "It's Taylor. Probably just letting me know she's back from her folks'. My mom's gone. Sorry," she repeated, pushing the green button. "Hey, Taylor."

"Are you okay? Are you in trouble or something?"

"Me? No. Why?"

"Two Galena cops were just here looking for you. I didn't tell them anything, but they said you had to call them tonight. . .or they'd be back to find you."

Steven's neck muscles turned rigid, his stomach roiled, as Jeanie's face paled in the moonlight. She turned her back and walked away from him, gripping a black wrought-iron fence and lowering her head as she talked.

He couldn't hear the rest of her answers. But he'd heard enough.

Burt had done more than he'd asked him to. Way more. The snap of her phone echoed in the silence. He walked toward her.

Eyes like black coals met his. "You told. . .your friend. . .to talk to Damon?" Her voice rasped, all but disappearing on the last word.

Sweat dampened his forehead, heat rose from his neck. "Burt was at the car show. I thought he might know the guy. Burt's good at getting people to talk. I thought if Damon admitted anything. . .anything Burt could tell the police. . ."

"You *told* him to call the police? Knowing they'd question me?" A sob swallowed her words.

"I told Burt not to mention you. You have to believe me, Jeanie. You know I wouldn't do that to you. I was just trying to protect you." He reached out with both hands.

Her arms crossed her chest, fingers clawed at her shoulders. Her eyes grew wide, her stare vacant. "All that talk about not controlling my life. . .what do you call this? I've spent twenty-five years keeping my past from hurting Angel or my mother. You just undid all of it. And if any of this hits the news, I could lose my scholarship to Bellouet Conseil." Her voice rose as thunder rumbled in the distance. "Did you think of that, Steven?"

232

Muscles contracted at the base of his skull. His pulse pounded at his temples. "Yes, I thought of it." Outstretched hands coiled at the sound of his own sarcastic words. "My little plan to keep you here wasn't working, so I thought if only I could disparage your character and ruin your reputation you'd—"

"Plan? You had a plan?"

"Jeanie, don't be ridiculous. Think. You know I'd. . ."

His words trailed off as she turned and ran. Across the bridge and into the dark.

Chapter 19

Overhead fans whirled in the pressed tin ceiling, an air conditioner hummed from a small, high window, but the clover-leaf rolls Jeanie pulled out of the warming cabinet were in danger of baking before they reached the oven.

She slid the pans onto racks, closed the oven door, and mopped her forehead with her sleeve. Her mother walked in, shot a sympathetic glance as she grabbed a tray of muffins, and turned up the worship song on the radio on her way back to the front.

With a sigh that made Taylor stop her noisy rummaging in a drawer, Jeanie stomped to the radio and turned the knob to the first clear signal. The weather station. Her head was not in a worshipful space this morning. She hadn't talked to God in a week.

She had, however, talked to the Galena police and the Dubuque police and a detective from Reno, Nevada.

And, in a matter of minutes, she'd talk to Angel. Because, thanks to Steven, she no longer had a choice.

"Arrrrh!" Taylor dropped a spatula into the drawer. "People die in heat like this. Where's the egg separator?"

"In the dishwasher."

Taylor kicked the open drawer. It closed with a strange grating sound then bounced open. "Uh-oh." She grimaced at Jeanie then eased the drawer open. From way at the back she pulled out a strange looking metal object.

Jeanie stared at the thing from across the room. "What is it?"

The object hit the backsplash behind the sink. "It used to be a sieve." Taylor's chest heaved. She covered her face with her hands and turned her back.

Jeanie ran across the creaking wood planks. "What's wrong?" Her arms went around the trembling girl.

"It's just. . .too creepy. That guy Mr. Vandenburg punched. . .and. . .Nevin. All at the same time. . .it's like a conspiracy." She pulled away, swiping at tears with the back of her hand. "I keep thinking. . .everywhere I go. . .are there people like that everywhere?"

"No, honey. It's just a coincidence those two guys showed up."

"You always say you don't believe in coincidence."

Jeanie tightened her hug. No words came to mind.

"I can't sleep. I keep having nightmares. I believed Nevin. How could I be

234

so stupid? I would have gone with him if you hadn't stepped in." Another shudder shook her and she struggled to catch her breath. "What if you hadn't been right there?"

Who knows but that you have come to this position "for such a time as this"? "But I was there. God put me in that place at that moment to protect you."

Taylor sniffed and nodded. "That's what I keep thinking. I don't always believe all that God stuff, but if anyone but you had been listening in, they might have thought he was offering me a real modeling—"

The sound of the side door opening drew her attention. Taylor's face morphed into a grin. Angel walked in, followed by Wade.

"Happy Birthday, Mom!"

෨෪

"You absolutely glow." Jeanie gave her daughter her fourth hug in an hour as Taylor peppered her brother with questions about the Grand Canyon while showing off her muffin-making skills.

"He's wonderful; marriage is wonderful." Copper curls shimmied as Angel shook her head. "And we made a decision I wanted to tell you in person." Her sun-kissed freckled cheeks rose as she smiled. "I'm selling the business."

Taylor stopped talking. "Seriously?" She and Jeanie asked the question in stereo.

"Seriously. I wrote up an ad and a wonderful Christian man answered. He and his wife have been event planners in Indiana for years and they'll run Pleasant Surprises the way I would. And. . ." Glittering blue eyes turned to Wade. "We're not moving to Chicago."

"Seriously?"

Angel laughed. "Seriously. We want to join Hands in Service and help Steven with fundraising. Wade is going to keep teaching at River Ridge. His apartment is still open, so we'll stay there until we find a house. I'll be here to help Bapcia while you're in Paris." She leaned over and planted a loud kiss on Jeanie's cheek. "Wade loves teaching here, and I just wanted to be back close to you. . .and my dad."

Jeanie swallowed hard. The thick, humid air closed in on her. *My dad.* She looked down, tried to shake the fuzzy feeling behind her eyes.

"Mom? Are you all right?"

"I'm fine."

"Sit down." Angel pulled out a stool.

Jeanie sat down. "I'm fine. Just hot and tired."

Taylor hopped down from the counter. She grabbed a bottle of water from the refrigerator and handed it to Jeanie. "Hot. . .and tired of talking to cops all week."

"What?" This time it was Wade and Angel in stereo.

Taylor gasped. Both hands flew to her mouth. "Sorry," she whispered.

Jeanie sighed, narrowing her eyes at Taylor. This wasn't the right time. But she had no choice. "Let's go sit in the office."

❧

"I wanted to wait. . .until we heard all about your trip." Jeanie took the cap off a pen, jammed it back on.

Angel put her hand in Wade's. "What's going on, Mom?"

A long, tremulous sigh rattled the sticky notes on her desk. "You. . .didn't live here in Galena until you were three. . ." She paused, not knowing where to go from there.

"I know. We lived in California."

"You were born in California." *On a scouting trip. I went into labor with two runaways in the backseat.* "But we lived in Reno, Nevada."

"O. . .kay." Angel leaned forward, freckles in stark contrast to her pale face. "What's all this got to do with you talking to cops?"

"Just hear me out. This isn't something I wanted you to know." *Ever.* Again, she rammed the pen into its cap. "When you were a baby I worked as a. . .for an. . .escort service in—"

"A real escort service? Or a cover-up for—"

"Yes."

Angel's gasp ricocheted off green walls. "You were a—"

"No. I was. . ." *Something worse.* "I was the person who. . .recruited girls to work for—"

"Are you kidding?" A wild-eyed look transformed Angel's features. She stood, pulling her hand from Wade's. "*My* mother? And where was I while you were. . .recruiting?"

"I was with you most of the time, honey. And the other girls watched you whenever I—"

"Other girls? So we lived with them?"

"Yes."

"My babysitters were streetwalkers and I'm just finding this out now? I don't believe this. How could you keep all this a secret? No wonder you didn't take any baby pictures. All this time I thought you were just too poor." Shoving her chair, she stepped past Wade. "All these years of preaching about integrity and honoring God and making me feel like I could never live up to you and all that time you were hiding. . .this? And you never intended to tell me the truth?"

"Angel, sit down, there's more you need to know."

"More?" Angel walked to the door. "I don't want to hear any more." She walked out with her husband behind her.

❧

Steven paced back and forth on the deck, working up a sweat as Burt lay in the hammock waxing philosophical.

"It was divine intervention, Steven. I can't explain it any better than I have about a hundred times already. That slimy guy with a bruised nose was so proud of his trashy little business idea it was like taking candy from a puppy. I just primed the pump. And after he spilled all his beans, I asked if he knew anybody in the area who'd ever done that kind of thing. *He* named Jeanie. I never said her name to him. Everything I told the cops I got straight from him."

Smashing an empty soda can on the deck railing, Steven glared at him. "I told you not to mention her name to the police."

"Okay, so I messed up. But you know God's in control." He sat up, rubbing a hand over short-cropped hair. "I know you don't want my opinion, but something good's gonna come out of this. You just wait."

Steven shot the soda can at a plastic bag hanging from the handle of the grill. "It's going to be a long wait. She won't answer my calls. I went into the bakery yesterday and she locked herself in the off. . .ice." His voice slowed as a black Ford Explorer pulled up next to Burt's Corvette. He waved and smiled for the first time in days. "It's Wade. . .and my daughter!"

"Hey, I'm out of here. It's gonna get mushy." Burt stood, ran down the steps, waved at Wade and Angel, and jumped into his car.

Like a much younger man, Steven leaped the railing with more grace than he'd ever landed in Burt's car. "Welcome back!"

The passenger door opened and Angel, eyes and hair spitting sparks in the sunlight, dashed out and into his arms.

"What's wrong?" Steven looked across the top of the vehicle to Wade, who answered with a helpless shrug.

"I was raised in a house of ill repute!" She hammered out the words. "That's what's wrong." Eyes the same color as his sons' blazed. "Did she tell you that?"

"Yes."

"And you're still. . .interested in her?"

Steven sighed and motioned toward the deck. "Let's sit down." He turned from Angel's glare and led the way up the steps.

Wade sat down on the hammock. Angel took a chair at the table under the umbrella. Steven pulled two sodas out of a mini refrigerator. "She had no choice, Angel. She was protecting you."

Her hands latched onto the chair arms. "Protecting me by luring girls into that kind of. . .disgusting work?"

Steven's lips parted. "She didn't tell you *why* she did it?"

"No." Angel's voice lowered, her brow furrowed.

Wade cleared his throat. "We didn't stick around to hear the whole story. Tell us what you know, Steven."

❧

The side door opened and shut slowly. Jeanie didn't look up from the cupcakes she was decorating. Only family or employees used that door, and she wasn't in the frame of mind to talk to either.

"Mom?" Angel's voice was no more than a whisper, very much like a scared little girl.

Quick, light footsteps crossed the floor.

"Steven told us the whole story." Her daughter's arms slid around her. "I'm so sorry. Sorry I didn't listen and sorry for everything that happened to you. I don't know how you survived, or how you could seem so happy all these years with the memories of everything. . . ." Angel's words picked up speed. "But you saved me and you have to know I'd never, ever hold anything you did against you. Steven said you were afraid of telling me because—"

Jeanie put her fingers up, millimeters from Angel's lips—the way she'd done so many times when she was little. *Shh, Angel. Now's not the time to cry. We must be very, very quiet and hide like little mice. . . .* "I've already ruined your first day back."

"And I ruined your birthday."

"Let's leave all this for later and go get ready for dinner. Bapcia's cooking all our favorites."

Wiping her face, Angel nodded. "Okay." She walked toward the door.

Jeanie switched on her airbrush compressor and picked up a cupcake. As sky-blue dye tinged a ring of frosting stars, she heard the door open.

It didn't close.

"Can we invite Steven?"

The weight that had settled on Jeanie's chest all week pressed harder. She didn't turn around. "No, honey, we can't. I'll explain all that. . .sometime."

The door closed. But a loud sigh followed. "Explain it now. No more shoving stuff under the rug. Steven told us why you're mad at him, and it doesn't make sense."

A clang from the door to the bakery made Angel turn. Taylor walked in, looked at them both, and shrugged. "Just getting angel wings." She walked, slower than she needed to, to the shelves on the far wall.

Angel turned back to Jeanie. "Steven didn't talk to the cops, his friend did. And they'll probably stop that guy who was stalking you because of it. That's a good thing. You should be grateful."

The compressor sputtered as it shut off. The cupcake tipped over when she set it down. Jeanie turned slowly on her stool to face her daughter. Her arms crossed over her tight chest. "Steven *told* his friend to talk to Damon and the police. That wasn't his call to make. It's my life, my decision."

Taylor, with a backward glance, walked out with a tray in each hand. Angel swiped a red-gold strand of hair from her cheek. "He did it because he was scared for you." She folded her arms at her waist. "And it's not just your life. It's mine, too. All your secrets are messing with my life. . .and Steven's." She took two steps, then stopped. "You know, if you'd been honest right from the start, before I was born, all of our lives would have been different."

Jeanie flinched. Her spine pressed against the edge of the metal table.

"Steven told us how you ended up with that. . .job." Angel paced toward the ovens, then back again. "You're always trying to protect everybody." One hand reached out. "That's a good quality, Mom, but sometimes it goes too far. If you'd told him you were pregnant instead of trying to—"

"That's enough. You have no idea what you're talking about."

Angel came closer. "I think I do." Her voice softened. She knelt in front of Jeanie. "We had a long talk with Steven. He understands that you tried to handle everything yourself because you loved him. But he should have been able to make that decision." Her voice hushed, almost to a whisper. "It was his life, his baby. It should have been his decision to make with you."

❧

Jeanie's head throbbed, her throat burned. Eyes half-closed against the pain, she lined cupcakes in white boxes. The bakery lights clicked off and Taylor walked into the kitchen with a bucket and a handful of rags. She walked to the sink without a word. After a moment, she turned around.

"I'm really sorry." She lifted the bent strainer by its handle. Her voice held none of its usual airiness. "Maybe I can bend it back."

Jeanie closed a box and rubbed both temples. "Just throw it out. It's too small. We haven't used it in years." When Taylor didn't move, she looked up and took a second look at the thing in the girl's hands. "Wait. Let me see it." She walked closer and stared at the strainer. The sides of the metal ring that held the mesh were bent toward each other. "No. . .I want it. . .just like it is. It'll fit perfectly into a canning jar like that. It'll save me a step when I want to strain seeds from my raspberry filling." She tugged one of Taylor's pigtails. "You turned this old thing into something useful."

Taylor stared at it and slowly nodded. "Kind of like what God did with all the junk from your past. He used it to save me and maybe catch that guy." She handed Jeanie the strainer. "He made something useful out of it."

Chapter 20

Switching hands on her rolling carry-on, Jeanie walked beneath the copper globe suspended from the white framework dome. Stars, stripes, circles, leaves—flags of every imaginable pattern and color lined O'Hare's international terminal.

She glanced at a clock. Three hundred and sixty minutes and she'd be off the ground. Six hours to fill with anything but second thoughts. Angel had dropped her off early because Toby was flying in from Boston. Two of Steven's children would meet face-to-face in a matter of minutes. Jeanie didn't stick around for the scene. She could have stayed at Pug's apartment and taken a cab, but this was her choice. Now she was here, checked in, and nothing would interfere with her departure.

She bought a Pumpkin Spice Frappuccino at Starbucks and sat down. Directly across from her, an elderly couple laced their hands together as they laughed and whispered. Jeanie pulled her MP3 player out of her bag and started a French lesson.

"*D'où est-ce que tu viens?*"

"Where do you come from?"

"*Je viens d'États Unis d'Amérique.*"

"I come from the United States of America."

She looked out the window at the red, white, and blue stripes on the tail of the AirFrance plane pulling away from the gate, and ripped off her headphones. She pulled a novel from her bag, stared down at the picture of an empty park bench on the cover, and stood up. With no destination in mind, she walked down the hallway. At the first shop, she bought a bag of trail mix and a *People Magazine* then found a seat at an empty gate. She sat with her back to the window and opened the trail mix.

Stale. She crunched the bag and shoved it in her bag. A long gulp of Frappuccino camouflaged the rancid taste. She opened *People* and scanned the contents page. WHO ENVIES JEN'S LOVE LIFE? CAMERON & JUDE: FRIENDS FOREVER.

The titles twisted in her head. She turned to a fashion article but couldn't make her eyes focus. "WHO ENVIES JEANIE'S LOVE LIFE?" The magazine landed on the chair beside her. "STEVEN AND JEANIE: FRIENDS FOREVER."

A rueful laugh huffed from her chest. She slipped low in the chair, resting her head on the back. Sleep—the escape that had eluded her for days—was what she needed. But closing her eyes didn't close the curtain on her doubts. Like a living collage, snippets of thoughts and conversations cascaded before her.

He did it because he was scared for you. . . . I thought we had honesty. . . . I thought. . . you knew me. . . . That wasn't his call to make. . . . If you'd been honest right from the start. . .all of our lives would have been different. . . . It's my life, my decision. . . . Kind of like what God did with all the junk from your past. . .He made something useful out of it. . . . It was his life, his baby, too. . . .

Overhead speakers announced final boarding for a flight to Berlin. A young woman stopped in the corridor. Bulging bag over one shoulder, baby on her back, she stared up at the departure and arrival monitors. Shadows hovered beneath her eyes as they darted back and forth. The baby fussed and she reached back and bounced the pack.

Hush, Angel. Mommy will get you out of here. We'll be free and no one will ever tell us what to do, ever again.

Truth seeped into her consciousness. Her hands closed over her face. Her first prayer in weeks was only a sigh. *Forgive me.* She was angry with Steven for doing exactly what she'd done to him. She'd tried to protect his future. He'd tried to protect her life. Staying mad at him wasn't rational, wasn't like her.

But it did guarantee she wouldn't miss her flight.

It protected her future.

Because she knew, without a doubt, if she wasn't mad at Steven she wouldn't be here.

She looked down at her passport and boarding pass sticking out of the pocket of her carry-on. *Lord. . .* Her second prayer floated on a soft moan. Sitting on the veranda in Reno, she'd set her mind on Paris. It was her symbol of freedom. *Someday I'll get there.* But giving up Steven for her goals wouldn't be freedom at all.

Ticket in hand, a man with a backpack slung over his shoulder dodged a wheelchair as he ran. Was he, like she was, running toward something he thought he wanted more than anything? What was he leaving behind? Was he, like she was, hoping what he left behind would still be there when he returned?

Lord, forgive me. Maybe it's wrong, but I want it all. I want Steven, and I want this chance. I want to go to Paris, and I want him to be just as in love with me when I return.

Putting it into words birthed a strange response. Tears sprang to her eyes, yet she laughed. *No one gets it all.* The woman with the baby, the man with the backpack, were both leaving something or someone behind. If she went to Paris, she'd lose Steven. *It's all about choices.* She glanced up at the Stars and Stripes hanging overhead. Freedom. She'd experienced life without it. Now she had the freedom to choose.

Your dreams and our relationship aren't mutually exclusive.

Her hand slid into her bag. She flipped her phone open and dialed. His voice on his cell phone voicemail message pushed her tears over the edge.

"Steven, I'm at the airport. My plane leaves at four twenty. I'm. . .so sorry. I know you did what you did to protect me, and I shouldn't have been trying to hide everything anyway. Maybe it's too late, but if you really did have a plan to keep me here, it worked. . . . I don't want to go to Paris without you. If you still want me to stay, I will. Just. . .call me." She dug a tissue out of her bag. "I love you."

❧

She stared at her phone. Three thirty-eight. Angel had called once, her mother twice. Just to cover all the bases, she'd left a message on Steven's home phone. His silence told her everything she needed to know. Opening *The Little Black Book of Paris*, she stared at a page of lists—Where to Eat, Where to Shop—and tried to recapture the allure of the City of Light. Flipping pages, she found a quote from Hemingway. "If you are lucky to have lived in Paris. . .wherever you go for the rest of your life it stays with you."

But the same was true of any town. . .if your memories were sweet.

She closed the book, tossed it in her bag, and walked to the restroom. Cold water did nothing for the dark circles and red-rimmed eyes. She reapplied her makeup and, as she took her place at the end of the boarding line, tried to look like the excited winner of the Grégoire Pâtisserie contest.

The couple who stepped in line behind her spoke French. She turned around and managed a smile at the woman with burgundy hair and the man with diamonds on his watch. "Je vais à Paris pour la première fois." *My first trip to Paris.*

"Ah. . . Vous tomberez en amour."

Jeanie nodded and turned away. Did they think she would fall in love with Paris or—

The room went dark. The woman behind her giggled.

Hands. Large hands covered her eyes.

Her bag dropped. She reached up and found what she was looking for. . .a tiny scar. "Steven!" She whirled around and looked up into meltingly blue eyes. "I tried calling"—her breath came in short, convulsive bursts. The man in front of her took a step toward the gate—"but you didn't ans—"

His finger tapped her lips. "I got your message and I jumped in the car. I—"

"How did you get past security?"

He held up a boarding pass and his iPhone. "Cheapflights. Hundred and ninety-eight dollars to Montego Bay." He tore the ticket in half. "Now will you let me talk before you get on that plane?"

"But I don't want to leave—"

Once again, his finger touched her lips. His smile engulfed her. "I have one question—do you still think you were designed to be single?"

Her shoulders shook. "No. Absolutely no."

Steven reached into his back pocket. "Then will you marry me when I come see you at Christmas?"

242

Her answer was a sob and a nod. The French woman sighed.

He pulled out a small square box, black velvet worn smooth on two corners. The cover creaked as it opened. A tiny diamond sparkled on a silver band.

Jeanie gasped. "It's beautiful."

"I talked to Lucas about replacing the diamond with something bigger, but he suggested a diamond wedding band that would wrap around. . .something serene, he said. Anyway. . ." He pointed at the ring. "This was all I could afford thirty years ago."

"*What?*"

He shrugged, smiling like a twenty-two-year-old. "I bought it for your eighteenth birthday."

A tear dripped onto the velvet lining. "And you kept it. . .all these years?"

"I tried to sell it several times, but I couldn't." He pulled it out. His hand shook as he slipped it on the end of her finger. "Wait. You didn't say yes."

With a laugh, she pushed her finger through the silver circle. "Yes."

"Happy Birthday, Dreamy." His arms wrapped around her and his lips found hers.

After a moment she pulled back. "But we're not getting married in Paris. I'm coming home at Christmas and someone else can have my apprenticeship."

He kissed her again. "We've got three months to figure out the details. Now tell me you love me and get on that plane."

"I love you. I always have."

The French couple clapped. The woman hugged Jeanie. "Vous tomberez en amour."

Steven slid her bag over her shoulder. "What did she say?"

With a final kiss, she whispered, "You will fall in love."

੭❧

The house smelled of sage and cinnamon. Steven opened the oven door and gave his boys a sneak peek at the turkey. Toby grinned his approval and took a handful of green olives from the relish tray. "Wonder how Angel feels about food fights."

"Don't even. . ."

"Hey, any girl who can sit in a tree stand for three hours can handle a little pumpkin pie in her face."

Griffin picked up a fistful of silverware. "Her husband's big enough to eat you for dessert, punk."

The phone rang. Steven looked up at the clock. Griffin rolled his eyes and strode out of the kitchen. Toby batted his eyes like a lovesick doe. "Wuv. Twoo wuv."

Steven grabbed the phone and turned his back. "Hello."

"Happy Thanksgiving."

"You, too."

"I wish." Jeanie gave a loud sniff. "I had crepes for supper."

"Next year." Steven eyed the sad excuse for a pecan pie on the counter. "Next year you'll be here to bake pies."

"Mom said she's bringing two pumpkin and a chocolate. You won't go pieless."

"Thank goodness. What did you do today?"

"I wrote a poem for you."

He walked toward the pantry cupboard, away from Toby's smirking face. "Read it to me."

"In four weeks and two days. At the altar."

"Tease. What else did you do today?"

"I made a cake."

He laughed. "You make a cake every day."

"But this one is different. This one said something to me."

"You made a talking cake?"

"Will you be serious for a minute?"

"You'll be home in twenty-three days. How can I be serious? Okay, I'll try." He couldn't stop a small snicker. "What did your cake say to you?"

An exaggerated sigh answered him. "We're working on sculpted cakes and I made a flag—an American flag—it's rippled like it's waving. I called it Freedom Cake."

"Has a nice ring to it." He couldn't resist the urge to sing it. "Let freedom riiiing. . ." On the other end of the kitchen, Toby jumped in on air guitar. "Let the white dove sing. . . ."

Jeanie finally laughed. Or cracked. "Listen to me!"

Waving Toby out of the room, Steven took a deep breath. He opened the refrigerator, hoping the cold air would steal his giddiness. But it only reminded him of being locked in a cooler with a beautiful woman. "I'm listening."

"You know how I keep saying I think God is nudging me to do something?"

"Yes. So God spoke through the cake?"

"Steven."

The threat in her voice only widened his smile, but he wiped it away. "I'm listening."

"The cake was like the final piece of the puzzle. I keep going back to what Taylor said about how God made something useful out of my life. But other than saving her and getting Damon sent to prison, I just don't feel useful."

"Being my wife is a very worthwhile endeavor, Dreamy."

Another sigh. "I know. That's my high calling, Mr. Vandenburg, and I'll be honored to dust your souvenirs for the rest of my life, but—"

"You want to serve God, not just me."

"You *do* get it."

The smile in her voice made him close his eyes and lean against the refrigerator. "I do. Hmm—like the sound of that. So tell me about the puzzle."

"I don't think God's gifted me to teach. I think He wants to use my past. I think everything happened the way it did this year to put me in a position to use everything I know, everything I was trying to hide. I want to work with you and Wade and Angel. I want to sell Freedom Cakes and donate all the proceeds to missions that take women off the streets and help them start new lives."

He couldn't really explain the sting of tears. Her past and her passion all clicking together. . . "That's. . .perfect." The rasp in his voice gave away his emotions.

"I was hoping you'd think so. My man's got a very tender heart."

"It's getting softer by the minute, thanks to you. Maybe after your husband retires, the two of you can get involved more directly. I think God could use those street smarts of yours."

Her silence made him wonder if he'd said the wrong thing. After a moment he realized she was crying. "Jeanie, I'm sorry. I didn't mean that to offend you."

"It didn't. It made me happier than you can imagine. I've been praying about doing something like that."

The doorbell rang. "Just a minute. Your mom's here. You can say 'Happy Thanksgiving' before we say good night." He opened the door and hugged Ruby. "Want to say hi to your daughter?"

Ruby handed him a pie carrier half as tall as she was and took the phone. "Happy Thanksgiving, honey." Steven watched her smile straighten. "I know, but it won't be long. Oh, just a minute. Something came in the mail." She reached into a bag and pulled out a thick envelope. "It's from Reno. From a Mrs. Anna Trudeau. It's marked 'Photos—do not bend.'"

From five feet away, Steven heard Jeanie's gasp. Eyes wide, Ruby handed him the phone and the envelope.

"Open it, Steven. Quick." Jeanie sounded like she was holding a very deep breath.

"Do you know what it is? Who is she?"

"She's the woman I took care of. She's Val's mother." Her voice was breathless. "Open it."

Tucking the phone on his shoulder, he pulled off the tear strip. A letter tumbled out. Words written by a shaky hand covered the paper. "Dear Jeanie— how strange to call you that. I saw your picture in the paper. The story was big news out here. Thank you, child, for doing the right thing. I have tried for years to forget. . .only God can help the memories. At least I have the chance to ask your forgiveness now. I can—"

"Are there pictures?"

"Just a minute." He shook the envelope. Photographs cascaded onto the table. Ruby gasped. Tears stung Steven's eyes. "Yes. Lots of pictures."

"Baby pictures?" Jeanie's voice was barely a whisper.

He picked up a photo of a toddling girl with red curls and wide blue eyes. "Yes."

Jeanie tried to say something that got swallowed up in sobs.

"I'll scan and e-mail them tonight." He set the picture down and put his arm around Ruby, who cried against his chest.

"O. . .kay." Jeanie seemed to be laughing and crying all at the same time. "You"—she blew her nose—"you go enjoy your turkey and give your boys and our daughter a hug from me, and I'm going to go cry happy tears to sleep and dream of you. I'll call you tomorrow. I love you."

"I love you, too. Sleep tight. Only thirty more nights to sleep alone."

☙

Beyond the low arched window at the front of the Galena Wedding Chapel, snow fell in big, lazy clumps. Jeanie took her bouquet of stephanotis and scarlet roses from her mother while Taylor arranged the bottom of her dress.

Angel, in an emerald green gown, leaned over the ivory satin skirt and draped Jeanie's braid over her shoulder, then adjusted the band of pearls and crystals encircling her head. "You're sure this'll stay in place after Dad gets done with you?"

"Angel! That sounds. . .you know." Jeanie's laugh betrayed her jitters. "I tried it last night. It'll be fine." She fiddled with the sweetheart neckline and smoothed her side-wrap skirt. Tiny gold stitches glinted in the light of two candelabras. "Do I look okay?"

A camera flashed. "You look gorgeous, sweet pea." Lucas put his arm around the woman beside him and handed her a camera lens. "What do you think?"

Leaning into him, Gretchen giggled. "I think she's absolutely radiant."

"Thank you." Jeanie's flowers shook. "Then I guess it's time to ask all of you to leave for a few minutes. Angel, will you—"

"I'll go get him."

The scroll in her hand dampened, but she knew the poem by heart. She tried not to disturb the dress, to move only her eyes as she waited.

White satin bows tied crimson roses to the ends of each of the six wooden pews. The gold-trimmed white staircase Steven would descend at the beginning of the ceremony was also graced with roses. Overhead, sixteen lights twinkled in a delicate gold chandelier.

The door at the end of the aisle opened. Steven, twenty pounds thinner than he'd been when she left, walked in wearing a black suit with a red satin tie. He took two steps and stopped. His lips parted.

She held out the hand that sparked with a tiny pinpoint of light. "Come here."

The look of awe didn't leave his face as he walked the burgundy carpet between the pews. "You're. . .so. . .beautiful."

"Thank you."

He stepped next to her, close enough for her to see the sheen of tears. His hand rose toward her face. "Can I. . .touch you?"

She laughed. "In a minute. I have to explain something first."

"Like why I get to break tradition and see my bride before the wedding?"

"Yes." She tucked the poem in her bouquet and took his hand in hers. "You know, from Angel's reception, that in a traditional Polish wedding the bride wears her hair in two braids, symbolizing that she is no longer one, but should always be mindful of her groom."

Steven nodded. Creases deepened between his eyebrows. "But you still have just one."

"Because. . .when I was seventeen I decided to start my own tradition. When I promised myself to you, I put my hair in one braid, symbolizing that I gave up my independence." She squeezed his hand. "I forgot that part a few months ago." She blinked, willing tears not to smudge her makeup. "I know I wasn't bound to that promise over the years"—she let go of his hands and lifted her braid—"but I never met anyone who made me want to change my hairstyle. Now that I'm fulfilling my promise, I will. *You* will."

Steven's eyes closed. A deep breath expanded his chest, but he lost the battle against the tears that had only shimmered a minute before. With trembling fingers, he pulled the band from the end of her braid and ran his fingers slowly through her hair until it fell around her shoulders in waves. He swiped at his cheek then touched hers. "I love you."

"I love *you*." She straightened the rose on his lapel. "Now let's get married."

"I have something for you first. . .after I apologize." He reached into the inside pocket of his suit coat. "I've been keeping a secret. And controlling your life again."

"Steven. . ."

He pulled out an envelope. "You're not going back to the bakery just yet. You're doing your apprenticeship. . .and I'm taking a sabbatical. . .in Paris."

A gasp, followed by a squeal, echoed off the ceiling beams as she wrapped her arms around his neck.

Steven's lips brushed her ear, sending tingles down her bare arms. "*Now* let's get married."

Morning Glory Muffins

2 cups all-purpose flour
1 ¼ cups white sugar
2 teaspoons baking soda
2 teaspoons ground cinnamon
¼ teaspoon salt
2 cups shredded carrots
½ cup raisins
½ cup chopped walnuts
½ cup unsweetened flaked coconut
1 apple—peeled, cored, and shredded
3 eggs
1 cup vegetable oil
2 teaspoons vanilla extract

1. Preheat oven to 350 degrees. Grease 12 muffin cups, or line with paper muffin liners.
2. In large bowl, mix together flour, sugar, baking soda, cinnamon, and salt. Stir in carrots, raisins, nuts, coconut, and apple.
3. In separate bowl, beat together eggs, oil, and vanilla. Stir egg mixture into carrot/flour mixture, just until moistened. Scoop batter into prepared muffin cups.
4. Bake in preheated oven for 20 minutes, until toothpick inserted into center of muffin comes out clean.

PURE SERENDIPITY

Dedication

To the Name above all Names. . .Jesus, the Author and Finisher of my faith; and our new grandson, Noah Q. Wienke, a gift from God.

Cathy

To my mom—who ran in the rain in a pink bathing suit, served hot chocolate in the snow, blinked the porch light, spoiled my kids, sent our books to all her friends, and showed me how to start the day. . .alone with the Lord.

I love you.
Becky

Thank you to Deb Kinnard, Margaret Trzop, and the entire 11:30 lunch table at Lutheran General Hospital in Park Ridge, Illinois, for Polish translations.

Thank you to Kristen for finding a man-sized chicken suit just in time to provide inspiration.

And thank you to Jan Glas, as always, for so willingly reading and catching goofs before we send our "babies" out.

Chapter 1

"Well, Lord, it's just You and me now."

Ruby Cholewinski brushed a stiff pewter curl off her forehead and scanned the reception area of Bernadine's Stillman Inn for anything out of place. A single burgundy petal peeked out from behind the base of a rose-colored marble pillar. She picked it up and tucked it into her purse next to the heels she'd discarded as her only daughter drove off in a car festooned with paper bells.

Snow obscured the afternoon light filtering through lace-covered windows. She kicked off her slippers and stared at the gray light patterning the floor. The room was clean, empty. . .and silent. Exactly the way home would be. Jeanie was on her way to Paris with Steven, starting a new life. There was no one to rush home to.

She lifted a spray of stephanotis off the cake top and eased the ivory-tinted layer into a cake box then picked up her keys. *No one to share a car with.* A splotch of frosting sat on her glove. *No one to share the washer and dryer with.* She glanced at her watch. *No one to wait up for.*

The day after Christmas, and she was all alone.

"Thank You, *Jesus*!" Keys twirled around her finger as stockinged feet did a polka hop-and-chassé across the dance floor. "It's about time!"

"Hey, I brought them back as fast as I could!"

Ruby's polka skidded to a slippery stop. Keys flew off her finger like David assaulting Goliath and landed in a large hand with a snake tattooed around its thumb. *"What?"*

"I said"—a loud sigh blew across the awkward few inches between them—"I brought the keys back as fast as I could, considering it's snowing cats and dogs out there."

The man loomed over her. Six feet plus an inch or two. . .or three. There had to be more than a foot between the tips of her fresh perm and the top of his shiny, bald head. Steely blue eyes squinted down at her. She found her center of gravity and stepped out of his personal space. "Those are my keys. What do you mean you brought them back?"

"Not these keys. *These* keys." His right hand opened, as wide across as the cake in the box. In it were two key rings. One sported a huge brass B. The other held the keys to Ruby's bakery.

"How'd you get those?"

"Jeanie gave them to me 'cause I know the flower girl."

Ruby felt a new wrinkle forming down the middle of her forehead. If it weren't for the fact that the man had given a speech about her new son-in-law at the reception, she'd be pulling her whistle out of her purse about now. On second thought, just because he'd been Steven's best man didn't mean he wasn't nuts. "There was no flower girl."

He rubbed a neatly trimmed goatee. "Well, whatever you call her. . .the girl from the flower shop."

"Sandy. The florist."

"Flower girl. . .florist. . .yeah, Sandy. She's my friend's daughter, and she had to put the flowers on the cake at the bakery after you closed 'cause she had to get to another wedding, so I said if Jeanie trusted me with the keys, I'd let her in. And she did, so I did, but I stuck the keys in my pocket, and I was sitting at the coffee shop just now when I remembered Steven's tux, and I said, 'Emma, I have to go back to the chapel,' and she said, 'It's probably locked,' and that's when I remembered the keys."

The new crease between her eyes actually hurt. Ruby had a sudden surge of empathy for the poor woman he'd left in the car. If the other set of keys belonged in his ignition, his wife was, at this very moment, freezing to death in front of the Galena Wedding Chapel while the man babbled.

She plucked her keys from his hand, "Thank you"—what in the world was his name again?—"Ernie."

"It's Burt." His eyes gleamed like blue-tinged hematite.

"Oh. Sorry. I'm Ruby Cholewinski." She dropped the keys into her coat pocket and held out her hand.

The snake tattoo engulfed her fingers. "I know. You've waited on me at your bakery a time or three. "I'm the two chocolate-covered and one raspberry-filled doughnut guy on Saturday mornings."

Her eyes narrowed. "You did look a little familiar, but—"

"I shaved my head for the wedding."

"Oh." What did one say to such a pronouncement? I love the style? What a nice shine? "You have a nice-shaped head." The wool coat suddenly prickled her arms. *Glupia. What a silly thing to say.*

He gave her hand a firm shake. Muscles bulged under a sport coat the same color as his eyes. She'd never met anyone with navy blue eyes. "Glad to officially meet you, Ruby. You make the best Bismarcks this side of North Dakota."

"Thank you." She didn't have the heart to explain they'd originated in Germany, not the Great Plains.

Burt nodded, his smile hinting at years of mirth and mischief, giving Ruby a glimpse of a younger man—with fresh tattoos and an untamed heart. Her hand stayed locked in his. Her pulse did a fluttery thing she'd have to mention to her doctor if she ever made that appointment. The grandmother clock on the fireplace mantel called attention to their lack of words. She cleared her throat,

252

pulled her hand away. "Well. . .I have to make sure the bride's room is in order." *And you have to keep that poor wife of yours from becoming an ice sculpture.* "Enjoy the rest of your weekend, Burt."

"You, too. I'll come in for a doughnut one of these days."

"You do that."

But one of these days, I'll be gone.

❧

Rose petals littered the floor in the Romance Room, remnants of a teenage melt-down. Ruby shook her head and took off her coat. She smiled as she replayed Taylor's tantrum in her mind. It wasn't the first display of temper she'd seen from her young bakery apprentice. The girl's immaturity baffled her. By seventeen, Ruby had already married the baker's son, flown from Warsaw to London to New York, and was keeping house in a two-room flat in Chicago and learning to bake Polish pastry with a baby strapped to her back. She stared down at the worn signet ring that now only fit on her pinky. *Fryderyck.* He'd been gone almost twenty-two years. She'd been without him almost as long as she'd been with him. She shook her head. Her mind wandered these days. That had been the first sign. When the headaches started a month ago, she didn't need an MRI to tell her what was wrong.

She rummaged in her oversized purse and pulled out a grocery bag. As she reached for the wastebasket overflowing with tissue, her likeness called from the giant mirror next to the canopy bed. Straightening, she stared at the image. The dress that matched her name reflected on her cheeks and gave her pale arms a glow. There were no outward signs of the brain tumor she knew Dr. Bartel would find. . .the tumor just like the one that ended her mother's life at sixty-two and her great-aunt's at the same age.

Sixty-two. . .she'd left that number behind a month ago. Every day from here on was a gift to be savored, minutes to be filled with living and loving with reckless abandon. *Lord, let me be a blessing in these few short months.* Another smile tipped her lips as she thought of the amount on the Visa gift card she'd hidden in her daughter's purse. Jeanie and Steven could live the high life in Paris thanks to Ruby's weekly deposits in her secret account. Forty-seven years is a long time to save for a wedding.

She picked up the grocery bag again, emptied the wastebasket, and reached down for the items that had apparently missed the basket. A lipstick-stained tissue, a piece of satin lace, and a box. As it dropped into the bag, the letters on the box leaped out at her. APT. *Accurate Pregnancy Test.*

"Who in the world would—*Angel!*" Tears prickled her eyes. "Lord, I'm gonna be a great-grandma!" She did the math in her head. "If she's a month along, that'll be August. But it could be earlier. It could be July. Lord, You'll give me till August, won't You? You'll let me see Angel holding her baby?" A tear fell, making a dark burgundy spot on the velvet. "I think it's a girl. I can see

Angel and Wade with a girl." They'd all wear pink for a four-generation picture at Grant Park. *Even if I don't know my own name by then, they have to take a picture.* She swiped her cheeks. "I will not be sad about this. This is a gift straight from You, Lord, and I'm going to enjoy every moment of this pregnancy. I'll get out my crochet hooks and—"

But what if the test was negative?

The thought parted her lips and deepened the new wrinkle on her forehead. She dug in her purse and pulled out another grocery bag. Black boots marched to the bathroom. She flipped on the light, spied the wastebasket, and swooped in on it like a private eye hot after clues. The contents cascaded into the bag. Q-tips, tissue, half an apple. . . "There!" The plastic wand fell, plus sign up.

"I'm going to be a great-grandma!" She glided back to the bride's room on feet that moved like wings.

A baby. . .new life. A reason to celebrate. And the news came on her first day of true empty nesting. "We need to do something crazy, Lord. What should we do tonight? Bowling?" Not too fun without other people. "I know. There's a concert at St. Michael's. We can listen to the glockenspiel choir. And then I'll dig out my dusty skates, and we'll go ice skating at Depot Park." Her boots skated across the rose petals as she hummed "The Skaters' Waltz." Her eyes closed, her head tilted back.

And a man coughed.

❧

Doesn't that just make You smile, Lord?

Burt stood in the shadows, Steven's tux slung over his shoulder, and hoped she didn't see him. What a beautiful sight—sheer joy wrapped in red velvet. He shouldn't be eavesdropping on her conversation, but the woman was mesmerizing. So full of life. . .and spunk. He loved the way she spoke to the Lord as if He were right there in the room watching her dance, getting ready to join her at the skating rink. A verse from Zephaniah popped in his head—*"The Lord your God is with you. . . . He will take great delight in you; in his love he will no longer rebuke you, but will rejoice over you with singing."* Did Ruby Cholewinski know the Lord sang over her as she danced? He had a feeling she did.

He backstepped quietly, but as he turned to leave, powdery crumbs of smashed baby's breath from the tux's lapel invaded his nostrils, starting paroxysms of coughing. Ruby gasped. Her foot slid on a mess of rose petals, and she tipped backwards. Burt lunged, still coughing, and caught her around the waist. "Ea. . .*hack*. . .sy. Steady there."

"Are you okay?" They said it together, like a well-rehearsed line. Eyes watering as he choked and wheezed on flower bits, he pulled his hands away.

Ruby squinted at him until he resumed somewhat normal breathing then covered her face with one hand and peered through her fingers. "Tell me you didn't see me dancing. . .again."

"Dancing? Were you dancing?" Tender skin on the top of his head tightened as his eyebrows neared his extinct hairline. Trying not to stare at the becoming pink rising in her cheeks, he waved toward the floor. "Looks like a greenhouse exploded in here."

"A teenager exploded here. Her parents said no to her. . .finally."

"Say no more. Raised three of my own."

"Wow. You deserve a medal. I barely survived one." Dropping to her knees on the pink carpet, Ruby began scooping petals into a grocery bag. Burt sat down beside her. He threw a petal in the bag and stared at her. Their height difference didn't seem so drastic from this angle. She smiled. "Can I tell you a secret?"

"Of course."

"I just found out I'm going to be a great-grandma."

"Congratulations. Wait. . .does that mean my buddy Steven is going to be a grandpa?"

"That's what it means. But don't say anything to anyone. I don't know if he and Jeanie know, though I'm guessing Angel told them at the wedding, and Angel doesn't know I know, so you have to pretend you don't know if they tell you."

"Right." He bit back a grin. The woman's mind didn't dance quite as smoothly as her body. "We should celebrate!"

"That's what I thought. I mean. . .that *I* should celebrate."

"Well, you can't celebrate alone. Let's see. . .I could take you to dinner."

He'd thought it just an expression when authors described a person's eyes snapping open. But he could swear he heard Ruby's.

"What about your wife? Oh. . .your wife! She's probably frozen by now!"

So maybe the dinner invite was a mistake. "I imagine she is." He chewed harder on the smile. Corrine would have loved this one. "She's been at Elmwood for eleven years now."

"Elmwood?" Ruby's red-tinted mouth gaped. "Cemetery?"

Burt nodded, letting his smile uncurl like a tightly wound flag.

"But who's in the car?"

Steven hadn't mentioned a word about his new mother-in-law being delusional. "What car?"

"Your car. The woman who said the chapel would probably be locked."

"Emma? Emma's not in the car. Not in mine anyway. We just met up for coffee."

"Oh. So she's not your wife or. . ."

"Anything even closely resembling one."

"I see."

"So I can take you to dinner? Or maybe you just want to get back to your carpet skating."

A flurry of rose petals pelted his face. "You *were* watching!"

And listening. He tossed one back, grinning and wondering how it had happened that retired Navy Rear Admiral Burton Jacobs found himself sitting cross-legged on a pink rug in a room called Romance, throwing rose petals at a woman with snapping gray eyes.

Chapter 2

"Feeling adventurous?" Burt opened the passenger door of a teal blue truck he'd told her was a 1968 Dodge. Wet snow sheeted off the window and onto his shiny, black dress shoes.

Ruby arched her left brow. "Absolutely." Adrenal flood-gates opened, sending tingles down her arms as she tapped her boot on the running board and hopped into the truck. Never in her life had she accepted a ride with an almost stranger. *Ride, nothing,* pomylona kobieta—*you just accepted a date!* Her mother's voice resounded in her head, calling her a crazy woman over the clack of windshield wipers arcing through the snow. Beneath the street lamp, rutted slush took on a yellowish glow.

Heat rushed through the vents, turning the white spots on her gloves to minipuddles. Burt brushed off the back window, singing, "Oh, the weather outside is frightful. . . ." His deep baritone lent a cozy feel to the frightfulness. The clamor he made getting into the truck—kicking shoes, slapping gloves, the clanging of the scraper when he threw it behind the seat—reminded Ruby once again just how long it had been since she'd kept company with a man.

"So. . ." He ran a hand over the damp spots on his head. "Sure you don't have a curfew?"

"I've got all night, mister." She silenced a gasp. The warmth crawling toward her ears didn't come from the vents. "To play. . .I mean. . .to do something fun." The heat converted to a full-fledged hot flash.

Burt's laugh didn't help. "Just so you know, this isn't my usual MO. I haven't had an actual relationship since my wife died. . .not that I'm saying this is a relationship, but I don't go around asking strange women—I mean women I don't know—out." His voice rasped on the last word. "What I'm trying to say is that I'm a man with scruples."

"I wouldn't be here if I didn't think you were a gentleman." Somehow she managed to make even the sincerest of statements sound coy and flirtatious. What had gotten into her? "You're my son-in-law's best friend. That tells me all I need to know. So where are we going?"

"My favorite steak place."

"Oh." Hard as she tried to swallow it, disappointment saturated that one word. His favorite was probably the same as her son-in-law's. Not that she didn't love the food at the Log Cabin, but, crumbs, she'd been eating there for forty years and knew her way around their kitchen about as well as her own. She fastened her seat belt and got ready for a ride that really wasn't going to be so wild after all.

"Need to stop at home for anything before we take off?"

Stop at home? She lived two blocks from the restaurant. "No."

"Okee-dokee." Burt grinned and winked. And the next thing she knew his right hand was brushing her left knee.

Ruby shrieked. Her right hand clawed at the door handle.

And the man leaning over her laughed like a hyena.

∂&

She sure was a skittish one. Burt tried stuffing his laugh back where it belonged, but it wasn't minding. What in the world did the little sprite think he was trying to do? He opened the glove compartment and pulled out his GPS. And Ruby slumped against the back of the seat.

"I. . ." The poor woman looked absolutely mortified. "Um. . .you have a GPS."

"I do." He turned it on, punched "recent locations," and clicked it into the holder mounted on the dash.

"You need a GPS to get there?"

"I like my gadgets. I suppose I could get us—" His back pocket buzzed like a swarm of angry bees. He took it out and squinted at the screen. *Not now.* "Sorry, the general's on the line." With a smile guaranteed to make him sound the picture of health and vitality, he snapped it open. "Candace, how are you on this blustery afternoon?"

"You're not home." Born on a naval base within earshot of barking sergeants, his oldest daughter was a product of her environment.

"That would be correct." He mouthed "my daughter" to Ruby, producing an empathetic smile. "Steven's wedding, remember?"

"The wedding was at eleven. And I know you haven't been home since because the mail was still in the box. I came over to bring you something to thank you for letting us borrow the truck, and you weren't home, so I waited. And waited. It's after four. *Way* after four."

"Huh. Wha'd'ya know."

"Where are you?" The sound of his firstborn's voice always made him want to salute.

"Still at the chapel. I"—he glanced sideways—"helped clean up."

"You could have let me know."

That I was picking up rose petals? The picture of Candace's first few gray hairs suddenly burgeoning made his diaphragm jiggle. "Well, you have a good evening. I have to get back to picking up. . ." *The mother of the bride.*

"The roads are terrible. Tell them you have to get home. I'll be your excuse. I have a meat loaf all ready to bake in your oven."

Unlike Pavlov's dog, the thought of this particular food dried up his salivary glands. Candace's version of meat loaf was a desecration of the name. Who was the airhead who first decided turkey could be ground? "I'm having supper with some friends, honey. Just stick it in the fridge. It'll taste great after church tomorrow." With a few strips of bacon and some barbecue sauce.

"Don't you let Jim talk you into going to Benjamin's. No pork chops. Promise?"

"No pork chops. I promise." *I'll stick to porterhouse.*

"Okay. If you don't call me by ten, I'm calling you."

"I'll call *you*." *Tomorrow.* "Go take a Vicodin, and say hi to Frank. Love you." He closed the phone on her protests. "I love *most* of my gadgets. This one feels like a tetherball and chain."

Gray eyes glittered in the light of the street lamp. "I don't own one. For the same reason. Sometimes a person just doesn't want to be reachable."

Sure, he was rusty at this stuff, but he'd have to be clinically brain-dead not to recognize the tip of the eyebrow over her left eye for what it was. Emma had been steadily cranking the winch for five years now, but he'd kept his grip on the wheel. The lady in the ruby dress, however, could prove to be a Siren. Well, whatever the slightly past-middle-aged Christian version of a Siren might be.

As he put the truck in gear, he analyzed how he felt about that possibility. He'd been alone for eleven years. He'd slogged through every stage of grief a few times over and maybe even invented a few. He'd lied himself right into believing he was happy on his own, filling his time with antique car shows, volunteer work, and hanging out with the other two members of the Sorry Widowers. But he'd been questioning everything since Steven got engaged. His driver's license might prove he was a few years past sixty, and his echocardiogram might show a little left-ventricle enlargement, but he didn't feel a day over thirty. He fishtailed onto the road, drove to the corner, and headed east on Highway 20.

"Where are you going?" The skittish look was back.

"My favorite steak place."

She peered through a swath cleared by the wipers. "I thought we were going to the Log Cabin."

That's your idea of adventure? He loved everything on the menu at the Log Cabin, but he'd eaten there more times than he could count using all fingers, toes, and the hairs on his head if he still had any. "Well, I guess we can."

"No. I just assumed. Anywhere's fine."

"Then hang on for—" His pocket buzzed. With a martyr's sigh, he pulled it out and opened it. "Hello."

"Dad. It's Bethany. Candace said you were out with Jim, but I just talked to Bella, and she's over at her dad's, and he's right there in front of her. And you're not. What's going on?" His middle child's voice rose to the pitch that had turned his hair gray.

Might as well start the drama right here and now. *Drum roll, please.* "I'm on a date, Bethy."

"A what?"

"A date." He winked at Ruby, whose black-gloved fingers poorly concealed her smug smile. "Man meets woman. Man asks woman to dinner. If you quit spending so much time hovering over your old man, maybe you'll experience one again before you turn forty."

"Har-har. May I quote? 'Dinner with Emma is simply dinner.' So quit with the date nonsense."

"It is a date, and it is not Emma, and it is definitely not nonsense." With a grin and a ceremonious flip of the wrist, he shut off the phone.

᠍᠍᠍᠍᠍᠍

"You have three girls, right?" Ruby studied his profile as he nodded. "Are you sure you don't need to report in to the third one?"

"My youngest is a cardiologist specializing in congenital heart defects. Divides her time between two hospitals, two hours apart. She's a busy lady. She was here yesterday but left right after we opened gifts. This weekend she's off somewhere with some colleagues working on a paper, so she's out of the daddy-gossip loop. She lives a little ways outside of Normal. Come to think of it, I think all my girls are a little ways outside of normal."

Ruby laughed. "If it helps you put things into perspective, today is the first time in my entire life I've been completely independent. I'm just about giddy with anticipation."

Burt turned to her. In the red glow from the dash lights, she could just make out the deepening creases in his white-stubbled cheek. "I hear you. My middle daughter, Bethany, just left home for the third time a month ago. You know, dinner just doesn't seem like quite enough to celebrate our independence. I'm thinking we need to be a bit more adventurous."

"I'm new at this, remember? What do you suggest?"

"Well. . ." He turned back to the road. Crevasses deepened on his face. "A little ducky told me you like to skate."

Ach. He had seen it all. What a bizarre sight that must have been—crazy lady in a red dress dancing on rose petals and asking God if He wanted to go skating with her. She groaned. "You asked me to dinner just to see what I'd do next, didn't you?"

"I have to admit you offer a certain entertainment value." His large hand left the wheel and slipped over her gloved fingers. After a slight squeeze, he said, "I can't really explain my actions. I've never been attracted to any of my friends' mothers-in-law before."

Attracted? People didn't get attracted to people in their sixties.

Oh really? Then what, exactly, should she be calling the way she felt when she stared at that profile? "I haven't skated in years."

"Me neither. But I know just the place. Perfect at Christmas."

"Where's that?"

260

"Millennium Park."

"The only Millennium Park I've ever been to is in. . .*Chicago*?" A car passed, illuminating Burt's mischievous grin. "You aren't serious."

"As a heart transplant."

"That's three hours away!" Her pulse revved, and a little voice inside whispered, *So what?*

"We'll be in Rockford anyway."

"We will?"

"Yeah. At my favorite steak place."

"Oh." *Oh-me-oh-my.* The night sounded absolutely carefree. And romantic. And then it hit her. *Lord, I can't do this, can I? I can't lead him on.*

Silver blue eyes left the road, waiting for an answer.

"Burt, I have to tell you something right up front."

"You're married."

"No."

"You're a vegetarian."

"No. I'm dying."

The truck swerved. Burt gripped the steering wheel like a bronco rider and pressed the brake. He pulled to the side, put the hazard lights on, and turned to her. "Ruby. I'm so sorry. Steven didn't say anything. This must be awful for them, especially Jeanie—going off on her honeymoon—six months in Paris when her mom's sick."

"They don't know. You're the only person I've told."

"Really? Wow." Burt rubbed his temple. "That was a selfless thing—letting her go and enjoy her new life."

"She wouldn't have gone back to Paris if she'd known I don't have long, and she's been looking forward to pastry school for thirty years. I couldn't do that to her."

Burt nodded. "What is it? Cancer?"

"Probably."

"Probably? That sounds a little vague."

Not if you've seen it. . .twice. Ruby glanced out the window at a pine branch bent to the ground by the weight of snow. "Well, it might not be malignant, but it can still be fatal."

"What can?"

"I have a brain tumor."

"Oh man, that's awful." Concern formed lines between his eyes. "How long have you known?"

"A couple weeks."

"What's the. . . What are the doctors saying? What's your prognosis?"

"I haven't seen the doctor yet."

"At all?"

Ruby looked away from the mesmerizing eyes searching her face. "I don't need to. I know the signs. My mother died the same way."

"But there are treatments. You need to see a doctor. If they get to it early—"

"It's inoperable."

"How can you be sure? New techniques are invented every day. And if they start chemo or radiation right away, they can shrink it or reverse it or—"

"I just want to enjoy the time I have left, Burt. But I didn't want you to get the wrong idea."

"Okay. I get it. But, man, you need a friend right now, don't you? I mean, I'm sure you have lots, but you could use—"

"Yes. I can use a friend. My daughter will try to control my life when she finds out. My granddaughter will be an emotional mess. I need someone who can help me laugh, who can help me live life to the fullest. . .however much I might have left."

The back of his large, rough hand brushed across her cheek. "I'm here to help, my friend."

Chapter 3

rgyle? For real?" Ruby laughed at the blue and yellow geometric pattern on the socks Burt handed her.

"We're not trying to make a fashion statement. In fact. . ." He pulled a purple paisley shirt off a hanger. "I think we're well on our way to the 'worst dressed' list, and we should embrace it." He put his burly arms through the sleeves and ripped a plaid beret off the Goodwill dummy propped beside the YELLOW TAG SALE sign. He held out his hand. "May I have this skate?"

Ruby fanned her face with a convenient sandal. And here she'd just been bragging to a friend that she hadn't had a hot flash in years. "You must wait, kind sir. As you can see, I am underdressed." She whipped around the end of a rack and lunged for the flashiest thing in sight. The bright red, pearl-encrusted sweater had a built-in pearl and gold necklace. She slipped it over her dress and lifted her chin. "Now I will skate with you."

His arm went across her shoulders. Hers slid across his back. Heat radiated through the paisley. He smelled like fresh-cut lumber. "Dum-dum-de-dum. . ." Burt's deep voice spilled down on her. His dress shoes slid across the rug. "Car. . .pet ska. . .ting along. . ."

"*Ahem!* We close in five minutes. Please bring your purchases to the register." The embroidered name on the saleslady's wide blue smock read SALLY. She didn't look like a Sally. She looked like a Brunhilde. Ruby squashed the temptation to shout "Ya' Vol!"

Burt gave Brunhilde a smile with enough wattage to make Ruby jealous. "Thank you, honey. We're almost done. I just need to find a pair of pants. Something wild. . .tie-dyed or leather maybe."

Clumpy eyelashes fluttered. "Are you going to a costume party?"

He looked at Ruby with a smile that far outdid the one he'd bestowed on the saleslady. "Guess you could call it that."

"Come with me." A pudgy index finger coiled and straightened. Burt's face blanched.

Ruby's hand on his back gave him a head start toward the beckoning finger. "Go ahead. I'll be fine." As she turned back to a rack of women's jeans, she smiled at Brunhilde's cackle fading in the distance.

She'd just selected a pair of jeans she was sure she'd worn in her twenties, when the strangest sound came from behind her.

"*Bawk, bawk, bawk–bawk–bawk.*"

Whirling around, she came face-to-face with a six-foot-something neon yellow chicken.

The tip of her chin touched the ruby heart that hung from her necklace. The man was completely *maniaki*. Why, then, did she have this overwhelming desire to throw her arms around his fluffy yellow belly? And why was she starting to laugh like she was as nuts as he was? "You're not skating in that."

"Why not?"

"Because. . ." Because she'd be embarrassed in front of a bunch of people she'd never see again in her short life? A bunch of people who probably weren't having half as much fun as the feathery man grinning down at her like the Cheshire chicken? "Because. . .I don't have a camera."

A calloused finger chucked her chin. "We'll fix that. Got everything you need?" Yellow arms rummaged through the tangle of skates and scarves in their shopping cart. He lifted the flowered jeans. "Do you have some. . .um. . .something warm to wear under these?"

"I thought I did, but they're too big." She pulled a pair of hot pink fleece pajama bottoms out of the cart.

"Perfect. Wear them over the jeans."

"You're a genius! It's exactly what I need to complement the sweater."

"Then, madam, let's be on our way to making memories to last a lifetime. . . however long that may be."

For a reason she never could have explained to a friend with a normal life expectancy, his words made her laugh with an abandon she hadn't felt in years. She held out her hand. "Let's go, Big Burt."

❧

Her red velvet sleeve rippled in the crook of her arm as she took a drink. Dangly earrings with red stones sparkled in the candlelight. Her cheeks were pink, her eyes bright. The woman sitting beside him didn't look like she was dying.

Burt gripped his chopsticks and focused on the shiny surface of the hibachi as a wave of sadness rolled over him. He would not let her see it. Everything about this night would be perfect. When he seemed to have a bridle on his emotions again, he lifted his water goblet. "To freedom."

Fine lines branched from the outside corners of her eyes as she tapped her glass to his. "To living life a little ways outside of normal." A sweep of her hand encompassed the entire Shogun restaurant. "This is not what I expected."

"Good. Just outside normal. . .that has to be our new motto. Every time we're together we can't do anything expected."

Fire leaped from gray eyes. Red-lacquered nails reached toward a square white dish. The next thing he knew, a slice of pickled ginger floated in his water glass like a dead pink fish. Not allowing a flicker of reaction, he calmly downed it and deftly dropped two edamame beans into her glass. Eyes straight ahead, with finesse equal to his, she sipped it down.

Their eyes met. "I like you, Ruby Cholewinski."

"And I like you, Bur—" Her eyes grew enormous. "Oh my gracious! I don't even know your last name."

"Jacobs."

"I can't believe it."

"You can't believe my last name is Jacobs?"

"I can't believe I said I'd go out with you before I even knew your name." Ruby rubbed the back of her neck. What was she thinking?

"It's not a date, remember? It's a. . .friend. . .thingy."

"So who goes on a friend thingy with a person they don't even know? I think I'm developing disinhibition syndrome."

"Disinhi*what*?"

"My mother had it. You start to lose your inhibitions and do inappropriate things. . .like going out with strangers in the middle of a snowstorm."

"So your granddaughter has it, too, I take it." One side of his mouth tipped up.

"Angel? No! Why would you say such a thing?"

"The way I heard it, she got stranded on the road one night, accepted a ride from a tall, handsome stranger, and now she's married to him. . .and carrying his child."

"Oh. You're right." Ruby's lips puckered as she fought a smile. "I don't know what scares me most. . .the thought that my granddaughter may have a brain tumor or the possibility that this syndrome leads to pregnancy." She shook her head, laughing until tears filled her eyes. "Burt Jacobs, I like you. You just may be the key to my dissolving sanity."

"Ditto, my friend. And look at it this way: If we're striving to live just outside of normal, you'd have an advantage on me if you had that diswhatever."

"You're right. I need to work it, don't I?"

"Absolutely."

"So this is your favorite restaurant, huh? I had you pegged for a steak man."

"I am. I'm just not a steak and potatoes man. I'm a steak, rice, seaweed, and cucumber kind of guy. My youngest daughter got me hooked on this place. She thought she was introducing me to some hip new food. But I spent three years in Vietnam. I've eaten more kale and rice than she'll ever dream of."

"You look like a navy man. Am I right?"

He nodded.

"What was it like over there?"

He'd walked right into this one. He thought of all the cleaned-up stories he'd told his girls. He didn't share war stories with anyone other than his vet buddies. Corrine had never asked. She'd just held him tight when the nightmares made him too scared to sleep. "I don't like to talk about it much."

She nodded. "I know what you mean."

Something in her voice told him she did. "Why?"

Her eyes closed for a moment. When they opened, he had the impression she wasn't seeing him or the restaurant. "I grew up with Soviet guards—"

"Dad!"

He blinked twice. "Kimberly!" Was he imagining her? Seeing specters of his daughters hovering everywhere he went? But the viselike grip was on his arm, not in his head. "What are you doing here?"

"What am *I* doing here? I'm staying at a hotel a mile away. What are *you* doing here in the middle of a snowstorm? Bethany said you were on a date." Deep green eyes lasered Ruby. "She didn't tell me you were running around the countryside."

Burt stood, needing, at the moment, to tower over his youngest. "Kimmy, I'd like you to meet Ruby Cholewinski."

Kimmy held out thin, tapered fingers. Her pale, reluctant hand reminded him of the pickled ginger fish floating belly-up in his stomach. "Hello."

Dabbing her mouth with her napkin, Ruby slid her chair back and stood. She clamped Kimmy's hand between both of hers. "Kimmy. . .or is that your daddy's name for you? Should I call you Kimberly?"

"I go by Kim." Reproving eyes shot the same warning she'd been giving him since sixth grade.

The admonition just made him smile. "'Kimmy' makes her sound like a child, and 'Kimberly' makes her think she's in trouble. I use them both."

Ruby laughed. "Be thankful you're not Polish, Kim. My daughter grew up hearing me yell 'Janka Augustynka Cholewinski, get your little *chodź tutaj* in here!'"

His daughter smiled. At least he thought that's what that was. It faded as quickly as it appeared. Her green gaze turned on him. "You're heading home soon."

How was he supposed to answer a question that wasn't even a question? Not with the truth, that was for sure. "How's the writing going?"

"Dad. The roads are terrible. Why don't I get you a room and—"

"Kimberly! It's not that kind of a date."

Next to restoring antique cars, exasperating his daughters was his favorite hobby. The payoff this time was spectacular. Her cheeks puffed; her lips clamped then rippled on a sigh. "I'll get *you* a room, and your date can stay with me."

Ruby's eyebrows pushed her forehead into her hairline. She politely excused herself and strode toward the sign pointing to the restrooms and phone. He hoped she wasn't calling for someone to come and pick her up.

He couldn't blame her for being terrified. Patting his daughter's arm with almost as much patronizing as she was giving him, he kissed the top of her blond head. "Thanks for worrying about us, Kimmy, but we'll get home safe and sound. Snow'll be done before we head back."

"No it won't. I checked the radar at the hotel. It's supposed to snow between here and the Mississippi until about four in the morning."

But not between here and Lake Michigan. With a bear hug and another kiss, he pushed her back toward the table of three waiting for her. "I'll call you the moment we arrive." *In Chicago.*

Thank the Lord for cell phones that didn't give away where you were. There were times that ball and chain really came in handy.

≈⚘

"He has a bad heart."

Ruby stopped straightening her panty hose and listened. No one responded to the dire proclamation. Maybe the flush of the toilet had distorted the words and she'd misunderstood. She smoothed her slip and let the red velvet fall over it then unlocked the stall door. "Kim!" She jumped back, banging her head into the swinging door. "What did you say?"

"My dad. Don't let him fool you. He's not who he appears to be. He has a bad heart."

Ruby stepped to the sink and sudsed her hands, eyeing Kim's scowl in the mirror. He's not who he appears to be? He's not kind, funny, thoughtful. . . . "You know, dear, sometimes parents act mean, but they really—"

"I don't mean like that. He's wonderful. He's the best father anyone could ask for. His heart is medically bad." Her sigh fluttered a strand of straight, wheat-colored hair. "He had a heart attack two years ago. Did he tell you that?"

"No. He didn't." Here he was the only person in the world who knew about her brain tumor, and he'd skipped over this little detail.

"He has left ventricle enlargement, and if he doesn't take his blood pressure seriously, he's going to have a worse attack." As if needing to hide her emotion, she walked to the sink and turned on the water.

"Does he know how bad it is?"

"He knows. He won't take it seriously. He exercises, but he completely ignores the diet I laid out for him." She cranked the handle on the paper towel holder. "I'm sorry. I shouldn't be dumping this on you."

Ruby shook her head. "Actually, I may be exactly the person you should tell." She cupped her hand over Kim's silken hair for a moment. *Because now I know your father and I have something in common. . .and there's no way I'm going to let it stay that way.* With a nod, she said good-bye, flung open the door, and strode to the table.

Burt grinned as she pulled out her chair. "I saw Kim go in after you. I was ready to come and rescue you."

"I can hold my own." She offered a sweet and innocent smile then looked down at the table. "Did you eat my shrimp?"

"I had the chef throw everything back on the grill to keep it warm." He signaled to the man in the white coat.

Within seconds, sizzling shrimp and jasmine rice appeared in front of her.

Her mouth watered. She stared across at Burt's hibachi beef, still oozing blood from its rare center. *Lord, grant me the courage and the stomach I'll need to save this man.* "In keeping with our unexpected theme"—she lifted her plate with one hand and his with the other—"we're going to switch."

Burt's jaw dropped, showing off two gold crowns. "But I don't like shrimp. I never order shrimp."

"You do now."

Chapter 4

Millennium Park, lined on three sides by trees aglow with tiny white lights, was a magical place on a winter night. "It's a fairy world," Ruby whispered into the breeze.

"Say what?"

Magical—except for the fact she was skating with a chicken.

"I said it's a scary world when they allow giant chickens on the ice rink."

Burt's laugh carried across the ice, giving even more people even more reason to stare. *Let them.* Ruby smiled up at her yellow friend, and his hand tightened on hers.

"We're pretty good together. You've got the grace, and I've got the moves." He dropped her hand, stuck his fists in his armpits, and skated backwards, wings flapping in time to "Jingle Bell Rock." "Getting tired?" He searched her face like a worried mother.

"Never felt better in my life."

It was true. Other than the thing that grew, hopefully very slowly, in her head, she was blessed with a strong immune system and not a single achy joint. And now, with none of her energy channeled into worrying over Jeanie, she felt like flapping her wings, too.

"Me too. I feel li—" Both hands shot straight up like a referee declaring a touchdown. Yellow arms backstroked. His face froze in a contorted smile. . .seconds before his tail feathers hit the ice and skidded under the hand-linked bridge of two teen skaters. He hit the Plexiglas wall with a soft *thump*.

From Ruby's perspective, the moment passed like a dream sequence in a low-budget comedy. One second he was standing; the next he was spinning on his bottom like a big yellow top. Behind him, the Cloud Gate sculpture hovered like a chrome-clad spaceship, reflecting the lights of the city. Loudspeakers piped "Silent Night" onto the skaters slowing to gawk at the grounded chicken.

"Burt! Are you okay? Did you hit your head?" She latched onto the railing and lowered to her knees. "Say something."

He blinked twice, rubbed the back of his head, and offered up a crooked smile. "Just livin' a little outside of normal."

❧

Ruby slowed her steps on the way to the truck, making it easier for Burt to pretend he wasn't limping. She liked the fact that he wasn't the kind of guy who wanted to be babied. But like it or not, he was going to get a little of it. "Where, exactly, did you get hurt?"

His embarrassed smile was endearing. "Right in the cell phone."

"That'll be an interesting bruise." The skin beneath her pearl-studded sweater suddenly warmed. How long would it be until disinhibition syndrome made her unfit to be out in public? "Is your phone okay?"

"It looked fine." With a not-quite-hidden grimace, he pulled it out and opened it. Something popped off, followed by a soft *tick* as it hit the ground.

"That can't be good."

Burt held out the phone. One piece in each hand. "Guess I have an excuse now for not answering my girls."

"I'm so sorry."

"It's a small price to pay for giving you a laugh."

"I didn't laugh! I was terrified. Watching you spin like a big rubber ducky across the ice, right smack between those two kids. . ." Her shoulders shook. "This is just nervous laughter."

"See, it was worth it." Burt opened the truck and tossed his phone and the chicken suit behind the seat.

She held out her hand for the keys. "I'll drive."

"I didn't hit my head."

"Just humor me."

He handed over the keys. "So what's next?"

"Getting you home."

"The night's still young." He rubbed his right elbow and winced.

She wrinkled her nose at him. "But we're not."

"Funny. It's only ten o'clock."

"Which gets us back to Galena after one."

Wrapping his arms around his broad chest, he rubbed his forearms. "I'm chilled. I might go into shock if I don't get hot chocolate. Soon."

"Get in." She pointed toward the passenger side. "One cup." *Skim milk, no whip.* She hopped into the seat, stuck the key into the ignition, and stared out the windshield. . .almost. Her entire field of vision was a half-moon of road beneath the steering wheel.

"Uh-oh." Burt's laugh filled the cab. "Houston, we got ourselves a problem. You sure are a little thing." He winked, warming her once-chilled face.

"*I'm* not the problem. It's your truck. Doesn't this seat adjust?"

"Sorry. I had to weld it in place. It's custom-made for a giant." Rummaging behind the seat, he pulled out the chicken suit, rolled it into a fuzzy ball, and handed it to her. "And be careful what you say about Lizzy. She'll get her revenge. She's got her flaws, but she's been good to me."

"Lizzy? You named your truck?"

"I name all my vehicles. My Corvette is Marilyn; my Chevelle is Sophia. They have personalities—they need names."

Ruby stuffed the suit beneath her and fastened her seat belt. As she pulled out of the parking space, she glanced at Burt. "Why not Joe or Ralph or Henry?"

"Shh!" He leaned forward and covered the dash speakers with his hands. "She'll hear you. Lizzy's no Ralph. She's as feminine as you are."

"Am I supposed to say 'thank you' to that or slap you?"

"Probably both."

They bantered about the personalities of every car they'd each owned until Ruby put on the turn signal, turned off on Highway 31, and found a coffee shop open until midnight. They walked in, and Ruby directed Burt to find a seat. "My treat."

It took forever to get the young, pierced girl at the counter to understand her order. How hard could it be to put a couple of shots of chocolate syrup in skim milk, heat it up, and top it with sweetened, foamed milk? She ordered a Double Caramel Cinnamon Crème for herself.

Burt's eyes were closed when she got back to him. Long legs stretched out, feet crossed on the ledge in front of a fireplace. His head rested on the back of an eggplant-colored love seat.

A love seat. Ruby set the drinks on a low table and studied the man. He'd taken his jacket off, and even in purple paisley, he could pass for a model in an AARP magazine. She didn't normally find bald men attractive, but on him it looked good. She stared at his arms, curious about the stories behind the tattoos. And they weren't small arms. These were biceps and triceps and whatever-other-ceps that either lifted weights or worked hard. What did he do with his time other than restoring cars with actresses' names?

He opened one eye, and she jumped. Burt grinned. "Just sittin' here dreaming about my next conquest."

She wasn't sure she liked the sound of that. "What are you conquesting?"

"I got my sights on a beauty." He opened his other eye.

Ruby picked up her Cinnamon Crème and took a step back.

"Sleek red lines, graceful curves. . ."

Her leg smacked the table. Burt's hot chocolate wobbled.

"Moves like a dream. . ."

Trembling fingers grabbed the cup. The heat from two cups and the man on the love seat sparked another hot flash.

"I'll call her Ruby." Deep Vs formed around his eyes.

Who was this man, and why was she still standing in front of him letting him talk about her like she was a—

"1960 Roman Red Corvette convertible with white cove and white soft top. When that girl's refurbished, she's gonna shine like a. . ."

With a splash of Cinnamon Crème and faux hot chocolate, Ruby sank into the love seat.

❧

"What is this stuff?" Burt took a second swallow of the insipid drink and lifted the plastic cover.

"Hot chocolate." The lady in red stared into the fire, a curious smile teasing her lips.

"Something's wrong with it. Is yours okay?"

"Yup. Fine. A red Corvette, huh? I thought you already had a Corvette."

"One can never have too many Corvettes, my dear. It's like women with their shoes and purses." He took another swig. The punk-looking girl behind the counter should be fired. If he weren't so comfortable, he'd get up and complain. At least it was hot.

"Hmm."

"Hmm? You're not a shoes and purses woman?"

She sipped her drink and stared at the gas-burning logs for a long time. "I'm not really an. . .anything woman. I'm a mother and a grandmother—and soon to be a great-grandmother—and a bakery owner and church volunteer and a member of the Red Hat Society. I think maybe one goal of my independence has to be to figure out just who I am apart from all the hats."

He got that. "I joined a grief support group after Corrine died. We spent a lot of time talking about finding a new identity. That's when the antique cars entered the picture. The facilitator asked what we'd choose to do if we had a month with no job or other obligations. I'd been stuck in this nowhere land, couldn't think straight or make decisions, didn't have a clue who I was. But the moment she asked the question, I suddenly pictured the Packard my dad and I restored when I was a kid. It became, as you'd say, the key to my dissolving sanity. Now I've turned it into kind of a therapy ministry. I invite guys who are going through a rough time to help me, and then we sell the cars—the ones I can bear to part with, that is—and donate the profit to missions."

He loved the way she turned to face him and leaned close enough for him to smell the cinnamon wafting from her cup of something that probably tasted tons better than his. As she tipped her head to one side, her right earring dangled in space, catching the light from the fire. "I love that. Gives me goose bumps."

"So what would you be doing if you had a month free?"

"Wow. . .that's a tough one. I haven't had a month free since I was fifteen."

"What about travel? Or have you already seen the world?"

"Oh no. I've seen a little corner of Poland, a glimpse of New York, some of Chicago, and all of Galena. That's the extent of my travels. I guess, if I didn't have a bakery around my neck, I'd want to do what Angel and Wade did on their honeymoon—take Route 66 all the way to California and stop at every little greasy spoon along the way. Or follow the Oregon Trail. I want to see both coasts. Ach! It's all a dream. I have a bakery around my neck."

Lord, look at her. . .she can't be sick. Just look at her. . . . He shook it off. "You

272

have a bakery; I have daughters. All I want to do is sell my house, buy an RV, and drive from one end of the country to the next, hitting every car show from Maine to Cal-i-for-ni-a. But it doesn't fit into my girls' plan for my life."

"So I need to sell my bakery, and you need—"

"To sell my daughters."

They talked until the overhead lights blinked. Burt glanced at his watch. They'd stayed much longer than he'd intended. The punk girl who hadn't mastered hot chocolate shut off the lights before they stepped onto the sidewalk. Sleet-laced wind hit their faces, and he instinctively put his arm around Ruby. "Temperature's dropped."

She nodded against his jacket.

"I'll drive."

"Are you sure you're okay?" Under the eerie glow of a halogen light, she stared up at him.

He couldn't resist humoring her concern. "Check my pupils."

Ruby stopped, turned him twenty degrees, and squinted into the cold, wet air. "I can't really tell in—" Her words ended in a gasp as his lips found hers. Warm and soft in spite of the weather.

❧

It wasn't a strained silence that filled the truck cab. Just a strange one. He didn't try to fill it with excuses or apologies. He had neither.

Sleet turned to snow as they neared Rockford. Hard, icy ruts covered with new snow made it slow going. Sandbags in the truck bed helped, but what he wouldn't give for four-wheel drive. He kept both hands on the wheel but tried to look relaxed. He didn't want Ruby to know the drifts ahead and the diminishing visibility made him irritated with himself for lingering in front of the fire.

Several minutes after the heat kicked in, she removed her gloves. He chanced a quick look at her expression. Her smile fit the theme of the night. . .unexpected. She turned, catching him looking at her. "Thank you," she whispered.

"For?"

"Making me feel like more than a doughnut maker."

He laughed. "Ruby, you are way more than a doughnut maker. You are funny, graceful, and the best kind of friend a guy could—"

Lizzy shuddered. The speedometer needle sunk to the left. His foot on the accelerator pressed all the way to the floor, and still she slowed. *No.* He'd just filled up on Thursday. *Candace! You little. . .* He steered to the side of the road just as Lizzy hiccuped to a dead stop.

Chapter 5

What happened?"

Burt closed his eyes, took a long, slow breath, and slammed his fist on the dashboard. "My daughter borrowed the truck on Friday. I mentioned Lizzy's quirks—one of them is a gas gauge stuck on F." Pressing his lips together so tight they numbed, he stared out each window. No house lights anywhere. No lights. No phone. No heat. *Lord, what do I do now?* "I'm sorry, Ruby. What a lousy way to end a wonderful night."

"Or life."

Her face was expressionless. Burt's stomach muscles cramped. She was right. If they tried to walk, they could die of hypothermia. If they stayed in the truck, it would simply take longer. "I'm so sor—"

The smile started in her eyes then spread slowly until it lit her whole face. "You're doing it again."

"I'm doing what again?"

She reached across the seat and grasped his hand. "Making me feel like more than the doughnut lady. This is an adventure. I haven't run out of gas since. . .1964."

Lifting his hand, he kissed hers. "I'll say it again. You are way more than a doughnut maker. So what should we do now?"

"First, we pray." Without waiting for his response, she bowed her head. "Almighty God, we acknowledge that all things happen for a reason. Nothing catches You by surprise. So we come before You and ask for Your protection and Your direction. Help us out of this predicament, and help us to make some memories along the way. Amen."

"Amen." He hoped she couldn't hear the emotion messing with his voice. The last time he had held hands with a woman and prayed with her, she died three minutes later. He cleared his throat. "I have a blanket behind the seat and an emergency kit under your seat."

Ruby bent down and pulled out a red plastic box. Burt opened it and sorted through the contents. Flashlight, flares, candy bars, space blanket, first aid kit.

"I don't want to waste the flares. We need something to tie around the antenna." He looked around the cab. His gaze landed on Ruby's knees. "Something bright. And pink."

"Wait till I tell the girls back home about this one." She wriggled out of the pajama bottoms and handed them over.

Only three cars passed. He hadn't had time to light the flare that waited on the dash. Not a one slowed when he leaned on the horn and flashed the lights. The pajama bottoms flapped in the ice-laced wind. Worthless. He should have let her keep them.

Burt glanced at the fluorescent hands on his watch. Three sixteen. Four hours until sunrise. His toes were numb. His breath hung like smoke over Ruby's head, snuggled against his chest. His arms ached from holding her, but sometime during the night he'd realized that the gnawing, aching emptiness he'd lived with for eleven years wasn't there anymore. Twelve hours with the woman who slept in his arms had brought forth a miracle.

Should he leave her here and try to find help? He'd asked himself that question a hundred times since Lizzy sputtered and died. Her warm breath against his shirt gave him the answer. He'd unzipped his jacket and tucked her arms behind his back. He could leave the jacket and take his chances, but without his heat she'd freeze. Three hours and someone would find them. They could hold on that long. Couldn't they? And if not, this had to be an easier way for her to walk into the arms of her Savior than what awaited her. *Lord, we're trusting You.*

Years ago, fighting for his life and someone else's freedom in Vietnam, he'd known the satisfaction that his death would be noble. Here, snuggled in a 1968 pickup with a woman in a chicken suit, all he knew for sure was that someone would get a laugh out of it. His daughters would be furious. The thought made him smile. *We did good, Corrine.* They were all a little uptight and obsessive-compulsive, but they loved the Lord and their families. He would have liked to see Bethy married. She'd come close twice, had her dreams crushed as many times. An hour or so ago, Ruby had mentioned praying for her daughter's future husband for forty-seven years. It had given him hope. Jeanie couldn't have found a better man than Steven. *Take care of my girls.*

Ruby stirred. "Mmm. I smell coffee."

Was she dreaming? Or was that another symptom of the unthinkable thing in her head? "Oh, really. Hazelnut? French vanilla?"

"What's your favorite?" She didn't move from her warm cocoon.

"Alterra French Roast. Straight-up black."

"Then that's what I smell. What should we have with it?"

So she wasn't delusional. Or if she was, he wanted the same disorder. "Belgian waffles."

"Cherries or strawberries?"

"Hot fudge."

"Ugh. Too early in the morning for chocolate. But I'll fix it for you. I'll have strawberries. And whipped cream. None of that stuff that comes in a tub."

He kissed the top of her head. Was that wrong? Life was short. In Ruby's case, really short. And she fit so perfectly in his arms. "I agree. I'll fix the bacon."

Resting his head on hers, he closed his eyes. Just for a moment. . .

Waking with a start, he looked at his watch. He'd slept more than half an hour. Not good. He needed to stay awake. Forty years ago he'd gone days without sleep and still kept his focus. The snake coiled around his hand was proof of his endurance under stress. He shook his head, took several deep breaths.

The movement woke Ruby. She yawned. "Where were we when Kim showed up at the restaurant? You were talking about serving in Vietnam."

I said I don't *talk about Nam.* "I think we were talking about you and Soviet guards. You grew up in Poland?"

"Mm-hm. I got married when I was sixteen and came to Chicago the same year. I didn't mean to sound like I understood what you went through, just that I know what you mean about not liking to talk about it. I've told Jeanie and Angel a lot about my childhood, but there are things I'll only talk about with my sister."

"I've heard stories about the breadlines in Poland after the war."

Ruby lifted her head and smiled. "That was my job. Every morning at five o'clock I had to be in line. How I hated that in the winter. But God brings good things out of adversity. That's how I met the baker's son—and married him and came here."

"How long have you been alone, Ruby?"

"More than twenty-one years. Fryderyck was a volunteer firefighter. He saved a little old lady from an apartment fire. He died saving her cat." She was quiet for a moment. "How did you meet your wife?"

"She wrote me a letter while I was in Nam. She was in a college group doing their good Christian duty by writing to soldiers. That's how the letter arrived—addressed to 'Vietnam Soldier.' The chaplain handed out letters like that to guys he felt sorry for. I just happened to get hers."

"Serendipity."

"Yeah. Guess you could call it that. She came to see me at Bethesda when—"

"You were wounded?"

He hesitated, knowing he'd have to answer and pretty sure she wouldn't stop at one question. "Not bad. I've got a nasty scar on my left leg, but nothing serious. Not like some."

"Were you shot?"

"Grenade. . .I think. I was on a PBR—proud, brave, reliable. It really stood for Patrol Boat, River. We were part of Operation Game Warden, patrolling the Mekong Delta. From first light to sundown we stopped and searched sampans, checking for weapons and supplies intended for the Viet Cong. Sometimes we found old men and their grandkids taking vegetables to market. We'd tell them American jokes and give them candy and gum. Sometimes we found deserters or VC with machine guns."

Ruby's hand gripped his arm. "You must have been terrified all the time."

"You develop an eye for detail. You look at a man's hands first. If they aren't cracked and calloused, he's not used to work in the fields. That's when you reach for your weapon. But yeah, I was scared all the time. Fear gets to be like white noise. Kind of a steady hum, you know? You never get used to it; you just live with it. We had skirmishes, but after a few months we got cocky. We were told we were winning. The Tet Offensive proved us wrong."

"Is that when you were hurt?"

If he closed his eyes, he'd be back there again. The sounds, the smells had never completely left. "The temperature was over a hundred that day. The guy I was with was getting on my nerves. I'm sure I was grating on his. Traffic was unusually light, as if the locals knew something was about to happen. All of a sudden it was like the end of the world. Rifle and machine gun fire erupted from the riverbank, followed by rocket-propelled grenades. We accelerated to thirty knots and let loose on them. But this wasn't a normal ambush; this was a full-scale, battalion-strength attack. The U.S. sent in Seawolf helicopters and ground troops, and we finally pushed them back. Then our job was to cut off their escape routes. That's when I got hit." The deafening explosion still echoed in his head. White light, blinding pain. He hoped she wouldn't ask for details.

"Were you a Christian then?"

"Furthest thing from it. I was a wild child of the sixties—not much I didn't try. I never gave God a second thought. Or a first, for that matter. But I sure prayed that night. What they say about no atheists in foxholes is true. Every time the other guy in the boat with me said a Hail Mary or made the sign of the cross, I copied him. I didn't know who I was praying to, but I wasn't about to take any chances on ignoring His help if He existed."

"Fire insurance."

"Exactly. And the next time the chaplain started talking about Jesus, I was way more ready to listen than if I hadn't just gone through the closest thing to hell I ever hope to experience."

Ruby pulled her arm out and adjusted the thin stadium blanket, pulling it high enough to cover his ears. "I prayed all the time in Krakow. I prayed for food and warmth and for my father's job at the steel mill. I prayed for a rich, handsome boyfriend to take my family to America." She laughed, her breath warm against his neck. "God gave me a poor boyfriend who snuck bread to me. And by the time my father lost his job, my poor boyfriend was my poor husband, and his family and my family came to live with his uncle in Chicago, and we all stayed very warm that summer. . .sixteen of us in a two-bedroom flat with one window."

Burt pulled her closer. "We have both had very full lives."

"We have. And if we freeze to death tonight, we will have even better lives. I'm sure there are chocolate-covered waffles in heav—"

A dim light bounced against the dash. Headlights. This time Burt moved more like the soldier he'd once been. Ruby slid toward the passenger window.

He grabbed a flare, lit it, and cranked the window down. The flare sputtered in the wind. The lights grew brighter, closer. And stopped.

After several nonbreathing moments, red and blue lights lit the inside of the cab like a carnival midway. Ruby cheered. Burt exhaled. "Never thought I'd see the day I'd be this happy to have a cop on my tail."

≈❧

"Strawberry waffles?" Burt projected over the truck heater that had been on full blast since he'd gotten it started. He pointed toward a sign advertising Galena restaurants. "We need a thanksgiving meal like the pilgrims who survived the first winter. We should have invited Officer Wilms. In the mood for thanksgiving waffles?"

Sorry, bud, that was all fantasy. "I have a better idea. I'll fix you breakfast at my house." *Egg-white omelet and dry toast. God kept us alive in the car. I'll do my part now.*

"What will the neighbors say?"

"They'll say, 'Hey, who woulda guessed it? Ruby Cholewinski's got a life.' Seriously, you don't really think at our age we're compromising our testimony, do you?"

"We'll turn on all the lights and open all the curtains so as not to be a stumbling block for other senior citizens in your neighborhood. You do live in a neighborhood, right? I guess we never talked about that. For all I know you have a cot in the storeroom at the bakery, Doughnut Lady."

"And for all I know, you sleep in the backseat of a Corvette." She pointed toward the lights of the Spring Street Bridge. "Turn up there."

As they crossed Park Avenue, Ruby swiveled to stare at Belvedere Mansion. "It's good to be home." *And alive, and feel my toes. Thank You, Lord.* It wouldn't be much of a story if she ever chose to tell it to Jeanie or Angel. . .or her great-grandchild. *Let me tell you of the night Great-Grandma almost froze to death in the wilds of Illinois. . .in a pickup truck. . .in the arms of a man she'd only just met.* She would not say "a man she hardly knew," for it no longer seemed true.

She turned her smile away from Burt and caught the first pink glow of dawn in the side mirror. Nestling back against the seat under the orange and blue blanket, she thanked God again for warmth. "Turn right on Main. I live two blocks past the bakery."

"Yes, ma'am."

In the gold first light, she studied him. It seemed impossible he'd been in her life less than twenty-four hours. He *fit* in her life. However long it might be. When they reached Meeker Street, where Main became Dewey, she pointed. "This has been one amazing night."

"It has." He found her hand under the blanket. "Let's make it a habit. Well, not all of. . .it." His last word was barely audible.

"What's wrong?"

He stopped in front of her house and turned on the brights, illuminating a silver van. "That's my daughter's van. That's—"

"Dad! Dad!" The woman's voice increased in volume with the sound of feet crunching snow.

Burt shoved open the door. "Candace! What in the—*Bethany?*"

More steps. More gasps. "Bapcia!"

Ruby got out of the truck. "Angel? What are you do—"

Ruff! Angel's Irish setter added his voice and a slobbery kiss.

"Mo*ther!*"

"Jeanie!" Ruby did a double take. "*Jeanie?*"

Her newlywed daughter, who should be having breakfast in bed with her husband before heading to O'Hare International, stood on the porch, hands on hips, steam billowing from her mouth.

"How *could* you, Mother?"

Chapter 6

Ruby sat on the couch. A good eighteen inches away sat her partner in crime. Their accusers stood in a half circle between them and the unlit Christmas tree in the corner. Scanning from one scowl to the next, Ruby tried to decide which one was the angriest. Angel, red hair in a tangled mass of postwedding curls, or Jeanie, dark circles under her eyes that should have come from her wedding night and not from worrying about her mother. And then there were Burt's girls. Candace, blond hair perfectly coiffed but a blue vein throbbing on her forehead, or Bethany, dressed head-to-toe in black as if she'd gotten a jump start in case her father hadn't returned.

Jeanie clicked her tongue. Candace sighed.

Ruby'd had about enough. "I don't think either one of us has another 'I'm sorry' in us. Angel, if I'd had the slightest clue you'd be checking up on me, you know I would have called you. I'm sure it was frightening to find my truck at the chapel, and I can only imagine what you thought when you found out I was with Burt." *But, oh how I wish I could have seen your face.*

Burt cleared his throat. The sound tinkered with the lock she'd put on the laugh that had been sneaking up her throat since her third or fourth apology had met with less than grace. She'd been wrong to think only of herself. But it hadn't been intentional. Well, the part about worrying her granddaughter and ruining her daughter's wedding night hadn't been intentional. "I'll make some coffee."

The jury didn't budge.

"Mother. . . What's gotten into you? Those jeans. . . It's like, I left for a few hours and you became a stranger. You're a Sunday school teacher, for crumb sakes. You've never gone anywhere without telling one of us. How could you think for a minute we wouldn't be worried? And then to find out you're with. . ." Jeanie gestured toward Burt, clearly unable to come up with a suitable label. "It's just not like you to do something so irresponsible, so. . . ." Again she seemed at a loss for the right word.

"So spontaneous? It's just not like me to be so impulsive and fun? Well, praise the Lord! 'Cause I don't want to spend the rest of my life being predictable. And you two had better get used to that. I'll do my best not to worry you, but I'm sixty-three, not sixteen, and if I want to spend the night in the arms of a handsome stranger, that's just what I'm going to do."

A quartet of gasps sucked the air out of the room, leaving a black hole silence, filled within seconds by a whoop and a knee slap from Burt. His laugh was contagious—but only to Ruby. Their children did not share their amusement. When Ruby finally found a sliver of self-control, she wiped her eyes. "Cut me a little slack, girls. I'm a big girl—"

"Actually, you're really not." This from Burt, a man already skating on ice much slipperier than at Millennium Park.

His commentary started the laughter again. "What I mean is. . .I'm not going to do anything dishonoring to you or the Lord and—"

Footsteps sounded overhead, someone walking in the bedroom above the living room. "Steven?"

"Or Wade or Taylor," Angel answered.

"A regular family reunion. Let's all have breakfast. Belgian waffles, anyone?" Ruby tried to get up. The glares held her in place.

"Mother."

"Sorry. Where was I? I was saying we had no intention of staying out all night, but—"

"But you had every intention of bringing *him* back here to your empty house." Jeanie's hands found her hips.

"What's going on?" Taylor's sleepy voice reached the bottom of the stairs before she did. "Ruby! You're home. Are you okay? What happened? This is the guy, huh?" Wide eyes sparkled.

"Burt, this is Taylor Ramsey, Angel's sister-in-law. Taylor, I'd like you to meet Burt Jacobs."

"Way cool." Taylor eyed Burt and nodded, her grin taking up half her face. "You were at the wedding. Wow. . .this is so cool, Ruby. I hope I'm still dating at your age. I bet it's even more fun 'cause you don't have to worry about—"

"*Ah—hem.*" Candace interrupted with a feminine version of her father's throat clearing. She shot Taylor a look that shut the girl's mouth. "Dad. . .this isn't. . .good for you. Besides all the obvious. . .missing sleep, almost freezing to death. . .you're too old to be cavorting around with a woman you hardly know. It's not good for your heart or. . ."

Ruby knew intuitively the second Burt had had enough—long before his oldest got to the "o" word. It happened on the first "this isn't good." Burt's large hands slapped his knees. The sound produced a detectible, though subtle, change in Candace and Bethany. Backs straightened; eyes widened.

Burt stood and looked down on both of them. "That's where you're wrong. This *is* good. Very good. I've laughed more since yesterday afternoon than I have since your mother died. It's good for my heart, and it's good for my soul. We're not doing anything immoral or anything that's going to bring shame on our families. I'm *sixty*-four, not eighty-four, and however much life is left in me is going to be a good life—and an unplanned and unexpected life—and my girls are just going to have to give me their blessing or back off!"

Burt sat back down, this time right next to Ruby. He put his arm around her shoulders and stared at his girls, waiting for a response he couldn't possibly predict.

Candace stood like a mannequin, her expression unreadable. Bethany, her pale face a startling contrast to the solid black from her chin down, suddenly started to laugh. "Okay, you win. I get it. Being single isn't fun—take it from an expert. As long as you promise to take care of yourself, you have my blessing, Dad."

Burt blinked back unexpected tears as Bethany—aloof and undemonstrative Bethany—walked toward him and threw her arms around him. After planting a kiss on the top of his head, she held her hand out to Ruby. "Glad to meet you, Ruby."

"Well, *I'm* not!" Candace turned her back to him, strode across the room, and picked up her coat and purse. "You're going to kill yourself acting like this." Without putting the coat on, she stomped toward the front door, yanked it open, and walked out.

In the awkward stillness that followed the slam of the storm door, Ruby patted his knee. Burt looked at Bethany and shrugged his shoulders. She rolled her eyes in response. They were both accustomed to what Kimmy had dubbed "Candascenes."

A low hum sounded from behind Bethany. The teenager sitting cross-legged on the floor near the television pressed her hands together. "We need to take a moment and clear the negative energy from the room." She closed her eyes.

Burt raised an eyebrow. "I think it just left."

Yoga girl ignored him.

Bethany looked from Angel to Jeanie to Ruby—"I'd really like some of that coffee you mentioned. Can I help?"

"I'll fix it." Jeanie, eyes red-rimmed and smudged with black, headed toward the kitchen.

A stair step creaked, and black socks and gray pant legs appeared on the stairs. Burt felt as though he'd just been given an ice water injection. The legs were attached to his accountability partner. Ruby stiffened. "How 'bout if all the ladies gravitate to the kitchen? Taylor, you, too. You can 'ohm' out there."

A sleepy, disheveled Steven stood at the bottom of the stairs. "You got a good explanation for wrecking my wedding night?"

"Steven." Burt stood, raked his fingers over the place where hair used to be. "This is awkward."

"Awkward?" Steven rubbed his face with both hands, walked toward an overstuffed chair, and sat down. "You spent the night with my mother-in-law. And I did *not* spend the night with my bride. I'm not quite sure 'awkward' covers it."

"I didn't 'spend the night.' I. . ." Burt dropped back onto the sofa and repeated the events of the night. "It was just a comedy of errors."

"Yeah. I'm not feeling the comedy at the moment."

"Don't you have a plane to catch? Grab your wife, and get out of here. Go to Paris or something."

Steven nodded toward the kitchen. "You really think I'm going to get her out of there?" His lips pressed together in a tight line. He leaned back in the chair and closed his eyes. After a few silent moments, his shoulders began to shake.

Leaning forward, Burt squinted at his friend. *Please don't cry, Steven.*

The sound began almost imperceptibly, a low, breathy sound, and grew in volume. Steven was laughing. But was it healthy laughter, or was he losing it?

"You spent the night with my mother-in-law!" Steven opened his eyes and shook his head. "Do you realize, man, if this relationship continues, I could end up calling you 'Dad'?"

⁂

"So, Bethany, where do you work?" *And what must you think of me that I spent sixteen hours with your father and never thought to ask?*

"I'm a competency resource manager for IBM in Dubuque."

"Oh my." Ruby felt her eyes crossing. Thankfully the unnecessary clanking of the coffee carafe against the sink and the banging of cupboard doors kept her awake. "I have no idea what that is."

"My job is to streamline resource management processes. I work with senior management to define and update business rules to ensure staffing objectives are met within the context of labor management and do data analysis to get at the root cause. . ."

Another headache. If only she could close her eyes and sleep. It began in her shoulders and slowly ratcheted up her neck until Ruby's skull felt encased in a metal helmet. The helmet grew tighter with each dart Jeanie sent her way as she smacked coffee cups and spoons onto the table. Could her daughter's frustration actually speed the growth of the tumor?

Taylor set out a plate of pastries. "Polish pastry reaches the heart." Interrupting Bethany, she quoted the tagline Ruby had created when they first opened Angel Wings Bakery. Was this the same girl whose bouquet had exploded in the bride's room?

Bethany picked up a *chruscik*. "Angel tells me you're a pastry chef, Jeanie."

Angel's eyes fluttered from half mast at the sound of her name. *Poor thing.* She sat at the kitchen table, chin resting in her hand. Ruby wanted nothing more than to send her pregnant granddaughter home, send her daughter packing, and crawl into bed.

Jeanie turned from the sink. "I'm supposed to be on my way to an apprenticeship in France as we speak." While she answered Bethany, she glared at Ruby.

"So go!" Ruby pointed toward the door. Conflicts with her daughter were fairly common, but usually they were about the bakery and were resolved quickly. Nothing about this made sense. "Your flight's not until four."

"It's not that simple!"

Ruby pushed out an empty chair with her foot and was surprised when Jeanie sat in it. Leaning across the table, Ruby took her hand. "What's this really about? We've explained and apologized till we're blue in the face. Do you think we made it all up? Should we call the cop who found us this morning? Do you want to examine Burt's broken phone? Or maybe the bruise on his—"

"*Mother!*"

That tone was getting old. "Well, what is it? There's nothing more to be said."

Jeanie tapped a spoon on the table. Each beat resounded in Ruby's head like clanging cymbals. Angel reached out, stilled the spoon, and laid her head on her arms. *Thank you, dear.*

"I just. . .don't feel like I can trust—"

The phone rang. Jeanie jumped up to answer it. Ruby chewed her bottom lip. *That's my phone. Tell me you weren't going to say you can't trust me.* She stopped her silent dialogue to listen to Jeanie's side of the phone conversation.

"He's still here. . . . Of course. . .I couldn't agree more. I was just about to say the same thing. . . . I'll get him." She carried the cordless phone into the living room. A moment later she was back. Turning to Bethany, she said, "That was your sister Kim."

Bethany shook her head and patted Ruby's shoulder. "Candace called her."

"Kim and I had a nice chat at the restaurant. Maybe she was able to reassure Candace that I don't have horns or—"

"That's irrational, Kimmy." Burt walked into the kitchen, gripping the phone as if it were the snake tattoo come to life.

This wasn't the way she'd imagined it. Burt was supposed to walk in, compliment her beautifully remodeled kitchen, and ask what he could do to help with breakfast. While he was distracted squeezing fresh orange juice, she'd whip up a heart-healthy omelet, and then they would hold hands and thank God for a peaceful end to an amazing adventure.

Burt pulled the phone from his ear and stared at it. He pushed a button and set it on the table. His top lip curled on the left. "Kimberly is on speakerphone. She'd like to participate in our cross-examination." His gaze landed on a stack of books on the kitchen counter. Picking up Ruby's burgundy leather-bound Bible, he winked at her and held it out. "Do you promise to tell the truth, the whole truth, and nothing but?"

Chapter 7

Rules?" They said it in unison, Ruby's tone perfectly in sync with his.

Burt couldn't choose between laughing and screaming. He made eye contact with Steven, who leaned against the refrigerator, hiding his grin behind a crumpled paper wedding bell. The man was no help.

"Guidelines. We need to know where you are and that you're coming home at a respectable hour. You had dating rules for us, Dad," Kimberly's static-filled voice reminded from the kitchen table.

"We're not dating." Again they spoke in duet.

"Well. . ." Bethany entered the ridiculous discussion. "Technically, if you're going skating and out to dinner and you're both single and it's just the two of you, it's a date."

Jeanie nodded. "Exactly. And you had rules for me, too, Mom."

"Wha. . ." Ruby's mouth parted. Gray eyes darted from her daughter to her new son-in-law. "Do I really need to remind you that you broke every single one of them?" She waved toward Angel. "I have proof!"

Angel opened one eye. "Leave me out of this. You guys are all nuts. I'm going upstairs." With a yawn, she stood and shuffled out.

"Hey, wait, all of you." The teenage girl whose name Burt couldn't remember raised both hands, palms out. "There's truth in what everyone's saying. If you just take the time to understand each other's motives and—"

"Taylor, there's a very comfy couch in the living room." Ruby nodded toward the door.

"Fine. I was just trying to bring a little peace and tranquility into this mess. Come on, Sunny." She stood and patted her leg. The dog rose with a whine from the rug by the back door. "We'll create our own serenity." Chin held high, she followed in Angel's footsteps.

The trial seemed a bit more fair with only two people on each side of the table.

"What's going on?" Static rose from the phone.

He'd forgotten about the unseen accuser. Still, three against two wasn't bad. "Just thinning the herd, honey." Burt rubbed his sternum where a dull pain had begun about an hour ago. His body reminding him he needed food and he didn't need the stress.

Kimberly's sigh echoed in the room. "Bethany, you haven't said much."

"You really want my opinion?"

285

"Of course."

"I think you and Candace have fallen off the edge." She shot a quick glance at Jeanie. "Do you honestly think Dad's going to run his plans by all three of us for approval and punch a clock when he gets home?"

"If he doesn't have the sense to not go out when the roads are terrible with some woman he doesn't even know. . ."

Bethany rolled her eyes. "He's still competent, Kimberly, still in charge of all his faculties. We can't make decisions. . .or *rules*. . .for him. It's none of our business what he does with his free time."

Burt chucked his daughter under the chin. Two against three. The odds were in his favor, unless Steven weighed in with his wife.

"None of our business?" Kimmy's voice rose to glass-breaking frequency. "If he has another heart attack and ends up in a wheelchair on oxygen, who's he going to live with? Are you going to sign the papers putting him in a nursing home for the rest—"

"Enough!" Burt grabbed the phone. "Courtroom is adjourned, ladies. I'm not going to sit here while you talk about me like a doddering old fool. I appreciate your concern, and I promise I'll go off to a nursing home without complaint if living my life like a free man wrecks my heart. But I am not going to live like the boy in the bubble. I love you, Kimmy, but good-bye." He shut off the phone and held his arms open to Bethany. "Thank you for your vote of confidence."

"You're welcome." She leaned toward him and even hugged back a bit. "I'm going home now." She pulled away. One eyebrow lifted. "Are you?"

He laughed. "I'll punch that clock as soon as I walk in the door."

"Bye, Dad."

"Bye, honey." With a sigh, Burt waved and turned a tired smile on Ruby. "I suppose I should get going."

"I should hope so." Jeanie stood. Both hands fastened to her hips.

"Jeanie. . ." Steven offered a quiet warning.

"This isn't your battle, Steven. My mother is my problem, and until she promises me she's going to let Angel know whenever she decides to leave town, I am not leaving the country."

Steven took an audible breath. Ruby slapped the table with an open hand and stood. "*Wychodź stąd!* Get out! I love you with every ounce of my being, but this is my house, and you are not welcome in it because you are going to walk over to that man you married and tell him you love him and you're sorry for being rude, and then you're going to drive to O'Hare, get on a plane, and start your life, and I'm going to stay here and thoroughly enjoy what's left of mine in any old way I please!"

❧

"You're one feisty doughnut lady." Burt rested his arm across her shoulders as they watched Steven and Jeanie's rental car pull out of the driveway.

"You're no slouch yourself, Big Burt." She rested her head on his chest, feeling as though she belonged right there in the shelter of his arm.

"Hard to believe. . .twenty-four hours ago I only knew you as the lady who owns the bakery."

"Serendipity."

"There's that word again."

"I love the sound of it. But I add my own twist—our meeting was a fortunate Godcidental discovery." Her arm slid around his waist. "Think about it. . . . I was still at the inn because I got distracted by the pregnancy test. You were only there because you forgot the tux."

"And your keys. So my absentmindedness isn't old age; it's God moving in my life?"

Ruby nudged him with her shoulder. "That could become a cop-out."

"It could. So when can I see you again?"

She turned just enough to look up into silver blue eyes. "When do you want to see me again?" Her head tipped to the side, adding sauciness to her coquettish tone. For a moment she felt like she was watching someone else. Who was this minx?

"You don't really want me to answer that, do you?"

"I do."

Two large, warm hands framed her face. He lifted her chin, smiling down at her like sunlight breaking through dark clouds. "If I weren't a man of God and if it weren't for His strength, I wouldn't leave." He lowered his lips and kissed her. Short, sweet, and dizzying. "I'll call you later." Grabbing his jacket from the back of a chair, he walked out.

Ruby stood by the storm door as her breath fogged the glass, watching the lights of the pickup turn on. "I said I wanted a change, didn't I, Lord? I was thinking more along the lines of dyeing my hair brown." With a final wave, she closed the front door and walked through the living room to the coffeepot Jeanie had never gotten around to turning on. The digital display next to the ON button told her she still had time to get ready for church.

A long soak in the tub and flannel pajamas warmed in the dryer were what she really wanted. "Don't worry—I won't give in to it." She walked back through the living room and picked up the velvet dress. A clump of yellow polyester fuzz drifted to the floor. She picked it up and closed her fingers around it.

❧

"Ruby!"

The voice blared across the church parking lot.

Ruby pulled her collar up around her ears. "Madora."

"I heard what happened to you yesterday." Gloved hands crossed, pinning a lace-covered Bible to her plaid coat, Madora Kingsley scampered toward Ruby's open car door.

Did you hear I skated with a chicken, Madora? Pass that one around on the prayer chain. Ruby tossed her purse into the front seat and lifted one boot toward the beckoning safety of the car's interior. "Morning, Madora. Good message this morning, wasn't it?"

The face that looked astonishingly like Julia Child's formed a prim smile. "I didn't expect to see you. Are you all right?"

"Never better. How's that acid reflux?"

"As long as I don't eat too late or—are you trying to distract me? So it's true, isn't it? Do we need to talk?"

Five or six years earlier, in one of the women's ministry's greater fiascos, Madora's name had been plucked out of a gravy boat along with Ruby's, and for one interminable year the two were "prayer sisters." Which translated into Madora stopping by the bakery six days a week to pray. . .and eat angel wings that Ruby felt obligated not to charge for. After the first week, when it became clear the two had very different understandings of confidentiality, Ruby had fought the temptation to make up a fantastical imaginary life filled with wild prayer requests.

Today she didn't have to. "I don't know what you heard, but I—"

"I heard you disappeared after Jeanie's wedding with my friend Emma Winters's boyfriend."

Emma. . . The woman Burt had met for coffee was Emma *Winters*? As in. . . the pastor's sister? The sister who hadn't gone to Ruby's church for over ten years because her pastor brother had told her to stop gossiping or leave?

Boyfriend? Ruby blew the thought away. Anything that left Emma Winters's lips and filtered through Madora Kingsley's colorful mind could not be trusted.

"How is Emma these days? Haven't seen her in years."

"She was just fine. Until Burt didn't show up for supper last night, and then this morning when her daughter talked to Burt's daughter and found out the two of you spent—"

"Madora, I hate to be rude"—she ducked and sat down in the passenger seat—"but I have a chicken waiting for me."

❧

"I'll expect you for dinner tomorrow?"

Emma gripped his elbow as she stepped off the curb in front of the church. Was it his imagination, or was she hanging on tighter than usual?

"Um. . .I'll have to get back to you on that." Burt took longer, more purposeful strides toward Emma's car. "I may be tied up."

"Candace coming?"

"No."

"Kimmy?"

"No." Before she went through his entire family tree, he'd better fess up. . .a little. "I might be meeting a friend for dinner." He didn't need to explain more.

He'd made it absolutely clear from day one that he was perfectly content baching it. The key word was "was." But she didn't need to know any of that.

Emma nodded. "I'm sure you do."

He recognized that tone—he'd learned a thing or two living with four females. The woman knew something. There was no safe answer, so he didn't try.

The grip on his arm became a tug. "Remember the warped seal around my back door that you said you'd replace? I could really feel the cold air seeping through there last night while I was mashing potatoes."

Mashed potatoes! "Em. . .I'm sorry. I completely forgot about dinner."

"I wonder why?"

"Well, I. . .was helping a friend"—*pick up rose petals*—"and I simply forgot."

"Burt Jacobs. I'm not a ninny. Your Kimmy called my Marie this morning. I know every little detail." Her accusatory look melted into a smile. She poked his chest with a mitten-encased finger. "And I have no problem with it. I know you're not interested in a serious relationship, and I don't mind at all sharing you with Ruby. . .as long as she doesn't think she can hog you. She and I are just going to have to sit down and have a little chat. The last thing I want is for her to be jealous of me."

Oh-boy. "I don't think that's really necess—"

"Why don't the two of you come over tomorrow night and help me eat that roast?"

Oh-boy-oh-boy.

Chapter 8

These muffins are. . .wonderful, Emma. Very light."

In the middle of Ruby's compliment, Burt's stockinged foot found a resting spot on hers beneath the embroidered tablecloth. She managed to finish the words before grabbing her bottom lip between her teeth.

"Well, coming from you, that's an extreme compliment. I think what I miss most about your church is Sunday morning fellowship time with your bakery goodies."

Not the soul-piercing sermons by your own brother? Ruby reached for another corn muffin to busy her mouth.

"Tell me about your childhood, Ruby. I hear your father was a Communist soldier."

Ruby gulped. The muffins weren't light enough to float around that one. Burt patted her back as she struggled to avoid blasting Emma with crumbs. "My father was a steel-worker. And a nationalist."

"Oh." Emma held out the gravy boat. "I guess I have to get my facts straight."

Emma's phone rang. She reached behind her and pulled it from its cradle. "Hello. . . Oh, hi. . .no. . .only Tuesday or Thursday this week. . .sorry, just the way it is. . . I'll make pork chops, and the shovel is in the garage. . . . Bye." She hung up the phone and turned back to them, looking oddly flushed. "So, Ruby, you were just a young girl when you came to the States, weren't you?"

Be nice, Ruby. This is a safe topic. At least she's not talking about Burt. "I was only sixteen."

"And pregnant."

The muffin in her hand crumbled. Light and crumbly—not tough enough to make a good weapon. "And married."

"Oh. . .of course. Tell me about your husband. Was it a fairy-tale romance?"

Burt picked up the roast-beef platter. "This is excellent, Emma. What's your secret? I can't make a good roast."

"Low temp and a bay leaf. Was he much older than you? Sixteen is so young to marry."

Ruby took the gravy that was still suspended between her plate and Emma's at the cozy little table. "He was nineteen. And it was very romantic. He stole bread from his father the baker and gave it to me for my family. The first five times I saw him, all I said was 'thank you.' And then he asked me out." She set the gravy out of Burt's reach.

"Ooh. . .a bit of a rogue, hey?" Emma's British accent missed the mark. "Where did you go on your first date?"

"We went to Mass."

Emma appeared to have a *bit* of trouble swallowing her own muffin.

Waving with a forkful of stabbed green beans, Burt pointed at the gravy. "I'll take a little more of that."

Tapping his foot under the table, Ruby shook her head. "No you won't. You have to save some room for the dessert I brought."

"Don't worry about Burt." Emma slid the gravy toward him. "He'll find room. He always does."

Ruby grabbed the bottom of the china bowl. "He's not supposed—" She stopped. She wasn't supposed to know anything about his heart condition. But she did know, and she'd seen him rubbing his chest more than once yesterday. "Stuffing yourself isn't healthy."

Emma grabbed the top. "Neither is not enjoying life."

"He doesn't need—"

"Hey!" Burt clamped onto the vessel like it was a football, trapping both of their hands. "That dessert you brought, Ruby—doesn't it have to be warmed up or something?"

She glared at him. "It's fresh fruit."

Emma laughed. "Here I thought you'd bring something from the bakery. Well, I've got fresh peanut butter cookies that will go just right with that fresh fruit. You'll want a glass of milk, won't you, Burt?" She winked at Ruby. "He loves to dunk my cookies."

I'd like to dunk your cookies, lady. Ruby pulled her hand away. "Cookies would be lovely." *Lord, I'm sorry. Jeanie's right—I've turned into somebody even I don't recognize.*

"This brings up a good point, Ruby." Emma's hand left the gravy and slid over Ruby's. "We need to coordinate things so we don't overfeed this boy."

"Um. . ." Burt pushed the gravy to the side. "I think—"

"We need a schedule." Emma patted Ruby's arm with her right hand then crossed her left hand over to pat Burt. "I'll take him on the even days. . .and you can have the odd ones."

❧

"I'd invite you in for coffee, but this is an even day." Ruby slammed the truck door and stepped onto the sidewalk.

Burt got out, walked around the front of the truck, and held out his hand. "Let's take a walk." His breath hung like a cloud between them.

She thought a moment. Did she really want to hear a "why can't we all just get along" lecture? But the hand stretched out to her looked inviting. "Okay."

They headed toward town. Ruby took in the familiar curving street, the red-brick buildings on either side. Lamp poles, covered in red and white, stood like peppermint stick sentinels. Red-bowed wreaths hung on every pole. Windows glowed with tiny white lights on swags of green. Even two days after Christmas, the sight brought an almost giddy kind of joy. Since her first year in Galena, the Christmas season had never seemed to last long enough.

"A nickel for your thoughts." Burt squeezed her hand.

"I was thinking of my first Christmas here. Janka—that's Jeanie's real name—was six. Chicago had been good to us. We'd worked and scrimped and finally had enough money to start our own bakery. We opened right after Thanksgiving. I put red and green sugar on our angel wings, and we sold out by noon every day. I was so tired and so happy. . . ."

Burt let go of her hand and put his arm around her. "We are blessed to have good memories."

"What's your favorite Christmas memory?"

He was quiet for half a block. They passed the Log Cabin restaurant and stood in front of the bakery, its tall windows outlined in small, white lights. Burt cleared his throat. "One, strangely enough, was on a ship in the South China Sea."

"Tell me about it."

"It was my first Christmas over there. On Christmas Eve we'd had a not-so-bad ham dinner, and we were sitting around on bunks, reading mail, passing around cookies from home. There's this dinky, really awful-looking artificial tree. . .and one of the guys pulls out a harmonica and starts playing 'Silent Night.' And one by one we all joined in. Maybe for the first time ever, the words meant something. I think it was that night—in the middle of a war—that God made the first little crack in my stone-cold soul."

She leaned against him. "He works in mysterious ways."

"Mm-hm. What's your favorite memory?"

"I have so many. Angelika's first Christmas with us was beyond anything I can describe. She was three years old, with all that wide-eyed wonder. Every morning she took the baby Jesus out of our crèche and hid him so Bapcia and *Dziadek* could find him. But my very best Christmas was in *Warszawa* when I was seven."

"Warsaw?"

"Oh. . .sorry. Yes. I was born at the beginning of the reconstruction. I only knew of the city's prewar glory by the stories my parents told. When I was seven, we had the biggest Christmas tree ever. Huge and green. . .and almost bare. My sister made paper ornaments, but for weeks I'd been praying for real glass ornaments like the ones my parents remembered."

"You were feisty even way back then."

"I guess I was." They walked across the quiet street and stood hand in hand in front of Poopsie's gift shop window. Ruby pointed to a *Christopher Pop-In-Kins* book. "I used to read that to Angel long after she was too old for it."

"Now you'll have to get one for your great-grandbaby."

Ruby nodded and allowed a contented sigh. Emma's name hadn't come up since they'd left her house with a bag of peanut butter cookies.

"Did God answer your prayer?"

"You'll see. I want to show, not tell."

"I'm intrigued."

They strolled past R Toys & Gifts. Engines, boxcars, and cabooses in primary colors wound through sparkling artificial snow. Burt put his face an inch from the glass. "I still feel like a six-year-old boy when I see a toy train. It's sad to think you never experienced anything like that."

"Most of the time my sister and I weren't aware we were so poor. If we had nothing but sauerkraut for supper. . .oh well. So did the kids next door. It was harder on the people who remembered the good times." She turned back toward home, and they continued walking.

"Makes me feel very spoiled. I was born ten months after my dad got home from Germany. He got an engineering job in Chicago. When I was two, we moved into a brand-new house."

"One of those cookie-cutter neighborhoods?"

Burt nodded. "Park Forest. So while I was growing up in the American Dream, you were living on sauerkraut."

"But maybe I should be feeling sorry for you instead."

"Why's that?"

"Because I experienced the American Dream firsthand. We came to Chicago with nothing—we left six years later with a down payment on a business. By the time Jeanie was ten, we bought our house."

"The same one you're in now?"

"Thirty-seven years in the same house."

"Wow. Can't imagine that. We moved seventeen times before I retired."

"My turn to say 'wow.' Can you name all the places you lived?"

"I could try." He took a deep, noisy breath. "New Orleans, Guam, Pearl Harbor, Charleston, Corpus Christi, Fort Worth, Norfolk, San Diego, San Clemente, Guantanamo. . ." He stopped for a breath. "Well, you get the idea. Ended up at Great Lakes Naval Base in Chicago and moved here after I retired. Kimmy and Bethany were on their own. Candace and her husband had moved here and had twins. Corrine wanted to be close to those babies." He was quiet for a moment. "She died a year and a half after we moved."

"That must have been awful. Had you gotten to know people here? Other than family?"

"A few. I worked part-time as a mechanic, and we were getting connected at church, but you know how tough it is to be the fifth wheel." His thumb ran across the back of her hand. "Let's talk about something positive. . .like how you get me on the odd days."

Ruby stopped. The action caused Burt to swing around to face her.

Lamplight danced in his eyes. His tongue made a small bulge in his cheek. Wriggling her hand out of his, she answered the dancing eyes by narrowing hers. "You're loving this, aren't you? Two women trying to outdo each other and probably ending up in a catfight."

"Seriously? You think it'll come to that?" He rubbed his chin. "Can't wait for that one."

Without a single premeditated thought, Ruby bent and scooped snow with both hands. She packed it hard and let it fly.

"Hey!" The snowball hit Burt smack on the nose.

"Bull's-eye!"

"Oh. . .just you wait. . . . I'm trained in hand-to-hand combat, girl. I eat pip-squeaks like you raw and by the handful—don't even bother to spit out the seeds." As he yelled like a drill sergeant, he swiped snow off the sill below a shop window. His hasty attempt disintegrated a foot from Ruby's ear and showered her with clumps.

"You call that combat, chicken man?" She dove toward a pile of snow mounded against a parking meter. "I'll show you—" The heel of her right boot went forward. The toe of her left went back.

Burt caught her millimeters before she split in half.

Gasping, laughing, sucking in air like she'd summited Mount Everest, Ruby flung her arms around his chest. "You s–saved me. And it's not even an odd day."

Lifting her to solid footing, he stared down at her. The lamplight faded from his eyes. "You do understand, I hope, that there won't be any catfight."

"There won't?"

"No."

"Why?" Her voice reduced to a squeaky whisper.

His lips lowered until his breath tickled her cheek. "Because you won that fight before it even started."

Chapter 9

The recliner felt like it was made for him. Yet it belonged to the little elf fixing him hot cider in the kitchen.

Burt surveyed the room. Nothing fancy. . .decorated in shades of brown. But Ruby's personality popped out everywhere. In one corner, a huge jade plant sat beside an old, carved-back rocking chair. Miniature ornaments that looked like old-fashioned ribbon candy decorated the jade plant.

On the coffee table sat an open Bible, devotional book, and one that looked like it could be a journal. A pair of glasses and a mug with "Bapcia" written in a child's hand sat next to the books. Furry, purple slippers rested on a stack of cooking magazines on the floor. Pictures of Jeanie and Angel took up one whole wall.

He got out of the comfortable chair and walked over to the Christmas tree. Only about as tall as Ruby, the tree sat on two wrapped boxes. It was covered with colored lights, old-fashioned tinsel, and more glass ornaments than there were branches. Gold and jewel-covered eggs, snow-covered houses, ladies in colorful skirts, snowmen, and colored balls weighed down the boughs.

So what would this room have told him if he'd never met the woman who lived here? That Ruby Cholewinski was a woman with a passion for God and family. . .and food and comfort. And she was a romantic.

A combination that could win battles over avowed bachelors before they even began.

He walked back to the recliner with the worn-smooth arms. On the table beside it was a framed portion of Psalm 139 done in needlepoint or cross-stitch—he'd never figured out the difference. He sat down and picked it up.

"My mother stitched that." Ruby set a mug on the table. As she walked to the couch, Burt read the passage silently.

> You have searched me, Lord, and you know me.
> You know when I sit and when I rise; you perceive my thoughts from afar.
> You discern my going out and my lying down; you are familiar with all my ways.
> Before a word is on my tongue you, Lord, know it completely.
> You hem me in—behind and before; and you lay your hand upon me.

He set it down and picked up the mug. "Good words."

"I used to repeat the last verse when I stood in the breadline or if I had to walk to school alone." She took a drink then set her mug on the coffee table.

295

"Which brings me to my six-year-old prayer." She turned toward the tree. "Two days before Christmas I woke to a thin layer of frost covering the blankets my sister, Freda, and I slept under. The sun was just coming up, shining through fernlike patterns in the ice on the windows. It was beautiful, magical, and I knew it was a sign. I ran to the parlor in bare feet, sure I would find the tree covered in real ornaments. But it was exactly as it had been the night before—mostly bare, with a few paper stars. I was so disappointed." Her voice roughened, and a sad smile lifted her lips.

Burt wished he was sitting beside her, but he didn't want to break the spell the memories had on her.

"Bapcia Borkowski, my mother's mother, lived three blocks away. My mother gave me a crock to take to her that morning. I hid my sadness until I was outside. Tears froze on my cheeks in tracks as I carried soup to Bapcia. There was a glass factory between our apartment and hers. I didn't like walking past it. The windows were boarded up, and there were holes where there should have been bricks, and it smelled bad, but men still worked there. I always held my breath and ran when I got near it. But this morning I couldn't run, or the soup would spill. As I walked past a doorway, it opened. A man stepped out. '*Dzien dobry*,' he said. I kept my head down, but I wished him a good morning, too. 'I have something for you,' he said. 'A Christmas gift.' He told me to wait there, and when he came back"—she stood and walked to the tree—"he held in his hands the most beautiful thing I'd ever seen in my life." With both hands, she lifted something red from a branch. "'It is not quite perfect enough to sell,' he said, 'but I think, for you, it is perfect.'" Cradling the ornament, she walked toward the recliner. "He wrapped it in a cloth and tied it with string." She laid the red and gold egg in Burt's hands. "I never saw the man again."

❧

The glass egg looked small in his large hands. Small. . .but protected. Burt looked down at it for the longest time, and when he looked up, there were tears in his eyes. The depth of empathy caused Ruby's next breath to shudder on its way out.

Shifting the ornament to his right hand, Burt reached up and took her hand. "It's beautiful."

"I never doubted God for one moment after that. He was real, and He cared about a poor little girl in Warsaw. That's all the theology I needed."

Burt placed the egg gingerly back in her hand. "I have a six-year-old grand-daughter. I can't imagine her walking alone in a war-torn city."

"Those were different times." She walked back to the tree and kissed the ornament as she always did before hanging it on the tree. "But those times made me who I am today."

"Then I am very grateful for those times."

She turned and smiled at the man who looked very at-home in her recliner. "I am afraid for Wade and Angel and the children they'll have. It's not good for a person's character if life is too easy."

Burt nodded. "I was a product of the easy life."

"Well, that shoots my theory all to pieces, doesn't it? You are a very fine product." She walked back to the couch, sat down, and arranged her lap quilt over her legs.

"The man I am today is the result of the hard life I created for myself because I was used to an easy life." Both brows raised in unison. "Try saying that one fast."

"Tell me about the old Burt."

A shadow crossed his eyes again. He rubbed his chest the way he had yesterday. Maybe it was just an unconscious thing he did under tension.

She didn't want to be the cause of his stress. "If that's too nosy, you don't have to answer."

He shook his head. "It's embarrassing, but, like you said, it's part of what God used to make me who I am today."

"Then, for whatever you are about to tell me, I am grateful."

A self-conscious smile touched his lips. "The old Burt lived for the moment and thought only of himself. My motto was 'Party hard, drive fast, and never get caught.'"

The screen door creaked. The front door flew open. Angel strode into the room. She looked from Ruby to Burt and back again. "Oh. Hello. I don't want to interrupt."

Ruby didn't buy the surprised look. Angel couldn't have missed the truck in front of the house. Was she here on a reconnaissance mission?

"Come in. Sit down." Ruby jumped up, ushered her granddaughter to the couch, and tucked the quilt around her legs. Up close, she noticed red-rimmed eyes and felt a twinge of guilt for questioning Angel's visit. "What's wrong? You two have your first marital spat?" *Or is this pregnancy moodiness?*

"Taylor and I had a fight. Not our first. Wade was at a meeting at church, and she wanted to go out with friends. I told her it was too late, and she went ballistic. After Wade got home, I just had to get out and let him handle her."

Burt leaned forward, folding his hands. "Taylor is the yoga girl who was trying to bring peace and tranquility into this house?"

"That's the one. She forgets about world harmony every time we say no to her."

"She lives with you and Wade?"

Angel nodded. "Wade's mom has a lot of health problems. She's supposed to avoid stress—which means avoiding her daughter. Taylor's been going to Wade's school and working at the bakery. She lived here with Mom and Bapcia for a while, but with the wedding, we thought she should stay with—" The phone rang.

Ruby jumped up. "There she is—calling to complain about you." She went to the kitchen and answered the phone.

"Ruby. It's Emma. I've been trying to call Burt. I don't imagine he's at your house this late."

Was that a question? It didn't sound like one, so maybe it didn't require an answer. "What do you need, Emma? Everything all right?"

"I need"—Emma huffed the words into Ruby's ear—"to talk to Burt. My freezer's on the fritz."

"Oh, that's too bad. Did everything thaw?"

"Not yet."

"Well, I guess that's one reason to be grateful for twenty-degree weather. You can stick everything in coolers outside, and it'll stay fine until morning."

"I'm not hauling all—is he there?" Exasperation made Emma sound much like a hissing cat. Burt could be wrong about that fight.

Ruby Janka, stop that this minute. Her conscience used her mother's voice. "As a matter of fact, he is." She glanced at the clock. Twenty minutes to an odd day. Emma was probably thinking the same thing. "I'll get him." She opened her mouth to call Burt to the kitchen but changed her mind and took the phone to him. Could she help it if she wanted to watch his face? "It's Emma." She held the phone out.

His eyebrows converged. He took the phone. "Em?" His gaze stayed locked on Ruby's as he spoke into the phone. "What's up?" A long, listening silence followed. "No problem. You go to bed, and I'll let myself in."

He had a key? Was he in the habit of letting himself in? After she'd gone to bed?

Movement to her left reminded Ruby her granddaughter was still there and pulled her thoughts off their jealous path. She sat on the couch and rubbed Angel's back. "Taylor's at a difficult age. When your mother was her age, she was—"

"Sneaking out to meet her English teacher in the woods." Angel rubbed her face with both hands. "I guess things could be worse. There's no boy in the picture."

Burt set the phone down and stood. "I'd better get going. Emma's freezer is on the fritz."

Did he have to use her exact words? "Of course."

"I'll call you." He darted a glance at Angel. If not for her granddaughter, this night might well end with a kiss.

Ruby stood and walked over to him. "All right. You can call the bakery any—" The phone rang again. "It must be Emma. No one else would call this late." *Or be this rude.* She picked it up and said a polite hello.

"Ruby? This is Kim."

Unbelievable. They really were going to stalk the poor man if he didn't punch the time clock.

"I'm sorry to bother you, but—"

"He's here." Ruby's words registered a few degrees cooler than the outdoor air.

A relieved sigh whooshed through the receiver. "It's awfully late."

"It's twelve minutes to twelve. I happen to know he doesn't turn into a pumpkin at midnight."

A nervous laugh answered her. "I know you think we're being overprotective." *As a matter of fact, I do.*

"Can you talk for a minute. . .without my dad listening?"

"Of. . .course." Ruby walked casually into the kitchen.

"Like I said at the restaurant, there's a reason we're so vigilant. And we could use your help with something if you're willing. He'll listen to you."

"O. . .kay."

"My dad missed his appointment with me last week. . .on purpose. He needs to keep those appointments. He could be walking around with a time bomb in his chest and. . ."

A curious picture flashed before her eyes—she and Burt side by side, staring at X-ray view boxes revealing round black cartoon bombs—one in his chest and an identical one, fuse lit and sparking, in her cranium. She shook her head. She'd missed several sentences. Her mind wandered so these days. "I'm sorry. What did you want me to do?"

"Convince him. Tell him to do it. For you."

Angel peeked in and mouthed good-bye. Ruby blew a silent kiss before answering Kim. "Sorry. What does he need to do?"

"I put in the orders. He just has to call me and work out a time."

Walking to the doorway, Ruby watched Burt put on his jacket. "Sure. I'll make sure he follows through with it. Bye."

She turned off the phone and floated into his open arms.

What, exactly, was 'it'?

Chapter 10

The Wednesday after Christmas dawned bright and clear. By midmorning, ice melted off the eaves in tiny rivulets that ran down the high windows of the bakery kitchen. Ruby restarted a CD of Christmas carols for the second time. Sue, her part-time help, groaned. "Christmas is over."

"Hush." Picking up a piping bag, Ruby defended herself while writing "Happy New Year" on a sheet cake. "I was too busy with the wedding to get enough of this."

"That's like eating stale popcorn after the movie's over." With a shake of her hairnet, Sue went back to unloading the dishwasher. "I think all that time you spent stuck in the car with Burt Jacobs affected your sense of timing."

"How did you. . .did Angel tell you?"

"Word gets around in this—"

Angel stomped in, marched over to the CD player, and turned off the music with a smack of her hand on the button. "Anybody get the memo Christmas is over?"

Sue cheered. Ruby flicked a dab of frosting at her granddaughter's pristine apron. Was that a tummy bulge already or just the huge silver belt buckle Wade had bought her in El Paso?

"Can you watch the front, Bapcia? I need to sit down a minute."

Ruby stared at Angel's face and set down the piping bag. She pulled out a wheeled stool. "You look pale."

"It's just tension. We had another knockdown, drag-out with Taylor last night. I have a headache. It's making me a little queasy."

What's making you queasy is not in your head, and Taylor has nothing to do with it, Angelika. "I've got some soda crackers in the cupboard." She rummaged until she found the box. "Something dry like this helps. If you go too long between meals, you're more likely to get sick."

Angel narrowed her eyes. "I had breakfast an hour and a half ago."

"You should carry some protein with you all the time for"—she walked quickly back to her cake—"energy. They say everyone should eat smaller, more frequent meals. It's good for—" The front door buzzed. "I'll watch the front." *Before I stick my foot in my mouth.* Life would be so much simpler if Wade and Angel would make their announcement. She whipped her hairnet off, scurried out of the kitchen, and slipped behind the counter, calling "Good Morning" before she could even see the customer behind the tea display.

"Morning, Ruby."

Madora. The air wafting through the slowly closing door was much colder than she'd expected. "How are you, Madora? What can I get for you? Coffee?"

"Just a moment of your time." She unbuttoned her plaid jacket and sat on a stool. "Those apple turnovers look good."

"Two-for-one special, just today."

"Hmm. Guess I'll skip it. I came to offer you something."

Needing to busy her hands, Ruby retied the bow at the back of her apron. "Oh?"

"Yes. I've missed our little accountability sessions, and I imagine you have, too. With all that's going on in your life, I think you could use someone to talk to. . .to act as a moral compass, so to speak."

The sudden spasm that interrupted Ruby's exhale created a hollow sound. "Gesundheit!"

Ruby turned away from the plaid jacket and the beady blue eyes focused on the apple turnovers and attempted to resume a normal breathing pattern. "That's so very thoughtful. But I already have a very supportive social network of Christian sisters. Oh! Guess what? I just remembered something." She stared down at hash marks on a notebook page and did a quick calculation. "Our thirty-eighth customer of the day gets two free apple turnovers." She ripped a wax bag from the box. "To *go*."

≈❧

December 31—5 p.m.

I've lived a simple, private life. I want to keep it that way. I've spent the past forty-eight years worrying over someone—Fryderyck, my mother, Jeanie, Angel. Now I would like to take care of only me. I repeat—I want to take care of me!! I don't want to be anyone else's burden until I have to be. And I don't want to live in a fishbowl. Why is everybody so fascinated with two ~~old~~ somewhat old people who enjoy each other's company? Well, the Emmas and Madoras of this world are going to find themselves bored silly because they're not going to find anything interest—"

The doorbell rang. Ruby closed her pen in her journal, smoothed her skirt, and answered it.

A chicken stood on her porch.

≈❧

The look on her face made up for the stares and snickers at the flower shop. Burt held out a bouquet of long-stemmed roses. "Happy New Year."

"You're kidding."

"You said you were wearing a costume, so I thought I would, too." He gestured toward her calf-length skirt covered with a pointy-hemmed white apron. She wore black lace-up boots and a fitted red jacket trimmed in green and gold

301

braid. "Very pretty, by the way. Very. . .Polish."

Ruby rolled her eyes, shook her head, and pointed at his fuzzy, yellow chest. "Very handsome. Very. . .poultry-ish."

"Thank you. And don't worry—I'm only wearing this to dinner."

"Funny."

He handed her the flowers.

"Thank you. I love red—how did you know?"

"Lucky guess."

He followed her into the living room and waited while she found a vase in the kitchen. Her Bible was open on the coffee table, and he picked it up. The gold edges were worn to white in spots. It was opened to Ecclesiastes. He looked down at the much-quoted third chapter—a fitting passage to read at the end of one year and beginning of the next. "There is a time for everything"—he read softly to himself—"and a season for every activity under the heavens: a time to be born and a time to die, a time to plant and a time to uproot, a time to kill and a time to heal, a time to tear down and a time to build, a time to weep and a time to laugh, a time to mourn and a time—"

"To dance." Ruby twirled in a tight circle, a knobby, white vase filled with roses held at arm's length at if it were her partner. Her traditional Polish skirt billowed around her legs. Once again he was struck by the almost-visible glow of her spirit. She was beautiful. Not in the skin-deep way he would have defined beauty thirty years ago, but she possessed a kind of splendor time couldn't touch. She set the vase down, walked over to him, and held her hands out, one at his shoulder, the other reaching for his hand. "Ready?"

Burt closed the Bible and clung to it. "Um. . .you should maybe know I've never polkaed."

"Ach. It's about time you learn." She laughed as she walked to the entryway and took her coat off a hook. "To everything there is a season. Got your permission slip?"

Burt patted his jacket pocket. "I have a special notarized dispensation signed by my daughters allowing me to stay out until 3:00 a.m."—he held out his hand for her coat—"and a new preprogrammed cell phone, courtesy of the three spies."

She slipped into her coat and turned around. With an impish grin, she looked up at him. "I'm just glad it's an odd day."

"Me, too."

⁓⧓

"Forget them." Burt pulled to a red light. "All of them—Emma, Madora, and every one of our nosy daughters. Tonight it's just you and me. Okay?" He pulled a paper blowout from his pocket and blew on it until the end uncurled and tickled Ruby's chin.

"I'm sorry. I whined your ear off."

"That's what friends are for. But I need you to be happy. If I'm going to end the year by stepping on your toes, I need to know you're in a forgiving mood."

Gray eyes sparkled once again. "I pre-forgive you for every bruise."

"And everything else?"

"No blanket pre-forgiveness. I'll offer it on a case-by-case basis."

The drive to Chicago seemed to take half what it usually did. Not that he ever minded driving, but he'd spent too many highway hours alone with his own thoughts. He put on his turn signal and picked a piece of yellow fuzz off his sleeve. He'd taken the chicken suit off before leaving Ruby's. It had accomplished its purpose. He turned right onto Erie and right again on North Wells, all the while watching Ruby's expression out of the corner of his eye. He hadn't told her where he was taking her for dinner.

He knew the precise moment she figured it out.

"You're kidding." Shock turned to laughter as she looked at the cement block wall advertising burgers and fries, and quoting the restaurant's founder— *Ed says, Shake it up, baby.* Her laughter died suddenly as she stared down at her skirt, picking up the edge of the scalloped apron. "I am not going in that place dressed like this."

Ignoring her, Burt drove around the block twice before he finally found a parking space. He got out, walked around the front of the truck and opened her door. She didn't budge. "There's only one way you're getting me into Ed Debevic's in this skirt." She reached in the backseat.

A flash of yellow hit him in the face. "Not on your life."

"Better think of something more of a sure thing than that. Put it on or take me somewhere else." She held her mouth in a tight line, but her eyes twinkled like the Christmas lights on the trees in front of Gino's Pizzeria across the street.

Burt tried to stare her down but lost the battle. "You're serious? You'd walk in there with a giant, bald chicken?"

"I would. They're going to ridicule you no matter what—why not give them some good material?"

"I thought we were going to live life a *little* ways outside of normal."

She didn't answer. She merely challenged him with silent, piercing, beautiful eyes. He put the suit on and marched, chin high, into the humiliation of Ed Debevic's diner.

Four waiters danced on the counter to the blaring music of the "YMCA" song. The gum-snapping hostess eyed Ruby up and down, and deadpanned, "You—stand over there. You're the next act." Cupping her hands around her mouth, she yelled, "Hey, Harry! Put on some square dancin' music. They don't get any squarer than this one." She turned to Burt and rolled her eyes. "How many times do I have to tell you chickens to use the back door? Follow me." She led them around chrome-legged tables to a gold vinyl booth. "Sit down. We'll pluck ya' later." She slapped their menus on the table.

Burt sat down and peered over the menu at Ruby. "Are we having fun yet?"

"I will punish you for this. Someway. Somehow." She reached over and pulled a tuft of faux feathers out of his sleeve.

"Ouch."

A gasp drew their attention to a twenty-something waiter wearing suspenders covered with buttons. His hair was slicked back, and thick, black-framed glasses with white tape on the bridge perched on the end of his nose. "So that's where my order for table two went. Sir, you're needed in the deep fryer." He turned to Ruby. "Could ya' get any shorter?" Spinning on his heel, he returned in seconds with a booster seat. "Oh. Wait. You're short, but. . .have we had too many chicken nuggets, deary? Hey, I know you guys want to order, but my shift ends in"—he stared cross-eyed at his watch—"three, two, one. Bye." Ripping the menus out of their hands, he left.

Eyes sparkling, lips pressing back a smile, Ruby glared across the booth. "Someway. Somehow."

❧

Somehow, someway, his feet were actually moving in sync with Ruby's to the "Hoop-De-Do Polka."

"You're good!" The same earrings she'd worn to the wedding bounced and swung as she smiled up at him. "This was going to be your punish. . .ment"—she took a moment to catch her breath—"but you're a natural."

He'd stared a Makarov handgun in the nose with less fear than he'd felt with his first footfall onto a dance floor full of Polish dancers. But the trepidation that caused his heart to skip beats had been a waste of nervous energy. "I think there must be a little Polish mixed in with my Welsh." He leaned down, pressing his lips to her ear. "There's definitely a little Polish mixing up this Welshman."

Ruby closed her eyes and shook her head. "You need a break. Let's get a soda."

They passed a long buffet table with covered dishes labeled with words Ruby had to pronounce for him. *Krokiety, barszcz,* and *flaczki* were not regular items at the restaurants he frequented. They got their sodas and found two empty chairs at a round table and watched couples moving in time with the music like well-oiled pistons. Most of the dancers were older than they were. Ruby clapped in time to the music. When a new song began, she sang along in Polish. Burt alternated between studying the woman in red and gazing enviously at a handful of couples who had probably been doing the polka together for forty years or more.

Reaching for his arm, Ruby pointed to the clock on the far wall. The hands converged on the twelve. The lights dimmed. A spotlight lit a mirrored ball hanging from the ceiling. "Ladies and gentlemen"—the band leader announced—"please join together as we count down to the new year. Ten. Nine. Eight. . ."

Burt slid his chair closer to Ruby. His arm slid around her shoulders. "Four. Three. Two. One. . ." Bending down, he found her lips and kissed her in a way that celebrated far more than the beginning of a new calendar. "Happy New Year, Ruby."

Chapter 11

On the third Monday of January, Candace arrived, as usual, twenty minutes early. Which meant she was standing in *his* kitchen eating one of *his* bagels when he came down the stairs at 6:20 a.m.

Burt, on the other hand, was NPO. He glared at the piece of cinnamon raisin bagel slathered with cream cheese and, in a purely gut reaction, swiped it out of her hand and tossed it at the wastebasket.

"Hey!"

"Hey yourself. Have a little empathy for a starving man. You girls talked me into this. If I can't eat, you shouldn't be able to either. At least not in front of me."

Candace rewrapped the cream cheese and stuck it in the fridge. She pointed at the remains of a Salisbury steak frozen dinner in the wastebasket. "What time did you eat that?"

"That was my supper." It was none of her business if it was his second supper. He'd taken the "nothing by mouth after midnight" instructions literally, microwaving the dinner at eleven thirty and polishing off a pint of butter pecan in the last minute of yesterday. He grabbed his jacket from the hook on the back of the door. "Let's get this thing over with."

Candace pushed the remote starter for her husband's new Toyota Highlander. "Where's your bag?"

"Bag?"

"Didn't they tell you to bring anything?"

"No. What. . . ? I have to provide my own specimen bottles or something?"

Candace sighed as only Candace could sigh. He'd been embarrassing the poor girl regularly since she was ten. "Let's go."

They walked out the back door to the SUV warming up in the driveway. "This is ridiculous, you know. I'm a big boy. I can drive myself." He got in the passenger seat and slammed the door. "Is it your goal to make me feel incompetent before my time?"

"It's our goal to make you follow through." She backed onto Stagecoach Trail.

"Go the other way."

"Why?"

"I need a doughnut for later. I'm going to be prepared the minute they finish my tests."

A Candace sigh filled the car. "They have doughnuts in the hospital cafeteria. Galena's way out of the way."

"It's eleven minutes from here, and if you jump on Highway 20, it won't add more than ten minutes. And considering you were twenty minutes early, I'll be early for my appointment *and* I'll have doughnuts."

"And you'll get to see Ruby. How convenient." Her words dripped with some acidic emotion, but she made a gravel-spitting U-turn.

"Want to talk about it?" *He* didn't, but he might as well invite the commentary he knew was coming anyway.

She was silent for a good mile. "I just. . .don't like it."

"Don't like it or don't like her?"

"Both. What's she after?"

"Oh, I don't know. Let me think. . . ." He rubbed his chin. "Um. . . happiness?"

He knew his daughter's fingers, though encased in Italian leather, were blanching white on the wheel.

"Or money."

It was his turn for clenched fists that squeezed the blood out of his fingers. How dare she? A quip he'd learned from his own father balanced on the tip of his tongue—*I brought you into this world—I can take you out.* He swallowed the need to blast her, took several controlled breaths, and resorted to sarcasm instead. "So Ruby arranged for me to forget Steven's tux at the inn so I would decide to ask her out? Very clever woman. All the more reason to like her."

"Dad"—*sigh*—"think about it. I know the attention is flattering, but you have to be realistic. Now that her daughter's married and she's all alone, she's. . .needy."

His hands couldn't clench any tighter. He pounded one tight fist against the window. The girl had crossed the fence this time. "Everybody's needy! God made us that way. . .relational. If you're not, there's something wrong with you." He hadn't meant it as a personal shot. Her flinch told him she'd taken it that way. *If the shoe fits, dance in it, girl.* "Your mother and I needed each other. And when she died, it left me needy. I've been needy for eleven years." He rapped his fist again. "It's gotten pretty old."

He sensed her stiffen even more, if that was possible, but Candace remained silent for miles. She turned onto Perry Street and parked the car next to the bakery. Burt yanked the door handle then turned for one parting shot. "If you—"
He didn't open the door.

Candace was crying.

≈◈

Lord, give me the right words. "I didn't mean—"

"I know Frank and I don't have the kind of relationship you and Mom had. I've tried. I'm just not like her. I don't. . .emote."

306

And what do you call this? Burt turned in his seat and put his hand on his daughter's arm. "You show your feelings in different ways than Mom did. She was verbal and physical"—he swallowed the lump in his throat—"you bake and entertain and keep a spotless house. Hospitality is your love language, and Frank sees—"

A loud moan erupted from his refined daughter. Crossing her arms on the steering wheel, she sobbed.

"Candy. . .honey. . .what's this all about?"

"Nothing." Coiffed blond hair splayed across her coat collar. "I'm fine. Go get your doughnuts, or we'll be late." She waved off his attempts to console her.

"I won't be long." He got out of the car and walked into a place he hoped would be eggshell free.

Angel stood behind the counter, bagging bagels for an elderly woman. She nodded at him but was apparently too busy to smile. He waited his turn. The woman left, and Angel nodded again. "Good morning." Her voice reminded him of his third-grade teacher when he came in late from recess. Apparently he was still on her "not to be trusted" list.

"How are you, Angel? You don't usually work this early."

"One of our employee's son is sick. I suppose you're here to see my grandmother."

"And buy some doughnuts. Which ones do you recommend this morning?" A little charm never hurt.

"They're all good."

Okay then. "I'll have two chocolate-covered cake doughnuts and a raspberry-filled raised."

Angel pulled a white bag out of a box and picked up a piece of bakery paper. She put the three doughnuts in without once looking up. "Anything else?"

Your grandmother? "That'll do it."

He held out the exact change.

She fanned her fingers toward the door. "I suppose it's on the house."

"Absolutely not." He laid the bills and coins on the glass countertop and waited.

And waited.

Angel cocked her head to one side and finally made eye contact. She pushed a copper tendril off one pink cheek. The girl was stunning. Probably enhanced by that glow of pregnancy people talked about. The thought made him cut her some slack. He'd witnessed more hormonal personality alterations in his lifetime than he cared to think about. The poor kid probably felt horrible, and being around the smell of food all the time couldn't help. He flashed a huge, indulgent smile. "Is your grandma busy? I mean, I know she's busy, but if I could talk to her for a—"

"I'll get her." She'd evidently had enough of him stammering like a schoolboy.

"Thank you." He took a seat on a stool and swiveled around to watch the traffic. Main Street was quieter now that Christmas was over. A man walked past the window and opened the door. When he pulled off his hat, Burt recognized him—the jeweler from across the street. Zemken. . .but what was his first name again?

"Morning, Lucas. Burt." Ruby walked behind the counter, wiping her hands on a towel. A streak of flour decorated her forehead. Her eyes held his several heartbeats longer than the jeweler's.

"Lucas." Burt extended his hand and moved over so the man could take the end stool. "How's business?"

"Slow." Lucas shook his hand. "Burt, right? I should get that right—the whole town's buzzing about you two."

Ruby covered her face with both hands and shook her head. When she pulled her hands away, she was grinning, and three new spots of flour dotted her face. "Don't people in this town have anything better to do? We're really not all that interesting."

"That's not how I heard it. Lucy McNeil said there was a giant chicken in front of your house on New Year's Eve."

Ruby grimaced as she set two pieces of pastry on a napkin in front of Lucas and poured him a cup of coffee. Lucas picked up both and slid off the stool. "Thank you. I'll bring the cup back later. I'll leave you two love*birds* alone." He laughed all the way out the door.

Shaking her head, Ruby leaned her elbows on the counter. "Thank you."

"For what?"

"For the past three weeks. For giving me a life. Like the rest of this town needs to get." She held up the coffeepot. "None for you, right?" Her bottom lip tilted out in a sympathetic pout.

"I'll take one to go. Even cold, it'll be better than anything I could get at the hospital."

"So they let you drive yourself like a grown-up, huh?"

"No. Candace is in the car."

"She brought you here?" Her eyes opened wide.

"Not willingly. That's a topic for tomorrow when I pick you up at three for dinner and the*atuh* at Playcrafters Barn in Moline."

Her left brow rose coquettishly. "You're assuming a lot, Mr. Jacobs."

"Oh, I'm sorry. You're right." He pointed at the chunky tear-off calendar on the wall. "Forgive me. Tomorrow's an even day. I guess I'll have to ask Em—"

The last syllable was lost when the owner of Angel Wings Bakery leaned across the counter and planted her lips on his. And at that moment, the front-door buzzer announced a customer.

Their lips parted abruptly, and they turned in unison.

"*Emma!*"

He was in no condition to have his blood pressure checked, let alone a stress test. He'd failed one of those already today when Emma shrieked and ran out of the bakery.

Burt stared at the gown the nurse's aide handed him and at the hospital bed behind her. He'd expected to see Kimmy at the clinic, not the hospital. He didn't like the look of this. Nor did he appreciate Candace's sense of humor when she'd left the room and said she'd be back to pick him up in the morning. If that girl wasn't back here by noon, he'd call a cab.

"You can leave your clothes in this locker." The lady in the sunflower-covered smock demonstrated the opening and closing of the skinny closet. *Thanks. Sure couldn't have figured that one out on my own.* His attitude was taking a dive.

The aide left, leaving the door mostly closed. Burt shut it the rest of the way. With his back to the door, which who knows who might pop through without warning, he undressed and put on the ridiculous faded teal contraption with snaps and straps in the oddest places. Every joke ever made about gaping hospital gowns was true.

Now what? No point in getting in bed. He wasn't sick. He turned suddenly to the dry-erase board under the clock where the aide had signed her name. Did they know that? What if they'd mixed his orders with someone else's and he was about to be prepped for removal of some organ he still needed? He hadn't actually read any of the mountain of papers he'd signed in the admissions office. His empty stomach manufactured a sudden dose of acid in response to the thought.

Pacing to the window, he stared up at a battleship gray sky and down at patches of snow surrounding air-conditioning units on the roof two stories below. Any minute now someone would walk through that door and slap a blood pressure cuff on his arm. Thanks to Candace's fear that she wasn't "enough" for Frank and Kimmy's fear that her father was no longer competent to make decisions about his own health care, his blood pressure would read something like three hundred over two hundred, and before he knew it, they'd be cutting his chest open and trading his heart for some poor unlucky pig's.

A tap at the door made him jump, turn, and grab the back of his gown. The door opened before he found his voice.

A cute little blond, younger than his youngest child, fairly skipped into the room. "Good morning. I'm Bridget. I'll be doing your blood draw this morning." She set a red plastic box on the bed. Did they have to make it red? Vials, some full, some waiting like little vampire bats, jiggled in their holders. "If you're ready to get started, sit down, and I'll raise the head of your bed."

If I'm ready? Get real. He did as he was told, wondering if he should tell her that raising the head of the bed might not be the wisest idea.

Bridget opened an alcohol wipe and rubbed the inside of his elbow. "That

309

looks like a nice one." She prodded a vein. The girl enjoyed her job way too much.

Bridget tied a tourniquet around his forearm. "Make a fist."

Burt turned his face to the battleship-colored sky.

"Okay. Quick sting."

Ouch. He counted stripes on the tan and gold curtains. *One. Two.* Bridget siphoned blood into a tube. *Three. Four.* The tourniquet snapped. *Five.* The room darkened. *Six. . .*

"Mr. Jacobs? Burt?" His name chiseled at the fringes of his consciousness.

"Huh?" He opened his eyes, blinked twice. Sunflowers danced before his eyes. A whole field of them. . .in January. Strange.

"Burt? You with me?"

"Of course." Where did she think he'd go?

"We're all done." This from a voice on the other side of the bed. Bridget. The vampire.

He looked up at her, kept his eyes open this time. "Good."

Bridget laughed, picked up her red box, and waved as she headed out. "You know what they say. . .the bigger they are, the harder they fall."

If he had a dollar for every time he'd heard that one. . .

Dr. Kim Jacobs-Smythe entered the room, followed by two scared-looking interns in new white coats. "Good morning, Mr. Jacobs." She winked then turned to the chart in her hand.

"Good morning, Kimmy."

She glared.

He grinned.

"We're going to ask you a few questions, take your vitals, and then we'll do your echocardiogram and an MRI to check those stents. At eleven thirty we'll do your prostate exam and. . ."

Not a single word registered after that.

Chapter 12

Ruby pushed the receiver against her ear. "I can hardly hear you."

"I don't dare talk much louder." Burt's voice, a strained stage whisper, sounded urgent. "You have to rescue me. I'm being held in the hospital against my will. Kimberly, my daughter. . .I repeat—my *daughter* is going to do a prostate exam. I didn't agree to that. What's that part of me have to do with my heart? I'm not—"

"I'll come get you." The phone shook with the laugh she tried to keep silent. "But you're two hours away."

"That's okay. After my ECG, I'll get out of here. If I have to hide somewhere, I'll call. . .wait—you don't have a cell phone."

Ruby untied her apron as she headed to the front. "I'll borrow one. Give me your number." She grabbed a marking pen off the counter and scribbled on the back of her hand. "I'll call you when I get in the car."

In something under three minutes, she had borrowed Sue's cell phone, explained about the list of orders to be packaged and the half-filled pan of muffins in the kitchen, and was headed toward Rockford Memorial Hospital.

She typed in Burt's number before putting the car in gear but didn't push SEND until after she turned onto Highway 20. She assured him she was on her way, tried not to laugh at his predicament, and drove out of town, her pulse feeling like it bested the number on her speedometer by a good fifty points. It was a silly rescue mission, but Burt needed her—and the knowledge was exhilarating. The irony wasn't lost on her. Three weeks after declaring her glorious independence, and here she was ecstatic about being needed.

"Lord, do I confuse You as much as I confuse me? I think for a change I'm just going to go with the flow and not try to figure it all out. You put Burt in my life, and I hate that it had to be at the end of it, but I'm just going to trust Your timing and enjoy every minute of it." She turned on a Christian music station and for the next hour sang along with every praise song she knew. She was just coming up to Freeport when Sue's phone rang. She pulled to the side of the road so she could see the caller ID. It was Burt. "Hi."

"Okay. . .so I have a little. . .problem. Don't laugh, okay?"

She was already starting to. "Okay."

"Somebody took my clothes."

She didn't laugh. She erupted. Tears streaming down her face, she attempted to speak but couldn't.

"When you get over your fit, will you do me a favor?" Burt sounded distant, as if he was holding the phone at arm's length to avoid the full force of her mirth.

"Of c–course. You w–want me to buy you clothes, right?"

"Yes." He rattled off sizes. "And shoes. Size twelve."

"Got it."

"Thanks. I owe you one," he answered in monotone.

"I'm getting paid in giggles. I haven't laughed this much in years."

"Glad I could help. I'll be the blue guy in a skimpy gown at the west door."

Ruby hung up the phone and continued on, her mind preoccupied with what to buy Burt. She liked him in blue—it brought out the striking color of his eyes. Then again, she liked him in chicken yellow.

She was just coming up to the first Rockford exit when the plan gelled. Could she find her way to the Goodwill store? It was worth a try. It was so worth a try. Deciding not to take a chance on failure, she stopped at a gas station and got directions.

The moment she walked through the doors, memories of her first few hours with Burt scampered through her head like playful puppies. She'd been enamored then. Three weeks later, her emotions were something altogether different.

As she looked through a rack of men's pants, a plaid pair with a wide white belt slipped under her fingers. Holding her breath, she looked at the size. Perfect. Well, maybe an inch too short, but what was an inch? Biting her bottom lip, she threw them in the cart and went in search of a shirt that didn't match.

❧

He was totally within his rights to check himself out. He'd just kind of skipped the "check out" part. That was a minor detail compared to the very real problem of getting to an exit on the first floor before somebody sounded an alarm. The note he'd left on the bed would at least assure Kimmy he hadn't been abducted. Not against his will anyway.

And he'd return the two curtain sashes he'd borrowed from his room.

Hovering in the stairwell between the second and third floor, he set his bakery bag on the floor and knotted his makeshift belt. Below him a door opened. He held his breath. Fast steps approached. What to say? A boy of six or seven froze four steps down from him.

The boy wore a smaller version of Burt's gown. His arm was in a cast. Dark brown eyes mirrored the shape of his open mouth.

"Running away?"

The boy shook his head. "Going to see my baby brother. He was borned yesterday. I jumped on the bed when I heard he was borned." He pointed to his arm. "I fell. They think I hit my head, too, so I have to stay so they can watch me, but I never did hit my head. You won't tell, will you?"

"Not if you don't tell on me."

"Are you hiding from the nurses, too?"

"I'm hiding from my daughter. She's a doctor."

The boy shook his head. "That would be bad. Can you tell me how to get to the baby floor?"

Burt bent down closer to the boy's eye level, knowing full well he'd embarrass his own fuzzy hospital socks off if anyone approached from behind. "Well, I do know how to get there. Two of my grandsons were born here. But the problem is we can't get there from here. They have lots of special locks on the doors to keep the babies safe. Maybe someone can take you to see him. If you have permission, they'll let you in the right door."

The boy's eyes shimmered. "No they won't. They said 'cause I'm a kid and I might have germs and give the babies flu I can't go in there."

"Well, I bet your baby brother will be coming home soon."

The boy wiped his nose on his arm. "He can't go home for a long, long time 'cause his birthday was supposed to be by my birthday, and that's Easter time, and he's really, really too little, and I'm going home today, and I wanted to see him 'cause I'm going home to my dad's house, and when he goes home by my birthday, he's going home to my mom's house."

An invisible fist landed squarely on Burt's diaphragm. How was he supposed to answer that?

"Wanna see a picture? He has my same hair." Shaking dark curls, the boy held out a photograph. "His name is Mikey." He pointed at the little red face. The baby was cradled in a man's hand. Tubes stuck out of his nose. His tiny arms were not much bigger around than the man's fingers. "He's kind of funny looking, but he's still a real people."

"He's absolutely a real people. Just like you and me."

The boy slipped another picture from behind that one. "This is his bed. It's kinda like a box. See? It says 'Baby Boy Williams.' Mom says I should have a sign that says 'Big Boy Williams' on my bed."

Burt looked down at a miniature ear below the preemie's pale blue cap. "He's. . .beautiful. You're going to have so much fun being a big brother."

"I know. I buyed him a ball already before he was borned. I know he can't play with it yet, but he can look at it."

Burt blinked back tears. Bridget-the-bloodletter's words rang in his ears—*the bigger they are, the harder they fall.* "He'll be throwing it to you faster than you know."

☙

Ruby pulled the getaway car up to a gas pump. She hadn't thought to look at the gas gauge when she'd asked for directions, but their escape would be short-lived if she didn't fill up. As she stuck the nozzle in the tank, Sue's phone rang in her pocket. She took it out and cringed at the name on the display. Angel.

Angel could be calling Sue. In a strange twist of life, Angel was now occasionally babysitting for her old babysitter's children. Ruby slid it back in her pocket unanswered.

Seconds later it rang again. Again "Angel" popped up on the screen. *Lord, don't let me lie.* "Hello?"

"Bapcia! Where are you?"

None of your business. "I'm in Rockford."

"Sue said there was an emergency. What's going on?"

"I never said anything about an emergency." *Although being stranded in a hospital gown in January certainly qualifies.*

"It's him again, isn't it?"

"*Him* has a name."

The sigh that tickled her ear made her stick her tongue out at her reflection in the backseat window. "You left work. You never leave work unless you're dying." *Hmm. . .*

Well, that would be my excuse this time then. "Burt was stuck in Rockford without a car—"

"Did he run out of gas again?"

"No. He was. . .visiting Kim and just wanted to get home earlier"—*than his prostate exam*—"than Candace was ready to leave. And I was going to go to Sam's Club"—*in Dubuque, on Saturday*—"anyway, so now I can kill two birds." *One being a very large chicken.* She put her lip back between her teeth where it belonged.

"Bapcia. . ." A drawn-out silence followed. "Are you two getting serious?"

"Serious" was a hard word to define. "We're becoming good friends."

"Are you in love with him?"

"We've only known each other a few weeks."

"That doesn't answer my question."

"I'm not going to run off and marry the man, if that's what you're worried about."

Another long silence. "I guess that is what I'm worried about." Her grand-daughter's voice lowered until she sounded like the curly-headed little redhead Ruby had rocked by the window too many years ago.

The pump stopped. Ruby pulled out the nozzle. "Why does that worry you? I don't jump into things foolishly."

"I know. I guess I'm scared of things changing. I know that sounds dumb. But that's part of the reason I left Chicago. I just like the idea of someday bringing my kids to your house so you can teach them to make angel wings and read Berenstain Bear books to them and—" A loud sniff followed.

"Angelika. . .if I have anything to say about it"—*and it doesn't appear I do*—"I'll still be right there making angel wings when your little one is old enough to stand on a stool. Okay?"

"Okay. I'm sorry—I'm just being silly."

"No, you're being normal."

"Just be careful, okay? I'm sure Burt's an okay guy. I just don't want him changing things. . .or you."

"I understand. Bye, honey." *I understand, but it's too late.*

Burt sneaked out of the shadow of a fake tree and into the hallway just as Ruby's burgundy sedan pulled up to the side entrance. Taking a deep breath, he darted toward the door.

"Hey! Wait!" A woman's voice called to him. "You can't go out without a coat! Security!"

With a quick glance behind, he lunged for the door handle. The heavyset woman in a pink smock started running. He heard her footsteps picking up speed as he charged through the hospital door. The car's back door was open. He dove in and slammed it behind him. "Go! Go!" For the first time all day, he laughed.

And laughed. And he wasn't laughing alone. "Your c–clothes are in the bag."

"Thank you. You are my hero. I owe you lunch and dinner and way more. You pick the place." He stuck his hand in the bag. "Candlelight, prime rib, you name—"

A lime green velour turtleneck hung from his fingertips. "You little. . ." He dug deeper. Plaid pants, blue-and-orange-striped socks, red and silver running shoes, and a Green Bay Packer jacket with a number four on the back. As Ruby sped out of the parking lot, he sank against the back of the seat and calmly opened his bakery bag. His teeth sank gratefully into a filled doughnut, and he smiled around the bulge in his cheek at the face in the rearview mirror. "I don't get mad, woman," he garbled. "I get even."

"Yeah, yeah. I've heard that before."

"Just you wait. Turn your mirror down, and give me some privacy back here." He pulled off the thick tan socks with treads the sunflower lady had given him.

"No offense, but you don't really look the modest type." She turned the mirror down with yet one more raucous laugh. He had one leg in the ghastly pants when his phone rang. Kimberly's cell, of course. His goal wasn't to make her worry, just to escape her latex gloves. With a voice that mingled self-respecting pride with sheepishness, he said hello.

"Where are you, and what's this all about?"

"I'm away from the hospital, and this is all about me not wanting my daughter examining my—"

"Dad! Good grief. I'm a cardiologist. *I* wasn't going to do it."

The sheepish feeling overtook his pride. "You said 'we.'"

"That's an expression. That's how 'we' in the medical profession talk."

Duh. He loved feeling stupid in front of his kids. "Oh."

"Now get back here."

"Sorry. Can't. I've made other plans. I'll make an appointment with my GP."

"*I'll* make an appointment with your GP. And I'll call an ambulance to pick you up."

"Fine." *You just try that, sweetie.*

"I suppose Ruby is involved in this."

"Could be."

"I'm being paged." Her sigh echoed through the phone. "We'll talk later." The connection ended.

Burt struggled into the horrible pants, mumbling all the while about kids running their parents' lives. . .while Ruby laughed. As he tied a silver shoe, he blew out the last of his frustration in a huge breath. "Okay, I'm done. I escaped with my life and some of my dignity, and we need to celebrate. I know a happening joint for lunch. You'll love it." He gave directions as he slid the turtleneck over his head.

Ruby did as he directed. Until she put on the signal for the final turn. Her foot found the brake. "Ohh. . .I asked for this, didn't I?" She pulled slowly into a parking lot.

Burt got out, opened her door, and held his arms out wide. "Welcome to Chuck E. Cheese's—where a kid can be a kid." He leaned in and tugged her sleeve. "Can we go now? Can we go? Can we, huh?" He jumped up and down. "I wanna climb in the tubes and slide down the slides and play games and throw balls and eat pizza and drink so much soda I throw up and—"

"Okay! We're even." Ruby got out of the car and pulled her jacket hood over her face. "I don't know this man!" she shouted.

"Oh no, we're not even. I owe you so much more for buying me these clothes. So much more."

Ruby's hands rose in the air. "I surrender. You got me. I'll take you shopping and buy you real clothes and pay for gourmet food."

"Surrendered, huh?" He took a half step closer. "I like the sound of that." Leaning down, he tilted her chin. "You just stay surrendered." He pushed back her hood. Her lips parted. He leaned closer, touched his mouth to the tip of her nose. "But we're still having lunch right where we are."

Chapter 13

The woman was not good for his health. The tests Kimmy had ordered showed that other than slightly elevated blood pressure and cholesterol, he was a healthy man. But Ruby could change all that.

Burt smashed his snake tattoo into the mattress, sat up, and turned his clock facedown. He felt like he'd spent the night sumo wrestling. He had, in fact, been wrestling, but he was his own opponent. A two-month-old conversation haunted every one of the few minutes he'd managed to sleep.

"I can use a friend," she'd said. But she didn't want him getting the wrong idea. "I need someone who can help me laugh, who can help me live life to the fullest. . .however much I might have left."

"I'm here to help, my friend." That's how he'd answered. . .right after kissing her hand. If he'd stopped at her hand, maybe he'd still be feeling like Ruby Cholewinski was just another buddy who happened to be female. Like Emma. Like half a dozen single women at church. What had possessed him? Even back in his brain-fried days, when he had no morals and even less common sense, he never kissed a girl on the first date.

And why hadn't she stopped him? The woman was a flirt. He might be rusty, but he wasn't dead. One minute she said she only wanted a friend, and the next thing he knew, she was falling into his arms. What was a guy to do?

He sat up, punched two pillows into the right position, and leaned against them. *I'm listening, Lord. Chew me out, big-time. I know I messed up. How many times have I told Steven I'd take loneliness over the complications of a woman in my life? And now look at me. I can't be leading her on like this.*

Why? The question seemed to come from outside his head. He looked around at the shadows in the room and tried to formulate an answer.

Ruby was dying. So what would it hurt if he 'led her on'? Maybe she'd live a little longer with some added joy in her life. Maybe she'd die with a smile on her face.

A shuddering gasp echoed in the shadowy blackness. It took a moment for him to realize he'd made the noise.

What would it hurt? It would hurt *him.* A wave of sadness tumbled over him. He righted the alarm clock, smacking it back in place on the nightstand. She'd be at the bakery now. Alone.

But not for long.

❧

"Open the eyes of my heart, Lord. . . ." Ruby sang as she cracked two eggs in

317

each hand and started the twenty-quart mixer that had been around since before Fryderyck died. In the middle of the chorus, she yawned. *I'm getting too old for this, Lord. I think You and I have to have a talk about retirement.* Picking up a measuring cup, she surveyed the room that had been her second home for more than forty years. Letting it go would be hard.

But freedom would be easy. Sleeping in would be easy. Not balancing the books or dealing with demanding customers would be a breeze. What would she do with all that time? All that freedom? *Is it really okay to just think of me. . . finally? Lord, I can't even imagine. . . .*

But she could. And for the next hour, she did. With the money she made from selling the business, she could travel, see the country. . .maybe with a good friend. A good, tall, bald friend. Or update her wardrobe or buy a new car— something sleek and low and quite possibly red.

Or pay for a spectacular funeral.

There'll be none of that. "Open the eyes of my—" What was that? She stopped feeding carrots to the food processor and shut it off. Someone was knocking at the front door. Who would knock at the door of a dark bakery at 5:00 a.m.? Nerve endings at the base of her neck prickled. She grabbed a rolling pin on her way.

The front of the store glowed red from the Exit light. As her eyes adjusted to the dark, she saw a face peering through the glass. She was about to scream when the streetlight glinted off his head.

Leaving the rolling pin on the counter, she scurried to open the door for the man she'd said good night to only eight hours ago. The stern set of his lips wiped the grin from hers. "What's wrong?"

Burt stepped inside. A light dusting of snow on his black jacket sparkled pink in the light above his head. "This has to work both ways."

She didn't like the tone of his voice. With no idea what he was talking about, Ruby stalled for time and pointed toward a table in the corner. Burt took the chair facing the wall, and she sat across from him. "What works both ways?"

"You told me to humor my girls and schedule that check-up. You said do it for you. And I did. So now you have to do the same for me." He unzipped his jacket and shrugged it off as if it were the thing causing his frustration. "I know you want to live in denial, but I can't."

Ruby turned from him to the view of Main Street waking up behind him. A light came on above Poopsie's. The short little man with the cocker spaniel who lived up there would be in at six thirty-five for a cup of coffee with two creams and a blueberry turnover. Zemken's jewelry store across the street would be dark for several more hours. Lucas Zemken came in later and later since he'd found himself a girlfriend. She blinked and brought her wandering thoughts back to the grim-faced man across from her.

So the future of their friendship hung on the size and aggressiveness of the thing in her head.

An hour's worth of dreaming disappeared as if he'd pressed her DELETE button. The pain at the base of her head that had been in remission since Monday chose that moment to metastasize to her temples and eye sockets. In between phone calls from the three girls they'd dubbed the "spy trio," they'd been living a fairy-tale life—taking walks, watching old movies, and talking until she couldn't think of much this man didn't know about her. But reality was about to turn it all into nothing but a couple of pages in a photo album. Maybe a few of the pictures would end up on a Foamcore board at her memorial service.

He wanted her to find out her prognosis. For him. And what would be his criteria for staying or leaving? Would they stay friends if she had two years to live but not if the doctor said six months? Would he vanish from her life if the clock were ticking down weeks and days but no more months? Ruby stared into intense silver blue eyes and gave him the only answer she could. "I'll make coffee."

Without a word, he followed her and sat on a stool on the other side of the counter. She turned on an overhead light, measured coffee, pushed a button, and took a heavy white mug from the shelf. A timer dinged in the kitchen. "I'll be right back." She hurried to her sanctuary of stainless steel counters and supplies in neatly marked containers. Morning Glory muffins greeted the day with a hint of cinnamon. She pulled four pans from an oven and set them on racks. From a warmer, she lifted a four-loaf pan of nicely rounded raisin bread and put it in to bake. When she'd run out of things to do, she leaned against the sink and made a second sweep of the world that, one way or another, she'd soon be leaving behind.

Massaging a tight cord on top of her shoulder, she almost laughed at the ridiculousness of the fantasies she'd played with just minutes before. Who was she to dream of seeing the country? And who was she to play with the emotions of a man who—

Stood in the doorway watching her. Ruby stifled a startled gasp.

"So this is where you create the magic." The way he looked at her made her feel heavy in the middle, like a fallen soufflé.

"Would you like a muffin?"

"In a minute." He took three steps toward her. "I'm not sure you understand why I'm asking you to get this checked out."

"I understand. I wouldn't expect you to hang around and watch me"—she sought a lighter word than the obvious—"fall apart. But there will be signs. . . plenty of warning. It won't take an MRI to tell you when things are getting bad."

A strange sound—deep and low—came from him as he crossed the old linoleum, closing the distance between them. "You really don't get it, do you? I don't want you to find out how long you have to live so I know when to hightail it out of here." He ran the back of his hand across her cheek. "I want to know how much time I have left to be in love with you."

Other than his daughters, he hadn't held a sobbing woman in his arms for more years than he could count. And this one couldn't seem to make up her mind if she wanted to laugh or cry, so the sound vibrating against his chest was a sweet combination of both.

After a while, she reached behind her for a towel and mopped her face. "How c–can this h–happen? It's only been two months, but I feel like I've known you for y–years."

"Maybe it's all part of that serendipity you keep talking about. When you're young and healthy, God gives you lots of time to grow in love. For us, He arranged it so everything is just compacted and sped up."

She pushed against his chest and made a space between them. "But I can't let you. . . . You can't fall in love with a dying woman."

"Too late."

"You're not in love with me."

"Wanna bet?"

The faintest smile teased at her lips then faded. "If we stay just friends—"

"It won't hurt so bad? That's a lie. And I don't think there's any chance I can rewind my feelings."

"Lost love is romantic in movies. In real life it just stinks."

"So let's pretend it's a movie and make it a happy ending, even if it's not the one we want."

She shaped her hand like a bracket and ran it along an imaginary line in front of her. "To be continued. . .in heaven."

"That works."

She turned around, facing the sink. "No. It doesn't. You're not going to spend the next few years or months saddled with me. My energy's going to fade, and I won't be able to do anything fun, and my personality may change. My mother got so angry and demanding and"—her fist hit the metal counter— "I won't do this to you. If you've lived with someone for years and they get sick, that's different, but you don't owe me anything, and you already went through this with your wi—"

"This isn't *your* movie."

She turned back to him, confusion etched on her tearstained face.

"You don't get to write the script by yourself. We've already done the first scene together. You don't get to write me off and walk into the sunset without me."

"But. . ."

"I know I have a choice. I could pretend I never met you and keep things just the way they were. I could keep on looking in the mirror every morning and convincing myself I love being alone. But I don't love it. You're right—sometimes life stinks, but in between it's beautiful, and I want to celebrate it—with you. And there's not a thing you can do about it. Unless you don't *like* spending time with me."

Another laugh-sob shook her shoulders. "So if I say you make me nuts and I can't stand being around you, you'll walk away?"

"Absolutely."

"Okay." She took a massive breath. "Burt Jacobs, you make me nuts. I told you I only wanted a friend, and then you went and turned it into something else. I was perfectly happy with my quiet little doughnut-lady life until you came along and made me laugh and showed me what fun is, and then you kissed me and made me feel like a woman again, and now I can't stand being around you. Because all I can think of is"—she stretched on tiptoes and touched her lips to his—"this."

Chapter 14

Burt patted his belly as he carried a folding chair to a corner of the church basement. Two pancakes, three sausage links, a pile of scrambled eggs, and a mess of hash browns had stuffed his stomach. The pastor's message satisfied his soul. And thoughts of Ruby filled his mind. He was a full man.

Jim Hansen set a chair next to his, and three other men joined the prayer huddle. As the clang of chairs and clamor of almost forty male voices slowly died, talk in Burt's circle changed from the Fighting Illini and the weather forecast to personal matters.

"How's your mother doing, Greg?" Jim took the lead.

"About the same." Greg Merton sandwiched his Bible between two large hands. "The hospice people are wonderful. I don't know how they do it day after day."

"We need to be praying for them, too. You know we're here for you and your family. Anything you need. . ."

"I know."

"Burt? How was your week?"

"I had a good week." How honest should he be? Jim, the third leg of the Sorry Widowers group Steven had deserted, knew some of what was going on in his life, but he hadn't shared a thing with the other guys. "Okay. . .before I say anything, let me just remind you all of our covenant of confidentiality."

"It's a woman." Bob Torelli crossed his arms over his expansive middle and slid back in his chair. "So you're finally going to fess up."

After everyone muttered something about which particular rumor they'd heard—stranded truck, giant chicken, or the great hospital escape—Burt nodded. "If there's a chance I'll get some serious advice."

Their promises came with less-than-believable looks of innocence, but Burt knew his confidences were safe. Just maybe not his patience. They were mercy-giving men who could be merciless with one of their own when it concerned a woman. He'd watched Jim suffer harassment for weeks when he'd first told them about Amanda, his long-distance girlfriend. In truth, he'd done a bit more than watch. With a deep breath for confidence, he told them about Ruby, leaving out the brain tumor part. If he broke that confidence, she'd never forgive him. "So what do I do about my girls?"

"No offense, but how sure are you that their concerns are unfounded?" Bob, happily married for forty-some years, had watched his daughter marry a man her friends and family begged her not to.

"I've never been so sure of anything in my life. She's giving me way more than she's getting out of this relationship."

"Then speak the truth in love to your daughters. Tell them you need to live your own life."

"You're not getting any younger."

"If you're sure this is it, ignore them. . .nicely."

The answers popcorned across the group for several minutes. And then Jim leaned forward and folded his hands. "You need to reassure your girls. They're scared of a lot of things most likely. . .scared Ruby's after your money or she'll replace their mother's memory. And after you reassure them, tell them as gently as you can to back off and let you make your own dumb mistakes." Jim grinned across the circle. "We'll start praying there won't be too many of them."

❧

Ruby hung up the bedroom phone and turned the calendar back to March. There, she'd done it. After skirting around Burt's insistence for weeks, she'd finally followed through on her promise. She'd said she'd make an appointment with Dr. Bartel, and she had.

But she hadn't promised *when* that appointment would be.

The date she'd written down was only a month away. The receptionist had asked if she was experiencing any problems. In truth, she wasn't. She hadn't had a headache in two days. And that one hadn't been as bad as the one two days before it.

Maybe she was entering remission. Or a holding pattern. Her great-aunt's brain tumor hadn't been malignant. Just inoperable. The doctors claimed it could have been growing slowly for many years. Ruby had decided days ago to convince herself that hers was the same as Aunt Lotty's. If she thought it loud enough, maybe the mass would listen. But maybe staring at the lurking shadow on an MRI would shock her system into speeding up the horrid thing's growth. She was in no hurry to stare truth in its ugly face. Denial was an art worth perfecting.

But, for Burt's sake, she'd cut her denial short. Just a little longer. . .

She walked upstairs and opened the hall closet. Three red hats waited on the top shelf. A sassy little number decorated with wispy purple feathers fell into her hand when she touched it. Setting it on her head, she walked in front of the mirror.

Her lip curled. The hat was exquisite. But she wasn't in the mood to look like she was trying out for *Hello, Dolly!* Back in the closet, she picked up a billed felt cap accented with brass studs. "Now that's class." She went back to the mirror. The whole picture wasn't classy. Her lavender blouse and white cardigan seemed to accentuate pale skin and the hint of shadow under her eyes. Was she getting paler? Were the under-eye circles getting purpler? She stepped closer and winced. "It's showing." Just like her mother, she was aging at an accelerating rate.

"Stop that." She marched back to the closet and ripped a bright red blouse off its hanger. With her back to the mirror, she put it on, set the cap at a rakish angle, and grabbed the tube of lipstick she'd bought just for Jeanie's wedding. Santa Red. Perfect. She didn't need a mirror to apply it after decades of practice. She spun around. "Much better." The red reflected on her cheeks, giving her a healthy glow. Exactly the deception she was after.

"Not bad for sixty-three."

But what was Burt thinking when he stared at her across a candlelit table? Was he seeing the shadows, the sallowness? More than once he'd told her she was beautiful. Was it possible that on any level he actually thought that? The term didn't apply to women her age, even unsick women. Unless the old cliché was really true and love gave a guy 20/200 vision.

The thought drew her eyes to the yellowed, framed picture on her dresser, taken a week before Jeanie was born. The smile on her face in the picture was not put there by a photographer telling her to say "cheese." It was there because of Fryderyck's words. . . . "Smile, my gorgeous ripe tomato."

If her husband had thought her waistless shape, moon face, and puffy ankles were gorgeous, there was a chance Burt could overlook the ravages of age and disease.

For a while.

"Ach! Enough!" She was thinking in circles like a crazy person.

Or a person with a horrid thing in her brain.

Grabbing her sweater, she marched down the stairs and put on her coat. Wanda Michaels was picking her up in fifteen minutes for their annual Red Hat Cabin Fever Brunch. She pulled her gloves out of her pocket and walked out the door. Fifteen minutes of cold air might numb her thoughts. She walked to the sidewalk and was about to turn left, when she noticed someone sitting on the curb across the street. *Strange*. It appeared to be a girl, but all she could see was black hair tumbling over her knees and arms wrapped around legs in a fetal position. Ruby stood still—staring, praying, wondering if she should walk across the street. The figure moved. One ungloved hand rose to the top of her head. The way she moved. . . "Taylor?" Ruby dashed across the street. "Taylor! Are you all right? What's going on?"

Taylor sat up. Beneath an open corduroy jacket, she wore a baggy T-shirt proclaiming "Peace Rocks." The face above the shirt appeared far from peaceful. Heavy black eyeliner surrounded reddened eyes. In the two days since Ruby had seen her last, the girl had reverted to the choppy cut and two-tone black and blond hairstyle she'd sported when they'd first met a year and a half ago. But this time the black was on top, the blond underneath.

Ruby had no idea what was wrong, but one thing was sure. The girl needed a hug. Ruby closed the distance between them, sat down, and enclosed her in her arms. Taylor leaned against her and sobbed. Ruby let her cry until her sobs turned to shuddery hiccups. "What's wrong?"

Sniffing, Taylor dried her eyes with her sleeve. "Everything. Everything I touch gets wrecked. My parents almost split over me, and my own mother can't stand being around me, and now Andy hates me, and this morning I got in a fight with Wade." Her shoulders shook; her chin quivered. "I'm like. . . poison."

Ten minutes was not enough time to solve all the problems of a poisonous teen. "Come on. You're freezing. Let's fix some hot chocolate." She stood and held out her hand to the girl who was more than a head taller than she was. The Red Hats could start healing from their cabin fever without her.

"Th–thank you." Taylor stood and gathered her jacket tight around her. "Wade and Angel are doing something at church, and I was with one of my friends, but she was sick of listening to me, so I told her to drop me here 'cause I thought maybe you'd understand, but then I wasn't sure if I should bother you." She sniffed and shivered, hugging her arms across her middle. "All my friends are on Andy's side. They think I'm the one being the jerk, and they won't even listen to my side."

"Who is Andy?"

The question brought fresh tears. They stepped up the curb in front of Ruby's, and Taylor stopped. "We've been going out since school started. That's what Wade and I got in a fight about 'cause he doesn't want me seeing him, but Wade only knows Andy's grades and stuff and not what a good person he is. So we had to find ways to see each other like how Jeanie had to sneak out to see Mr. Vandenburg when she was my age."

Oh no. "Taylor, you're talking to Jeanie's mom, the one she disobeyed when she snuck out. Don't expect any sympathy here. What Jeanie did was wrong, and she's the first to admit it. It may sound romantic, but disobeying your parents— or in your case, your brother—is only going to land you in trouble."

"But I wouldn't be in trouble if—"

A tan SUV pulled into the driveway, about six feet from where they stood. Wanda rolled down the window and poked her frilled red hat out. "Ready?"

"Something came up. I'll join you later."

Taylor groaned. "You have a Red Hat thing, don't you? I'll leave."

"No you won't." Ruby put her hand on Taylor's sleeve. "What's going on with you is more important than those old ladies."

Wanda laughed. "She's right. We just sit around and cackle and talk about our gall bladders."

Straight black locks floated over blond layers as Taylor shook her head. "No.

I'm not going to wreck your life, too. You go have fun. I'll call. . .my friend to get me." She sniffed and turned and ran.

"Taylor!" There was no point in running after her. Ruby's short legs were no match. With a bewildered sigh, Ruby walked around and got in the car.

Wanda put the car in gear. "What was that all about?"

"Drama. Hormones. A stubborn kid with a broken heart."

"Anything serious? I thought she was all into loving Mother Earth and all that. She looks kind of rock star-ish today."

"Taylor tries on personas like we try on hats." Ruby sighed again, this time with less intensity. "What's new in your world? How was Hawaii?"

"Wonderful. Grandkids loved it. But in my opinion, Christmas without snow is pointless. But let's not talk about me yet. Let's talk about you. You're way more interesting. Do we need to be praying about our Ruby?"

Will it never stop? "As a matter of fact, you do." She'd try a distraction. "I'll let you in on a secret. It's not public knowledge, but I'm going to be a great-grandmother."

"Congratulations! Wow, what a life you have. . .two weddings in a row and then a great-grandbaby on the way and a new man in your life. . ."

"Oh, please." Ruby closed her eyes. "What have you heard?"

"Wonderful things."

Ruby relaxed her shoulders and let her back conform to the leather seat. "Who is he?"

"His name is Burt Jacobs. He's Steven's best friend."

"So he's younger than you are?" Wanda's tone wasn't judgmental, just blatantly curious.

"No. He's older than Steven. He's sixty-four."

"And you like him?"

"Yes." *Way more than I will admit to you.*

"Does he love the Lord?"

"Yes."

"And he's good for you?"

"Very."

"Then I'll be praising God and praying for both of you." She squeezed Ruby's hand.

"Thank you." Ruby squeezed back. "You're the first person with a positive reaction."

"Seriously?"

"Seriously. Jeanie and Angel and Burt's daughters all think there's something wrong with two old people being. . .friends."

"Well, you just ignore every one of them and just listen to the Lord and your old friends. We couldn't be happier for you."

"We?" Ruby grimaced.

Wanda laughed. "Opal called us all as soon as she heard. . .just to tell us to pray for you, of course."

"Of course."

"Your secrets are safe with the five of us."

Chapter 15

P ut me to work." Burt turned on a swivel stool and used his rationed half of a chocolate-covered doughnut to point toward the cash register. "I'll take Taylor's place if she doesn't show up."

"You're serious." Ruby stuck a label on a cake box and slid it into a display case. "Taylor waits on customers."

"I know that. What. . .you think I don't have people skills?"

She tried to picture an ex-Navy man behind her counter—wearing an apron, with shirt sleeves rolled up, revealing a skull and crossbones and a cobra winding across his hand. Would children run screaming from Angel Wings? Taylor was claiming to be sick, and Angel was staying home to keep an eye on her. She needed the help. "I think you'd do great." She brushed off second thoughts and pointed to the restroom. "Go wash up. Instructions for hand washing are next to the mirror."

"Sixty-four years old, and someone's finally teaching me how to wash my hands." He headed toward the back.

Ruby waited on two customers and took a phone call before he returned. She walked out of the kitchen with an apron and met him in the hallway outside the office door. "You may be the first employee in the history of health laws to take those instructions seriously."

"One thing the Navy taught me was to follow orders."

Ruby shook out the apron, found the loop at the top, and stood on tiptoes to slip it over his head. As he tied it, she leaned up for a kiss. At that moment the back door opened.

"Bapcia. Please. . ." Angel walked in with a pale-looking Taylor behind her. "What if someone walked in? That's. . ."

Lucky for her, she didn't finish the sentence, though her unspoken "disgusting" hung in the air. Ruby's fingers tightened on Burt's arms. "What if?"

Under his breath, Burt let out a low "Shhh," stepped a respectable distance away, and greeted Angel and Taylor.

It is to a man's glory to overlook an offense. Ruby took a calming breath. "Taylor, how are you feeling?" She hadn't seen her since she'd run from her house. The poor brokenhearted girl looked worse than two days ago. She was taking this breakup hard.

Taylor shrugged. Angel answered for her. "I gave her an option—go to work or stay in bed."

"I'm glad you're here." Ruby put her arm across Taylor's shoulders. "Burt's going to work with you, so show him the ropes."

Taylor's eyes brightened dramatically. "I get to train him?"

"You get to boss him around and—" The buzzer sounded on the front door. Ruby looked up and felt her bad day take a sudden turn for the worse. "Madora. Taylor will be with you in a moment."

The woman in the plaid coat walked to the counter. "Actually, I just stopped in to say 'congratulations'."

An odd sensation buzzed through Ruby's belly—as if she'd swallowed a beehive. "Madora. . .would you like to try our fresh filled do—"

"When are you due, Angel?"

The bees stung. All at once.

Angel turned to Ruby then back to Madora. "What do you mean?"

A pink-gloved finger waggled from the sleeve of the plaid coat. "Oh! Is your pregnancy still a secret? Don't you worry. . .I won't tell a single soul."

Not a single *soul. Maybe dozens of souls.* Ruby narrowed her eyes at Madora, willing her to disappear.

Angel laughed. She was playing this well. "I don't know what you heard, but I guarantee I'm not pregnant."

"I heard it straight from Merna Olson, who owns that little antique shop, and she heard it straight from Opal, who's in your grandmother's Red Hat club. I've known you since you were a little girl, Angel. You can tell me."

"I'm serious, Mrs. Kingsley. There's no secret. I'm not—"

"*I'm* pregnant."

Taylor slid to the floor and began to cry.

≈❀

Burt handed a box of muffins to an elderly man and looked up at the back wall for the hundredth time. Finally the fat baker with a clock for a belly announced they'd survived until six. The muffin man left, and Ruby locked the door and turned over the Open sign. She leaned against the door and rubbed her temples. Burt's chest tightened. She claimed her headaches were less frequent, but he wasn't fooled. He could tell when they hit, and this was a bad one.

Angel and Taylor, both pale and bedraggled looking, walked out of the kitchen and sank into chairs at a square table. Ruby untied her apron. "Thank you, all of you. We got a lot done. . .considering."

Angel nodded and rubbed the back of her neck. "She's still talking abortion."

Ruby dropped into a chair across from Taylor. Burt plopped down beside her.

Taylor pulled a damp tissue from her pocket and blew her nose. "I know what you're all thinking. But you all believe the way you do because of what you've been told at church. That doesn't make it the absolute truth. I've researched it. This. . .thing. . .is only like the size of an appendix. People have appendixes taken out all the ti—"

"Wait just a minute." Burt slammed his fist on the table. "You are not going to sit there and tell us you don't believe what's growing inside you is a human being."

Taylor pulled a sugar dispenser toward her and ran trembling fingers up and down its sides. "It's a *potential* human being. It couldn't live on its own for a long time." A tear rolled down her cheek and dripped onto the table.

Burt stared at the track left by that one tear and felt something soften. *Lord, give us words.* His fist relaxed, and he slid his hand over Taylor's. "Neither could you." He'd lowered his voice and tried to temper it. "You need Wade and Angel and your parents and Jeanie and Ruby to give you a warm place to live and to feed you and protect you. But just because you can't fend for yourself yet doesn't mean you're any less human."

Slowly Taylor raised her head. "But that's different. The ba—fetus isn't fully formed. It doesn't have feelings or emotions. If I take care of it now. . ."

She kept talking, but Burt's thoughts took him back to a little boy in an echoing stairwell. *He's still a real people.* "I have an idea." Three sets of eyes turned to him. "I'd like all of us to take a little trip on Saturday."

"Where to?" Taylor blew her nose again, eyeing him suspiciously over the tissue tented on her nose.

"You'll see. Just promise me you won't make a decision until then. Promise?"

Messy black and blond hair swayed as she nodded. "I promise."

ॐॐ

Walking out of the back door of the bakery just after noon on Thursday, all Ruby could focus on was the thought of a nap. Her head throbbed, the pain localized at the base of her skull. She'd spent half the night on her knees pleading for the life of Taylor's baby. The other half she'd spent in doubts about putting an apron on the handsome bald man who was beginning to feel as comfortable as her old purple slippers.

Denial about him wasn't working. In spite of everything he'd said, her guilt was growing faster than a tumor ever could. She couldn't do this to him. She needed to set him free to find something lasting. But just as she began scripting the best way to tell him, a pale blue pickup pulled around the corner.

"Hey, beautiful. You want a ride?"

The script vanished. She squinted through the pain and smiled. "Where you headed, mister?"

"Walmart. Picking up a case of antifreeze. Wouldn't mind some company."

"Can't turn that one down." She was almost out of Aleve anyway. She got in the truck.

"You've got a headache."

"Just a little one."

"Sure it is." He cupped her chin in his hand. "You're pale as a dog. How long until your appointment?"

"Not long."

"*How* long?"

Ruby pulled away and stared out the side window. She'd avoided a direct answer up to now. "Three weeks."

"*What?* Did you tell them how much pain you were in?"

She shrugged.

Burt stepped on the accelerator with more force than he needed. He drove in silence until they got out of the truck at Walmart. As they headed into the store, he took her hand. Suddenly Burt stopped. Coming out of Walmart with a bag in each hand was Dr. Bartel. Burt waved.

"Stop that!" Ruby pulled but couldn't free her hand.

"Did your doctor ever mention he's an antique-car fanatic? Hey, Kirk!"

"Burt! Ruby! How are you. . .two?" Behind dark-framed glasses, Dr. Bartel's gaze landed on their linked hands. He came nearer.

"I'm fine. Ruby's not doing so well."

She yanked her arm, still to no avail.

"Ruby? What's going on?"

She shrugged. "I've just been having occasional headaches."

Burt cleared his throat. "Her mother and a great-aunt died of brain tumors. She needs to get these headaches checked out."

"Absolutely. Today." Dr. Bartel looked over the top of his glasses. "I'm on my way to the clinic. Since I know you well enough to know you won't make the call, I'll have one of my girls call you with an appointment. Do we have your cell number?"

"I don't have one."

Burt released her hand. "I'll make sure she calls."

"Good. Ruby, I'll see you in my office this afternoon." With a wave, he walked away.

Ruby waited until he was out of earshot. "You had no right to do that." Her arms folded tightly across her chest.

"Oh, yes I did." Burt put a hand on either side of her face. "You can be mad all you want, but loving you gives me that right."

❧

Cold sweat prickled her sides. The vise had returned to her head, tightening at her temples with each jerk of the waiting room clock. Yesterday was a blur of blood draws, lights in her eyes, neurological tests, and an MRI. Minutes from now, all denial would be shattered, and the man whose hand encased hers would have a decision to make.

Stay and watch, or leave and be free.

"Mrs. Cholewinski?"

Ruby stood on trembling legs and pulled Burt to his feet. He hadn't said a word since he'd prayed with her in the truck. He was as visibly scared as she was.

331

The nurse led them to Dr. Bartel's private office. They sat in cherrywood chairs in front of a huge desk and stared at a picture of a sailboat silhouetted against a setting sun. Dr. Bartel walked in and sat down. He shook Burt's hand across the desk, greeted Ruby, and opened her file. The only sound in the room was the turning of pages. The doctor stroked his chin. "Ruby, what was going on in your life when the headaches started?"

She thought for a moment, back to the first one. "It sounds a bit like a soap opera, but it was the day before my granddaughter got married. My daughter revealed, after twenty-eight years, who the father of her daughter was. I had headaches for a few weeks then, but that was over a year ago. They went away until a few months ago. . .when my daughter started planning her wedding and her move to Paris. . . ." *Add in Burt's daughters' resistance, competition with Emma, Madora the town gossip, and now Taylor. . . .* Somewhere in the back of her pounding head, a light went on. "So this. . .thing. . .is aggravated by stress?"

Dr. Bartel nodded gravely. "Stress will definitely aggravate your condition. So will lack of sleep or too much excitement of any kind. But"—he lowered his head, peering over his glasses—"there is no 'thing.'" A slow smile spread across his face. "Your MRI is negative, Ruby. You don't have a brain tumor. In fact, I can't find a thing wrong with you other than slightly elevated LDLs." He closed her file and leaned forward. "What you suffer from. . .what I can see you are experiencing at this very moment. . .is clinically known as a muscle tension headache."

Chapter 16

I'll leave you two alone." Dr. Bartel slipped out of his office.

Ruby's mouth still gaped like the open MRI tube. She stared at the sailboat gliding past the setting sun. "Sailing would be fun."

"Uh-huh." Burt seemed to be experiencing his own version of shell shock.

"I'm not dying."

"Huh-uh."

"That means I'm. . .living."

"Uh-huh." A silent moment stretched long but was suddenly broken by an eardrum-shaking laugh-shout-groan. Burt jumped up, reached down, and pulled her to her feet. "You're not dying! Did you hear that?"

The vibration started at the bottoms of her feet and quickly overtook her entire body. Every cell shook, every nerve quivered, and there was nothing she could do to stop the shaking—until six-plus feet of muscled man engulfed her in his arms. Lifting her, jelly legs and all, off the ground, he twirled in a tight circle, stopping only when the toe of her shoe toppled a framed portrait of Dr. Bartel's family. He set her down slowly.

And the tears started. Hers. And his.

They picked up their jackets and left the clinic. The clouds that had littered the sky an hour earlier had blown away. The air whispered of spring. Burt squeezed her hand. "Let's walk."

Minutes later they'd somehow ended up in Grant Park. They passed flower beds where tulip bulbs waited beneath the dirt for longer days and warmth. Down the hill, snow melted off swings and slides. . .the playground coming to life. The world smelled of damp ground and hope. Ruby led Burt up the stairs of the gazebo where Angel and Wade had recited their vows. They leaned on the wall and looked down at the sidewalk that curved past empty water fountains and park benches.

Ruby swiped her hand across her cheek. Had she been crying since the clinic? She had no idea. "I should know what to say right now, but I don't. I feel so incredibly stupid and foolish. What I put you through. What I put me through. . . All because I jumped to conclusions, all because I was too stubborn to listen to you."

"All because you were scared." He turned her by the shoulders until she had no choice but to face him. "Okay, I wish you would have listened to me. I wish you wouldn't have made us both lose sleep. But look what happened because of it. We embraced life, we acted silly, we laughed and set our priorities right." His Adam's apple dipped and rose, and he cleared his throat. "Because I thought I only had a short time with you, I didn't waste time admitting how I feel about you."

Ruby nodded, her throat too tight for words. She closed her eyes and breathed in the smell of spring and the crisp, clean scent of aftershave. "You didn't leave me."

"No, I didn't. But. . ."

She opened her eyes and didn't dare breathe. Her heart forgot to beat. Once. Twice. Her vision blurred. "But what?" she whispered.

"Maybe now that you know you may have another thirty years, you don't want me around. That's an awful long time to be. . .friends."

Thirty years. Three decades. A lifetime. An unstoppable laugh started deep inside her and lifted to the domed roof above them. She stepped away from him and twirled in a circle, hands outstretched, eyes closed. "What shall we do for thirty years?"

He grabbed one hand and then the other. Eyes locked on hers, he turned her in slow, dizzying circles. "We'll do the unexpected."

❧

They sat on a park bench, moonlight turning the last few clumps of honeycombed snow blue. Burt pulled her scarf up over her ears. "Going to church in my pajamas."

"Might be a little over the top. Make it the grocery store."

"Okay. Your turn."

"Dyeing my hair back to the color it was when I was twenty."

"It's pretty like this." He yanked at her bangs. "But go for it. And I'll grow my hair long."

"Can I confess something?" She smiled up at him. "I like guys with ponytails."

"Ponytail it is, then. Can't you see it trailing in the wind when I'm driving my little red Corvette named Ruby?"

"I can picture it. Maybe I'll grow one to match."

"People won't be able to tell us apart."

Ruby gave him an elbow in the ribs. "Let's get serious here. I want to walk down Michigan Avenue and give money to every single person who asks for it and not worry about whether or not they're scamming."

"I like that. We should think of more things like that—acts of kindness."

"I'll give Madora free pastry every time she comes in."

Burt laughed. "Now that's sacrificial giving. I can't think of anything I can do to match that." He opened his mouth to continue when "Praise You in This Storm" floated out of his jacket pocket. "That's Emma. I'll get it later."

"You have something to hide?" Ruby raised her eyebrow as far as it would stretch.

"Fine. I'll answer it." He stuck his tongue out at her. "And you can just sit there and be jealous." He pulled it out. "Hi, Em, what do you need?"

Is that the way he always answered her calls?

"Thank you. Sounds delicious. I'll pick it up on my way ho—" His eyes swooped up to the moonlit sky. "Um. . .now?" A mischievous smile tugged at his lips. "How would you feel about setting another place?" His fingers tapped his knee. "Yes. . .oh. . .you're right. Don't want to miss that. Hope you find some good deals. Bye, Em." He turned and grinned. "She invited me for pie, but then she suddenly remembered there's a sale at one of the boutiques in town and it ends tonight."

"So she didn't want to share you."

Burt shrugged. He was clearly making a valiant attempt to restrain a smug smile. "I guess that's what it amounts to."

"Can't say I blame her. I'm warning you, that catfight is still a-comin'."

He nuzzled her ear. "I'm looking forward to it."

"So Emma has her own ringtone, huh?"

"Yes."

"Oh." Ruby squeezed all the jealous inflection she could into that one word.

"So do you."

"What's mine?"

" 'Free to Be Me.' "

She sighed. "Has a nice ring to it."

"Cute."

"I like it. It fits. . .if people would just let me be free to be me. Now where were we?"

"Acts of kindness. I was about to say I can't get that little kid at the hospital out of my mind. Maybe we could volunteer at a hospital."

"You'd make an adorable candy striper."

"I would, wouldn't I? Especially with the ponytail."

"I could bake healthy cookies."

Burt's arm tightened on her shoulders. "I wonder if they'd let us hand them out."

"In a chicken suit."

"Perfect." Burt tousled her hair. "We'll call it the chicken ministry."

"I love it!" She leaned up and kissed his chin. "And I love you."

"Enough to wear a chicken suit?"

"Not a chance."

"But Big Burt needs a mate."

❧

"It'll be okay," Ruby whispered through her paper mask. Above her own pale green mask, Taylor's eyes grew wide with apprehension.

Kim motioned for them to follow her. She'd pulled some strings to make this happen.

Burt's arm slid around Ruby's shoulders, and she leaned into him. They wouldn't be here if not for this man's huge heart. She couldn't imagine loving him more than she did at this moment.

Stopping in front of a glass window, Kim reached out for Taylor's hand. She pointed to an incubator. "That little guy was born at twenty-seven weeks. He weighed eight hundred and twenty-six grams. That's about twenty-nine ounces, less than two pounds. But all his little organs are perfectly formed. He just needs a safe place to grow and develop."

Just like you. Ruby stared at Taylor and tightened her arm around Burt's waist, knowing he was thinking the same thing. Taylor didn't move a muscle, just stared. After several minutes, she took a step forward and put her hand on the glass. Kim stepped beside her. "We can come back here if you want, but I'd like to show you the transitional nursery."

Taylor nodded. Kimberly punched in a code next to the double doors at the end of the hall. They followed her to another glass window. They all stood back and let Taylor stand in front. On the other side of the glass, surrounded by incubators, sat four white rocking chairs. Two of them were occupied by women about Ruby's age rocking preemies. Kimberly tapped on the window, and the women looked up. Both grinned.

"These babies have been released from intensive care, but they're not ready for the regular nursery. They need catch-up time, emotionally as well as physically. After all the tubes and poking and prodding, they need some TLC." She looked at her father. "These women are volunteers. We call them Cuddlers. We have a dozen or so men and women in the program. They're carefully screened and trained just to rock our babies. Some of them sit here for hours. The nurses say it's hard to get them to go home at night."

Ruby stared at the glowing faces of the two women. She was still coming to terms with not becoming a great-grandmother. Burt rubbed her back, as if reading her thoughts. "We could do that," he said.

"We could."

Taylor turned slowly. She looked from Ruby to Burt. "Would you do that. . . for my baby?" Tears fell in a steady stream. "My mom can't help, and I want to finish school, and I don't want to be a burden to Wade and Angel, but if I had help. . .if I had"—her mouth lifted in a long-absent smile—"if my baby had cuddlers. . ."

A group hug engulfed Taylor and swept Ruby literally off her feet in the arms of a big, strong, softhearted man.

❧

"Hi, Mom."

"Janka!" Ruby snugged the phone closer to her ear and set down the bottle of highlighting solution she'd been arguing with for ten minutes. She hadn't talked to Jeanie in weeks. "How are you, honey?"

"We're wonderful. Paris is wonderful. I'm loving work. . .and Steven. It's incredible. Hey, I just talked to Taylor. Good news. We've been praying so hard."

"She's got a rough road ahead. I don't have to tell you that."

"We'll all be there for her. Um. . .Mom, I'm worried about you. Angel said you're looking pale and tired."

"That was a temporary thing. I'm fine now." She stared down at the dusty rose blush she'd just bought.

"And I heard you bought new boots. With heels. And black jeans."

"Aren't you proud of your old mom?"

Silence stretched from Paris to Galena. Ruby waited it out.

"That's not like you, Mom."

Where had she heard that before? "Well, sometimes a person has to do the unexpected."

"Mmm. Angel said Burt is working at the bakery. That's unexpected."

Ruby massaged the back of her neck. "Yes."

"I don't like it."

"He's doing great. People love him."

"No. I mean I don't like what's happening to you. I know you like the attention, but if you have to change yourself just so he'll like you, something's wrong."

The muscles at the base of Ruby's skull clenched along with her fist. *The only thing wrong here is a daughter trying to tell her mother how to live her life. Deep breath. Again.* "I'm not changing myself to get his attention." *Breathe.* "I'm buying new clothes and changing my hair because I've worn the same styles for ten years and I'm bored with it. Life is short, and it's meant to be celebrated, and that's what I intend to do, with or without your approval. What if I said you should still be braiding your hair—you should never have changed it for Steven?"

The empty space that followed filled with twinges of guilt. She'd been a bit too snippy.

A sniff echoed through the phone. "You're right. I just don't want you turning into somebody I don't even recognize. I don't want to lose you."

An ironic statement, considering the news Dr. Bartel had delivered. *All this over black jeans and boots with heels.* Ruby shook her head and smiled. "You're not going to lose me, honey."

"Has he. . .asked you to marry him yet?"

"No. We're just good—" She stopped short. That one wasn't going to work anymore. "No, he hasn't."

Not unless you count "Big Burt needs a mate" as a proposal.

Chapter 17

Praise music played softly in the living room as powdered-sugar snow drifted onto the bushes outside the window. If the forecast was right, they'd be cutting the evening short and shoveling their way to Palm Sunday services tomorrow morning.

Burt lit yellow candles and rearranged the pastel confetti he'd sprinkled on the tablecloth. The grill was lit and melting snowflakes on the deck. The house smelled of baking potatoes and a corn-casserole recipe he'd found online. A green salad waited in the fridge next to the raspberry cheesecake he couldn't wait to show Ruby.

Walking over to the china cabinet, he pulled out four plates and set them around the table. At six on the dot, there was a knock, and the front door opened. Ruby stomped in, her boots, black coat, and hair covered with snow. She handed him a square plastic container. "Happy spring."

"Always the optimist." He straightened his tie and took the container.

"Wow! Haven't seen you this spiffy since the wedding." Ruby slipped out of her boots and took a little hop onto the rug. She unbuttoned her coat, revealing a slice of red.

With one hand, Burt helped her out of her coat. She wore the red velvet dress, only this time it ended just below her knees. The woman had legs. Very nice legs. Very *not* senior citizen legs. His pulse turned up a notch. "Beautiful."

Out of her purse she pulled a long piece of matching fabric and wrapped it over her shoulders. "Couldn't waste it." She smiled up at him, eyes twinkling like the tiny red stones that swung from her ears.

"When did you have time to sew?"

She laughed and planted a kiss on his cheek. "Sleep-shmeep. I'll sleep in heaven."

"I doubt it. You'll be too busy dancing—doing the heavenly polka."

Ruby did a hop-skip-twirl and ended with a curtsy. "Something smells delectable."

He took a step toward her. "It's you."

Her arms slipped around his waist. "Like it? It's a Balenciaga *parfum*." She fluttered her eyelashes. "Steven and Jeanie sent it. It's called 'Prelude.'"

An almost audible gulp contracted Burt's throat. He glanced over his shoulder at the table, reassuring himself that there were, indeed, four plates taking up space on the tablecloth. "Jim and Amanda should be here any minute." The reminder was for himself, not her. He ran his lips across her forehead and pulled her tight with his free hand. "What did you bring?"

"*Pierogis, ptysie*, and ham-stuffed mushrooms."

"At least there's something I can pronounce. Come out to the kitchen."

But he didn't get her any farther than the dining room. Ruby stopped and let out a long, slow whistle. "One of your girls did this, right?" A fingertip touched a tulip in the bouquet in the center of the table.

"What are you implying?"

"That a manly man like you—" Her compliment ended in a laugh. She reached toward the china cabinet and picked up the magazine he'd forgotten to put away. She turned the cover toward him, displaying a picture that looked almost identical to the table set before her.

He shrugged. "So I needed a little help." He pointed the way to the kitchen and followed her. He set the plastic box on the counter. "I think I deserve props just for buying a women's magazine."

Ruby turned to face him. "You do." Her shoeless feet padded silently across the pine plank floor. Her hand slid into her purse and pulled out an envelope. "Here."

He lifted the flap. A downy yellow feather drifted out. "Uh-oh." He slid the card out. On the front was a squat cartoon chicken with real feathers glued to its tail. Above its head were the words "I admit. . ." He opened it and read the inside. "I'm a little chicken to say I love you." In tiny letters at the bottom, she had printed "But I do."

Burt set the card on the table and opened his arms. Tiny feet stepped lightly onto his shoes, raising her two inches closer to his lips.

His hand slid to the back of her head. His lips touched hers, lightly at first, and then—

The phone rang.

Ruby stepped down, her face flushed, her eyes wide. Burt nodded, acknowledging the same sense of tantalizing wonder mixed with a touch of shyness. He backed away from her and picked up the phone. "Hello."

"Hey. It's Jim. Amanda's plane was delayed. I thought we'd be able to make it in time, but we're still trying to cross the river. There's an accident on the bridge, and they've closed both lanes. The roads are getting slick. I'll call you when things start moving. You guys go ahead and eat; just save some for us."

"We'll wait for a while. I haven't put the steaks on yet."

"Sounds good. Hope to see you in a bit."

"Drive safe." Burt closed the phone and looked at the woman he'd just been kissing. "They're stuck in traffic."

Ruby smiled, nodded, and walked toward him.

And he did the only thing any red-blooded, God-fearing man would do.

He opened the refrigerator.

"See? Cheesecake. Raspberry swirl. Made it myself." Burt pointed at a spring-form pan and then at a glass bowl. "And Jell-O. I found a recipe online that called for cran-raspberry juice instead of water, and I added the leftover rasp. . ."

The man was scared to death. Of all the sweet and tender things he'd done, this was by far the most endearing. "Burt. Get out of the fridge. Let's heat up the appetizers while we're waiting." She tempered a laugh. "And *only* the appetizers."

He closed the door. On the front of the fridge was a picture of him and Emma. *That will have to go.* She turned her focus back to the poor man who stood rubbing his chin and grinning at her.

He shrugged. "I always thought when you got to be this age. . ."

"You'd be half dead?"

"Yeah. Passion is for the young, right? I used to hear of older people getting married and think how nice it was that they'd found companionship."

Married? She gave herself a mental slap on the wrist. He was talking about other older people. "I know." *Now what? Do we lay it all on the table? Do we have to state the boundaries? That's ridicu—*

"Maybe my girls are right. Maybe we need some rules."

Was he being funny?

"And the rule for right now is appetizers." He opened the cover of the plastic box.

"Right." She breathed a sigh. "Let's microwave just enough for the two of us."

Burt opened a cupboard, got out a stoneware plate, and handed it to her. She ran her finger across the raised pattern circling the edge. Pink houses with blue roofs. It matched the wallpaper border. All very feminine. And very nineties. Her stomach muscles tightened. Corrine had picked these out.

She'd been to Burt's house twice but never for dinner. He'd shown her the kitchen, but they'd sat in the living room where a green-and-brown-striped couch and two masculine leather recliners faced the fireplace and the huge flat-screen TV above it. A manly room. She put her other hand on the plate. "This is a nice pattern."

"With four women, I never had a say in much of anything kitchen related. Except the walls." He pointed toward the pale blue wall behind the kitchen table. "Even after the girls moved out, they had more say in things than I did. They all voted for pink. But they wanted me to do the painting. Wasn't happening."

Ruby nodded, picturing the scene, and suddenly, for no explainable reason, felt like crying. She blinked hard and busied herself filling the plate with half-moon-shaped potato dumplings, ham-and-cheese-filled mushrooms, and "stuffed swirls." She closed the cover on the container and looked up to find Burt looking down on her, arms folded, a tender smile on his face.

"Come here." He held out his hand.

"I should. . .wash. . ." She walked to the white sink and pumped liquid soap from a house-shaped dispenser. She took a steadying breath, rinsed her hands, and dried them on a pink and blue towel. Hand in hand, they went to the living room and sat on the couch. A fire blazed in front of them.

Burt folded one leg, rested his arm on the back of the couch. "Talk to me."

This time the blink only pushed the tears over her lashes. Burt bent back and pulled a tissue from a box on a side table. He tucked it in her hand. "I just all of a sudden get how your girls feel. . .how they'd feel if they walked in and saw a stranger in their mother's kitchen. How upsetting it must be to see you with someone else."

His hand played with the back of her hair. "It has to be hard for them." His voice grew as soft as the firelight. "But if it's easier for them to see me alone, that's nothing but selfishness."

He was right. But it only helped a little. "Angel was pretty honest with me a couple of weeks ago. She doesn't want things to change. She's already imagining bringing her kids to Bapcia's house. I want that, too. I love traditions. I've lived in that house since Jeanie was little, and if I leave—" She stopped, suddenly realizing she might be talking about something that hadn't yet entered his mind. "I didn't mean. . ."

"You didn't mean to imply that there's a possibility the two of us might someday make this friendship of ours a binding contract?" His right eyebrow rose, teasing her.

The heat in her face didn't come from the flames licking the logs on the iron grate. "I. . ."

"Jeanie, Angel, Candace, Bethy, and Kimmy are all going to be affected if you and I stay"—the other eyebrow lifted—"friends. I'm sure I sound heartless, but my attitude is 'deal with it.' I know my daughters. They may throw their tantrums and pull some manipulative schemes, but when it comes right down to it, they'll accept it. And once they decide to give you a chance"—the back of his hand brushed across her cheek—"they'll come to love you. Like I have."

Ruby stared up into silvery blue eyes. *Lord, what have I done to deserve this man?* She blew her nose and mopped her face. "Jeanie's coming around. Angel will give you a chance because you're her dad's best friend. And they'll come to love you. Like I have." She ran her fingers across his goatee and raised her lips to his.

And the phone rang.

Burt laughed and kissed the end of her nose. "I think Jim's working for my girls." He got up and answered the phone.

He had the strangest look on his face when he got back. Instead of walking to her, he walked to the window. "They're not coming." He pulled the drapes all the way open. "He said there are cars in the ditch all over on 20 west of Galena." He turned around. "He said I shouldn't let you go home tonight."

❧

Burt's phone swung from Ruby's fingers by its antenna. She stood by the window, mesmerized by the horizontally blowing snow. From the corner of the room, the grandfather clock struck ten. It was now or never.

She turned around and stared at the man whose feet were propped on his coffee table. "That was a wonderful dinner."

"You said that. A few times."

"I really should help you with dishes."

"You really should make that call."

The phone stopped swinging. "Angel will call your number if she can't reach me."

Burt took a sip of decaf from a dark blue mug. "Is that your decision then?"

"Yes. Maybe." She sighed. "She'll probably make Wade borrow his neighbor's snowmobile and come get me."

Mischief danced in blue eyes. "I have a little secret."

"What's that?"

"I have a snowmobile." He gestured toward her red velvet with his mug. "You'd make quite a sight flying through the snow in that dress." He pointed at the phone. "Call her. If you don't, it'll look like we're being sneaky. We're not doing anything wrong. She'll agree that—"

The phone rang. Ruby gasped and almost dropped it. Holding it like a dead mouse, she walked to the couch and gave it to Burt. He said, "Hello" and "Yes, she is," and handed it back to her. "Angel," he whispered.

"Hi, honey."

"I was hoping you'd be there."

Seriously? "I actually just had my hand on the phone to call you." *Or not.*

"We're at your house. We had dinner at The Irish Pub. We weren't planning on staying this late, but we ran into some people Wade teaches with. When we came out, the roads were horrible. There's ice under the snow, and it's even hard to walk. We're staying here tonight, and you'd better stay right where you are. I know that's awkward, but people will understand under the circumstances. . . ."

Ruby curled her finger, stuck her knuckle in her mouth, and bit down hard to quell a squeal of joy. Her eyes were riveted on Burt.

"Bapcia? Are you okay with that? Do you feel safe there? If not, Wade has a friend with a huge four-wheel drive truck. . . ."

"No. I'll be fine here. I'll just curl up on the couch."

"Thank you."

Thank you? "Thank *you* for watching out for me. Is Taylor with you?"

"She's at her folks'."

"Good. You two need a break. Pretend you're at a bed-and-breakfast, only you'll have to fix your own breakfast. There are extra blankets in the hall closet if you need them."

"Okay. Thanks, Bapcia. I'll talk to you tomorrow. 'Night."

"Love you." Ruby pushed OFF then double-checked it before releasing a sound that was an undignified mix of sigh and giggle. "She told me to stay here." She grinned at Burt. "All that worry for nothing."

"See? I told you so." A slight quiver shook Burt's words.

Ruby narrowed her eyes. "What's wrong?"

"Nothing." His eyes left her and began studying his decaf as if there were tea leaves at the bottom of his cup.

"Are you worried?" *Don't laugh, Ruby. Don't you dare laugh.* But the little-boy fear on the big, strong man's face was adorable. And made her knees weak. Maybe she should be scared, too. "Are you worried about us?"

The left corner of his mouth turned up. The skewed smile was kissable. "A little." He sighed and set the cup down. "Before I met you, I would have said I was the picture of self-control. A widower in his sixties is a popular man. My pastor did a little demographics study just for the Sorry Widowers."

"The who?"

"I never told you about that? Jim Hansen and Steven and I formed a group soon after Steven moved here. We called ourselves the Sorry Widowers and made a pact to keep each other on the straight and narrow. We also made a vow to shave our heads and fast at the wedding of a Sorry Brother."

"So that's why. . ." She patted the top of her head. "But you're still shaving it."

"I like the idea of being intentionally bald."

"Hmm. I like it, too." The throaty tone was not what she was aiming at. No wonder the poor guy was scared. "So what about the demographics?"

"Sixty-eight percent of the women between sixty and seventy in our church are single."

"Wow."

"Yeah." He ran his fingers through invisible hair. "It's a dangerous world out there. So you see, I've had lots of practice in the self-control department. But when I'm with you. . .things are different. It's too easy to lose focus."

"At the first sign of weakness from either one of us, I'll jump on that snowmobile and get out of here."

Burt smiled, but the concern was still in his eyes.

Lord, let me mean what I'm about to say with every ounce of my being. "You're safe with me."

"Thank you." Silver blue eyes pierced to the very core of her soul.

Lord. . .protect me, surround me. As He so often did, the Lord protected her with laughter. Her very next thought broke the spell of the entrapping blue eyes. "But your reputation will be toast."

A warm, rich laugh filled the spaces between the crackles from the fireplace. He patted the couch next to him. "We need a game plan. First, we get you some comfy clothes. Bethy left a couple boxes upstairs after her last move. Then we make popcorn and pick out movies. One chick flick, one action. Sound fair?"

"Sounds fun. I haven't been to a slumber party in years."

A sputtery cough sloshed the contents of Burt's mug. "Please don't use those words to anyone but—" The phone rang again.

"Uh-oh. Angel just realized what she said."

"Answer it."

She pushed TALK. "Hello."

Silence.

"Hello? Angel?"

A long pause. "This is Emma." The voice was cool and measured.

Ruby shivered and grimaced at Burt. "Emma. How are you? What a storm, huh? My granddaughter just called and told—"

"Let me talk to Burt."

Chapter 18

Ruby paced the floor in Burt's socks, Bethy's extralong sweater, and gauchos that fit her like long, baggy pants. Outside, a motor roared to life, and a loud whine split the air as Burt's snowmobile sped across the front yard.

White knight to the rescue.

Only he was rescuing the wrong woman. "It's an *odd* day, Emma! *My* day!" Ruby stomped to the grandfather clock and stared it in the face. "If they're not back here in half an hour. . ." *Calm down, woman. Emma has no control over her furnace.* Or does she? She bantered with her internal voice. "She probably turned the gas off herself. Some slumber party this is going to be."

You think God had nothing to do with this? Her conscience startled her with truth. "Okay, Lord. I know I'm supposed to thank You for this."

He's your White Knight.

Her lips parted. "You are, Lord, aren't You? I asked for protection. I just didn't expect it to come in the form of Emma Winters." She turned away from the expressionless clock face and walked to the kitchen. Did Emma drink coffee or tea? She had no idea. After two tries, she found baking supplies and pulled out cocoa, sugar, flour, baking soda, and vanilla. Next she headed for the refrigerator.

Forty-five minutes later, when the snowmobile whined back home, hot cocoa warmed in a pan, and the stove timer counted down the last five minutes of baking time for a chocolate sour cream cake. "Nothing says 'welcome home' like something warm and chocolaty." She gave herself a mental back-pat for saying it without a trace of bitterness. She and God had had a little talk while stirring cocoa. As usual, He'd won.

Boots stomped at the back door, and Ruby hurried to open it. "Emma, come in." Ruby looked behind her. No Burt. "You must be freezing."

"Not at all." Emma's rosy cheeks rose in a grin. "I hung on tight to Burt all the way, and he blocked the wind." She unzipped a snowmobile suit that Ruby knew—but hopefully Emma didn't—had once belonged to Corrine. "It was exhilarating."

Honor one another above yourselves. Practice hospitality. Live in harmony with one another. Ruby calmed herself with verses from the twelfth chapter of Romans. *If your enemy is hungry. . .* "I've got cocoa on the stove and a chocolate cake ready to come out of the oven."

Emma stepped out of the suit. "Actually, I'm allergic to chocolate."

Of course you are. "Well. . .I warmed up one of Burt's sweaters in the dryer for you. I'll get it for you."

"That won't be necessary." Bluish lips smiled tightly. "I'm just fine, and I brought my own tea bags." She pulled a plastic sandwich bag out of her pants pocket. "All I need is some boiling water."

Practice hospitality. Practice hospitality. Practice-hospitality-practice-hospitality. . . . "Of course."

Emma made herself at home on a stool at the kitchen counter, and Burt walked in.

"Mmm. . .chocolate. The language of a man's soul."

A snuffly noise came from Emma. "Thought you were all worried about his cholesterol."

Live in harmony. "Well, once in a while a man needs a little something sweet." *Sweet. . .know what that is, Emma?*

Burt kicked out of his boots and unzipped his coveralls. "It's miserable out there." He rubbed his arms.

Ruby glanced at Emma's frozen smile and back at the cold man who stood at the door. "I've got just the thing to warm you up." She slipped into his laundry room, opened the running dryer, and pulled out the sweater. Back in the kitchen, she held it up to him. "Slip into this quick, and come have some cocoa."

"How very hospitable." He didn't actually wink, but Ruby picked up the tiniest quiver in the muscles around his right eye.

The stove timer buzzed. Ruby took a toothpick out of a box on the counter. Burt pulled mugs off hooks beneath the cupboard, standing so close their stockinged feet touched. Out of Emma's sight.

Filling a mug with cocoa, Burt looked over at Emma. "Marshmallow or whipped cream, Em?"

Both eyebrows rose. Her head tilted to one side. "I'm allergic to chocolate."

"Oh yeah, that's right. I forget these things. Ruby, you like whipped cream with a sprinkle of cinnamon, right?"

"Right." *What a slumber party this is going to be.*

☙

"Process. P-R-O-C-E-S-S. Triple word score, which brings it to thirty-three points." Ruby wrote down her score, totaled it, compared it to Emma's, and took a massive forkful of chocolate cake. It was mighty good, if she did say so herself. The poor woman sitting across from her at the kitchen table and trailing her by thirty-eight points didn't know what she was missing. Ruby turned the board to Burt.

Reading glasses perched on the end of his nose. She'd only seen him wearing them a few times. In restaurants with poor lighting, he used them to read. He looked rather professorish. A nice look. He stroked his goatee. "I've only got one vowel."

The ringing phone interrupted his concentration. He stood and walked to the wall phone. Ruby glanced at the grandfather clock. It was twenty after one. "Whoever that is, it can't be good." She glanced at Emma. "Unless it's someone calling about your furnace. Were they going to work on it tonight?"

"No." Emma hadn't been much for conversation the whole night.

"Will it turn over?" Burt spoke to the person on the phone and waited for an answer. "Let me talk to him." He asked several questions in car mechanic language and after a minute said, "I can be there in ten minutes." Hanging up the phone, he let out a tired sigh. "Taylor and Andy 'borrowed' Angel's truck."

"Taylor's supposed to be with her parents this weekend. The little. . .*errr*! What happened?"

"They got stuck in a drift out in the middle of nowhere, about five miles from here, and then the truck stalled."

"I'd bet Angel doesn't know anything about this. You're going to help them, aren't you?" *My white knight.*

"Can't leave 'em out there. Sounds like an air control valve or maybe a fuel filter."

"Don't you go trying to dig them out. Your ticker's not up for that."

Emma tilted her head to one side. "What's wrong with his heart?"

Nothing I can't fix.

"Nothing's wrong with my heart. Ruby's a worrywart like my girls." His right eye did another almost wink. "I'll strap a shovel on the snowmobile, and let the kid do the manual labor." As he talked, he walked into the laundry room and came out with his coveralls. "You ladies feel free to turn in." He looked from Emma to Ruby and bit down on his bottom lip. "There are two guest rooms upstairs."

Not a chance she was going to bed first. Ruby smiled tightly, sending a message she was pretty sure he received. "I'll stay up."

Emma picked up her teacup. "Me, too." She took a long swig and pulled out another tea bag.

So that's how it's going to be. She had a momentary picture of two catty women fighting over a teapot and a bathroom, seeing who could outcaffeine the other. *Emma, would you like some warm milk? You're getting sleeeeepy. Your eyes are getting heavy. . . .*

"Ruby?" Burt stared at her, hands on hips.

How long had she been lost in plans to hypnotize Emma? "Yes?"

"What should I do with her?"

With who? "Oh! Um. . .bring her here, I guess. I'll call Angel and tell her to call Taylor's parents. I wouldn't trust her to go back to Wade and Angel's. . . alone. Let the boy take the truck and—is it safe for her to be on a snowmobile in her condition?"

"What condition?" Emma leaned over her coffee cup. "Is she—"

Ruby held up her hand to stop the question.

Burt shrugged. "I'll go slow." He zipped up his coveralls and put on his boots.

"Do you have an extra jacket and hat and mittens for Taylor? The girl dresses like she lives in Miami."

"I'm sure I can find something." He turned toward the laundry room then stopped. "Come give me a hand, Ruby."

Sliding out of her chair, Ruby stood. "I'll be right back."

It took her eyes a moment to adjust to the dark room. Burt leaned against the dryer. In his hands were a pair of gloves, a hat, and a scarf. A fleece-lined jacket lay on the washing machine. He crooked his finger. "Come here," he whispered. "Help me find what I need." His arms went around her; his lips brushed hers.

"You be safe out there."

"I think I'll be safer out there than you'll be in here. No catfight until I get back, okay?"

"No promises." She rose on tiptoes and kissed him.

And a *huff* sounded at the door.

What a slumber party this is going to be.

☙❧

Ruby looked up at the clock. Thirty-two minutes had passed since the snowmobile whined across the yard. And at least twenty of those minutes Emma had spent in the bathroom. She was still in there.

Ruby walked through the back hall, past the laundry room, and stood outside the bathroom door. Should she say something? What if the woman was sick? What if. . . Ruby's stomach flipped. What if she'd taken something? Or found a razor blade. . . She took a step closer, raised her fist to knock, but stopped when she heard a muffled noise. Emma Winters crying?

And it was all her fault. If the poor woman hadn't witnessed that kiss. . . Ruby opened her mouth to call to her when another noise filtered under the bathroom door. Laughter.

What in the world? Like any concerned woman would do, she put her ear against the door.

". . .until tomorrow. . .apple. . .cherry. . .bag of salt. . .driveway. . ."

Emma was talking on the phone. At three in the morning? She pressed her ear tighter to the door and heard a snap. Like a phone closing. She jumped away and scrambled down the hallway, sliding into the stove like a batter acing home plate. Needing to look purposeful, she turned on the oven as Emma walked into the room. "Are you feeling all right? I was starting to get worried about you."

"I'm fine." Emma pointed to the oven. "Another cake?" Her tone implied Ruby was doing something very wrong.

"No. I just thought I'd. . .make a. . ." A what? There was still more than

348

half a cake left. "A batch of muffins for breakfast. I guess baking is in my blood. When I'm sad, I bake; when I'm worried, I bake."

"When you're trying to get a man, you bake." Emma stood at the window, her back to Ruby.

"Ex. . .cuse me?"

"You heard me. Don't think I don't know how you wormed your way between Burt and me. You did it with food. One chocolate-covered doughnut at a time until *poof!* he's out of my life."

"Emma! I did not 'worm' my way between the two of you. I didn't have designs on him—it just happened."

"Just happened," Emma mocked in a singsong voice.

Hands curling into fists, Ruby glared at the woman's back. "The way we met was pure serendipity. God designed it, not me."

Emma whirled around, fire in her eyes. "How dare you bring God into this. I want you out. I had him first. Leave him alone."

Twilight Zone music played in Ruby's head. "Don't you think Burt should be the one to decide that? I'm not budging until he tells me to back off."

Index finger raised and pointing like the witch in "Hansel and Gretel," Emma advanced.

Ruby held her ground. "This is ridiculous."

Emma passed the breakfast bar.

"We're two mature Christian women."

Emma reached the stove.

"We're acting like children."

Emma closed in on the refrigerator. The arm with the pointy finger on the end rose; the hand formed a claw. . . .

Ruby screamed.

Emma pulled a photograph off the refrigerator.

And Burt walked in.

⍦

The grandfather clocked struck four. Emma stood in front of the window, her back to the room. Burt added another log to the fire. Ruby spread another blanket over Taylor's legs. "Need more?"

Taylor shook her head, eyes on the boy who huddled under a quilt in Burt's recliner. "I'm warming up."

Closing the fireplace screen, Burt whispered, "Wish I could say the same about the other women in this room."

Ruby huffed softly. "I'll meet *you* in the kitchen, mister," she whispered back and strode into the next room. She opened a cupboard and took out the flour for the second time then opened the refrigerator with no idea what she was looking for. Something orange showed through a drawer. Carrots. She'd make carrot muffins. She dug through cupboards until she found a grater. She'd washed, peeled, and grated them all and was cracking eggs when Burt finally showed his face.

He stood and stared at her for a long, drawn-out moment. "Emma said she was just grabbing a picture off the fridge." A bump revealed his tongue pushing his cheek.

"Probably to hit me with it." Ruby picked up a carrot she didn't need and chopped off its ends.

"She was trying to make you jealous."

"It didn't work." She picked up the peeler.

"It shouldn't work." He snatched the peeler out of her hand. "What are you doing?"

"Baking. When I'm upset, I bake."

"Well, this time you can't." He reached across the top of the stove and turned off the oven. "This time you have to pray instead. Because you and I have a job to do."

"We do?"

"Yes, we do. Taylor just asked me to explain God to Andy."

An egg slipped out of Ruby's hand and smashed on the counter. "Taylor doesn't believe in God. . .at least not in just one."

"I know. She just said that. But she thinks that now that they're having a baby, they should figure it out together. So they want to ask us some questions."

"Oh my. . .we need to pray." She pushed the grated carrots aside. "*This* is doing the unexpected."

"Did you know Andy's parents are divorced?"

"Yes. He's living with his father."

"He was. Until about five hours ago. His dad just found out about Taylor and kicked him out."

"Which is why he's sitting in your recliner."

Burt nodded. "Serendipity." He took her hands in his and closed his eyes. "Heavenly Father, we come before You seeking wisdom. Please help us to be sensitive, to not push too hard, but to not treat Your Word too lightly. Soften their hearts, and use our words."

Ruby let all her Emma frustration out in one breath. "Forgive me for my attitude toward Emma, Lord. Grant me an opportunity to ask her forgiveness and make things right. Please give us hearts of genuine compassion for Taylor and Andy. In the Name of Your Son. Amen."

"Amen."

Burt squeezed her hands. She squeezed back.

As they walked toward the living room, they heard steps on the stairs. Emma had gone to bed.

Chapter 19

Ruby handed a mug of hot chocolate to the boy with the tousled blond hair. Andy mumbled something that was probably an expression of gratitude in teenspeak. Taylor whispered her thanks and snuggled deeper into her blankets. Burt sang—"Oh the weather outside is frightful"—as he repositioned a glowing log with a poker. Sparks floated up, dancing a counterpart to the snowflakes that bounced off the windowpane.

"Kind of cozy, isn't it?" Ruby tried to sound calm and natural as she curled her feet under her on the couch next to Taylor and pulled a lap quilt over her knees. She wasn't the slightest bit calm.

"It feels way more like Christmas than Easter." Taylor glanced at Burt and pointed to a wooden crèche on the coffee table next to a bowl of plastic eggs. "And you still have Christmas stuff out."

Burt nodded. "I keep that out until Easter for my grandkids. Helps me tell them the whole story."

Taylor folded her hands across her belly. "I think it's cool Jesus came as a baby." She tipped her head to one side. "I wonder what Mary and Joseph thought when they found out she was pregnant with God's Son. That had to be so awesome."

Who was this girl, and what had she done with Taylor, the girl who just weeks ago was asking the universe to make everyone just get along? Ruby exchanged glances with Burt and hid her shock from Taylor. "Actually, I think they were probably both about as scared as you two."

Burt pulled a Bible off a bookshelf. "Want me to read about it?"

"Yes." Taylor stared up at him, eyes wide like a preschooler at story time.

Silhouetted against the snowflakes lit by the porch light, Burt opened the Bible and began to read from the book of Luke. When he got to the part where the angel spoke to Mary, Ruby tiptoed out of the room to find a box of tissues for Taylor.

By the time Burt read, "The shepherds returned, glorifying and praising God," Taylor had used up half a dozen tissues. She sniffed and blew her nose. "That's so beautiful. I kind of identify with Mary." She glanced up at Andy then back at the bowl of eggs. "Since I'm going to give birth to a son, too."

Andy blinked, narrowed his eyes. His lips parted, but nothing came out.

"I had an ultrasound this morning. I was waiting for the right time to tell you." She reached in her jacket pocket and pulled out a stack of pictures. "It's a boy."

The grandfather clock struck five. Still holding the ultrasound pictures, Andy dozed in the recliner while Taylor continued to chatter. She picked up a green plastic egg. "Why are there numbers on these?"

Ruby locked eyes with Burt and gave up all hope of getting any sleep before dawn. "They're resurrection eggs. They tell the story of Jesus' death and resurrection. The Easter message."

"Find number one." Burt pointed at the bowl. "And open it."

Taylor fished out a pink egg. When she pulled the two halves apart, a cotton ball fell out. "Smells good. What's on it?"

"Perfume." Burt told her the story of the woman who anointed Jesus' feet with perfumed oil.

"Wow. Imagine loving somebody that much."

Ruby picked up the cotton ball and held it in her palm. "Jesus explained that the woman loved much because she had been forgiven much."

A shadow crossed Taylor's eyes. She opened a blue egg. Three play-money coins fell out. Burt explained about the money Judas was paid to betray Jesus.

One by one, Taylor opened the eggs until a row of eleven items lay in front of her on the coffee table. A piece of purple cloth, a strip of leather, a thorn. . . each item representing a part of the story. Ruby had never seen Taylor able to focus this long.

Burt got up and walked to the couch, sitting on the other side of Taylor. "The last egg tells the most important part."

Taylor pulled the halves apart. The egg was empty. A tiny gasp escaped her lips.

"I get it. I *get* it."

❧

"I'm ready." Wearing a pair of flannel pajamas Ruby had dug out of a box, Taylor walked into Burt's back guest room where Ruby was turning down the covers on one of two twin beds.

Ruby fluffed the pillow. "Do you want the night-light on or off?" She stepped back, making room for Taylor to walk by her.

"Off." Taylor crawled into the bed. "But I meant I was ready for Jesus to run my life."

Breath catching in her throat, Ruby nodded. Taylor patted a spot next to her on the bed. Ruby sat down.

"But there's still something I'm scared about. I know that God loves us just the way we are, but what if I keep doing stupid things even though I try not to? Will I do to God what I did to my mom and what I'm probably going to do to Wade and Angel? Will I frustrate Him so much He'll just. . .send me away?"

Ruby's chest tightened. *Lord, help! How do I explain Your infinite patience?* She scanned the room until she found a pocket New Testament sitting on the desk in the corner. She got up, picked it up, and opened to Romans. "The apostle Paul was handpicked by Jesus to serve Him. At the time God chose him, Paul's main goal in life was to persecute Christians. But here are some words he wrote *after* he became a follower of Christ: 'For I have the desire to do what is good, but I cannot carry it out. For I do not do the good I want to do, but the evil I do not want to do—this I keep on doing.'"

"Wow. Sounds like me."

"And me. And Burt. And every other person who loves God and desperately wants to do what is right. But God chose Paul. . .and me and Burt. . .and *you* in spite of that."

A sweetly innocent smile touched Taylor's face.

"Just talk to Him, honey. Tell Him exactly how you feel."

Taylor nodded, folded her hands on her lap, and closed her eyes. "God, there's a lot I don't understand, but I believe You're there, and I want to belong to You. I guess You already know everything I've done. I'm sorry for all of the bad stuff. Thank You for loving me and choosing me even when I don't deserve it. I want You to change me and. . .I guess just keep loving me and my baby boy. Amen."

⁊❦

Ruby padded down the steps, expecting to find Andy sound asleep on the couch. Instead, she found him standing in the living room with his arms wrapped around a pillow, still talking to Burt. She took a few steps back up the stairs—where she could see and hear but not be seen.

"So what did you do?"

Confusion registered on Burt's face for a moment. "You want a list of my sins?"

"I guess."

"Well. . .I drank, I smoked—legal and illegal substances—I treated women like dirt, I ditched friends if they didn't do things my way, I lied to cover my tracks. . .and I justified all of it because it made me happy. And I was happy. . . just as long as I wasn't alone. I didn't dare let the party stop, or I'd have to face the truth that deep down I was miserable. Any time I got a glimpse of my reality, I tried something new."

Andy's arms wrapped tighter around the pillow.

"Anything in that list you can identify with?"

The boy looked down at the floor. The grandfather clock chimed the half hour. "Pretty much all of it. Except the happy part." He ran his hand through a mop of unruly waves. "So how'd you get your stuff together?"

"I didn't." Burt shook his head. "When I finally decided to let God run my life—even though I wasn't absolutely sure He was real—He started changing me. Like the song says—I once was lost, but now I'm found; I was blind, but now I see."

353

The boy looked down at his socks.

"No one's pushing you to make up your mind on anything right now. Just think over what we've talked about. Anytime you've got questions, you know where to find me or Ruby."

"Thanks. It's hard to think with all this on my mind. I don't have a job or a place to live, and I don't know the first thing about being a dad."

"Do you like old cars?"

After a slight jerk of his head, Andy nodded.

"I'm refurbishing a car I just bought, and I could use a hand, but the hours I have to work on it are pretty sporadic. Since you don't have any other commitments, would you consider doing me a huge favor and staying here for a while to help me work on it?"

"Yeah. Yeah, I guess I could do that."

"Great. Thank you. Sleep well."

"You, too." With a smile, the boy carried the pillow into the living room.

Ruby walked down three steps, and Burt looked up and met her eyes. Taking her hand, he led her to the kitchen and closed the door to the living room. "How much of that did you hear?"

"Enough to know that boy's not going to be out on the street. . .and you bought a new car."

"Yeah. . . So much for empty nest. It just felt right. Crazy, huh?"

"Not any crazier than me inviting Taylor to come and live with me. Right after she gave her life to the Lord."

"Really?"

"Really. The eggs got to her."

Burt grinned. "Andy said he was listening in on that, too. Gives a whole new dimension to our chicken ministry, doesn't it? We should take the eggs to the hospital next week." Burt opened his arms, and she stepped into them. He kissed the top of her head.

Ruby rested her head on his chest. "What a slumber party this turned out to be."

Chapter 20

Weather like this called for the flouncy red hat with the purple feathers. Ruby tucked newly highlighted hair behind her ears and donned the hat. From her red and purple collection, she picked out a wide, beaded bracelet to accent her red cotton V-neck sweater. "Voila! What do You think, Lord?" She twirled in front of her bedroom mirror. "No more bags under the eyes, and I lost four pounds. Not too shabby, huh?"

In her quest to de-stress her life, she'd hired another baker, and Burt was taking over a few of her jobs at the bakery. She now worked nine to five, three days a week—except today, when she took off a whole Wednesday—because she could. On the nights when she and Burt didn't stay out too late, she slept like normal people, and with an always-hungry, pregnant, live-in cook, she hardly had to lift a finger at home. Three weeks had passed without a confrontation with Jeanie, Angel, or any of Burt's daughters, and Ruby hadn't had a headache in all that time. Best of all, she was a woman gloriously in love. And it showed on her face. The only minor stress was the knowledge that she had likely ruined any hope Emma Winters had of happily-ever-after. But her conscience was clear. She'd won the man fair and square.

"Life is good." Blowing a kiss at the lady in the mirror, she picked up her purple purse and walked out the front door.

With her hand on one of two white columns supporting the corner of the porch roof, she took a moment to stare up at the cedar tree in the front yard that towered over the power lines. When they'd bought the house, Fryderyck had used a stepladder to put a star on the top at Christmas. "Four decades is a long time to live in one house." She patted the column. "It's been a good house, Lord. But I don't think I'll be needing it much longer. If being this bold isn't what You want me to do, please stop me and give that man a nudge. No, a shove. We're not getting any younger."

As she walked down the four steps, she waved at Lucas Zemken. "I was just on my way to see you."

Lucas walked across the street and met her on the sidewalk. "Pretty dressy for a Wednesday. Is this just for a trip to the jewelry store, or are you off to join the mad hatters?"

"We have our spring fling at Vinny Vanucchi's." She looked up one side of the street and down the other and whispered, "Is it done?"

"All polished and ready. Gretchen's manning the store—she's expecting you." Lucas tapped the brim of her hat. He wore his best "I've got a secret" smile. "You're pretty confident, little lady. Sure I'm not going through all this work for nothing?"

"I couldn't be surer."

"So when are you going to do this thing?" The gleam in his eyes brightened.

"This afternoon. He's picking me up at Vinny's, and he's making dinner for our girls. How's that for perfect? The dinner was his idea. His girls will be in town for the middle one's birthday tomorrow, and Burt said he just wanted to spoil the women in his life. But if he says yes, we won't have to put off the announcement, and we can start making plans right away."

"And you think all your girls are going to be okay with this."

Ruby waved her hand as if shooing a fly. "They've all gotten used to us being together. It's been five months."

Lucas clamped his bottom lip with his top teeth. "Promise me you'll call the very second he says yes. I'll be home all night."

"You'll be the first, I promise."

"Okay. Don't be late now." Bending over, he gave her a hug. "Be happy, little lady."

❧

Burt ran his hand over his smooth scalp. After weeks of watching his hair grow around the naturally bald spot on top of his head, he'd ditched the ponytail idea. Ruby hadn't seemed to mind. "Mmm. . .smell that." He took a deep breath as he walked out of the garage. The air was pungent with the scent of apple blossoms. "The sweet, sweet smell of spring." He threw a polishing rag at Andy. "Think she's ready?"

Andy laughed and pointed at the little red car. "*She's* ready. I don't know if the real Ruby is ready."

"Oh, she is, believe me. Hints have been falling like raindrops lately. At least now she'll forgive me for spending more time with you than I have with her the past few weeks."

The boy smiled then quickly looked down and began rubbing a spot on a fender that Burt was pretty sure couldn't get any shinier.

"Spill it, kid. If there's anything in that head of yours, you'd better let me in on it."

"I kinda. . .made a decision. Taylor's mom and dad want her to try living at home until after the baby's born—we're just not ready to get married. I want to be able to support them good, you know? So I've been listening to you, and it got me thinking."

"About God?"

Andy laughed. "Yeah, about God. How could I not think about Him, hanging around you? But what I started to say is I'm going to join the navy."

Burt took a step back. "You?"

"Hey, don't look so shocked. You're not the only one who could look cool with no hair. And they say it makes a man out of you. Who knows, maybe I'll find God in the navy just like you did."

"Who knows?" Burt held up his hand for a high five then wrapped the boy in a bear hug. *Lord, You know.* "I'm proud of you, Andy. Real proud."

Ruby fingered the edge of the checkered tablecloth and tried to focus on the conversation at the table. The four other women decked out in red hats chatted about daffodils and irises as the white umbrella above their table flapped in an unseasonably warm early May breeze. Ruby stared down at the remains of her Uncle Paulie's Baked Mostaccioli in a vermillion-colored bowl. As amazing as it tasted, she couldn't finish even half, thanks to the butterflies taking up space in her stomach. She flagged a waitress and asked for a box.

When the three other red hatters got into a heated discussion about the best time to prune forsythia bushes, Wanda leaned over her Fettuccine Carbonara. "So, I hope you're sufficiently repentant that it's all your fault Emma had to find someone else to fill Burt's spot on her schedule. Was she maaaad." Both eyebrows wiggled up and down.

"Schedule?" Ruby turned in her chair to face Wanda squarely. "I have no idea what you're talking about."

The eyebrows break-danced. "I volunteer at the food pantry with Emma—known her for years. What I didn't know until last month was that her Burt was your Burt. Well, Emma was out of her bipolar meds because of the storm, and she showed up at the food pantry in a manic—"

"Emma's bipolar?" Flashbacks ran through her brain—a wild woman descending on her, claw raised, ready to corner her in Burt's kitchen and club her with a photograph. "That explains so much."

"Yeah, you don't really want to be around her when she's on one of her swings."

"Tell me about it."

"Anyway, she was ranting to everyone who'd listen how she'd found her even-day guy kissing some other woman and how now she'd have find somebody else to fix her dryer because her odd-day guy only did yard work."

"What?"

"You seriously didn't know? She had three men on her schedule, leading them all on. Oh, she feeds them, but if they're hoping for more, they're going to be disappointed. Yeah, she's got free snow plowing and lawn mowing and repair work. One of them even does her vacuuming, since poor Emma suffers from sciatica and. . ."

The phone calls during dinner, the murmurings in the bathroom during the storm, the "You can have him on odd days"—it all made sense. Then again, none of it made sense. "What a. . ."

"Conniver? That's what I call her. And if Burt didn't tell you about it, I'll bet none of the guys knows about the others. Shrewd. In a sick kind of way."

Ruby sat in stunned silence while Wanda turned back to her pasta. But the more she thought about it and pictured Emma with a big eraser wiping Burt out of her life, the funnier it became. She covered her mouth with her hand and tried to control the spasms shaking her shoulders.

"Let it out, woman," Wanda garbled over a mouthful of noodles. She turned to Ruby, eyes glistening. She gulped and laughed. "If you don't laugh, I'll do it for both of us."

Ruby complied. Wiping her eyes, she reached for her water glass. "I just can't believe. . ." A streak of red, a dash of yellow on Main Street caught her eye. By the time the yellow part registered, it had disappeared. *Oh no. He wouldn't.*

"Did you see that convertible?" The voice, female and youngish, came from the table behind her. "There was a chicken driving that car!"

❧

It worked. Exactly like he'd hoped. Ruby stood in front of Vinny Vanucchi's Italian Ristorante bawling like a baby in front of her gaping red-hatted friends. "So, you like it?"

Nodding, crying, wiping her face with both hands, she stepped off the curb and ran her fingertips across the white letters—spelling out RUBY—splashed across the spit-polished fender. "She's beautiful."

"She's yours." He held out a key chain with a large gold *R* on the end. "Get in." He opened the low driver's-side door with a flourish. Ruby took the keys, stretched up on tiptoes, wrapped her arms around his yellow belly, and kissed him. Her flouncy hat went sailing. He kissed her back and ran after it. When they were settled in the leather bucket seats and the motor was purring, he turned on the GPS he'd mounted on the dash, punched in "recent selections," and said, "Just do what she tells you."

The time to their destination was supposed to be twenty-eight minutes. Before they reached the bridge spanning the Mississippi, Ruby had cut three minutes off their ETA. The lady apparently liked speed. He kept his eyes on her, turning only when she pointed out flowering trees or two Holstein cows with their calves silhouetted on a hill. The day was unexpectedly warm, and the countryside waking up to spring was a beautiful sight. But not quite as beautiful as the woman behind the wheel.

"Give me a hint. Just one."

Burt stroked his goatee. "Okay, just one. It's another step toward freedom."

❧

As she crossed the bridge, Ruby glanced at the little round clock on the dashboard. Her pulse picked up speed with each passing mile. Anticipation vied with distress. Whatever this surprise was, she knew she'd love it, but it had best not interfere with her plan. She tightened her grip on the steering wheel. The little car fit her. And it was named after her. A sure sign that the man would say yes.

Blinking hard to prevent any more tears, she studied the metal lattice work arching over the road then peered down at a barge. The Mississippi looked blue today, reflecting the sky. She tried to focus on the scenery for the next few miles.

Five hundred feet to go. "Turn right. Turn right," the snooty British GPS lady commanded. Ruby looked up at the sign. And her heart clunked against her ribs. *Hawkeye Boat Sales.*

She'd never been on a boat in her life. The thought terrified her. *This* was freedom?

"Park over there." Burt grinned as he pointed. His expression clearly said, "Won't this be fun?"

She strained her lips into something like a smile and turned the key. "A boat. How"—swallow—"fun." Her voice quivered, betraying her.

"A boat?" Burt's grin dissolved. "You want a *boat*?"

"Well, I. . . Isn't that why we're here?"

"No! I spent way too many years on a boat. We're here to look at those."

She followed the line of his arm and gasped. "RVs! We're here to look at RVs?"

"Maybe."

"Maybe?"

"Well, I'm not writing this script all by myself, you know. You get a say in this, too. But I thought. . .if you like the idea. . ." He opened the glove compartment and pulled out a shapeless package wrapped in bright orange paper. It felt like a pillow. She tore it off. A fuzzy yellow bundle lay in her hands.

A chicken suit. And attached to the zipper was an orange plastic egg.

"Open it."

With shaking fingers, she pulled the two halves apart. The inside was lined with velvet. A diamond peeked out of the folds.

"Lucas designed it." Burt pulled out the ring, took a moment to wipe the tears from her face, and said, "Like I said before, Big Burt needs a mate. I was thinking maybe, if you like the idea, we could take our chicken ministry on the road. There are hospitals all along Route 66, I hear." He steadied her hand and slid on the ring. "So, what do you think?"

"I think. . ." The raised, round diamond glittered in the sunlight. She laughed, sniffed, and laughed again. "I think you spoiled my plan."

His lips parted. His eyes darkened.

Ruby reached deep in the pocket of her sweater and took out a box. "I was going to propose to *you*." She opened it, revealing a narrow gold band. "Lucas designed it. It's the first-ever manly engagement ring. When we—if you accept, that is—when we get married, there's a matching ring that he'll fuse to this one." She pushed it onto his finger. "Burt Jacobs, will you marry me?"

Wiping his eyes on his fuzzy yellow sleeve, he smiled. "I asked you first."

Chapter 21

Ruby took the biscuits out of the oven. "I think we're ready," she called to the girls in the living room. "We are, aren't we?" she whispered to the man ladling creamed chicken into a pink and blue soup tureen.

"We are so ready."

"Are they?"

"Of course. Think positive."

The girls were sitting down when Burt and Ruby carried out the food. Burt sat at one end of the table. Ruby took the open chair at the opposite end. Candace and Angel sat on one side. Kimberly and Bethany were on her left. *Lord, what a beautiful sight.* This spoiling-Burt's-women night could turn into an annual tradition. And next year Jeanie would be here, too.

"Smells wonderful." "This is so special." "Dad you're a slow-cooker whiz." "Ruby, those biscuits look divine." The cheerful chatter continued until Burt clinked his glass with his spoon.

"Let's pray." He folded his hands. "Lord God, we acknowledge that all things come from You and You work all things according to Your perfect plan. Thank You for these amazing girls You have blessed Ruby and me with. Thank You for the food You have provided. And tonight I thank You especially that Ruby has agreed to be my wife. In the precious Name of our Lord. A—"

A glass crashed. Angel yelped and jumped out of her chair. Candace, face the color of snow, slammed her fist on the tablecloth. "How could you?"

Bethany wrapped her arms around Burt's neck. "Congratulations, Dad! That's awesome."

"How can you say that?" Candace waved toward the china cabinet where Corrine's china stood on display. "Don't you know what this means? Everything changes now. Christmas, holidays, traditions. . .everything."

A sob rose from the corner where Angel had landed when she jumped. With the front of her blouse soaked, she looked like a sad little girl.

"Angel?" Ruby stood, head spinning. "Come here, honey."

"It's okay, Bapcia. I'll be okay." She held up both hands, palms out. "I just have to. . .adjust. I'll be okay."

Ruby turned to Burt. Peering out from the circle made by Bethany's arms, he stared at Kimberly, who still sat at the table. In an apparent catatonic state.

Lord, help!

Burt studied the feisty lady slamming cold baking powder biscuits into a plastic bag. She had a headache again. He could tell by the pinched look on her forehead. He spooned barely touched creamed chicken into a bowl. "We have to live our lives, Ruby. They're grown-ups."

"I know. I'm just mad. All they were thinking about was themselves. If it weren't for Bethany, I think I would have kicked them all out of your house. I pictured calling Jeanie and putting her on speakerphone so she could share the love and we could all discuss wedding plans together. If it were up to me, I'm not sure I'd even invite them to the wedding. Ach!" A biscuit missed the bag and rolled on the floor. "At least you won't have to cook for a week. . .or two." She bent down and grabbed it and chucked it at the wastebasket.

Burt sealed the bowl, slid it in the fridge, and turned to wash his hands. As he squirted soap into his palm, his gaze landed on something sitting on the windowsill. Something he'd put there hours ago. He rinsed the soap off his hands. "Come here."

She walked toward him, brushing crumbs off her black skirt.

He held out the wishbone. "We don't need them to make wedding plans. We have our own methods. Whoever wins gets to set the date."

Ruby stared at the chicken bone, a smile crinkling the corners of her mouth. She rubbed her hands together then blew on them like a batter getting ready for his turn. "You're sure about this?"

"I'm sure. Are you? You'll go along with my idea if I win?"

"Yup." She grabbed one end of the wishbone between two fingers, spread her feet wide apart for support, closed her eyes, and took a deep breath.

"On the count of three. One. . .two. . .pull!" The bone snapped.

Ruby won.

Burt swallowed hard. He'd made a promise, but now he wasn't so sure. "Congratulations." He walked over to the kitchen desk and took the calendar off the wall. Handing it to her, he said, "Pick a date."

She smiled, lifted May, stared at June, turned to July. . . .

Lord, increase my patience.

August and September joined the others. She looked up at him. "Know how much I love you?"

Enough not to torture me into the winter? "How much?"

The pages dropped. Her index finger circled and landed on a date. "This much."

Burt choked on his own saliva, coughed, and sputtered, "*Tomorrow?*"

"It'll probably have to be Friday because we can't get the license until tomorrow, but as soon as we can."

Still coughing, he picked her up and twirled her around.

"Does that mean yes?" She rubbed her nose on his cheek.

He set her down. "Yes! Absolutely yes!"

"So what would you have picked?"

"I was being very patient." His lips skimmed her hair. "I was going to say next Saturday."

~❧~

"Lord, it's going to be the three of us from now on." Ruby twirled in a very reserved circle. "Thank You."

From the edge of the Eagle Ridge Resort patio, she looked out over Lake Galena. She couldn't have dreamed of a more perfect day. In less than ten minutes, Burt and the pastor would be here. They were taking a bit of a risk getting married so close to home, but by the time the gossip made its way to their girls, it would be a done deal. She'd already be Ruby Jacobs. "Mrs. Burt Jacobs." She rolled it around on her tongue. How strange it would be to have a name everyone could pronounce.

She smoothed her red skirt. The blouse she wore was the one her mother had been married in. Its wide sleeves were edged in lace and embroidered with large red roses and green leaves. All she'd bought new were her shoes—soft, flat, ballet-type slippers. Perfect for dancing. . .alone with her husband.

Footsteps sounded on the patio. Two sets of footsteps. She closed her eyes. *Lord, just this once. . .not the chicken suit.* She turned around. Her breath caught in her throat. Burt wore black pants, a black dress shirt, and a bright red tie. In his hand was a single red rose. Her knees wobbled.

He walked toward her, gave her the rose, and took her other hand. "What do you think of my gorgeous bride, Pastor?"

"You look absolutely radiant, Ruby." Pastor Carl kissed her on the cheek. "I'm so happy for you. And I've enjoyed talking to this man of yours. I like him."

"That means a lot, Pastor. I kind of think he's a keeper."

"So. . .we have the rings, the license. . . . God is in His heaven, and all is right with the world. If you'll both face me, we'll get started." He opened a small black book.

"We are gathered here today before God alone to join you, Burt, and you, Ruby, in holy matrimony, which is an honorable and solemn estate and therefore not to be entered into unadvisedly or lightly, but reverently and soberly." He looked up and smiled at Ruby then Burt. "Who gives this woman to be married to this man?"

Oh no. Ruby bit her bottom lip. She did not want to look back and remember giggling at her wedding. *Wrong page, Pastor. Wrong ceremony.*

"I repeat. . . . Who gives this woman to be married to this man?"

"We do!" Angel popped around a hedge, followed by Taylor and Wade. Laughing and breathless, Angel held her phone over her head and ran toward them.

"And so do we"—the voice coming through the phone made tears spring to

Ruby's eyes—"I love you, Mom. We wish you all the best."

"But how. . ."

Angel wrapped her in a hug. "Taylor found some scribblings on a paper in your Bible. She gave every one of us a little talking to—the little peacemaker." She kissed Ruby's cheek and stepped back to Wade, who pointed a video camera at Burt.

"And who gives this man to be married to this woman?"

"We do!"

A laughing mob of husbands and children led by Burt's three daughters stepped onto the patio. Ruby turned and watched her husband-to-be's face crumple. She reached in her pocket and handed him her handkerchief. They turned back to the pastor.

"Now. . .if we can continue. . ." Pastor Carl blinked several times and cleared his throat. "If anyone can show just cause why these two may not be lawfully joined together, let them speak now or forever hold their peace."

Burt turned back to face their witnesses. Ruby did the same. Angel held her hands up in surrender and grinned. Kimberly mouthed, "Love you." Candace swiped her face with both hands, shook her head, and blew a kiss at her father then one at Ruby.

"If you two will face each other, we'll try to get through this." Pastor Carl laughed. "Burt Jacobs, do you take Ruby Cholewinski for your lawful wedded wife, to live in the holy estate of matrimony? Will you love, honor, comfort, and cherish her from this day forward, forsaking all others, keeping only unto her for as long as you both shall live?"

Burt wiped his face with the lace-edged handkerchief. Silver blue eyes looked straight into her soul. "I will. And I'm praying that's a long, long time."

CREAMED CHICKEN WITH BAKING POWDER BISCUITS

(Save the wishbone and only serve to people who will stay and eat!
But it's great reheated, too.)

BISCUITS

> 2 cups sifted flour
> 3 teaspoons baking powder
> 1 teaspoon salt
> ½ cup butter or shortening
> ½ cup milk

Heat oven to 450 degrees. Mix dry ingredients well in bowl. Cut in butter or shortening until mixture looks like "meal." Stir in almost all the milk. If dough does not seem pliable, add enough to make a soft, puffy dough easy to roll out. Turn out on lightly floured board, and lightly knead for 30 seconds, enough to shape. Roll to ½ inch thick, and cut with 2-inch floured biscuit cutter. Bake on ungreased sheet in middle of oven for 10 to 12 minutes.

CREAMED CHICKEN

> ¼ cup finely chopped onion
> ¼ cup butter
> ¼ cup all-purpose flour
> ¼ to ½ teaspoon salt
> ⅛ teaspoon pepper
> 2 cups milk
> 2 cups chopped cooked chicken
> Minced fresh parsley

In a large skillet, sauté onion in butter until tender. Stir in flour, salt, and pepper until blended. Gradually add milk; bring to a boil. Reduce heat; cook and stir for 1 to 2 minutes or until thickened. Stir in chicken and parsley; cook until heated through.

Split biscuits; top with creamed chicken. Makes 6 servings.

A Letter to Our Readers

Dear Readers:

In order that we might better contribute to your reading enjoyment, we would appreciate you taking a few minutes to respond to the following questions. When completed, please return to the following: Fiction Editor, Barbour Publishing, Inc., P.O. Box 719, Uhrichsville, OH 44683.

1. Did you enjoy reading *Illinois Weddings* by Becky Melby and Cathy Wienke ?
    - ❏ Very much. I would like to see more books like this.
    - ❏ Moderately—I would have enjoyed it more if _____

    _____

    _____

2. What influenced your decision to purchase this book?
    (Check those that apply.)
    - ❏ Cover   ❏ Back cover copy   ❏ Title   ❏ Price
    - ❏ Friends   ❏ Publicity   ❏ Other

3. Which story was your favorite?
    - ❏ *Pleasant Surprises*   ❏ *Parting Secrets*
    - ❏ *Pure Serendipity*

4. Please check your age range:
    - ❏ Under 18   ❏ 18–24   ❏ 25–34
    - ❏ 35–45   ❏ 46–55   ❏ Over 55

5. How many hours per week do you read? _____

Name _____

Occupation _____

Address _____

City _____ State _____ Zip _____

E-mail _____